C000130646

Hal Spacejock
Just Desserts

Book Three in the Hal Spacejock series

Copyright © Simon Haynes 2012

spacejock.com.au

Cover images copyright depositphotos.com

Stay in touch!

Author's newsletter:
spacejock.com.au/ML.html

facebook.com/halspacejock
twitter.com/spacejock

Works by Simon Haynes

All of Simon's novels* are self-contained, with a beginning, a middle and a proper ending. They're not sequels, they don't end on a cliffhanger, and you can start or end your journey with any book in the series.
Robot vs Dragons series excepted!

The Hal Spacejock series for teens/adults

Set in the distant future, where humanity spans the galaxy and robots are second-class citizens. Includes a large dose of humour!

Hal Spacejock 1: A robot named Clunk
Hal Spacejock 2: Second Course
Hal Spacejock 3: Just Desserts
Hal Spacejock 4: No Free Lunch
Hal Spacejock 5: Baker's Dough
Hal Spacejock 6: Safe Art
Hal Spacejock 7: Big Bang
Hal Spacejock 8: Double Trouble
Hal Spacejock 9: Max Damage
Hal Spacejock 10: Cold Boots (2019)

Also available:
Omnibus One, containing Hal books 1-3
Omnibus Two, containing Hal books 4-6
Omnibus Three, containing Hal books 7-9
Hal Spacejock: Visit, a short story
Hal Spacejock: Framed, a short story
Hal Spacejock: Albion, a novella

The Robot vs Dragons Trilogy.
High fantasy meets low humour!
Each set of three books should be read in order.

1. A Portion of Dragon and Chips
2. A Butt of Heads
3. A Pair of Nuts on the Throne
4. TBA (2019)

The Harriet Walsh series.

Set in the same universe as Hal Spacejock. Good clean fun, written with wry humour. No cliffhangers between novels!

Harriet Walsh 1: Peace Force
Harriet Walsh 2: Alpha Minor
Harriet Walsh 3: Sierra Bravo
Harriet Walsh 4: Storm Force (2019)
Also Available:
Omnibus One, containing books 1-3

The Hal Junior series

Written for all ages, these books are set aboard a space station in the Hal Spacejock universe, only ten years later.

1. Hal Junior: The Secret Signal
2. Hal Junior: The Missing Case
3. Hal Junior: The Gyris Mission
4. Hal Junior: The Comet Caper

Also Available:
Omnibus One, containing books 1-3

The Secret War series.
Gritty space opera for adult readers.

1. Raiders (2019)
2. Frontier (2019)
3. Deadlock (2019)

Collect One-Two - a collection of shorts by Simon Haynes

All titles available in ebook and paperback. Visit spacejock.com.au for details.

HAL SPACEJOCK
JUST DESSERTS

SIMON HAYNES

Bowman Press

This edition published 2012 by Bowman Press

Text © Simon Haynes 2011
Cover art © Simon Haynes 2012

ISBN 978-1-877034-04-6 (Ebook)
ISBN 978-1-877034-10-7 (Paperback)

2nd Edition published 2007 by Fremantle Press
1st Edition published 2004 by Bowman Publishing

This is a work of fiction. Names, characters, places and incidents are either the product of the author's imagination, or are used fictitiously. Any resemblance to actual persons, living or dead, business establishments, events, or locales is entirely coincidental.

This publication is copyright. Apart from any fair dealing for the purpose of private study, research, criticism or review, as permitted under the Copyright Act, no part may be reproduced by any process without written permission.

Dedicated to my family

Hal Spacejock Just Desserts

A mysterious sealed crate, a pair of shady mercenaries with more guns than brain cells and the amnesiac robot which may or may not be on a secret mission ... Only interstellar ignoramus Hal Spacejock and the unflappable Clunk could turn a straightforward cargo delivery into space opera with clowns.

Three simmering planets, two cocky spacemen and one huge mess: **Just Desserts**, for your pleasure.

The Oxed system

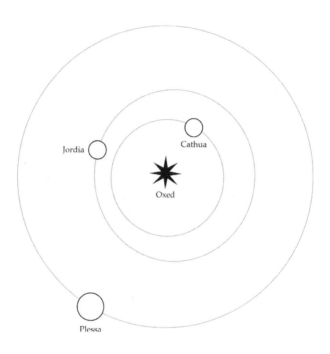

Jordia

Cathua

Oxed

Plessa

The *Volante*'s engines roared as the ship descended towards Cathua, one of three inhabited planets in the Oxed system. In the flight deck, Hal Spacejock was paying as much attention to the coffee mug balanced amongst the instruments as he was to the approach. He could survive without watching the landing, but he only had one mug.

The screen changed suddenly, and in between the sponsor logos and pop-ups Hal could just make out the mottled blue surface of Cathua. As they got closer the oceans and continents gave way to a patchwork of contrasting squares, but the popups and banner ads didn't give way to anything - they just multiplied.

'You can tell it's a garden planet,' said an even, male voice. 'They grow produce in those fields.'

Hal glanced at the battered bronze robot sitting to his right. 'Clunk the co-pilot. Useless data on demand.'

'Facts are important. Without them we could land in the ocean.'

'Again.' Hal gathered his mug and made his way to the rear of the flight deck, where a coffee maker sat in pride of place. It was a huge, chrome-plated model bristling with spouts, and the control panel was more complicated than the one Clunk was using to fly the ship. 'You keep your eyes on the screen,' said Hal, as the robot turned to watch. 'You're supposed to be navigating.'

'I don't want to miss the fun.'

Hal patted the machine. 'You're just miffed because I installed it myself.'

'Not miffed. Worried.'

Hal requested a white coffee. The machine gurgled and spluttered, then filled the mug with orange goo.

'Order orange mucus and it might give you coffee,' said Clunk helpfully.

Hal emptied his mug and tried again. This time he got yellow foam with blue sprinklies.

Clunk tried not to smile. 'Would you like me to calibrate it?'

'Shut up and land the ship.' Hal tried a third time and got something that looked just like coffee. Unfortunately it tasted like rocket fuel. There was a snort from the console, but by the time Hal had finished gagging Clunk was feigning interest in the viewscreen. There was a grey spot on the map now, a patch which grew into a linked cluster of landing pads and buildings. A flashing green cross tracked one of the landing pads, which was marked with three pulsing circles and a floating sign which said 'Land Here'.

'That's ours,' said Clunk, pointing it out in case Hal had missed the subtle clues. 'The cargo should be waiting for us.'

'It's fresh food, right?'

'Correct.'

'I told you that stasis controller was a good idea. It'll make us a fortune.'

Clunk pressed his lips together. 'Freezing time is a complex process, Mr Spacejock. If anything goes wrong ... '

'Jimmy Bent gave me a three month guarantee. Everything's covered.'

'That's Bent Jimmy, and the only guarantee where he's concerned is that the goods are stolen.'

'Get away. Next you'll be saying he gave me change in forged credits.'

'You took change from Bent Jimmy?'

'He said he couldn't break a thousand.'

Clunk sighed.

'Hey, no sweat. I'll pass the dodgy credits onto someone else.'

'What about the dodgy stasis controller?'

'If it fails we lose someone's lunch order. Big deal.'

'It *is* a big deal. This cargo is worth half a million credits.'

Hal almost dropped his mug. 'How come?'

'Beef from hand-reared cattle, organic vegetables from genetically purified seed ... it's very, very expensive. Worse, they're paying us a pittance to carry it.'

'Six thousand credits isn't bad.'

'After fuel and costs we'll make about five hundred.'

'Don't fret. Once word gets around we'll be fighting off customers.'

'Given our record, I think you mean *with*.'

'All right, Mr Negative. You fly the ship and I'll book the jobs.'

'I'd be only too happy with that.' Clunk turned to the screen, where the landing pad was growing rapidly. 'Speaking of flying, we're about to set down. You'd better drink up.'

Hal made a few slurping noises, pretending to drink his coffee. Then he dumped the mug and plonked himself down in the pilot's chair. 'All right, hit it.'

The engine note changed and Hal's weight increased sharply. Moments later there was a gentle bump and the engines throttled back.

'Landing fees deducted,' said the Navcom.

'Welcome to Cathua,' said Hal drily.

'Arrival tax paid. Ground clearance fee debited. Bank charges levied. Oxygen excise –'

'All right, that's enough of that.' Hal frowned. 'Every time we land it's like ten thousand ants are nibbling me to death.'

'Should I book the pest controllers?'

'Don't talk to me about fumigations,' muttered Hal darkly. He eyed the airlock. 'How's the atmosphere, Clunk? I could use a breather.'

Clunk sniffed. 'Traces of burnt insulation, caffeine and a lot of dust.'

'Outside,' said Hal patiently. 'I meant outside.'

'Ah.' Clunk checked the console. 'Petrochemicals, carcinogens and temperature of four hundred and seventy-five degrees Celsius.'

'Is that safe?'

Clunk's eyebrows rose. 'Safe? It's like a crematorium without the bricks.'

'People do live here?'

'Certainly.'

'So where did the reading come from?'

'This particular sensor is near the starboard thruster.'

'How near?'

Clunk turned to the console and checked. 'Very close, as a matter of fact.'

'And the engines are off?'

The robot threw a switch. 'Now they are.'

'And the atmosphere?'

'Twenty-five degrees, oxygen normal. It's safe to go out.'

Hal entered the airlock. The outer door opened and he dragged in a couple of lungfuls, then gagged on the stale, oily taste.

'That's the petrochemicals and carcinogens,' said Clunk, who'd followed him into the airlock. 'They haven't cottoned on to clean energy sources here.'

Hal rubbed his watering eyes and took in the landing field, which was ringed by derelict warehouses, run-down factories and boarded-up shops. The spaceport terminal was a two-storey building with a tall, arched roof and walls of tinted glass. It looked impressive, but a closer inspection revealed broken panes and a mad scramble of overlapping graffiti. 'We should never have come here, Clunk. It's a dump.'

'There wasn't another food job within twelve parsecs.'

'That far?'

'Long,' corrected the robot.

Hal frowned. 'I thought a parsec was a measure of distance?'

'It was, once. The meaning was altered some time ago.'

'Bloody revisionists.'

'There's the cargo,' said Clunk, indicating a column of delivery trucks approaching the ship. Their flanks were plastered with brand names and colourful logos: H. Turo Hydroponics, Dave Gornov Pies and R. Soles & N. D. Bits Smallgoods.

'Makes me hungry just looking at them,' remarked Hal.

'We have food.'

'Sure, if you like frozen crap.'

'The AutoChef doesn't serve frozen –'

'You're right. It warms it up first.' Hal pointed at the terminal. 'I'm going to find something to eat. Can you supervise the loading?'

5

'I thought you were handling customers from now on?'

'You can't expect me to work on an empty stomach.' Ignoring the robot's protests, Hal strode down to the landing field and made for the spaceport terminal.

Clunk watched Hal go with mixed feelings. He was annoyed at being left to do the work on his own, but also pleased to be free of interference. The human meant well, but loading would take half the time without him. He made his way to the cargo hold and operated the controls, lowering the ramp until it was level with the floor. Just outside, almost within arms reach, there was a rugged little freighter with a rust-streaked hull. Clunk pressed his lips together at the sight. A huge empty landing field, and ground control had to set them down right next to a dented old bomb like that. If they so much as scuffed the *Volante*'s paint . . .

The first truck reversed up and a platform slid out to meet the *Volante*'s ramp. Once they connected the entire cargo emerged in a block: silver crates stacked five high, three rows across and half a dozen deep. They moved across the platform and rode onto the ramp, rumbling past Clunk and vanishing smoothly into the hold. Now empty, the truck drove away and another took its place.

Clunk leaned against the doorway and watched the intelligent floor dividing the cargo and moving it around the hold, filling the available space quickly and efficiently. Despite his misgivings he decided the job would probably work out, even if the profit was small. He'd been critical of

Mr Spacejock's stasis controller, but deep down he knew his objections stemmed from a fear of newfangled machinery. The stasis controller wasn't a direct threat to his role aboard the ship, but surely it was only a matter of time before some other piece of equipment came along to replace him.

◆

The spaceport concourse had been grand once, but that was long, long ago. The marble flooring was stained and dusty, and the ticket counters were staffed by nothing more than fading hopes. There were boarded-up kiosks reminiscent of ornate crypts, and Hal passed one empty vending machine after another, their fascias faded and peeling, their contents long since excreted.

He'd almost given up hope when he spotted a tatty wooden sign protruding from the worn brickwork. It was a confectionary shop, and Hal decided a couple of choccy bars would go down a treat.

The door opened reluctantly, admitting him to an unlit room the size of a large cupboard. There was a counter just ahead of him, with a customer service bell fixed to a cracked wooden base. Behind the counter, a wall of uneven shelves overflowed with faded boxes, their once-garish logos reduced to sepia by whatever sunlight managed to sneak through the grimy windows.

Hal stepped up to the counter and reached for the bell, but before he could use it a door creaked open, admitting a faceless serving droid. 'Good evening, sir,' it said, in a poorly synthesised male voice. 'What can I do you for?'

'Do you carry Tastee chocolate bars?'

The droid gestured towards the shelves. 'All our products are tasty, sir.'

'Yeah, twenty years ago,' muttered Hal, eyeing the dusty cartons. He raised his voice. 'I meant the Tastee brand. You know, Munch after lunch?'

The droid put a finger to where its lips would have been. Lacking a mouth, the gesture failed to evoke the genteel air its programmers had strived for. 'I believe we may have some out the back. Wait a while, I shall return momentarily.'

Hal glanced through the dirty window and saw a wasteland dotted with rusty junk and weeds. It was almost dark, and for all he knew a gang of thugs was sizing him up at that very moment, working out where to dump his body.

The droid came back, brushing dust and rat droppings from a battered cardboard box. 'Here you are, sir! The last one.'

'It looks like the *first* one. Ever.'

'This is a fine product, sir. Tastee bars age well.'

Hal sighed. 'How much?'

'Thirty-seven credits.'

'What, for one Tastee bar?'

'No, for the whole box.'

'I don't want a box, I just want a couple.'

'But we only sell bulk, sir. We're a wholesale company.'

'Wholesale?' Hal stared. 'What are you doing in a passenger terminal?'

'The rent's cheap.'

'Whatever you're paying, it's too much.' Hal leaned across the counter. 'Listen, sell me a couple of bars and I'll pay double for them. Okay?'

'I can't break the pack, sir. Doing so would render it unsaleable.'

'It's unsaleable now.'

'Retail outlets won't buy open packs.'

Hal waved at the shelves. 'They won't buy this mouldy old crap, whether it's open or not!'

The droid hung its head. 'I know it's not much, but it's all we have. My owner isn't well, and –'

'I'm sorry,' muttered Hal. 'I'm sure it's not all mouldy.' Suddenly a thought zipped into his head like a double-speed Tastee bar jingle. 'Listen, did I mention I was thinking of opening a sweet shop?'

The droid perked up. 'Really?'

'Oh yes. I'm, er, doing market research. Trying to decide which products to stock.'

'Now that I can help you with.' The droid set the Tastees on the counter, turned to the shelf and began pulling down boxes. 'These are my favourites,' confided the sales droid, ripping the lid off the carton. 'Maya Swell aniseed balls. Would you like one?'

Hal eyed the gaudy packet. 'Maya Swell, eh?'

'You see? Marketing genius. And take these . . . ' the droid tore into a yellow carton and held up a handful of glossy brown sweets. 'Spaceman's Little Helper.'

'What sort of name is that?'

'They were going to call them Spaceman's Friend, but it was already trademarked.'

'They look like hard-boiled turds in dandruff.'

'Well yes, but they have a strong market presence.'

'Strong doesn't begin to cover it,' said Hal, after catching a whiff of the contents. He glanced through the windows at the darkness outside. 'Look, I need to get back to my ship. Can I grab a few samples and settle up?'

'You can't leave now. I still have lots to show you!'

'Sorry, I really must. Could you hand me a couple of those Tastee bars?'

The droid turned its blank face towards him. 'You're not really opening a sweet shop, are you?'

'Er ...'

'I see.' The droid tipped the Spaceman's Little Helpers back into the torn carton and tried to piece the faded lid back together. 'I didn't really believe you. I suppose it was more hope than anything.' It raised its head again. 'Hope is bad for robots. Did you know that?'

'I guess so,' muttered Hal, looking at the floor.

'I'll lose my job over this,' said the droid. It gathered a stray Spaceman's Helper and held it up between finger and thumb. 'Junked,' it said, crushing the sweet with a snap.

'Is there anything I can do to help?'

The droid hung its head. 'I doubt it.'

'How much are these?' asked Hal, tapping the Maya Swell box.

'Twenty-two fifty,' said the droid in a dull voice.

'And the Spaceman's thingies?'

'Nineteen eighty.' The droid looked up. 'You mean ...'

'Bag 'em up,' said Hal gruffly. 'I'll take the lot.'

2

Loading was complete by the time Hal returned to the *Volante*, and he found Clunk moving amongst the stacks of silver crates with dozens of blue data cables looped over his arm, plugging them into sockets one by one. 'How's it going?' asked Hal, holding the decrepit cardboard box behind his back.

'Not bad,' said Clunk. 'I'm just connecting the crates, and then I'll calibrate the controller.'

'Excellent. Fantastic.' Hal hesitated. 'Do you want a hand?'

'No thanks,' said Clunk quickly. He spotted the box. 'What did you get?'

'Oh, this and that.'

Clunk came over and lifted the flap. 'Spaceman's Little Helpers?'

'Spaceman's Friend was trademarked.'

'They look like dried leavings in dandruff. Are you sure they're edible?'

'I'm not going to find out.' Hal frowned at his purchases. 'All I wanted was a couple of lousy chocolate bars.'

Clunk sniffed. 'Looks like you got a whole box of them. I don't know why you eat the things. They'll rot your teeth and make you fat.'

'Now you're a health nurse?'

'I'm merely concerned about your well-being.'

'You are?'

'Yes. If you die, who else am I going to look after?' Clunk reached for the bill. 'How much did you spend?'

'None of your business,' said Hal, snatching it away.

'That much? Really?'

'The place was very run down,' said Hal defensively. 'The owner was sick and they had this pitiful little serving droid minding the shop.'

'Faceless. About so high?'

'How'd you know?'

'A very successful model, I'm led to believe. Their software has no effect on me, which is why we don't leave every spaceport with a shipload of musty old stores.'

'Wait a minute. What do you mean successful?'

'You went in for two chocolate bars and came out with half the shop.'

Hal's jaw dropped. 'You mean I was set up?'

'Evidently. These products are inedible and worthless, and yet you paid for them.' Clunk frowned. 'I should have gone with you.'

'I don't need a minder.'

Clunk eyed the stack of confectionary. 'I guess you don't, with that many Helpers.'

'I got something else too.' Hal reached into his pocket and took out a small black button. 'It's a commset. Neat, eh? The charger and stuff's in the bag.'

'What's the contract like?'

'Contract?'

'Monthly payments. Billing.'

'Oh, not too bad,' said Hal vaguely. 'Pretty standard.'

'What was a sweet shop doing selling electronics?'

'It was a special offer. They give you the thing for free and charge you …'

'… Hundreds of credits a month for the contract,' finished Clunk. 'A very special offer indeed.'

'It'll be useful. You'll see.' Hal glanced around the hold. 'How long till we leave?'

Clunk held up a bunch of cables. 'An hour or so.'

'That long? What am I supposed to do?'

'You could always grab a coffee,' said Clunk innocently.

◆

Hal entered the flight deck, dumped his cardboard box on the pilot's chair and plugged the new commset in for a charge. Then he took a screwdriver from the *Volante*'s toolkit and approached the coffee maker with a determined gleam in his eye. The cover came off after a brief tussle, two gouged fingers and a smattering of paint flakes, and Hal brushed a few spots of blood away as he contemplated the insides. The machine resembled a nuclear bomb crossed with a perpetual motion device - not that Hal was familiar with either, but they sounded complicated and complicated was what he was staring at.

'What the hell are all these thingumabobs for?' he asked nobody in particular.

'Have you checked the manual?' replied the Navcom.

Hal glanced at a thick volume sitting nearby. The cover was plastered with bright friendly pictures that gave the impression an untrained chimp could obtain warm drinks from the machine using nothing but blind luck and brute force. Neither had worked for Hal. 'You must be joking. That thing's as useful as a lifebelt on a space station.' He tapped a couple of brass pipes with his screwdriver and tugged at a loop of wire. It came free, and he hurriedly reconnected it. 'All it has to do is make coffee and spray it through the nozzle things. Why's it so complicated?'

'You *did* purchase the super deluxe model.'

'Of course I did. It came with the froth attachment and a free bumper sticker.' Hal found a hidden button and pressed it. As he did so, the overhead lights dimmed.

'Don't do that again,' said the Navcom.

Hal did it again.

'I said –'

Hal pressed the button repeatedly, getting nothing out of the coffee maker but a gargling sound. The lights flickered again and again, until the machine expired with a loud fizzing noise.

'I *told* you not to do that again,' said the Navcom. 'Now you've destroyed the overload protection module.'

Hal flapped at the smoke. 'Well, we'll just have to get another one.'

'You can't, not with that model. It's a non-serviceable part.'

'What if we –' Hal broke off as the lift pinged. 'Oh hell, that's all I need.' He slammed the cover back on the coffee maker and rammed home a couple of fasteners. 'Don't mention this or Clunk will be lecturing me for weeks.'

'But –'

'One word and I'll run your cooling pipes through the sewage tank.' The doors opened and Hal whipped the screwdriver behind his back. 'Hey, old buddy! What's happening?'

'Old buddy?' Clunk raised one eyebrow. 'Have you been drinking coffee again?'

'No, he hasn't,' said the Navcom. 'Not a drop.'

'That'll do, Navcom,' said Hal sharply. He glanced at Clunk. 'Are we ready to leave?'

Clunk sighed and shook his head. 'I'm afraid not. We have a problem.'

'I'm sure Mr Spacejock can fix it,' said the Navcom. 'He's very good with a screwdriver.'

'What kind of problem?' asked Hal hurriedly.

'The stasis controller is only rated for forty crates, but we've got two more than that. We'll have to cancel the job.'

'I'm not giving up six grand,' said Hal flatly.

'But there are too many crates. It won't run them all at once.'

'You'd better show me.'

'What for?'

'In case I can help, of course!'

Clunk looked doubtful, and was about to elaborate when he paused to sniff the air. 'Can you smell burning?'

'No, not me. Must be your imagination.' Hal ushered him towards the lift. 'Come on, I want to have a look.'

◆

Hal entered the *Volante*'s hold, following Clunk past the neat stacks of crates to the rear of the ship. Each crate had a winking red light on the front, and the effect was that of a stadium full of red camera flashes. The cargo ramp was down and Hal glanced at the elderly ship parked behind them, wondering whether they'd spare him a cup of coffee. His train of thought was interrupted when Clunk nudged him.

'There, Mr Spacejock. See for yourself.'

15

Hal looked. The stasis controller was a large white cylinder covered in heatsink fins. Nestled amongst them was a status screen and a hefty power switch, and a thick black cable ran from the base to a junction box, which was connected to the silver crates via the blue wires. There were two empty sockets on the box, and a couple of blue wires were draped over the top, their plugs dangling loose. 'What's the problem? That box thing still has room for the plugs.'

'That box thing is a hub, and it has room because it can be used with larger stasis controllers.'

'Have you tried switching it on yet?'

Clunk shook his head.

'What's the worst that can happen?'

'Do you know what an overload protection module is?'

Hal pictured the stricken coffee maker. 'I've had one or two dealings with them.'

'Well, if we switch on the controller we could blow the module.'

'And that's non-serviceable, right?'

'Actually, no. You can replace them easily.'

Hal shrugged. 'Let's give it a shot then.'

'Are you sure? I mean –'

'Of course I'm sure. If it hangs together we're out of here. If it doesn't, you can replace the module thingy and we'll think again.' Hal patted the stasis controller, almost slicing his hand on a heatsink fin. 'This is quality gear, not some cheap piece of junk.'

Clunk hesitated. 'I'm still not sure.'

'It's only two crates over the limit. Are you telling me they didn't allow for a bit of give and take?'

'Manufacturers generally allow for a margin of error,' said Clunk slowly. 'However –'

'Can't you tweak the margin a bit? Upgrade the parts or something?'

'I don't know the first thing about this machine, and you'll lose the warranty if I so much as open it.'

'There's your answer then. We'll plug it in, and if anything happens I'll get a replacement from Bent Jimmy.'

'He's five days travel from here, Mr Spacejock. If anything happens we're stranded.'

'Nothing's going to happen. Watch.' Before Clunk could raise any more objections, Hal plugged in the loose wires, put his hand on the chunky power switch and pulled it down.

Chack! The controller's status screen lit up with pulsing yellow bars, and as they climbed higher and higher the fins began to radiate serious heat. Hal glanced around the hold and saw green lights on all the crates. 'It's working!'

'For now.' Clunk touched one of the fins and winced. 'But will it last three days?'

'Sure it will,' said Hal. 'Come on, let's go!'

'I've got to organise clearance first, and then –' Clunk broke off. 'What was that?'

'What?'

A second or two later Hal could hear it too: a gentle hissing, gradually getting louder. 'Is that supposed to happen?'

The controller's display exploded with a loud crack, and the glass was still rattling on the deck when Clunk pushed Hal behind a stack of crates. There was a thunderous boom and the near side of the controller disappeared in a vivid white flash, sending half a dozen fins spinning into the hold. Clunk was knocked clear off his feet, and the force of the explosion hurled the heavy cylinder out the back of the ship, leaving a bunch of torn cables whipping around in its wake. Hal's ears were still recovering from the blast when a second, deeper crash blasted his ears.

Through the swirling smoke he saw Clunk sitting up, brushing fragments of glass from his chest. 'It's all right,' called Hal. 'I'm okay.'

Clunk glanced at him, his face expressionless. Then he stood and walked to the rear of the hold, stepping carefully over the sparking cables. He stopped at the doorway and leaned casually on a hydraulic piston, gazing out onto the landing field.

'Just as well it's on wheels,' said Hal. 'We can push it back and try again.'

Without turning, Clunk beckoned.

Hal walked over and looked down. Through the billowing smoke he could just see the controller lying next to the old ship parked behind the *Volante*. The metal fins were bent in every direction and the exposed heart was a blackened knot of tubes, wires and electronics. Smouldering cables radiated outwards like arms on a barbecued squid, and flames flickered around the thick black connecting cable, which was now a strip of molten slag. 'Doesn't look too good,' he remarked.

'Oh, it gets much worse,' said Clunk, pointing higher.

Hal looked. The flying cabinet had smashed into the parked ship, leaving a huge square dent in the engine housing. Various fluids were leaking out, running down the hull and dripping on the stasis controller: fuel, coolant or sewage, whatever it was, if there was anything more likely to damage the controller than hurling it at the nearest spacecraft it was soaking the thing in toxic liquids. At any second an irate pilot was likely to burst out of the ship, and it wouldn't take a detective to follow the trail of destruction back to the *Volante*. 'We'd better fetch it and get out of here,' said Hal.

18

'What for? It's ruined.' Clunk turned and spread his hands, encompassing their cargo. 'And so are we.'

Hal caught his breath as he saw flashing red lights all over the cargo hold. 'Okay, so we need another controller.'

'You won't get one here.'

'Parts, then. You can fix anything.'

Clunk's lips tightened. 'Build from scratch, you mean.'

'Think of the challenge! A lone robot working against pressing deadlines. The desperate human waiting breathlessly in the wings. The triumph of success. Fame. Fortune.'

'That's the problem with humans,' remarked Clunk. 'You're all full of –'

'Hey, come on! You said the protection module was easy to replace. I'd never have switched it on otherwise.'

'Are you blaming me for this disaster?'

'Well –'

Clunk bunched his fists. 'Because if you are, I'm leaving.'

'No, never!' said Hal, backpedalling. He tripped over a cable and sat down on a crate. 'Thing is, you're my only hope. I'll never get out of this one on my own.'

Mollified, Clunk crossed his arms. 'Things will have to change around here.'

'Anything.'

'No more impulsive behaviour. We stick to the rules.'

'Sure.'

'No meddling with electrical equipment.'

Hal pushed the coffee maker out of his mind. 'Right. Anything you say.'

'Very well. I will stay on as co-pilot as long as you keep your word.' Clunk jabbed his finger at the damaged ship. 'I'm going to exchange insurance details with the pilot. You're going to sit in the flight deck and touch nothing.'

'Insurance?' Hal frowned. 'Is that a good idea? I mean, what about the excess?'

Clunk's eyes narrowed.

'Yeah, insurance. Good idea.' Hal jumped up. 'I'll be in the flight deck.'

'Sitting still.'

'Absolutely motionless,' said Hal.

Clunk relented slightly. 'You can have a coffee, Mr Spacejock. But go easy on the sugar.'

3

Clunk jogged down the *Volante*'s cargo ramp, his mind in turmoil. Had he really threatened to walk out on Mr Spacejock? He went cold at the thought. What other human would give him a home, would rely on his advice and help daily? All right, so Mr Spacejock didn't so much rely on advice as completely ignore it, but he was thoughtful and kind. Actually, on second thoughts, Clunk realised Hal was rather thoughtless, and any kindness was usually accidental. Regardless, Clunk needed a roof over his head and a socket to charge by, and the *Volante* was all he had.

Lost in thought, he crossed the landing pad to the rugged little vessel, where he levered the controller upright and stood it on its castors. Once he'd hooked up the blackened cables he glanced up at the ship to inspect the damage, drawing in a sharp breath as he saw the deep square dent in the engine housing. Their insurance would cover it, but the excess would empty their account and the subsequent hike in premiums would make it impossible to earn a living.

What if he repaired the damage himself? There was a loose flap of tin which he felt he could straighten without too much trouble, but when he touched the flap it promptly fell off. There was a crash as it hit the ground, and a coiled tube burst free of the engine, whipping around and spraying thick brown oil in a mad, random pattern. Clunk jumped clear, but not before he'd been iced with a chocolate-coloured lattice. The pipe continued to flay around, battering delicate components with abandon while the ship settled lower and lower on the ground, and Clunk felt he should step in and grab it before it did even more damage. Then again, he'd clearly made things worse by approaching the ship, and the longer he stayed the worse things were going to get, so the obvious course of action was to leave, and as soon as possible.

The internal debate was still raging when he spotted a faded yellow sticker plastered on the ship's nose cone: *This abandoned vessel has been reported to the authorities.*

Relieved beyond measure, Clunk put his shoulder to the controller and pushed it across the concrete to the *Volante*. After a decent run-up he forced the controller up the ramp, over the lip and into the hold. Once inside he closed the door and turned to the stasis controller to evaluate the damage. The remaining fins were bent, but that needn't affect their operation. The screen he could live without, but the large hole in the case and the blackened components inside were definitely a concern. He could replace them, but first he had to work out what they did.

Within moments he'd mapped all the circuits to determine the purpose of each component, pinpointing the likely sources of error. He also spotted several places where he could use up-rated components to squeeze a little more performance out of the controller, hopefully enough to run the two extra crates. Once he'd listed the parts he needed he contacted the Navcom. 'Can you put me in touch with an electronics supplier?'

'Not until tomorrow. They closed at five.'

'All of them?'

'There's only one.'

'But that means we're stuck here overnight! Are you sure we can't get parts?'

'Not until the morning,' said the Navcom.

Clunk eyed the flashing red lights all around him. The food would survive a few hours, but he wouldn't like to leave it much longer.

◆

While Clunk was retrieving their makeshift ship-to-ship missile, Hal had been busy in the flight deck. The robot's threats had really shaken him and it was five whole minutes before he was able to pick up a screwdriver and resume his attack on the coffee machine.

He'd barely got within a metre of it when the Navcom chimed in. 'Clunk said not to touch anything.'

'I'm not. I'm using the screwdriver.'

'Semantically correct, but I don't think that's quite what Clunk meant.'

'He should have been more specific.' Hal shrugged. 'Anyway, he'll never believe this thing blew up before the fuss downstairs. All I can do is fix it before he finds out.'

'But if he catches you messing with it –'

'I'll be wearing my nuts for earrings.' Hal whipped the cover off the coffee maker and peered inside. 'Come on, advise me. What do I have to do?'

'My recommendation? Put the screwdriver away and sit down.'

'You're not helping much.' Hal poked around inside the machine, generating fat blue sparks as he prodded high voltage terminals with the metal tool. 'It's a wreck, isn't it?'

'You said it.'

Hal swore. 'All I wanted was a cup of coffee.'

'Did you know the spaceport has an online shop? You could order a replacement machine and have it delivered to the ship.'

'You're really trying to land me in trouble with Clunk, aren't you? What's he going to say when a courier rocks up with a new coffee maker? It'll be the short-of-money speech with three encores and a curtain call *and* I'll be wearing my nuts for earrings.'

'I thought you were in charge of the ship?'

'I am.' Hal pictured Clunk's angry face. 'Sort of.'

'Shall I bring up the shopping interface?'

Hal sighed. 'I guess there's no harm in looking.'

'What style of mall would you like? Retro, classic or bargain basement?'

'Bargain sounds good.'

'Complying. Five credits deducted.'

The main screen flickered and a dingy-looking arcade appeared. The signs were crooked, the windows were boarded up and several derelict robots were shuffling around aimlessly. 'Welcome to Rhone!' said a hand-painted banner across the entrance.

'I'm not using that dump. Give me the classic one.'

'Accessing classic node.' There was a burst of white noise and the same image came back. 'Five credits deducted.'

'I said classic.'

'This is the classic.'

'How come it's the same as the other one?'

'All nodes lead to Rhone.'

'Another bloody fiddle.' Hal squinted at the gloomy image. 'Is that an appliance shop?'

The screen jumped and a store front appeared. It was a rough hack with glaring white lines where the textures didn't quite fit and a jerky waterfall animation with pixellated spray. The virtual windows were filled with poorly cropped images of white goods, overlapping to form an eye-watering montage. 'Welcome to the Hand-E-Mart virtual store!' said an excited voice. 'Make your selection from the following menu: housewares, homewares, hosiery, hardware, handicrafts or pets.'

'Homewares,' said Hal.

'You chose . . . pets. Is this correct?'

'No.'

'You chose . . . no. Is this correct?'

'Yes.'

'You chose . . . yes. Is this correct?'

'Yes,' said Hal, through gritted teeth.

'Thank you. Please make your selection from the following menu: housewares, homewares –'

'Housewares,' said Hal.

'You chose . . . homewares. Is this correct?'

'Close enough.'

'Please say yes or no.'

'Yes.'

'You chose . . . yes.' There was a delay while a fancy animated 'Yes' danced around the screen. 'Thank you. You are now entering the Hand-E-Mart virtual warehouse. Remember, every item is on special and delivery is included at no extra cost.'

Hal drummed his fingers on the console as a progress bar crawled across the screen.

'Your warehouse is ready!' said the mall software brightly. 'Would you like to buy this item?'

Hal looked at the large blue toaster displayed on the screen. 'No.'

'You chose ... no. Are you sure about that?'

'Yes.'

A frilly, ivory-coloured bathmat appeared. 'Would you like to buy this item?'

'No way.'

'You chose ... no. Are you sure about that?'

'I just want a coffee maker.'

The screen flickered and a squat, orange appliance appeared. It had several gleaming spouts, two dozen chrome knobs and a big warning sticker with a black lightning bolt.

'That's it!' said Hal. 'Do you have it in white?'

The bathmat reappeared. 'Would you like to buy this item?'

'Show me the coffee maker!'

The orange monstrosity flicked up. 'Would you like to buy this item?'

'How much?'

'One hundred and twenty credits. Would you like to buy this item?'

'Yes,' said Hal.

'Would you like one or two hundred?'

'Just one.'

'Order accepted. Would you like pickup or delivery?'

'Delivery,' said Hal.

'You chose delivery. Are you sure?'

'Yes.'

'You are calling from the *Volante*, docked at the Cathua spaceport. Is this the delivery address?'

'Yes.'

'Thank you for shopping with Hand-E-Mart virtual store. Your order will arrive within twenty-four hours.'

Hal sank back in his chair, feeling like he'd just gone three rounds with a debating team. He spotted the battered cardboard box under the console, flipped it open and grabbed a Tastee bar. Unfortunately, the chocolate had turned into a chalky white lump, and when he checked the terms and conditions on the back he discovered faulty product could only be exchanged on Plessa. 'Navcom, where's Plessa?'

The main screen displayed a system map with planets Cathua and Jordia orbiting near the primary star, Oxed, and Plessa all alone near the periphery. 'Plessa is the richest planet in the system,' said the Navcom. 'It has the biggest economy, the busiest spaceport and the largest population.'

'Oh, that's great,' muttered Hal, throwing the chocolate bar back in the box. 'It'd cost us ten times this load of crap in fuel.'

'Not to mention port fees,' said the Navcom.

Hal sighed. 'I'm going to check on Clunk before I turn in. I'll see you in the morning.'

'Good night.'

Hal paused near the lift. 'This wasn't a bad idea about the new coffee maker, you know. I'm glad I thought of it.'

The Navcom wisely said nothing.

4

A green cab made its way along Cathua City's busy main street, the light from the packed stores gleaming off its frost-rimmed windshield. Inside, the driver's eyes spent more time on his passenger than they did on the road. His fare was a tall woman with hair cropped to a blonde fuzz; her strong jaw and thin lips spoke of a driven, determined nature. Her figure-hugging white dress was a poor choice for the freezing weather, but given the eye-popping figure it was hugging, the driver wasn't about to complain.

He hadn't complained about their route either, even though they'd just passed the Post Office for the third time in fifteen minutes. After two laps he'd realised he had a loony on his hands, but he didn't mind loonies if they were good for the fare. 'Round again, love?' he said, tearing his gaze from the woman's shapely legs.

His passenger didn't answer. She was staring straight ahead, and with a shock the cabbie realised she wasn't even blinking. Gawd. Had she carked it? 'Er, miss? Hello?'

The woman turned a blank stare on him. 'Yes?'

'Round again?'

A look of confusion crossed the woman's pale face and her eyes narrowed as she studied the meter, the shops and the busy street. 'Where are we?'

'The high street.'

'No, which planet?'

The driver's heart sank. She wasn't just a loony, she was an out-and-out whackjob. 'Cathua, love. This is a cab, not a rocket ship.'

'Take the next left.'

The driver obeyed, steering into a narrow street lined with apartment buildings. Alongside him the woman sat motionless, as if she were carved from marble.

'Stop here.'

As the cab pulled over, the woman opened her purse and took out a handful of credit tiles. Without looking at them, she dropped the lot into the driver's outstretched hands, got out and closed the door. He watched the ghostly white figure move towards the nearest building, her outline wavering and shimmering through the frost-laden windshield. Then she was gone.

The driver glanced up at the street number and did a double-take. They were back where they'd started! 'Total nutjob,' he muttered, shaking his head. Then he looked at the money in his hands. There was over a thousand credits in high-denomination tiles.

◆

Jasmin Ortiz stood in the apartment building's lobby, looking around in confusion. She knew she lived here, but while the surroundings were familiar she couldn't remember which flat was hers. In fact, when she dug deeper she realised she couldn't remember anything before the cab ride. Her memory was completely blank.

She crossed the lobby to a row of mailboxes near the lifts, expecting to find a clue amongst the name tags, but to her annoyance they only had numbers. She put her fingers into the nearest slot and tried to ease the door open, hoping to find a letter inside addressed to the occupant. Crack! The reinforced plastic splintered like balsa, scattering shards on the marble floor. Stunned, Jasmin examined her hand, clenching and unclenching her fingers, and with every movement her ultra-sensitive ears picked up the faint but distinctive whine of micro-motors. She examined the other hand, then her arms, her elbows ... and although her skin was incredibly realistic, she realised with a jolt that all her parts were mechanical. She wasn't human!

There was a flash inside her head as she relived a sequence of vivid memories. Cold air and bright lights as she emerged from a tank. Masked strangers bending over her, bringing her to life with nutrients and high voltage. Pain, too. Physical and mental, tearing apart her circuits and -

When Jasmin came to she was lying on the cold marble floor, the red handbag close to her face. She frowned at it, then sat up and wrenched it open. Inside she found more credit tiles, a small metal key and a swipe card. Both the key and the card carried the same number: fifty-two.

The key fitted a mail box, which contained a wad of advertising flyers. Jasmin stuffed them in her bag, then called the lift and selected the fifth floor. Moments later she stepped into a carpeted hallway with doors at regular intervals. Fifty-two was the first on the right, but as Jasmin readied her keycard the door on the opposite side of the hall opened and an old lady in a faded pink dressing gown peered out.

'Back already, dear? Did you forget something?'

Did I ever, thought Jasmin. 'Do you know where I was going? Was there anyone with me?'

'No, dear.' The lady looked at her in concern. 'Are you feeling all right?'

'I have to sit down.'

'Good cup of tea, that's what you need.'

'I'll bear that in mind.'

'Did you like your apple pie?'

Jasmin weighed up the two possible answers and chose the safest. 'Yes. Lovely.'

'You didn't see Petey downstairs, did you?'

'Petey?' Who or what was Petey? Jasmin desperately tried to remember. Husband? Cat? Toy boy? 'I don't think so.'

'I sent him out for milk an hour ago and he's not back yet.'

That ruled out a cat, thought Jasmin. 'Does he usually get lost?'

'Oh no. He's as regular as clockwork.' The old lady put a hand to her mouth. 'Oh, I didn't mean that in a nasty way. I mean, I know robots are sensitive about that sort of thing.'

Jasmin stared. Did this old woman know what she was? Did everyone?

'Not that Petey is sensitive, of course. Poor dear, it's all he can do to walk properly.'

And that ruled out the toy boy. 'Never mind, I'm sure your husband will turn up soon.'

'I hope not. He died twenty years ago.'

'But Petey ... '

The old lady turned pink. 'You *know* Petey's my robot. There is *nothing* improper in our relationship, and I'll thank you not to spread rumours.'

'Oh no, I didn't mean –' Jasmin stopped, because the old lady had just retreated into her apartment and slammed her door. Turning quickly, she swiped her card and hurried into her own apartment before she could insult the rest of her neighbours. That was the worst part about being a deep cover agent AND a robot ... the way they messed with your head after every mission.

Jasmin froze. Where had *that* come from? She poked around in her mind, but there was no way to trace the thought. Deep cover agent? Mission?

Suddenly she realised she was standing in the dark. She gestured at a pickup and soft lighting illuminated the apartment, which consisted of a small lounge flanked by a very small kitchen. At the back of the lounge thick curtains covered the wall, while alongside there was a door to the bedroom. Jasmin looked around, but there was nothing to indicate it was the lair of a master spy. No computer terminals, no consoles with throne-like command chairs from which to direct minions ... not even a doomsday machine with a big red button and a digital countdown. With a wry grin, she realised that as far as the chain of command went she was probably at the henchwoman end of the scale. Henchdroid, rather. Lower than low. Dispensable. Cannon fodder.

Pushing such thoughts from her mind, Jasmin went to inspect the bedroom. The double bed looked as new as the day it was installed and the huge collection of lightweight dresses in the wardrobe only emphasised her immunity to the weather. The bathroom had a toilet, a basin and a shower cubicle, none of them used.

She tried the kitchen, where a pristine workbench was flanked by a small refrigerator and a cooktop. Brand new cups hung from two rows of hooks, clean and shiny and clearly unused. There were no jars of coffee or sugar, no tea towels, no unwashed plates ... no signs of life whatsoever.

On a whim, Jasmin opened the fridge. The door held two cartons of milk, while the shelves were laden with apple pies. There were at least two dozen of them, ranging from fresh through somewhat furry to completely fossilised. Clearly, pie wasn't her thing. Nothing was, she realised as she closed the fridge, because she didn't have to eat.

In the cutlery drawer, Jasmin found a length of flex with a glossy black plug on each end. One plug matched the wall socket, but the other was a complex affair that didn't fit anything she could see. Frowning, she replaced the cord and closed the drawer.

She looked around her apartment once more. As far as she could tell there wasn't the slightest hint as to what she was supposed to be doing. Hadn't she left herself anything? Not even a note? A sudden thought occurred to her. Could her orders be on a time delay? Was a mysterious visitor going to knock on the door and explain everything?

She glanced at the curtains covering the end wall, then walked over and drew them aside to reveal a glass door leading onto an enclosed balcony. Out on the balcony was a large metal box, two metres tall with a smooth shiny surface that was cold to the touch. There was a narrow control panel near the bottom of the nearest side, with a status display and a keypad. Secure storage, then. Did this box contain her spy kit? Her past?

'You seem to have found the shipment,' said a female voice. 'Would you like to proceed with your mission?'

Jasmin looked around for the speaker, but the apartment was empty. Then she realised the voice had spoken within her, inside her head. 'Who are you?'

'I am your controller. My job is to guide you during your mission, and to ensure its successful completion.'

'So who am I?'

'You are Jasmin Ortiz, and you work for the good of Plessa.'

'What am I doing on Cathua?'

'Working for the good of Plessa.'

Jasmin frowned. The controller was obviously of limited intelligence. 'Yes, but what am I supposed to *do*?'

'You must complete your mission.'

'Which is?'

'You will be told as it nears completion.'

'How can I complete it if I don't know what it is?'

'The mission will be revealed in stages. At the successful completion of each step, you will be given the next.'

'What if one of these steps goes wrong?'

'That is not an option.'

'You mean I can't improvise?'

'Improvising is not an option. You must complete each stage as detailed.'

'You don't need a spy for something like that. You might as well use a mindless robot!'

'Precisely.'

Jasmin's face took on a stubborn look. 'What if I refuse?'

Immediately, her body was wracked with agonising pain. Jets of fire scorched her skin, which shrivelled and blackened under the intense heat. Then the pain was gone and her skin returned to normal. 'That was just a taste,' said the controller. 'The real punishment lasts forever.'

Jasmin took a ragged breath. Earlier she'd remembered the pain of birth, but this was the fiery agony of death. A protracted, never-ending death.

'Your first task is to arrange a delivery,' said the controller. 'The shipping crate on your balcony must arrive on planet Jordia within forty-eight hours.'

Jasmin eyed the crate, which was big enough to contain a body. 'What's inside?'

'That does not concern you at this stage.'

'How do I pay for the freight?'

'There is a bank account in your name. It contains more than enough funds to complete your mission.'

'Do I get to keep the rest?'

The controller ignored her. 'I am about to unlock a data package held in your main storage area. This knowledge pertains to your mission, including contact details and account numbers. I will also patch your personality.'

Jasmin's vision dimmed, then returned to normal. She felt the same, but now there was more information at her disposal. 'What's this about a suitcase?'

'You'll find it under the bed. It contains items you will need further into your mission.'

Jasmin went into the bedroom and pulled the suitcase out, laying it on the bed. 'It's locked.'

'You cannot open it without the correct combination,' said the controller. 'If you try, it will self destruct.'

Jasmin lifted the case and shook it. It seemed to get heavier and heavier, until she could barely hold it, and then she realised all her movements were slowing.

'Your energy levels are low,' said the controller. 'Would you like a recharge?'

'How?'

'Insert your finger into your navel.'

'Same to you, you –'

'That's the opening mechanism,' said the controller patiently. 'Insert and twist.'

Jasmin did as she was told. There was a hiss as her abdomen parted, and a wrench of torn fabric as the dress split from her neck to the waist. No wonder she had so many spares in the wardrobe, she thought. Bending slightly, she examined her belly and saw tightly packed components joined by thick copper tubes. In the middle was a rounded box, and in the centre of the box there was a power socket. It was a match for the cord in the drawer, and when she returned to the kitchen and plugged it in a row of indicator lights began to pulse. There was a jolt from the feed, and Jasmin felt a heightened perception as the power surged through her. She stood there, absorbing enough electricity to run a sports stadium, and decided that booking a courier for the crate could wait a while.

Barely had she closed her eyes when there was a knock at the door. 'Miss Ortiz, it's me. Mrs Beatty.'

Jasmin checked the time and realised with a shock that it was the middle of the night. She gestured at the door, which opened silently, and saw the old lady from number fifty-one in the corridor, clutching her dressing gown around her skinny frame. 'What is it?'

'Petey's not back yet. I'm really worried.'

Jasmin felt a flash of irritation. 'Mrs Beatty, it's two in the morning. I have better things to worry about than your missing robot.'

'But he's so old!'

'So are you, and you should be in bed.'

'He went out in his old suit, you know. Oh, I do hope they don't mistake him for one of those tramps.' Mrs Beatty squinted at Jasmin's chest. 'Why, your dress is all torn! Were you attacked, dear?'

Jasmin pulled the ends together, covering the charge cable. 'It's nothing. I caught it on the door handle.'

'Would you like me to fix it? I'm ever so good with a needle.'

'Mrs Beatty, go home.'

Ignoring her, the old lady entered the apartment. 'I could mend that in two shakes of –'

Irritation flared into hot anger. 'Leave me alone, you interfering old bat!' roared Jasmin.

Round-eyed, the old lady stared at her. 'B-but, but –'

'Get lost, and take your lousy apple pies with you!' Jasmin pulled the fridge open and Mrs Beatty vanished just as two pies splashed above the door. Jasmin hauled out two more and threw those, laughing aloud as they stuck to the wall. When she ran out of pies she threw the milk cartons, which exploded with a satisfying squelch, splashing the carpet and armchairs.

Jasmin kicked the fridge shut, unplugged herself and flopped into the nearest armchair. 'Hey, controller! Did I pass another test? Is scaring old ladies another stage in my precious mission?'

The controller remained silent.

5

'Good morning, Mr Spacejock,' said Clunk brightly, as Hal emerged from the lift.

'Morning,' mumbled Hal, wiping sleep from his eyes. The previous night's events were still a blur, but he distinctly remembered Angry Clunk and Really Angry Clunk. 'Everything okay?' he asked, playing it safe.

'I have some good news for you. I made progress during the night.'

Hal brightened. 'Really?'

'Yes, I've almost completed the repairs.'

'You little ripper! You mean we don't need any parts?'

Clunk smiled. 'Absolutely. When I examined the machine I discovered the thermal overload had kicked in, preventing damage to the thermostat by modulating the –'

'Excellent. Magic. When can we leave?'

'Leave?'

'Yeah. I mean, if you've fixed the thing we don't have to hang around here any more. Right?'

Clunk frowned. 'I don't understand.'

'We're stuck here because the stasis controller needs parts,' said Hal patiently. 'If you've fixed it without them, we can go.'

'Oh, I wasn't referring to the stasis controller.'

'What did you fix then?'

Clunk pointed towards the rear of the flight deck. 'The coffee machine.'

Hal's face fell. 'Oh.' Mentally, a small but pertinent fact clicked into place. 'Hang on! Who told you about that?'

'I found an error report in the Navcom's logs.'

'Oh great.'

'Aren't you happy? I mean ... coffee!'

'All right, fire it up then.'

'I haven't run any tests yet,' warned Clunk. 'It might not work properly.'

Hal passed him the cup. 'You promised me a coffee.'

Clunk held the mug under the spout and pressed the button. There was a roar as a jet of blue flame hissed out, knocking the mug from his hands, and when Hal gathered it up he saw a neat hole in the bottom.

'I can adjust the temperature,' said Clunk. 'It won't take a moment.'

'I wouldn't bother.' Hal put the mug down and sat at the console. 'Navcom, give me the news.'

'Lead item. Cathuan President to attend robot trade fair on Jordia.'

'Anything a little more racy?'

'Cathuan President cancels tax breaks on robot research.'

'Taxes? Politicians?' Hal shuddered. 'Next.'

'Plague of birds on Plessa?'

Hal shook his head.

'Supernova in the Carolie quadrant?'

'Shipping news is boring.'

'You're supposed to be a pilot,' said Clunk. 'You have to know these things.'

Hal shrugged. 'If a supernova went off round here it'd be too late, wouldn't it? We'd all be in little bitty pieces before it made the news.'

'You'd like to know if there was a bird plague on the planet you're heading for, wouldn't you? How else would you know to avoid their meat pies?'

'You start buying meat pies and I'll start listening to the bird forecast. Next.'

There was a lengthy silence as the Navcom scanned for interesting news. 'What about this one? Laboratory staff questioned as experimental robot continues to evade capture.'

Hal snorted. 'Enough with the robot stories. Next.'

'Jordian trade embargo stretches into third month.'

Hal sighed. 'Don't you have anything better?'

'Define better.'

'Oh, I don't know. Solid gold asteroids spotted in the vicinity. Free food if your name is Hal. That kind of thing.'

'I do have a store of such items.'

Hal sat up. 'Now you're getting warm. Hit me with it.'

'Story mode activated. Once upon a time –'

'Oh, give me a break,' groaned Hal, slumping back in his chair. Suddenly he frowned. 'Clunk, why were you fixing the coffee maker? We're grounded because of the stasis controller.'

'I need parts, and the shop doesn't open until eight.'

Hal glanced up at the clock. 'It's eight now.'

'Fifteen seconds to.' Clunk tilted his head. 'And unless I'm mistaken, that's our cab.'

'What cab?' asked Hal, as he heard a faint toot.

'For the parts centre. I'm going to use off-the-shelf components to replace those damaged in the explosion.'

'Will that work?'

Clunk gestured at the airlock. 'I won't know until I try.'

They left the ship and walked down the ramp to a dilapidated yellow cab. Clunk got aboard, tipping the car dangerously to one side, and then Hal leapt in, balancing the vehicle.

The cabbie glanced over his shoulder. 'Parts centre?'

'Correct,' said Clunk.

The driver slammed his foot down, hurling them forward in a cloud of dust. The car gathered speed rapidly and shot across the apron, skimming potholes and leaving vaporised puddles in its wake. The terminal buildings loomed ahead, until it seemed they were going to ram them. Just as Hal was leaning forward to alert the driver to their impending doom, the car shot down a ramp and entered a dark tunnel. Their passage was illuminated by the odd flash from the car's exhaust and the occasional dirty skylight overhead, and these flashes showed ragged, grimy brickwork and rusty pipes hemming the car in from both sides.

Hal saw a spot of light in the distance, which grew larger until they were back outside, hurtling down a narrow lane lined with boarded windows. The cab sped through a pair of gates and turned left, accelerating rapidly and leaving the spaceport behind.

A few minutes later they turned into a car park, stopping in front of a navy-blue building. 'Parts centre,' said the driver. 'That'll be ten credits.'

'Can you wait?' asked Hal. 'We'll only be a moment.'

The cabbie glanced in the mirror, eyeing Hal's well-worn flight suit. 'I'll hang around, but you got to settle up first.'

'You think we're going to do a runner?'

The driver took in Clunk's battered appearance. 'Not run, exactly.'

'So wait here, then.'

'Only if you pay first,' said the driver stubbornly.

'Oh, don't bother,' growled Hal, tossing a credit chip into the cab. 'Go on, get lost.'

'Hey, what about a tip?'

'Brush up on customer service.'

The driver departed at speed, and they hurried into the parts centre to avoid the choking cloud of dust. Inside they found a large room festooned with thousands of spares in bubble-packs, shelf upon shelf of battered cardboard boxes with cryptic labels, and floor displays containing lengths of plastic piping, angle iron and metal rods. A track worn into the green carpet tiles led to a counter squashed between a scale cutaway of a jet engine and a huge barrel overflowing with rubber grommets.

As they approached the counter Hal pointed out a display of oil cans. 'You could use one of those.'

'What for? I'm a sealed unit.'

'I was thinking about the ship,' said Hal. 'You could give my chair a squirt for a start.'

'Is that so,' said Clunk flatly.

'Yeah, it's got a squeak. And the cargo hold door's a little stiff.'

'I'll tell you what else we can do with an oil can,' said Clunk, reaching for the biggest model. 'If you'll just –'

Hal raced him to the counter, where he leaned on the button recessed into the scarred plastic surface.

Nothing happened.

Hal pressed the button again, straining for the slightest sign that his action was having an equal and opposite reaction.

No dice.

He was just about to apply himself to the button for the third time when the door burst open, admitting a sturdy young man in faded green overalls.

'Watcher keep pressing it for?' demanded the man, settling on the stool.

'I tried rubbing it but nothing happened,' said Hal. Behind him, Clunk snorted.

'Watcher want, anyway?'

Hal motioned Clunk forward. 'This is where you take over.'

'Ready?' said the robot.

The youth held his pen over a pad and nodded.

'That's one 6E board, three FN D8s, one L4-2 with an OG controller and one BF-36.'

The attendant looked each item up in a bound catalogue and wrote down the details. 'Be right back,' he said, grabbing a cardboard box and vanishing through the door.

'I'd better check the parts before we leave,' remarked Clunk. 'I want to make sure they're of a suitable quality.'

'They'll be all right.' Hal pointed to a sign on the wall: *This company is acredited.*

'Accredited has two c's, Mr Spacejock.'

The door opened and the attendant came back with the box.

'These aren't official parts,' said Clunk, as he inspected the bubble-packs.

The attendant shrugged. 'Made in the same factory.'

'But not to the same standard.' Clunk took the last item out of the box and peered inside. 'Where's the BF-36?'

'We don't have any.'

'How long will it take to get one?'

The youth reached for a desk planner, which was still set to the previous month. He flipped two pages, and scanned the print. 'Next delivery is Tuesday week.'

Hal stared at him. 'You're joking!'

'Has to come from Plessa. There's an embargo, but this guy slips 'em through for me.'

'Tuesday week!' said Hal incredulously. 'I'm not waiting until then! My cargo will be ruined!'

'Go and get it yourself then,' said the attendant, shutting the desk planner. He summed up the total and held out the slip. 'That'll be two hundred and ninety-five credits.'

Hal paid for the parts and they went outside. 'There has to be a way to get one of these BF things.'

'Of course there is. We can fetch it from Plessa ourselves.'

'You want to take a 200-ton freighter on a round trip for a crummy little spare part? Have you any idea how much that's going to cost in fuel? Not to mention the landing fees and all those taxes.'

'We could take a passenger liner.'

'Oh yes, and we'd better go first class. They serve the booze in real glasses.'

'We don't have to travel first class. Third is much cheaper.'

'How much?'

Clunk paused to retrieve the info. 'Fares to Plessa - three thousand credits each.'

'Well that's out, then.' Hal looked around for inspiration, and his eyes narrowed as he spotted a flickering neon sign above a narrow doorway. 'What about the pub? I'm bound to get help if I hit the space bar.'

'Don't bet on it,' said Clunk.

'Why not? I could offer to navigate in exchange for a ride.'

'I wouldn't emphasise that particular skill.'

'What would you suggest? Toilet cleaning?'

'Do you know how?'

'No, but you could come with me.'

44

Clunk shook his head. 'I'm going back to the ship to fit these parts to the controller.'

'What for? We're stuck without the BF thingo.'

'I've got an idea, although the probability of success isn't very high.'

'What idea?'

Clunk shook his head. 'It's probably nothing. You'll have better luck in the bar.'

'Will do.' Hal rubbed his chin. 'If I don't get a lift, at least I can get plastered.'

'No alcohol,' warned Clunk. 'You're not allowed to fly under the influence.'

'Fly?' Hal snorted. 'Fly where?'

The bar was small, with thick hangings covering the windows and deep carpet on the floor. Around the walls, fake candles shimmered and flickered, casting pulsating pools of light on the dark, chunky furniture. The only bright spot was behind the bar, a thick slab of plastic running across the full width of the room. Here, assorted drink logos shone amongst back-lit bottles and racks of snacks.

Hal eyed the shadowy figures engaged in deep conversations and furtive deal-making, taking in the weathered clothing, ragged self-inflicted haircuts and the distant stares of those more used to deep space than candlelit tables. He felt the hairs on the back of his neck rising at the sight of free enterprise in action. Spaceport bars were the nerve centre of galactic civilisation, places where the

45

real business of space was thrashed out, and Hal decided he would frequent them more often, no matter what Clunk thought.

He approached the bar and took a stool next to a man with a sculpted goatee and a tailored mane of straw-coloured hair. As Hal sat down the man raised his drink and watched him over the rim, sizing him up with bloodshot eyes. Hal looked away and attracted the serving droid with a snap of his fingers. 'How much is the orange juice?'

'Nine credits, sir.'

'I'll have one, thanks.'

While the robot whirred off to assemble his drink, Hal felt in his pocket for change.

Alongside him, the elegant customer cleared his throat. 'Broke, huh?'

'Are you talking to me?' asked Hal evenly, keeping his eyes on the robot.

'I was just like you once. Hauling worthless junk from one end of the galaxy to the other, struggling to pay the bills.'

'Worthless junk?' Hal turned to face the man. 'For your information, my ship is carrying half a million credits worth of cargo.'

Across the bar, a dozen conversations were cut off mid-sentence. The man leaned forward eagerly, his voice loud in the sudden silence. 'Precious metals? Gemstones?'

Hal shook his head. 'Fresh food.'

The bar erupted with laughter.

'It's organic!' shouted Hal over the uproar. 'Beef from hand-seeded cows!'

The laughter got even louder, and Hal turned his back on them and hunched over his drink, his ears burning. 'Better than hanging around in bars for a living,' he muttered, just loud enough for the man sitting alongside to hear.

The man frowned. 'I don't know what you mean.'

'Oh yeah? Waiting for customers, are we?'

'I'm a pilot, first class.' The man tapped his chest. 'Kent Spearman of the *Luna Rose*.'

'Hal Spacejock, *Volante*.'

'Freelance?'

Hal nodded.

'Figures. I've yet to meet one of your kind who wasn't surviving on frozen food while lurching from one repair to the next.'

'It's not like that,' snapped Hal.

'Oh, so you're not here to cadge a ride? Pick up spare parts on the cheap? Borrow some fuel?'

'I don't know what you're talking about.'

The serving droid rolled up to the counter and delivered a glass of clear liquid. 'Your drink, sir.'

'What's that?' demanded Hal.

'Nine credits.'

'No, I mean what the hell is it? It looks like water.'

'It's your orange juice, sir.'

'But it's not orange.'

'It is,' said the droid, nodding vigorously.

'It can't be. It's clear.'

'All our drinks are filtered and purified, sir. Best quality guaranteed.'

Hal glanced along the bar. All the bottles held transparent liquid.

'That's nine credits,' prompted the droid.

Hal withdrew a bunch of tiles and slid a couple across the counter. 'Keep the change.'

The droid tilted its head. 'Thank you, sir.'

'Fifty-credit tips?' said Kent, who was looking at Hal with respect. 'Boy, did I get you wrong.'

With a shock, Hal realised he'd handed over the wrong tiles, but with his pride at stake he could only watch the drinks robot vanishing with the bulk of his cash. 'Fifty?' he said, forcing a smile. 'I usually bung them five hundred.'

'It's only money, eh? Course, I've been known to throw the cash around myself. Back home they call me the Big Tip.'

Hal raised his glass and was just about to gulp the drink down when he noticed the smell of alcohol. He took a sip and almost choked on the fumes.

'Problem with your drink?' asked Kent as Hal coughed and spluttered.

'I wanted orange juice, not rocket fuel.'

'You mean real juice?' Kent grinned. 'That's a first around here.'

'What do you mean?'

'Pilots aren't allowed alcohol before flying, right?'

Hal nodded. 'That's why I'm drinking juice.'

'Yes, but ships fly themselves these days. The old rules don't make sense.'

'So?'

'So we have an arrangement.' Kent tapped his mug. 'I order milk, I get beer. A can of cola is wine. Order orange juice and you get neat gin.'

'Are you telling me you fly under the influence?'

'My computer does everything. All that hands-on flying is for old farts.' Kent drained his glass and tapped the counter for another. 'You should try a real ship one day. Push a button to take off and another to land. Minimal interaction.'

'Buttons?' scoffed Hal. 'I haven't seen buttons on a ship for years.'

'Of course, when I say buttons I mean motion sensors.' Kent took a fresh drink from the robot and tipped it back. 'The President was most impressed. Nice bloke once you get to know him.'

'President?'

'He runs this planet.'

'Oh, a politician. I thought you meant someone important.'

'He's slightly more important than a cargo of food.' Kent turned his glass slowly on the counter. 'What are you doing here, anyway? You've got a ship, you've got a cargo and you obviously don't drink. Are you looking for something?'

'Not me,' said Hal, shaking his head. 'Just a bit of R&R.'

'Only I've got a couple of positions to fill aboard ship. Menial work, but if you're after a ride to Plessa –'

'Why don't you use robots?'

'Got four of those doing the engines.' Kent glanced around then lowered his voice. 'Want to hear about a neat money maker?'

'Sure.'

'Robots are trusting, right? I take 'em on and promise them freedom after a couple of years. Instead of wages, that is.'

'Sounds fair to me.'

'You think like a robot,' laughed Kent. 'After three or four years they start getting antsy, and that's when I ask them to polish the airlock doors. Whoosh! Time for another robot.'

Hal looked shocked. 'You space them?'

Kent shrugged. 'They're old anyway. And like I said, they're getting freedom.'

'Don't the rest object?'

49

'I don't tell 'em.' Kent glanced at him. 'So, do you want the job?'

'I'm not looking for work,' snapped Hal.

Kent shrugged. 'It's your funeral.' There was a buzz from his jacket, and he pulled out a miniature commset and held it to his ear. 'Yeah? What, both of them? Excellent. Sign them on, get 'em some uniforms and make sure they sign the disclaimers. Catch you soon.' Kent stuffed the commset back in his pocket and patted it. 'Don't need you after all.'

'Crew?'

Kent nodded. 'Pair of desperate no-hopers most like, but even these clueless morons can make up the numbers. Can't fly without a full complement, you know. Regulations.'

'Speaking of flying, I'd better check with my ship.' Hal took out his new commset and dialled the *Volante*. 'My co-pilot is smart but he needs watching.'

'Don't they all?' muttered Kent.

Through the static, Hal just picked out Clunk's voice. 'Captain Spacejock to the *Volante*,' he said crisply. 'How's it going?'

'What did you say, Mr Spacejock?'

'How's it going?' repeated Hal, louder.

'Are you well? Your voice sounds funny.'

'Excellent. Is everything ready for departure?'

'Of course not. I'm still deciphering the misprinted instructions on these parts, I've stripped a thread on the cover plate and we're still missing the –'

'I don't care what the Emperor said, we're doing it my way.' Hal rolled his eyes at Kent, who was obviously impressed but doing his best not to show it. 'He'll pay the full rate or he can ship his grub with a common courier.'

'Are you listening? I said –'

'See you later, Clunk.' Hal disconnected, and was about to put the commset away when Kent held his hand out.

'Can I see it?'

'Why?'

'They're quite good for cheap knock-offs. Work like crap but look the same as the real thing.'

Reluctantly, Hal passed over the button-sized commset.

'Ah, yes,' said Kent, peering at it closely. 'One of those cheap fakes.' He patted his pocket. 'Mine cost me three grand. Guy called Jimmy Bent fixed me up.'

Hal laughed. 'He sure did.'

'I can call the *Luna Rose* from here,' said Kent defensively.

'I just spoke to the *Volante*.'

'Yeah, but the *Rose* is in orbit.' Kent slid Hal's commset along the bar and stepped down from the stool. 'I gotta get things shape-shipped. Oh, and give the Emperor my regards. We go way back, him and me.'

Hal watched him leave, then finished his drink and set the glass on the counter. Not bad going, he thought. Not only had he blown fifty credits on a lousy orange juice, he'd also turned down a ride to Plessa. How was he going to explain to Clunk?

— 6 —

Jasmin ran full tilt through dense woods, ducking branches and leaping over tangled undergrowth as she tried desperately to stay ahead of her pursuers. They'd cornered her several times already, but when they opened fire their weapons had turned into torches, blinding her with beams of light instead of blowing her apart. Each time this happened Jasmin stumbled away, crashing through bushes and tripping over roots while her internal compass spun crazily.

KNOCK KNOCK.

Jasmin stopped dead. People were calling out, branches were cracking underfoot and she could hear the sound of torches being reloaded, but that last had sounded distinctly like someone tapping on a door.

KNOCK KNOCK. 'Hello? Anyone home?'

Jasmin's eyes flickered open. She was sitting in her lounge room, without a leaf or a blade of grass in sight. A dream? She remembered the guns and the way they morphed into torches. No, it had been a nightmare. She had a splitting headache, fuzzy vision and a metallic taste in her mouth. Apart from the taste, which was to be expected, the others were new experiences and not ones she was keen to repeat.

KNOCK KNOCK!

With a start, Jasmin realised it was a repeat of the noise which had woken her. She stood, gathering the torn edges of her dress as she walked to the door. Her feet slipped on the puddles of milk and the remains of the apple pies, and her balance compensator worked overtime to keep her upright.

The apartment lacked a door camera, spy hole or intercom, so she put her mouth to the frame and shouted. 'Who is it?'

'Courier. I'm here for a shipping crate.'

Jasmin glanced at the mess. 'Wait there, I'll bring it out.' She hurried to the balcony, put her arms around the crate and lifted it easily, reversing up to the front door with the dead weight in her arms. The door swept open and she put the crate down and tilted it so the courier waiting outside could get his trolley underneath.

'Thanks, miss. Going to the spaceport?'

'Yes, the cargo depot. I'll call through the name of the vessel when I have it.'

'I'll let 'em know,' said the courier, pulling on the trolley. It didn't budge so he tried again, and his face turned red as the crate lifted a couple of millimetres, the trolley's wheels splaying under the enormous weight. Puffing with the strain, he staggered down the hallway towards the lifts.

Jasmin watched him go, idly rubbing her shoe on the doormat to remove a chunk of pie crust. The lift creaked alarmingly as the courier got the crate inside, and once the doors closed on him Jasmin returned to her apartment. Now to find a ship.

◆

Hal strode up the *Volante*'s landing ramp, much more comfortable in the familiar surroundings. Going planet-side was like braving a storm in an open boat, tossed upon the whims and wiles of bureaucrats and conmen, whereas on board the ship he was answerable to nobody but himself. He'd enjoyed the duel with Kent though, and was pleased he'd put the jumped up throttle jockey in his place. Big Tip was right - a tip full of rubbish. And fancy anyone getting done over by Bent Jimmy!

As he entered the flight deck he saw Clunk kneeling on a suitcase, desperately trying to fasten the catches. He looked relieved when he spotted Hal. 'Thank goodness you're back!'

'Is everything okay?'

'It is now.' Clunk snapped the catches and stood up. 'I managed to put a temporary fix in place with the stasis controller. You see, there are parallel circuits with zero-state transistors, and by overriding the ... ' He noticed the blank expression on Hal's face and decided to summarise. 'It'll keep the food fresh while we're gone.'

'Good. Well done.'

'However, had you returned a little earlier you would have found me in a state of disarray.'

'Why?'

'Packing,' said the robot. 'I can never decide what to take.'

'Clunk, you don't have to pack.' Hal rubbed his forehead. 'I didn't get a ride.'

'Oh, I've arranged everything.' Clunk gestured at the suitcases. 'We must leave right away. The ship departs from the Orbiter in one hour.'

'Ship?' Hal stared him. 'What did you get, a day trip on a garbage scow?'

'Nothing like that. This is a modern liner with all the amenities. The brochure was very professional.'

'Are you out of your mind? I told you we're not paying for tickets!'

'That's the best part. They're paying us! I tried everything to get us a free trip to Plessa, and I was just about to give up when I came across a job listing. I signed us both up on the spot.'

A warning bell tinkled in the back of Hal's brain. 'Tell me it's not the *Luna Rose*!'

Clunk gasped. 'How did you know?'

'I just spent an hour chatting to the captain while he soaked up enough alcohol to sterilise a hold full of surgical instruments. I was right there when he took the call. A pair of clueless morons, he called them.' Hal paced the flight deck. 'You'll have to cancel this thing.'

'I can't. It's a binding contract.'

'Tell them I broke my leg.'

'They'll want a medical certificate.'

'Tell them someone hocked your batteries for lottery tickets.'

'They won't believe a lie. They'll want proof.'

'Who said it was a lie?' Hal stopped pacing. 'We're not going on the *Luna Rose* and that's flat. I told the captain we were mates with the Emperor. He'll never believe me now!'

'Mr Spacejock, be reasonable. We must have this part for the controller, and this is the only way we're going to get it.'

Hal resumed his pacing with short detours around the luggage. 'Maybe we could have him arrested for drunk in charge. Or we'll get him paralytic, and you can fly the ship.'

'Why are you so concerned?'

'You want me to put my life in the hands of an over-confident drunk!'

'And?'

'And I'm never happy when someone else is at the controls. They might screw up.'

Clunk raised one eyebrow. 'You're worried when you're *not* flying?'

'I didn't say that,' snapped Hal. 'Anyway, why do we both have to go? I'll stay here, you fetch the part.'

'They hired us both.'

Hal looked down at the suitcases, which bore large dents from the robot's knees. Clunk had gone to a lot of trouble, and how bad could a trip aboard the *Luna Rose* really be? 'I guess you did right,' he said gruffly. 'And Clunk?'

'Yes, Mr Spacejock?' said the robot hopefully.

Hal gestured at the cases. 'You ruined my goddamn luggage.'

There was a buzz from the console. 'Incoming call,' said the Navcom.

'Main.'

The screen fizzed and crackled and a sparse lounge room appeared, with a tall, attractive woman in a classy red dress standing alongside a chrome-plated table. She looked at Hal and smiled. 'The port commander tells me you have a freighter for hire.'

'We do indeed.'

'I understand you're good. The best.'

'Oh, I am.' Hal straightened his flight suit. 'And you are?'

'Sadly mistaken,' murmured Clunk.

'Jasmin Ortiz,' said the woman.

'So, Jasmin. How can I help you?'

'I have a cargo for Jordia. One item, overnight delivery. It will arrive at your vessel before eleven am tomorrow.' She paused. 'Are you getting all this?'

'My first officer is taking down every word.' Hal nudged Clunk. 'Every word, right?'

Clunk nodded.

'It's vital this delivery arrives on time,' said Jasmin. 'Otherwise there will be ... consequences.'

'Don't worry, it'll be there.' Hal paused. 'Where is there, exactly?'

'Just land at the spaceport and my people will be in touch.'

'What about payment?'

'Cash on arrival.'

'How much?'

'Thirty thousand credits.'

'Oh, is that all?' said Hal in a strangled voice.

Jasmin's eyebrows rose. 'Very well. Make it forty.'

'Forty thousand credits?'

'That's my last offer. Take it or I'll get someone else.'

'We'll take it,' said Hal hurriedly.

'There is just one thing,' said Clunk. 'What's in this item?'

Jasmin frowned. 'I'm paying you to carry it. The contents do not concern you.'

'Is it legal?'

Hal cleared his throat. 'What he means is, how much does it weigh?'

'No I don't,' said Clunk. 'I mean – ow!'

'Two hundred kilos,' said Jasmin, while Clunk rubbed his side.

'What about customs?'

'They'll be expecting you.'

'That's what I'm worried about.'

Jasmin shook her head. 'There'll be no trouble from that direction, trust me. Now, is there anything else?'

Clunk opened his mouth, but Hal got in first. 'Eleven o'clock tomorrow and forty grand. That's all I need.'

'Excellent.' Jasmin gestured at the screen, cutting the call.

'Wow,' said Hal, staring at the darkened display. 'All my birthdays in one go.'

'Forty thousand is four times the going rate,' said Clunk. 'Something isn't right.'

'Sounds like the perfect job to me.'

'It's someone else's job.'

'You don't know that.'

'Listen.' Clunk opened his mouth, and a recording of Jasmin's voice emerged. 'I understand you're good. The best.'

'So?' demanded Hal.

Clunk stopped the playback. 'I am a loyal and enthusiastic supporter, Mr Spacejock, and I have tremendous faith in your abilities. However, I would not be comfortable describing our little outfit as 'the best'.' He shook his head. 'It's a case of mistaken identity, pure and simple.'

'By the time she finds out we'll have her cash in the bank.'

'You're forgetting something. We already have a cargo job!'

'Now we have two.'

'And we don't have the part for the controller.'

Hal nudged a suitcase with the toe of his boot. 'We will soon.'

'But –'

'If you think I'm letting this one slip, you can think again.'

'There must be a catch. It has to be illegal.'

'Nonsense. She's just a cut above our usual customer, that's all. Rich. Throws money around like water.'

'In my experience, rich people don't pay any more than they have to. Not only that, she looked like a member of the armed forces.'

'The short hair, you mean?'

'Short? It looked like carpet!'

Hal shrugged. 'Rich and fashionable. The perfect customer.'

'But –'

Hal made a zipping motion across his lips. 'Enough. We'll dash over to Plessa, get the part and be right back here for delivery tomorrow morning.'

There was a ring from the console. 'Delivery for Mr Spacejock,' said the Navcom.

'What?'

'A delivery. They're waiting outside.'

'But –'

'I think I see what's happened,' said Clunk. 'Her shipment must have been waiting at the spaceport depot, and they're delivering it already.'

'No kidding. Did you work that out on your own?' Hal strode into the airlock and opened the door. The courier waiting outside held out a pen and clipboard.

'Mr Spacejock?'

'That's me.'

'Sign please.'

'Why?'

The man shrugged. 'Company policy. Can't hand over the goods without a signature.'

Hal looked past him and saw a large truck parked at the foot of the ramp.

'I haven't got all day,' said the driver.

Hal took the pen and scrawled on the docket. The driver tucked the clipboard away, and together they walked down the ramp to the truck. In the back there was a pallet swathed in plastic wrap. Hal reached up and poked a hole in the plastic, but all he could see was an expanse of orange cardboard. 'What's in it?'

'How should I know? I just deliver.'

'I only just finished speaking to your boss. That's some operation you have here.'

The driver glared at him. 'It's not my fault! There was a mix up with the delivery address.'

'Really? It's still amazingly fast.'

'Sarky bugger,' muttered the driver. He slid a collapsible lifter out of the truck, shook it open with a flick of his wrists and set it down on four tiny wheels. Then he raised the hook over the pallet, connected the straps to the corners and jerked it off the back of the truck. 'Stand clear,' he called as it swung round, narrowly missing Hal's head. The pallet thumped on the ground, and the driver unhooked it and folded the lifter up. 'Save the complaints next time,' he said, hopping into the cab. The truck roared into life and rumbled away, leaving Hal staring after it with a puzzled expression on his face.

'What's the cargo?' called Clunk from the top of the ramp.

'How should I know? It was just delivered.' Hal widened the gap he'd made in the plastic until he could see printing: 'Caution, hot water is dangerous!' With a sinking feeling he hooked his fingers under several layers of wrapping and pulled with all his might, ripping away an entire section. Then he groaned.

The pallet was crammed with Hand-E-Mart coffee makers.

— 7 —

Jasmin rinsed the mop and applied it to her floor, removing the last traces of apple pie. Not that she was particularly bothered about the mess, but for all she knew her next task would be to invite some dignitary to her flat for blackmail material, and it'd be hard going if he slipped over and knocked himself out.

Despite being kept in the dark about her mission, Jasmin had to admit she was enjoying herself. Her tasks were simple, and the only sour note was the taste of punishment the controller had given her. Still, she wouldn't have to worry about that if she continued to perform.

She'd just finished mopping up when her controller chimed in. 'It is time for the next stage.'

'Go ahead,' said Jasmin, leaning on the mop.

'You must employ two delivery drivers. You may spend up to twenty-five thousand credits, and ideal candidates will have criminal records and access to weapons.'

'Weapons? What kind of mission is this?'

'Are you questioning orders?'

'No, of course not. Just curious.'

'Curiosity is a luxury you cannot afford. Now, these men will be travelling to Jordia with you, but the destination must be kept from them.'

61

'How are we getting to Jordia? Passenger liner?'

'No, you will travel with the crate.'

'I didn't ask Spacejock about passengers! He's not expecting any!'

'You will arrive at the spaceport before he leaves. Offer additional funds, to a limit of twenty thousand credits.'

'That should do it,' admitted Jasmin. 'But where am I supposed to find a pair of criminals?'

The controller didn't reply.

Jasmin frowned. Trust her to crow about simple tasks. Look what she'd been given now! She thought for a moment, then realised she could turn to the same place everyone did when they wanted something questionable, immoral or completely illegal: Galnet, the massive network of interconnected computers that spanned the galaxy. It was a huge collaborative effort containing thousands of years of human history and knowledge, and the average person *still* used it to download music. Jasmin reasoned that if they could get away with such a heinous crime against humanity then finding a couple of toughs for hire would be easy.

Her initial searches returned endless links to music and little in the way of actual killers, but once she filtered out names of common bands and singers the results looked more promising. Eventually she discovered two sites based on Cathua. Rent-a-killer turned out to be a pest control company, and she doubted they'd fall for the it's-just-a-bigger-pest line. She selected the other, 'Mercs R Us - we do anyone', and was surprised when a stocky man with cropped grey hair popped up on the screen. His thick forearms rested on a scarred wooden table and his muscled torso strained his camouflage T-shirt, although a cynical observer might point out that anyone wearing clothes a size or two on the small side was going to fill them only too well. Behind him sat a skinny teenager with huge baggy trousers, a T-shirt with a gigantic zero in the middle and a cap with the peak hanging over one ear. He was wearing a bandolier stuffed with spare batteries, and his belt was laden with compact grenades.

'Welcome to Mercs R Us,' said the grey-haired man. 'Who do we do?'

'You're not a used car salesman, are you?'

'Nah, miss. It's Barry and Ace, guns for hire. I'm Barry, he's Ace.'

'G'day,' said Ace.

'And you kill people, do you?'

'Sure. Lots.'

'Have you been doing this long?'

'What's with the questions, lady? You got a job or not?'

'It's not whether I have a job, it's whether you can handle it.'

'Course we can. What is it?'

'I'm embarking on a trip and I need support crew. There may be shooting.'

'No sweat.'

'What experience do you have?'

'Football hooligans, vandals, rent-a-mob, violent debt collectors, standover men –'

'You handle all those things?'

'No, miss. We *are* all those things.'

Jasmin smiled. 'Excellent. Meet me at the spaceport tomorrow. Eleven am.'

'Wait a mo! You don't know our rates yet! And where are we going?'

'The destination is a secret, and I'll pay double your going rate. Just be at the spaceport with your weapons.'

'We want overtime,' said Ace, 'and meal breaks.'

Barry shushed him. 'Which vessel?'

'The *Volante*,' said Jasmin. 'And don't be late.'

◆

Hal shot into the flight deck and skidded to a halt in front of the console. 'Navcom, get onto that Hand-E shop. There's been a terrible mistake.'

The screen whirled and the Hand-E-Mart logo appeared. 'Do you want orders or payment?'

'Neither. Complaints.'

'Connecting you now.'

A grubby office appeared, complete with a battered filing cabinet, sagging desk and dog-eared piles of records. Sitting at the desk was a large, bearded man in shirtsleeves. He was toying with a pen, and as he spotted Hal he dropped it on the desk and reached for a sheet of paper. 'Mr Spacejock?'

'Yes, I just got –'

'Bob Knutchem, Hand-E-Mart. My people tell me there's a problem with your delivery.'

'Damn right there was! I ordered one of your coffee makers and –'

'No, a problem on *our* part. The driver should have collected your payment.'

'But I wanted one machine and you sent a whole pallet of the things!'

'It's a popular model. One of our best-selling items.'

'Not to me they're not. I want them picked up.'

Bob frowned. 'Picked up?'

'Yeah. I'll keep one, but the rest have to go.'

'We don't do pickups.'

'So hire someone who does.'

'We don't take returns. All sales are final.'

Hal shrugged. 'I'm going to leave them outside my ship. Either you collect them or they'll get burnt to a crisp when I leave.'

'Mr Spacejock, I don't care what happens to your coffee makers. It's the money I'm interested in.'

'Send someone over and I'll pay them.'

Bob smiled. 'It's so much better when people are reasonable.'

'I'm only paying for one,' warned Hal.

The smile vanished. 'Ah.' Bob took up the pen and tapped it lightly on the desk. 'This is where things get unpleasant.'

'Don't threaten me, buster. If you want to blame someone, get hold of the idiot who programmed your shop.'

'My shop works perfectly.'

'It's rigged!'

'Say that again and I'll sue for slander.'

'I'll bet you get every sucker who lands here. Increase the order, ship the stuff out and hide behind the local laws.'

'Mr Spacejock, you placed an order and I delivered the goods. Unless you pay me immediately I shall resort to other methods.'

'Get stuffed, you cheap crook.'

The pen broke with a splintering sound. 'You'll regret that,' snapped Bob.

'What are you going to do, send the boys around for a little chat?'

'I wouldn't call them little, mister, and they don't talk much.'

'I'll be gone before they're anywhere near me,' said Hal, thumbing the disconnect. The screen cleared and he drummed his fingers on the console, deep in thought. Bob's enforcers didn't worry him, but Clunk's reaction when he uncovered the bill for the coffee makers was going to be truly frightening.

At that moment the lift opened and Clunk entered the flight deck. Hal glanced at him fearfully, but the robot's face was only mildly disapproving: in other words, normal.

'I've secured Jasmin's cargo, Mr Spacejock. Oddly enough, it was twenty kilos lighter than expected.'

Hal stared at him. 'Jasmin's ...?' Suddenly he realised a golden opportunity had presented itself. If Clunk thought the coffee makers were Jasmin's, why correct him? Explanations could wait until later. Much later. 'Very good. Excellent.'

'I confess, I don't understand why anyone would pay forty thousand credits to ship coffee machines to Jordia.'

'We're couriers, not economists. And she told us not to worry about the contents.'

Clunk shrugged. 'Perhaps there's a shortage.'

'Forget about Jasmin. We've got a shuttle to catch and time's running out.'

'You're right. Can you give me a hand with the luggage?'

Hal reached for the nearest suitcase, then stopped. 'Hey, wait a minute. We're only going for a few hours, aren't we?'

'Correct,' said Clunk.

Hal tapped his suitcase with his boot. 'So what have you packed?'

'Winter clothing, in case it's cold.'

'And the other one?'

'Summer clothing, in case it isn't.'

'What about yours?'

'A few tools and spares.'

'Put it all back. We're travelling light.'

'But –'

'If we need anything, we'll buy it.'

'But –'

'No buts. Put it away and meet me outside.' While Clunk struggled into the lift with the cases, Hal extracted his battered cardboard box from the locker and took the ramp to the ground. He saw movement at the far side of the landing field, where a wedge-shaped shuttle was getting ready to leave, with navigation lights flashing and heat-haze rising from its slatted vents. The ship's engines fired, and thunder rolled across the landing field as the nose tilted up. It hung in mid-air for several seconds, getting louder and louder, until there was a massive thunderclap and the ship streaked into the sky atop a blinding flare of light, leaving rolling clouds of dust and smoke in its wake.

'Wow,' muttered Hal, squinting at the receding shuttle in awe. He'd be travelling aboard a similar vessel, and if the ride was anything like that he was in for one hell of a trip. He felt the ramp move and looked round to see Clunk shutting the airlock. As the robot finished Hal sought out the shuttle, which was now just a flickering speck in the sky, bright against the deep blue. He gathered his cardboard box as Clunk came down the ramp. 'All set?'

The robot nodded at the box. 'I thought we were travelling light?'

'I am,' said Hal, handing it over. 'You're travelling with this. Come on, we don't want to miss our flight.'

◆

Hal and Clunk entered the terminal and followed the signs to Departures, navigating lifeless escalators and unattended security checkpoints. Upstairs, they found a waiting area with rows of hard plastic seats and a 180-degree view of the landing field. There were no passengers to be seen, and the only person in evidence was a cleaner rearranging dust with a large broom.

'Excuse me!' called Hal. 'We're booked for the *Luna Rose*. Can you tell me where the shuttle leaves from?'

The cleaner jerked his thumb at the window.

Hal looked out. Apart from the *Volante* and the derelict freighter, the landing field was empty. 'So where is it?'

'What do you mean?'

'I asked you where the shuttle is.'

'No you didn't.'

'I did!'

'You didn't. You asked where it leaves from.' The cleaner pointed to a bare patch of concrete. 'And it leaves from there.'

'Okay, wise guy. Where's the ship?'

The cleaner pointed to the sky.

'It hasn't landed yet?'

'Landed?' The cleaner shook his head. 'It just left!'

'You must be mistaken,' said Clunk. 'They employed us for shipboard duties. It can't have left.'

'He's right. It's gone,' said Hal. 'I saw the damn thing taking off while you were messing about with all that luggage.'

'But it wasn't supposed to leave until eleven thirty!'

'Some bigwig made them take off early,' said the cleaner. He fished a bedraggled toothpick from his breast pocket and stuck it in the corner of his mouth. 'President, they say. Going to Jordia.'

'So how do we get to the Orbiter?'

'There's always Joe,' said the cleaner.

'Joe?'

'He runs the ship shop on the other side.' The cleaner nodded towards the landing field. 'Always moving his stock around. If you ask nicely he might take you up.'

Hal glanced across the field. On the far side he could just make out a garish sign with the words 'Joe's Ships of Distinction' above an image of a rocket ship.

'It's a long walk,' said Clunk. 'Do you think we could hire a taxi?'

'That's my money you're throwing around.'

'But if we don't get to the Orbiter in time we'll miss our flight to Plessa.'

'I'm just saying you could be a bit more frugal.'

'Who bought a whole box full of mouldy confectionery? Who signed up for a commset without checking the contract? Who –' Clunk lowered his voice. 'Who bought a self-exploding stasis controller from Bent Jimmy?'

Hal's gaze dropped to the ground below, where a collection of service vehicles were parked in a neat line. 'No need for a cab, Clunk. Come on.'

8

'Are you sure you don't want me to drive?'

'Shut up and get on,' said Hal, who was sitting at the controls of a luggage truck, revving the engine impatiently.

Reluctantly, Clunk climbed aboard and lowered himself into the passenger seat. As he was reaching for the seatbelt, Hal rammed the truck into gear and pressed the accelerator to the floor, launching them across the landing field in a series of fits and starts.

At the far side he parked the truck under the Joe's Ships sign and killed the engine. They jumped down and hurried into the sales office, which was set up like a lounge room. There were comfortable armchairs, side tables laden with sales material, a bubbling coffee maker and a large desk. As they entered, a fat man in a lemon yellow suit sprang up and hurried across to greet them. 'Good morning, sir! Welcome to Joe's Ships of Distinction!'

Hal shook the pudgy ring-laden hand. 'Are you Joe?'

'That's me. Need a ship - just ask Joe. I got everything from hoverbikes to megafreighters and my prices can't be beat.' He glanced at Clunk. 'You're not going to offer that as a trade?'

Hal shook his head. 'He's my co-pilot.'

'Fallen on hard times, eh?'

Clunk frowned at him. 'What did you say?'

'Leave it, Clunk.' Hal cleared his throat. 'Look, we have to get to the Orbiter, and –'

Joe groaned. 'Not another one.'

'Can you help us?'

'No way. Serious buyers only.'

Hal looked thoughtful. 'As it happens, our fleet does require an additional freighter.'

Clunk looked surprised. 'It does?'

'Sure. You're always moaning about the cost of fuel. We could use a small ship for the little jobs.' Hal glanced at Joe. 'Can we have a look at the stock?'

'Well of course, but you've caught me a little short at the moment. The bulk of our ships are spread amongst the other branches, and the big stuff is up there.' Joe jerked his thumb at the ceiling.

Hal looked up. 'What, on the roof?'

'Ha ha. Sir has a wonderful sense of humour.'

'So where do you keep them?'

'In orbit, sir. Our largest vessels are not suitable for planetary landings.'

'We're not interested in big ships. I want to see the smaller stuff.'

'As I said, we're a little short of stock right now. However, if you'll come this way I may have just the ship you're looking for.'

'Do you have anything available for immediate purchase?'

Joe grinned. 'Everything's for sale, sir. Now, if you'd like to pass into the hangar, I'll fetch my notes.'

As Joe trotted off, Hal and Clunk strode towards the hangar doors, which were open a metre or so.

'What are you playing at?' hissed Clunk. 'Acquire a vessel for our fleet? What kind of -?'

'We need a ship,' whispered Hal.

'We can't afford to buy one!'

'He doesn't know that, does he?'

'Not yet, but the penny will drop when it comes to paying the bill.'

'No it won't,' said Hal, with a chuckle.

'Ah. So what's the plan?'

Hal tapped the side of his nose. 'Just play along, Clunk. Don't contradict me.'

'I never do that, Mr Spacejock. I just straighten out the occasional misunderstanding.'

'Well leave them bent.' Hal glanced into the dingy hangar and whistled at the sight of a huge rusty hull. 'If that's small, I'd hate to see the bigger stuff.'

They approached slowly, craning their necks as they took in the ungainly craft. The rounded nose cone was covered in thick heat shielding to withstand re-entry temperatures; there was a large air intake in front of each stubby winglet, and behind the trailing edges the body of the ship flared out to incorporate an oversized engine. The joint was pierced with a double row of rivets, and beyond the rivets the rest of the ship was just a huge, rusty exhaust cone.

Clunk reached up and scraped several layers of grit from the compliance plate. 'Alpha II class,' he said, with a faraway look in his eyes. 'This vessel belongs in a museum.'

'I think it just came out of one.'

Clunk studied the rivets. 'It wouldn't have looked like this when it was new. Someone's cut the back off the original hull and welded on the booster rocket from a Titanic-class orbital insertion module.'

'Is that good?'

'It's powerful,' said Clunk. 'I wonder how they modulate the thrust?'

Hal walked to the back of the ship and peered up at the exhaust cone. 'This is bigger than the ones on the *Volante*,' he said, his voice echoing inside the hollow shape.

Clunk nodded. 'Titanics were used for very heavy payloads. They used to have six of these jets.' He looked at the ship through half-closed eyes and shook his head gently. 'Totally impractical. Heavy on fuel and a pig to fly.'

'Will it do?'

Clunk stared at him. 'Do? It's a grab-bag of spare parts assembled by a home mechanic with a death wish.'

'I kind of like it. It's quirky.'

'The word you want is lethal.'

Hal pointed to a bulge running the length of the hull. 'I wonder what that is?'

'I don't believe it!' said Clunk, staring in horror. 'They put the fuel tank on the outside!'

'Just look at the size of it. It must have a terrific range.'

'At least ten kilometres.'

'Eh?'

'Yes. If you land heavily, you'll destroy everything within a ten kilometre range. And I don't have to remind you about your landings.'

'You can handle that part.'

'I don't think I'd care to try.'

'Anyway, we don't need to land. A quick blast to the Orbiter and we're set.'

'Gentlemen, I see you've discovered the *Phantom-X1*!'

Hal glanced around and saw Joe entering the hangar. 'Clunk reckons this thing's a death trap.'

'Nonsense, man. The *X1* is a spacer's dream! Open the throttles on this baby and you'll be peeling your eyeballs off the rear wall. Treated right she's as gentle as a lamb, but when you need the power you just dial it in and ...' Joe thumped his fist into his cupped hand. 'Boom!'

Clunk raised one eyebrow. 'It blows up?'

Joe glared at him. 'Why don't you go and polish yourself. The captain and I have to talk business.'

Clunk leaned forward. 'You are speaking to a chief financial officer. Wouldn't you agree that 'sir' is a more appropriate form of address?'

'Oh,' Joe blinked. 'But certainly, sir.'

Hal smothered a grin. 'How much?'

Joe weighed him up. 'For you sir, a mere one point eight.'

'Gack!' Hal's grin vanished. 'Two million for that piece of junk?'

'Junk? This fine vessel was recently serviced!'

'Salvaged,' said Clunk. 'And they forgot to sweep the cobwebs out of the exhaust cone.'

'If the price is beyond your means, feel free to make an offer.'

'One two-fifty in cash,' said Hal firmly. 'And that's with a full load of fuel.'

Joe turned pale. 'That's not an offer, it's an insult! Why, you couldn't replace the engine for that!'

'You can't replace the engine at all,' said Clunk, tapping the side of the ship. 'It's welded in place.'

'Even so, one two-fifty is preposterous.'

'It does seem a little low,' said Clunk.

Hal glared at him. 'Maybe you *should* go outside and polish yourself.'

'One six-fifty,' put in Joe.

'One four.'

Joe mopped his brow. 'It's going to kill me, but you have a deal.'

'Thank you.   Could we have the rego transferred immediately? We're in a hurry.'

'Takes a week, sir. That is, unless ...'

'One four-fifty.'

'She's all yours. A pleasure doing business with you.'

'There's just one thing ...'

'Yes?'

'I'm not buying this ship without a test flight.'

'Aha!' exclaimed Clunk. 'Now I see what you're –'

'Just a quick trip up and down,' said Hal hurriedly.

'I'll have the ship prepped. Would you like a drink in our customer lounge while you wait?'

'Sounds good. I could use a coffee.' As they left the hangar Hal glanced back at the rusty old vessel. 'I wonder who gave it such a dumb name? *Phantom-X1* sounds like something out of a trashy science fiction novel.'

Clunk nodded. 'A very astute observation, Mr Spacejock.'

◆

The *Phantom*'s triangular flight deck had a console wedged into the pointy end and banks of poorly fitted lockers across the rear wall. Above the console was a concave viewscreen with a rippled surface and a yellowed plastic border. Multiple lines of text scrolled by on the screen, listing system failures, the precise distance to the nearest hospital and the likelihood of the whole shooting match exploding in a raging fireball the minute the engines were started. 'In case of fire,' said a sign at the rear of the flight deck, prominently displayed above an axe in a locked cabinet.

Hal crossed the flight deck, ducking his head to avoid the low roof. He sat at the console, and while he looked over the flickering lights and faded gauges Clunk settled into the co-pilot's seat alongside him. There was a loud creak and the robot sprawled on the deck as his chair sheared off.

'That never happened before,' said Joe, kicking aside fragments of crumbly metal. 'I'll have it fixed.'

Clunk inspected the broken support. 'Metal fatigue. Stress fractures. Rust.' He looked at Joe. 'Exactly how old is this vessel?'

'It's been refurbished.'

'According to these instruments, this ship is overweight and underground.'

Joe ran a finger around his collar. 'Would I be here if it wasn't safe?'

Hal finished inspecting the scarred console and reached for a recessed knob. 'Everyone ready?' He pulled the knob without waiting for a reply, and a dull roar shook the *Phantom* from nose to tail. 'What the hell was that?'

Clunk frowned at him. 'You just activated the afterburners.'

'Really? I hope nobody was behind the ship.'

'If they were, you just saved them the expense of a cremation.' Clunk pushed the knob back in. 'Don't touch that again. It'll drain the fuel tank in less than fifteen minutes.'

Joe cleared his throat. 'I don't want to teach you guys your job, but there's a checklist for taking off.'

'There is?' Hal looked around. 'Where?'

Joe mopped sweat from his forehead. 'First, you have to clear the area.'

'I think we can skip that part,' said Clunk.

'Not with the engines. You have to announce your intention to depart.'

Hal cupped his hands around his mouth. 'Listen up everybody. We're about to leave, so grab on to something and hang on tight.'

Joe shook his head. 'Through the microphone.'

'This one?' asked Hal, grabbing a stalk on the console.

'No,' said Joe, as the ship tilted. 'The silver one with the black grille on top.'

'Got it.' Hal leaned closer to the microphone. '*Phantom-X1* departing. Please vacate the area immediately.' He glanced at the salesman. 'Okay?'

'You didn't switch it on.' Joe saw Hal's expression and continued quickly. 'But I'm sure it won't matter just this once.'

'Damn right,' said Hal. 'Clunk, get this thing moving.'

'Yes, Mr Spacejock,' said the robot smartly. He leaned forward, flipped a couple of switches and pressed a button. 'This console reminds me of your old ship,' he said, as a multitude of red lights began to flash.

'The *Black Gull*?' Hal looked around. 'What, solid and dependable?'

'No, incredibly dangerous.' Clunk looked up from the instruments. 'We're ready to leave. Do you want to do the honours?'

'Sure.' Hal cleared his throat. 'Computer? Can you hear me?'

A crackle emanated from a battered speaker grille. 'Waddya want?' growled a male voice.

'Hello, I'm Hal.'

'Oh great. Another human.'

Hal frowned. 'I beg your pardon?'

'Last time I had one of your lot on board it took a week to get the stains out.'

Hal heard footsteps, and looked round to see Joe halfway to the exit. 'Where do you think you're going?'

'I'm going to leave you guys to it. Lots of paperwork to do. You understand.'

'Aren't you supposed to keep an eye on us?'

'I'll watch from the ground,' called Joe as he hurried from the ship.

'Probably has this thing insured for twice its value,' muttered Hal. He turned back to the console. 'Computer, take us to the Orbiter.'

'Get stuffed,' said the computer with a flash of the console lights.

Clunk looked apologetic. 'Mr Spacejock, I'm afraid this ship doesn't work like that.'

'Oh?'

'It's a manual system. Everything by hand. You know.'

'I jolly well don't,' said Hal. 'Perhaps you could enlighten me?'

The computer chimed in. 'If you want to go someplace, you damn well find it yourself.'

'Okay, how's this for manual?' said Hal, bringing his fist down on a large green button. There was a cough from the back of the ship, followed by a howl from the engine as it sucked in fuel and blew it out the exhaust cone in a jet of super-heated plasma. The deck flexed visibly as the roaring pounded Hal's ears. 'Whoo-hoo!' he yelled. 'That's what I call a lift-off!'

Clunk raised an eyebrow. 'We haven't left the ground yet. That's just the warm up.' He nodded towards a T-bar set into the middle of the console. 'Push that forward to advance the throttles.'

'How far?'

'You have to balance the thrust requirements with local gravity, fuel load and atmospheric pressure.'

Hal stared at the lever for a moment or two, then shoved it forward to the stop. The ship responded immediately, hurling itself into the air like a shell from a naval gun, trailing streamers of unburnt fuel, a ninety-metre tongue of flame and enough noise to shatter a mountain. There was a bone-jarring crash as it burst through the hangar roof, and Hal was thrown off his seat, landing heavily on the deck. He tried to get up, but the engine kept pouring out power, howling like a wounded animal as it blasted the ship into space.

Lying flat on the deck, Hal struggled to remain conscious against the crushing force of gravity. And failed.

9

Hal opened his eyes and tried to lift his head, only to discover that he was glued to the flight deck. Dust fell from the roof onto his upturned face, and the itchy, gritty feeling led to an explosive sneeze.

Clunk's face loomed above him. 'Mr Spacejock, thank goodness you're awake.'

Hal raised his hand, and with Clunk's help he managed to fight the crushing gravity and get to his knees. The flight deck whirled around him and multicoloured lights flashed all over his vision. 'I must have copped a real whack.'

'Sorry?'

Hal twirled his finger. 'My head's going round and round and there's flashing lights everywhere.'

'That's not your head, Mr Spacejock. The ship is spinning out of control.'

'I see.' Hal rubbed his chin. 'Where's the escape pod?'

'There isn't one.'

'Emergency exit?'

'Negative.'

'Seatbelts?'

Clunk shook his head.

'We're screwed.'

Clunk nodded.

'Oh come on, there's always a way out.'

'Not this time. And the Orbiter is dead ahead.'

'How far ahead?'

Clunk glanced at the console. 'Pretty close, actually.'

'So stop the ship.'

'I can't,' said Clunk. 'The throttle's stuck on full ahead.'

Hal's eyes widened. 'Computer! Show me a visual!'

A dense starfield appeared on the main screen. The Cathuan Orbiter was dead centre, a rotating spoked wheel whose many inhabitants were blissfully unaware of the spaceship now bearing down on them. There was a large hub in the centre of the wheel, with a number of brightly lit docking bays, and as the Orbiter grew larger and larger Hal could see helmeted workers inside the bays. They all seemed to be staring at the *Phantom*.

'Computer, that's close enough. You can stop zooming now.'

'I'm not zooming anything. That's a static image.'

Hal staggered to the console and grabbed the throttle lever. Muscles bunched, he braced his feet against the console and gave an almighty heave. The lever slid easily, banging against the stop, and the momentum hurled him backwards across the flight deck. He slammed into the spiral staircase, bounced off and dropped full-length onto the decking. 'You told me it was stuck!' said Hal, glaring accusingly at Clunk.

'Yes, under the console,' explained the robot. 'They used proprietary fixings and I don't have the tools to open it.'

Hal stared around wildly, then let out a triumphant cry as he spotted the fire axe. He darted across the flight deck, raised his arm and drove his elbow into the glass cover. Crack! The glass remained intact and Hal doubled up, clutching his throbbing arm and swearing under his breath. Meanwhile, Clunk undid the catch and opened the glass door. Hal recovered, yanked the axe from the clips and ran to the console, where he rained frenzied blows on the front edge. The axe rose and fell, chipping pieces of fake woodgrain off the console that zinged around the flight deck like angry hornets.

Hal stopped to examine his handiwork. The edge of the console was a twisted mess, with bright gashes where the axe had done its work. On screen, the Orbiter was getting bigger by the second. Throwing aside the axe, he dug his fingers under the front edge of the console and hauled upwards with all his might. 'Come and help!' he shouted to Clunk.

The robot stood alongside, and they strained together. Suddenly Hal felt the slightest of movements. 'Harder!' he yelled, redoubling his efforts. There was a creak as the console lifted, then a long, drawn-out groan as the entire cabinet rolled over and fell flat on its back with Hal and Clunk sprawled on top of it. They stood up hurriedly, and Hal gestured at the jumble of dusty, sparking cables. 'Your turn.'

Clunk reached into the tangled wires. After a moment or two the main drives cut out, then came back on with a deeper roar. Despite the artificial gravity, Hal was thrown against the console, and the metal surface dug painfully into his chest.

'We're not going to make it,' said Clunk calmly, looking up at the screen. 'We're going too fast.'

'Rubbish,' said Hal. 'We'll use one of those docking bays.'

'Only briefly.'

Hal stared at him.

'Whoosh!' said Clunk. 'Right through the back wall.'

'That's it!' cried Hal. 'Aim for the gap between the spokes!'

Together they hauled the console upright, and Clunk used the controls to fire the side thrusters. Ever so slowly, the Orbiter inched away from the centre of the screen. For a split second it seemed they would slam into the nearest spoke, a huge steel lattice packed with tubes, cables and access shafts, but somehow the ship rocketed through the narrow gap, engines howling.

They came to a halt several kilometres beyond the Orbiter, motors idling. In the ensuing silence Hal's heavy breathing sounded like a punctured life support system.

'D'you think they saw us?'

'Saw us?' Clunk stared at him. 'Mr Spacejock, that little stunt will be the lead item on every news service in the galaxy.'

'Really? Hey, maybe we should hang a 'Spacejock Freightlines'banner out the back and do it again!'

'I don't think that's a very good idea,' said the robot. 'People might get the idea their cargo is less than safe in your hands. Plus the banner might tangle on one of the spokes, and the publicity you'd get by accidentally towing the Orbiter into the local star doesn't bear thinking about.'

Hal thought for a moment. 'Okay, tell 'em we had a computer failure. Doddery piece of junk almost killed us.'

'I heard that,' said the computer.

Hal turned to the console. 'Come on, I need your help.'

'Why don't we tell them the truth?' asked Clunk. 'The throttle got stuck because you treated it roughly.'

'We can't tell them that! They'll think I'm an idiot!'

There was a long silence.

'And ... and it was your fault anyway.'

'Eh? Mine?'

'You had the controls, didn't you? I was out cold.'

Clunk opened his mouth, then closed it again.

Hal gestured at the console. 'Computer, you're with me on this one, right? That's two votes to one.'

'Incoming message,' said the computer.

'Who is it?'

'The Orbiter. Department of Infringements and Public Relations.'

'Do you want to take it?' Hal asked Clunk. There was no reply, and when he glanced to his right he saw the robot's eyes gleaming wildly through a shimmering veil of super-heated air. Somewhere, a fan was rattling as it strove to cool the robot's circuits, and there was a series of squeaks as Clunk clenched and unclenched his fists. 'I'll take it,' said Hal hastily, turning to face the main screen. It flickered and buzzed, then showed a spartan, white-painted office with a grey-haired man sitting at a desk. He did not look happy.

'It was my robot,' said Hal. 'He treated the throttle roughly and it got stuck.'

'I'm sorry?'

'Me too. Won't happen again. Bye.'

'Names please.'

'Er ... Smith.'

'And who's that with you?'

'My robot. His name is, um, Datoid.'

'Well, Mr Smith, I'm not really interested in your robot. My business is with you.'

'Business?' Hal's ears pricked. 'You have a cargo?'

'More of a burden.' The man glanced at his terminal. 'Excessive speed, dangerous manoeuvring, failure to obey signals ...' he frowned at Hal. 'And one of your landing lights is out.'

'But the throttle got –'

'I don't want to hear it. Your ship will be impounded pending payment of a five thousand credit fine. Please dock immediately to accept your punishment.'

'I object!' shouted Hal as the screen went dark. 'Hey! Come back!'

'They'll have your pilot's licence for this,' said Clunk.

'Pilot's licence, eh?' Hal looked uncomfortable. 'Wouldn't want to lose that. Most inconvenient.'

Clunk stared at him. 'Please tell me you have a licence.'

'It's not my fault,' said Hal, shuffling his feet. 'They doubled the price a few years back, and I didn't have the money.'

'A few years?' said Clunk faintly.

'Then you came along, and I figured I could share yours.'

'You just figured that, did you?'

'Look, the payment for this cargo job will cover my licence. Happy?'

'Not particularly.'

'Situation normal, then.' Hal gestured at the screen. 'Forget the fine. We'll bypass the Orbiter and catch up with the *Luna Rose* in deep space.'

Clunk reached for the controls, but before he could touch them classical music began to play from the speakers. 'Oh dear. Too late.'

'Why? What's that racket?'

'Docking manoeuvres initiated,' said the computer. 'This ship is now under Orbiter control.'

◆

Hal watched the screen as Clunk reversed the *Phantom* into the docking bay. Thrusters fired, lights flashed and buzzers beeped, but the robot seemed unfazed as he guided the ship into its berth. Halfway through the manoeuvre there was a gentle scrape, prompting a slight hiss from Clunk.

'What was that?' demanded Hal. 'What did we hit?'

'Nothing,' said Clunk. 'Everything is going smoo –' His voice was drowned out by the sound of rending metal, exactly like train tracks being fed into a blender. He shot Hal a worried glance, then turned his attention to the console. 'Computer, show me a visual.'

The main screen flickered into life, showing an expanse of stars. As the sound of tortured metal continued, the stars disappeared from the sides as if someone were drawing a pair of jet black curtains.

'It's the docking bay doors!' exclaimed Clunk, relief evident in his voice.

Hal looked at him. 'What did you think it was?'

'Oh, er nothing.'

'Go on. You thought we were scraping the side wall, didn't you.'

'That's a negative,' said Clunk firmly.

'You looked worried enough.' Hal winced at a particularly loud screech. 'How come we can hear it, anyway?'

'The noises are being transmitted through the metal frame of the space station.'

The stars vanished and the ship rocked as the huge doors met in the middle. Concealed lights came on, illuminating the rust-streaked paint, and Hal frowned as he saw liberal splashings of graffiti. 'How the hell did they get up there?'

Suddenly a synthesised voice crackled from the speakers. 'Greetings star travellers, and welcome to the Cathuan Orbiter! For your convenience this simple, easy-to-use menu will present you with all available options and interpret your voice commands. To make a selection, speak the option clearly and concisely.'

Hal got up and strode towards the airlock.

'Where are you going?' asked Clunk. 'You haven't heard the menu yet.'

'Stuff that.' Hal entered the airlock, walked to the outer door and checked the display. Green. He frowned. Was that air, or no air? Mentally tossing a coin, he operated the door and took a deep breath. Okay, green was air. Rank greasy air, but breathable all the same.

Hal stepped from the airlock and strode down the *Phantom*'s ramp to the oil-stained decking below. At the foot of the ramp he found a narrow door, which opened to his touch. Inside was a dingy, cramped airlock, and after negotiating the familiar controls he found himself in a circular space with grey-painted walls and a computer terminal. The floor was a metal grid, and looking down he saw a similar floor several metres below, another beneath that, and so on until they faded into darkness. In places the metal grid shone with fresh welds as if it had recently been repaired. Looking up, he saw the ceiling was the same.

The terminal screen flickered into life and an angry face appeared. The lips moved forcefully, but no sound came out, and when the man finished the terminal displayed a terse message: 'Ship Impounded. Five thousand credit fine.'

Hal grinned at Clunk, who'd just hurried in. 'They can get that out of Joe.'

'We were in control of the ship.'

'Oh no we weren't. You said so yourself.' Hal nodded towards the exit. 'Come on, let's find the *Luna Rose*.'

10

Hal and Clunk hurried along the Orbiter's carpeted passageways, following overhead signs to the *Luna Rose*'s boarding gate. At every sign they passed Hal expected the status to change from 'boarding' to 'departed'. At the gate his fears appeared to be confirmed - a thick red cord stretched across the airlock doorway and there was no sign of either staff or passengers.

'Don't tell me we've missed it.'

Clunk shook his head. 'They're probably cleaning up after the last run.'

'Cleaning up?'

'To be precise, hosing down. For the average traveller, space sickness and zero gravity aren't the best combination.'

Hal winced.

'On the plus side, there'll be plenty of hot meals going around.'

There was a snick, and Hal saw a smartly dressed woman removing the red cord. 'You cut it fine. We're just leaving.' She looked at them expectantly. 'You are flying with us today?'

'More than just flying.' Hal gestured at Clunk. 'He signed us on. We're crew.'

The woman's eyebrows rose, and Hal copped a double blast from her attractive green eyes. 'Crew?'

'Positions 14-69 and 24-T,' said Clunk. 'They were advertised on Cathua.'

'Kent wanted the best,' added Hal. 'And he got us.'

'But,' said Clunk.

'But what?'

'But he got us. Not and.'

Hal bared his teeth in an attempted grin. 'Bloody robots, eh? Precise to a fault.' He waved Clunk towards the boarding ramp. 'Go on, off you go. You'd better get settled.'

'I'm sorry?'

'I'll be along in a minute. Go on, vanish.'

Clunk glanced at Hal, then at the woman, then back at Hal. Without a word, he left.

'Is that your robot?' asked the owner of the stunning green eyes.

Hal nodded. 'Unfortunately.'

'You don't look like a steward.'

'I'm not,' said Hal. 'I'm a pilot.'

'Okay.'

'No, really. You should see my ship.' Hal spread his arms. 'It's big and white and goes like the clappers.'

The woman laughed. 'I'd stick with manly silence if I were you.'

'I didn't mean ... I wasn't ...' Thoroughly flustered, Hal gave up and fled along the boarding tunnel, not slowing until he saw Clunk waiting near the grey hull of the *Luna Rose*.

'So, when's the wedding?' asked the robot.

'Shut up,' growled Hal. He pushed past Clunk and entered the ship, sniffing at the strong smell of disinfectant. Inside, two narrow aisles divided rows and rows of seats, all of them occupied.

'Other way,' said Clunk, as Hal turned for the front.

'They have the flight deck at the rear of the ship?' Hal laughed. 'Trust Spearman to fly it backwards.'

'Flight deck? We're going to the crew quarters.'

'Of course, we have to sign on. Okay, lead the way.'

Clunk shot him a puzzled look, then turned and strode along the nearest aisle. At the rear of the ship they passed through a curtained doorway, entering a small area lined with locker doors. At that moment, a familiar voice crackled through the cabin speakers. 'This is your captain, Kent Spearman. We're cleared for departure and will be leaving shortly. Our flight to Plessa will take four hours, and you're welcome to take advantage of our delightful cabin staff during the trip.' He laughed, and most of the passengers giggled politely.

'Oh, ha ha,' sneered Hal. 'What a greaser.'

'There will be inflight entertainment, but I must remind you that the cashpoint on your seat doesn't give change. I trust you enjoy your trip, and I hope you'll take the *Rose* in future.'

'Take offence, more like,' muttered Hal.

Kent's voice crackled through the speakers again, this time confined to the crew quarters. 'Doors sealed and checked, departure imminent. Find your places guys, this is the real deal.'

'We'd better hurry up,' called Clunk.

'No hurry. He can't leave until we're up there.'

Clunk opened a locker and pulled out a bundle of clothing. He checked the tag, then handed it to Hal. 'Should be your size.'

'What's this?'

'Uniform. It's part of the agreement.'

'What's wrong with a flight suit?'

'You can't serve dressed like that.'

'Serve? What, as in the Navy?'

'No, as in dispense food and drink.'

Gripped by a horrible suspicion, Hal examined the clothing. It was a steward's uniform.

⬦

One hour later the *Luna Rose* was in deep space, having made the first of several jumps towards its destination. Hal and Clunk were in the galley near the back of the ship, separated from the passenger cabin by a curtain.

'Your turn,' growled Hal, as a buzzer rang overhead.

'That's not fair!' protested Clunk. He was standing alongside a drinks trolley, dressed in a trim uniform with a cap perched on his gleaming head. His metal hands poked out of the sleeves like crabs emerging from a pair of drainpipes, and his big flat feet were crammed into a pair of shoes. 'You have to help. I can't keep up!'

'I don't care.' Hal glanced down at his own clothes. 'Nobody's seeing me like this.'

'If you don't perform they'll charge you for the trip. Three thousand credits.'

Hal got up. 'I'll need one of those trolley things. And no dicky wheels.'

Clunk wrestled a serving trolley from its alcove and manoeuvred it into the aisle. 'Remember, you're just a faceless nobody. If you don't draw attention to yourself they'll forget you the minute they leave the ship.'

Hal grabbed the handles, took a couple of deep breaths, then plunged through the curtain into the passenger cabin. 'Listen up!' he called. 'I'm a pilot, right? I ended up in this embarrassing situation because I lost a bet with a mate.'

All the nearby passengers turned to look, and Clunk buried his head in his hands.

'If anyone gets clever, I'll space them. If anyone monkeys about, I'll beat them up and then space them. Got it?'

Everyone nodded.

'Good. We understand each other.' Hal pushed the trolley up to the first passenger and stopped. 'Drink?'

'N-not for me,' said the timid-looking man.

Hal turned to the other side. 'You?'

A woman and her companion both shook their heads vigorously.

'Good,' growled Hal, proceeding up the aisle.

Clunk watched him go, wondering whether perhaps he *should* have coped on his own. Hal's idea of award-winning customer service was to include a napkin when he handed clients their own head on a plate, and Clunk was still debating whether to drag him back into the safety of the galley when a loud voice caught his attention.

'Hey, robot! Gimme a drink!'

Clunk turned to see a large man in a floral shirt sitting in the aisle seat. His face was flushed, and the overhead lights bounced off his stubbly scalp. 'Certainly sir. What would you like?'

'Gearbox oil on the rocks,' said the man. He gave a shout of laughter and slapped his thigh. 'Kills 'em every time, you gotta laugh.'

'Tee hee hee,' said Clunk, his face set. 'What would you really like?'

'Hydraulic fluid!' said the man, looking around to judge the effect his words were having on the other passengers. 'No! Make it battery water with a twist of lemon!'

'I only have these beverages, sir.' Clunk gestured at the trolley, which contained a range of sugar-laden drinks in garish cans. 'You're welcome to any of these.'

'I don't want any of those.'

'In that case, perhaps you'd let me serve the other passengers.'

'You stand there until I say so.'

Clunk's hands tightened on the rail which ran around the top of the drinks trolley, squeezing it out of shape. 'I have to serve the others.'

'You're serving me.'

'But you're not ordering anything I can help you with.'

'And there's nothing you can do about it,' said the man triumphantly. 'If you don't obey I'll report you to the captain.'

'You think so?' Clunk tore the rail from the drinks trolley, clamped the man's wrist to the armrest and trapped it with the rail.

'Hey, you can't do that!'

Clunk finished the stiff metal off with a neat bow and repeated the process with the man's other arm. Then he took a roll of cloth tape from his chest compartment.

'Let me go, tinpants!' yelled the man, straining against the improvised cuffs. 'Let me go or I'll –'

'Go to the captain. So you said.' Clunk tore a decent strip off the roll and slapped it across the man's mouth, cutting him off mid-cry. 'Sit tight. I'm going to serve the other passengers.'

'You can't leave him like that!' said the woman across the aisle.

'You're right, he'll get thirsty.' Clunk took a can of drink, popped the seal and set it on the man's table. Then he selected a straw and punched it through the sticky tape covering the man's lips. 'Problem solved.' He straightened and looked down the aisle. 'Now, would anyone else like a drink?'

Nobody took him up on the offer.

Clunk returned to the trolley, and as he set off down the aisle he spotted a young boy watching his every move. The boy was clutching a cowboy teddy bear dressed in a tatty suede jacket, with a wide-brimmed hat on its head and bandoliers across its chest. 'Would you like a drink?' asked Clunk, crouching in the aisle alongside.

'N-no sir!' said the boy, shaking his head.

'Where's his gun?' said Clunk, tapping the bear's empty holster.

'One night, it got lost.'

His mother leaned across. 'We don't encourage violent tendencies.'

'I'm afraid it's in the genes,' said Clunk. 'Better if they work it out of their system as youngsters.'

'Oh, so your programmers were experts on child rearing?'

'I have adaptive intelligence,' said Clunk. 'I learn from my environment.' He looked down at the boy, who had tied the bear's arm to the chair and was force-feeding it salted nuts.

'Like a child?' said the woman scornfully.

'Just like a child,' said Clunk. Suddenly he tipped his head to one side. 'What was that?'

'What? Is something wrong?'

'No, I'm sure it's nothing.' Clunk set the brake on the trolley and hurried back to the galley. That flutter he'd heard - was his hearing playing up, or was it an engine running hot? He found the crew intercom and pushed the button, but there was no reply. Frowning, he examined a safety diagram of the ship.

The engines weren't accessible from the passenger cabin, and so his best chance was to alert the captain.

Pushing through the curtains, he squeezed his way past Hal as he made for the front of the ship.

'Where are you going?' asked Hal.

'I have to speak to the captain.'

'What happened to serving passengers?'

Clunk ignored him and pushed through the curtains into the deserted first class section, hurrying past comfy armchairs, side tables laden with glossy magazines and a huge video screen. He tapped politely at the door leading to the flight deck, then knocked slightly harder, then gave it a right banging with his fist. He was just about to kick it down when he saw the intercom. 'Hello, is Mr Spearman there?' he said, pressing the button. 'I'm Clunk, one of the crew.'

The door hissed open and Clunk saw Kent sitting at the console, working on a floating keyboard. Kent pushed the keyboard aside and spun his chair, sizing the robot up with a glance. 'How can I help you, metal man?'

'I don't mean to impose, but I noticed the port engine was running hot. It's two percent over optimum and burning more fuel than it should.'

'It's two point two percent, and I'm well aware of the problem.' Kent tapped a display. 'Crappy fuel from Cathua. Literally. They distil it from manure.'

'It's better for the environment.'

'Yeah, but you try flying a ship on cow farts.' Kent shook his head. 'I have to strip the injector array twice a month. Now that's a crappy job if ever I saw one.'

'You do it yourself?' asked Clunk, impressed.

'Only when I'm short handed. This baby takes care of herself pretty good, but a decent pilot has to do more than yank the stick. Know what I'm saying?'

'Indeed.'

'Are you getting gyp from the passengers? You being a robot and all.'

'A little. Nothing I can't handle.'

'Experienced, huh?'

'Actually, I'm a qualified pilot. First class.'

'Really?' Kent looked impressed. 'That's rare, these days. Most folk prefer a human at the controls.'

'Yes, well humans are odd creatures.' Clunk looked mortified. 'Oh, I didn't mean you!'

'I'll take that as a compliment,' said Kent with a grin. 'Hey, how'd you like to handle the docking?'

'Me?'

'Sure, it's a snip.'

'I'd better tell Mr Spacejock what I'm up to. He might –'

'Tea-with-the-emperor Spacejock? My cargo's worth half-a-mil Spacejock?' Kent pointed at the door. 'He's out there serving drinks?'

Clunk gasped. 'I wasn't supposed to say!'

'I'm glad you did. So, what's his story?'

'We're fetching a part from Plessa. Our stasis controller failed.'

'I've heard about those. Flaky pieces of junk.'

'That's what I said to Mr Spacejock, but he insisted.'

'So you're his robot.'

'No, we work together.'

Kent stroked his beard. 'I shouldn't really say this . . .'

'What?'

'In the bar, Spacejock told me he was looking for someone to take you off his hands.'

'He did?' Clunk blinked. 'Why?'

'Said he preferred to work alone.'

'But –'

Kent slapped him on the shoulder. 'Hey, don't worry about it. I've got a solution.'

'What's that?'

'You do twelve months with me, award wages, and I'll grant your freedom at the end of it. What do you say?'

◆

After Clunk dashed past, Hal continued to work his way towards the front of the passenger cabin. His drinks trolley was emptying fast, and he'd almost completed the run when he noticed the price list peeping out from a pile of peanut flavoured snacks. With a start, he realised he was supposed to be charging the passengers. No wonder they'd helped themselves to three or four drinks and handfuls of snacks at a time! Hal glanced back down the aisle and saw most of them busy munching and slurping before their good fortune was reversed. Oh well, he thought. At least they're happy.

He passed the last few rows and stopped at the set of velvet curtains stretched across the aisle. Uncertain whether he was supposed to go beyond them, he poked his head through for a quick look. His eyes widened at the sight of the luxurious lounge with its soft lighting and hushed ambience, and he shook his head as he scanned the empty seats. What a waste.

He pushed the trolley through the curtains and adjusted them to cover the gap. A few moments later he was relaxing in a chair with his feet on the table and a refreshing drink in his hand. He found a dinner menu and a headset in the seat pocket, and was tossing up between the curried lamb and the grilled fish when the door at the front of the lounge swished open and Clunk came in. The robot was looking thoughtful, but his expression turned to anger when he saw Hal. 'What do you think you're doing?'

Hal lowered the menu. 'I'm entitled to a rest break, aren't I?'

'Rest break? What happened to serving passengers?'

'Hey, you abandoned yours first.' Hal gestured at the door. 'What were you doing? Giving Spearhead a bit of personal service?'

'For your information, the port engine was running hot. I went to advise the captain on the correct course of action, but he was already aware of the issue. That's because he's a qualified pilot, unlike some I could mention.'

'Qualified drunk, more like.' Hal waved the menu at him. 'Here, can you grab me one of these curries?'

Clunk's face darkened. 'Can I what?'

'I thought I'd get in before the rush down back. Oh, and a bottle of red if it's not too much trouble.'

'Not-too-much-trouble? Mr Spacejock, if Mr Spearman finds you in here we'll be in more trouble than you can possibly imagine.'

'He won't though, will he?' Hal nodded towards the door. 'He's up the pointy end waggling his joystick.'

'Did you ever hear of autopilot?'

'That's where the ship flies itself, isn't it? Here, watch out!'

Tired of arguing, Clunk had simply grabbed Hal by the shoulders and hauled him from the chair, scattering the headset and menu. He manhandled him to the trolley, pushed him back into the aisle and pointed towards the back. 'Serve,' he said, before stalking off to retrieve his own trolley.

Hal straightened his jacket and rolled his eyes at the nearest passenger, a woman in a trim suit. 'Robots, eh? Can't take a joke.'

'I'd like a scotch on the rocks.'

Hal poured the drink, looked up the price then doubled it. After giving away most of the stock for free he had some catching up to do.

11

The *Luna Rose* arrived safely at the Plessa Orbiter and docked without loss of life or limb, despite Hal's best efforts. In the crew quarters, he tore off his uniform, kicked off the shoes and donned his flight suit and boots. The hubbub from the passenger compartment died down as the passengers left the ship, and when the last bag had been retrieved from the overhead lockers and the last inflight magazines had been shoved back into the seat pockets, Hal stepped out of the stairway and headed for the exit.

'We should talk to Mr Spearman before we leave,' said Clunk.

'No bloody way.'

'He seemed eager to speak to you.'

Hal stared at him. 'You told him I was aboard? Are you crazy?'

'Not at all. He seems like a nice man.'

'Nice? Kent three-grand-for-a-commset Spearman?'

'Are you sure we're talking about the same person? The man flying this ship was very polite and efficient.'

'Yeah, well you want to watch yourself around him. Stay away from airlocks if you know what I mean.' Hal pushed aside the curtain but stopped as he saw the captain waiting near the exit. 'Oh hell.'

'Hey, it's Hal Spacejock, intergalactic drinks waiter!' Kent eyed him up and down. 'Seen any emperors around lately? Or were you too busy serving my customers?'

'I did this for a dare,' growled Hal. 'And now that it's over I'd just like to say –'

Clunk cleared his throat. 'Mr Spearman, we'd like to confirm our return trip.'

'Sure thing, metal man. Just keep Spacejock here away from the booze. Anything stronger than orange juice and his brain melts.'

Hal took a step towards him, but Clunk grabbed his arm and hauled him off the ship.

'You shouldn't have interfered,' said Hal as they strode along a padded tunnel. 'I would have knocked that smarmy grin right off his face.'

'What about the trip back?'

Hal brightened. 'You're right! I'll wait until we get to the other end.'

'That's not what I meant.'

'Come on, we don't want to miss another shuttle.'

The padded tunnel led to a small departure lounge, with deep comfortable chairs and brand new carpet. The air was cool and fresh, and after a few deep breaths Hal sank into one of the armchairs and put his boots on the polished coffee table, almost knocking a dish of peanuts onto the floor.

'We can't stop here,' said Clunk. 'We have to get down to the planet. We need to book fares.'

'Look, my feet are killing me. Why don't I wait here while you organise them?'

Clunk looked at him doubtfully. 'Will you be all right?'

'Fetch the tickets. I'll be fine.'

After Clunk left Hal set to work on the peanuts. Before long the dish was empty, so he moved to the next table and started on a fresh supply. As he was busy munching a cleaner bot rolled into the lounge. Low and rounded, it ran on three small castors with a large rubber driving wheel. A flexible tube protruded between a pair of optical sensors, with a vacuum head which seemed to have a life of its own. The cleaner darted around the lounge, picking up specks of dirt and litter with sharp sucking noises. Hal lifted his feet as it approached the table, and the device cleaned up several spilled nuts. When the floor was clear, it sat and waited.

Hal transferred a handful of nuts to his mouth, and as he tilted his head back he saw the bot watching him. Unnerved, he spilled several peanuts.

The cleaner got them before they hit the ground.

Hal reached for the bowl and scooped up the last handful of nuts. He picked one out and flicked it across the lounge, grinning as the cleaner darted after it. As it came back Hal flicked two more, and for several minutes he had it gathering nuts from all points of the compass.

Then the peanuts ran out. 'Sorry lad,' said Hal, spreading his hands. 'All gone.'

The bot waited.

'No more nuts,' said Hal. 'Shoo.'

The bot turned its sensors on the empty bowl. There was a moment of silence, and then ... whoosh! It blew the contents of its dust bag all over the table. When it had finished, the bowl was overflowing with sweet wrappers, dust balls and ... peanuts.

Hal grinned and reached for a handful.

'Mr Spacejock, I'm back!' Clunk hurried into the lounge waving a pair of tickets. 'Look, I got two for the –' He jumped back as the cleaner bot whizzed past, pursuing a speeding nut. 'What's going on? Are you all right?'

'Fine, fine.' Hal looked around, gradually becoming aware of the damage to the lounge. It was a ruin - half the tables were overturned and there were empty bowls and crushed peanuts everywhere. 'Time to go,' he said, jumping up.

The cleaner bot stopped its pursuit and looked at him.

'I'm off now,' explained Hal. 'Can you clean this up on your own?'

The cleaner surveyed the room, moving its lens from one torn chair to the next, across the battered tables and over the powdery coating of lint, dust and crushed nuts. Then, without a sound, it turned and scurried away.

'You're unbelievable,' said Clunk as they made their escape. 'I can't leave you alone for five minutes, can I?'

'It was just a bit of fun,' said Hal defensively. He gestured at the tickets. 'So, when does the shuttle leave?'

'We're not taking the shuttle,' said Clunk. 'These are for the space elevator. It's cheaper.'

Hal snorted. 'Why don't we just throw ourselves out the nearest airlock and float down to the surface? It won't cost anything.'

'Mr Spacejock, the space elevator is the pinnacle of engineering know-how. It was constructed from A-grade recycled materials and the seasonally adjusted safety record is one hundred percent.'

'What else does it say on the back of the ticket?'

'No liability admitted for injury or death, and no refunds.'

'In that case, I'm going by shuttle.'

'But we don't have enough money left for two tickets!'

'I only need one. You're taking the elevator.'

Clunk's face fell. 'I thought you'd enjoy the view.'

'What, from a glass box on a rope? How long does it take, anyway?'

'Half an hour.' Clunk looked hopeful. 'You mean you'll come?'

'Just this once.' Hal held his hand up. 'But if I end up a seasonally adjusted statistic, you're going to be A-grade recycling material.'

They left the lounge and made their way to the boarding gate, where they found a line of people waiting. Hal went to join them, but Clunk pulled him aside.

'We don't have to queue. I purchased first-class tickets.'

'What happened to cheap?'

Clunk looked embarrassed. 'First class seats are next to the windows. I thought the view would be better.'

'So now we're tourists?' Hal shook his head as he followed Clunk along the line of passengers. They glared at him enviously, and he caught several comments about privilege and silver spoons. One or two asked him for a drink.

At the end of the line, the wall was pierced with a pair of archways. The right hand one was marked 'First Class Only', with a plush red cord strung between a pair of chrome stands. A young man in company uniform was waiting patiently nearby.

Clunk stepped forward and offered the tickets, which the man tore into ragged halves. Then he unclipped the cord and gestured them through the arch. 'Enjoy the drop.'

The elevator capsule was circular, with plush, outward-facing armchairs around the perimeter and narrow, unpadded benches crammed into the middle. The outer walls were huge glass panels that looked out onto a dark, starry sky. In the centre of the capsule, a thick steel column passed through the floor and out the roof.

'Cable guide,' said Clunk. 'Come on, we're on the far side.'

Hal followed the eager robot to their seats, where he saw a six-point harness securely anchored to each padded chair. 'What are those for?'

'I'm sure it's just a precaution,' said Clunk lightly.

Hal leaned against the glass and looked down. Far below, sunlight glinted off the slender elevator shaft where it curved gently into the clouds. 'Where's the toilet?'

'Back on the Orbiter.'

Hal raised his voice slightly to counteract the hubbub from the other passengers. 'You know, I don't really want to travel on this thing. What if the brakes fail?'

'We have brakes?'

Hal looked alarmed. 'You're not serious! How do we stop?'

'Very suddenly.' Clunk grinned, enjoying himself. 'Look at you! Ace pilot and interstellar navigator, scared of a little drop.' He grabbed for the armrest as the overhead speakers crackled.

'This is your flight director speaking,' said a cheerful voice. 'On behalf of the captain I'd like to welcome you aboard the *Icarus*. Our journey will take a little under sixty minutes, and drinks will be available to first class passengers as we pass the halfway point. I'd like to remind everyone to remain seated throughout the trip, as sudden changes to weight distribution may have detrimental effects on the braking mechanism. Finally, I look forward to seeing you back for the return journey.'

Hal looked around the capsule. 'Where's the crew, anyway?'

'Aboard the Orbiter,' said a man in the next seat. 'They release us by remote control.'

Clunk turned round. 'Have you travelled this way before?'

'Yes.' The man patted his harness, which was securely fastened. 'Don't forget this little beauty.'

Hal looked surprised. 'I thought they were for show.'

The man nodded at the ceiling, which was covered with dents. 'So did they.'

Clunk and Hal moved in unison, fastening their belts, snapping the buckles and tugging hard on the straps. When they'd finished, they were gripped securely to their seats.

Suddenly a buzzer sounded. 'On my mark. Three ... '

Hal gulped.

'Two ... '

Clunk gripped the armrest, crushing the plastic.

'One!'

There was a loud click and the capsule dropped from the Orbiter, shaking violently. Lights glared down through clear panels in the roof, and Hal saw the Orbiter receding at speed. He glanced down as he heard a grinding sound, then nudged Clunk. 'You'll break it off,' he hissed.

Clunk loosened his grip, releasing several shards of plastic from the broken armrest. They shot past his face and stuck to the roof, and a gritty haze filled the air as the capsule plunged downwards. As the acceleration wore off, dirt rained down on the passengers.

'We're in freefall now,' said the man in the next seat helpfully.

'I know.' Hal gestured at Clunk and himself. 'We're seasoned space pilots, we are.'

106

The man sniffed. 'Sure. And I'm a waiter.'

'We are! We're just fetching spare parts for our ship.'

'Right,' said the man, taking out a book. 'Would you excuse me? I prefer my fiction in written form.'

'Cretin,' muttered Hal. He grabbed for his armrest as the capsule lurched to the left, shaking all the passengers in unison. 'What was that?'

'Atmosphere.' The man in the next seat lowered his book. 'Just wait until we hit the thicker stuff, it'll really get bumpy. Of course, as a seasoned pilot you knew that.'

Hal stared at the book the man was holding, debating whether to pluck it from his hands and beat him around the head with it. He'd just made up his mind when Clunk distracted him with a loud cough.

'Mr Spacejock, they have capital punishment on this planet.'

'It'd be worth it,' growled Hal. He glanced up as a searing white flash lit up the capsule.

'Those would be clouds,' said the man in the next seat. 'You know, water vapour.'

There were several more flashes, and Hal became aware of a thin wailing sound.

'Air,' said his self-appointed guide.

'Listen buster, unless you want to experience a lack of it ...' Hal felt a restraining hand on his arm, and turned to glare at Clunk. 'You stay out of this.'

'I thought you might like to see the ground.'

'Why?'

'It's arranged in a particularly impressive spherical configuration.'

'Really?' Hal leaned forward and looked down. 'Where?'

'See the curvature of the horizon?' Clunk pointed. 'Look.'

Hal turned away from the window. 'Are you telling me this planet is round?'

'Yes.'

'Do you know of any non-round planets?'

Clunk thought for a moment, then shook his head.

'So you want me to look out the window and gawk at a planet which is just like every other planet we've ever landed on?' Hal turned to glare at the man in the next seat. 'Assuming we're pilots, of course.'

'As if,' muttered the man.

Hal indicated his flight suit. 'What d'you think this is, prison garb?'

'My gardeners wear overalls like that,' the man sniffed. 'Theirs are cleaner.'

Hal opened his mouth to reply, but a buzz from the overhead speakers stopped him.

'This is your flight director speaking,' said a scratchy voice. 'You are now passing the midway point of your journey. Braking will begin shortly, and I would like to remind all passengers to tighten their seat harnesses. Now that the capsule is within planetary jurisdiction, first-class passengers are invited to use the onboard drink dispensers. These are located in the armrest alongside your seat. Unfortunately, due to currency laws, change cannot be given.'

Hal examined his armrest. The top was hinged, and underneath he found a tray full of plastic straws and a spout above a stained plastic bowl. There was also a keypad with a modest selection of drinks, a flush button and a slot for payment. Hal stared at the filthy bowl in distaste, then closed the lid and put his arm back on it.

'Not thirsty?' asked Clunk.

Hal shook his head. 'How long until we –'

The rest of his words were lost in a sudden burst of screaming. A young man on the far side of the capsule was struggling to pull something from his jacket, while several passengers were trying just as desperately to stop him.

The man prevailed, and a slim blaster appeared in his hand. Immediately, the passengers melted away from him. 'Everybody down!' yelled the man, waving his gun. 'This is a stick-up!'

— 12 —

The young man took a bundle of fabric from his jacket and shook it out. 'I'm gonna move round amongst you,' he said, waving the gun. 'You put your valuables in the bag and I won't shoot. Deal?'

Most of the passengers stared at him as if he'd just materialised out of thin air. One or two nodded.

Hal glared at Clunk. 'I told you we should have taken the shuttle.'

Clunk ignored him. His eyes were fixed on the gun, tracking every motion.

'Hey, don't try anything,' muttered Hal. 'No heroics.'

'You're carrying the money for the spare part,' murmured the robot. 'He'll take it all.'

Hal's eyes widened. 'You've got to stop him, you hear?'

Clunk watched the man moving amongst the passengers, taking their wallets, cash and jewellery. 'They'll be waiting for him at the bottom,' he said suddenly. 'He'll never get away.'

The man in the next seat snorted. 'Bet you fifty credits there's a micro-fibre parachute and a breather in his hand luggage.'

The young man spun round. 'Shut up over there. Wait your turn like everyone else.' Suddenly he grinned. 'First class passengers, eh? Maybe I'll make an exception.'

As he approached, Hal saw Clunk's hand sliding towards the restraint on his harness. There was a muted click as the catch separated, and a clatter as the straps fell down either side of the robot's thighs. Then the man was upon them, standing in the aisle between the windows and the front of the seats. He gestured at the man with the book, who reached into his jacket and withdrew a leather wallet. His face was set as he dropped the wallet into the open sack.

'And the book,' said the young man.

'I haven't finished it!'

The young man placed the muzzle of his gun against the passenger's head. 'Buy another copy. I'm sure you can afford it.'

Sweat broke out on the passenger's forehead, and he dropped the book into the sack. The young man turned his attention to Hal, looking him up and down in surprise. 'What are you doing in first class dressed like that? Are you his gardener or something?'

'Yeah,' growled Hal. 'And I don't get paid for this nonsense.'

The young man turned to Clunk. 'I don't suppose you get paid at all?'

'Not a bean,' said Clunk.

'Any possessions?'

Clunk shook his head.

The young man reached into his sack. 'Here, have a book.'

'That's not yours to give.'

'It is now. Enjoy.' The young man tossed the heavy book to Clunk, who caught it one-handed and flicked it back again, whacking the young man in the forehead. The blow knocked the thief into a bench full of passengers, and willing hands grabbed him while Clunk leapt up.

In the confusion, Hal swept the blaster under his seat with his boot.

'Stand clear of the perpetrator,' said Clunk loudly. Blows continued to rain down on the hapless thief, so he waded into the crowd, pushing people aside until he was standing over the young man. After checking his pulse, Clunk seized the man's lapels and hauled him upright.

'Break the little bastard in two,' growled a male passenger.

'There will be no further violence,' said Clunk, staring the man down. 'Please return to your seats, I have custody of the offender.'

'What about my wallet?' demanded a passenger.

'And my cash,' said another.

'Wallets are easy, cash is a problem,' said Hal. 'Hands up everyone who got robbed.'

Many hands shot up, including dozens in a section of the capsule the robber hadn't been near.

'All right, forget it.' Hal shook the bag. 'I'm giving this to the authorities when we land. You can fight it out with them.'

'They'll keep our money!' shouted a man on the far side of the capsule.

'Hands up everyone who thinks we should sort out the wallets and jewellery, and give the cash to charity.'

Several hands shot up.

'Okay, you lot are out of luck. The rest of you, line up and tell me what you lost.'

There was some grumbling, but a while later the sack was empty save for a handful of credit tiles. Hal stirred them with his finger. 'Just enough for a coffee,' he said. He scooped them out and handed them to an elderly man seated nearby, then dusted his hands off. 'All done. How's the prisoner?'

Clunk shrugged. 'Out cold.'

There was a crackle from the overhead speakers. 'We trust you're enjoying the voyage. Braking manoeuvres will commence shortly, and all passengers must now be seated.'

Hal took his seat, reached underneath and slipped the blaster up his sleeve. Then he fastened his harness just as a grinding noise began to echo throughout the capsule. He felt himself settling into the chair, and he spared a brief thought for the passengers on the hard benches behind him. The capsule creaked alarmingly as it slowed, and the air grew warm as the massive brakes heated up. There was a smell of hot metal, mixed with burning rubber.

Hal gritted his teeth. 'H-how much longer?'

'Five minutes or so.' Clunk looked down at the thief, who was lying motionless on the floor under his feet. Then he looked at Hal in alarm. 'The gun! Where -?'

'I have no idea,' said Hal.

Clunk held his hand out. 'Wouldn't want them to find it on a passenger. There are heavy penalties for smuggling weapons.'

Hal shook the gun onto the seat and Clunk whipped it away. There was a snick, and it vanished into a compartment in the robot's hip.

'I don't know where you put it all,' said Hal. 'You must have hollow legs.'

Clunk nodded.

Hal looked round as the groaning sounds stopped. A movement outside caught his eye, and he turned to see a metal gantry sliding past the windows.

'Almost there,' said Clunk.

There was a shudder as the capsule came to a halt, followed by a loud hiss as the seals were opened. Warm air blew round the interior, carrying a strong smell of hot steel and rubber and the tiniest hint of spice.

Hal threw off the harness and stood up. 'Come on.'

'What about the thief?'

'He's not going anywhere. I want to be out of here before they start asking questions.'

Clunk followed Hal through the milling passengers. They flashed their ticket stubs at the door and then they were out, hurrying along a curved walkway towards the terminal building.

◆

The walkway encircled the space elevator like a ring, and through the inward-facing windows Hal spotted a group of security guards leading the groggy thief away. One of the guards was interviewing passengers, and Hal turned away in case they pointed him out as a witness.

He was halfway to the exit when he realised Clunk was no longer with him, and he turned to see the robot gawking at the elevator through the curved windows.

'What a remarkable feat of engineering,' said Clunk, visibly impressed.

'What's remarkable is that we got down in one piece,' growled Hal. 'Come on, keep moving.'

At the end of the corridor they found a wider passage with marble-clad walls and fresh, clean air with a faint spicy tang. There were colourful tapestries at regular intervals, and both sides of the passage were lined with lush palm trees that erupted in green splendour from polished bronze pots. Soft music played from overhead speakers, completing the soothing effect.

'Wow,' said Hal, staring around in amazement. 'Is this posh or what?'

Clunk glanced at the lustre on the nearest bronze pot, then looked down at his scuffed, grimy skin. 'I feel quite out of place.'

'You and me both.' Hal watched a group of travellers walk past, followed by a conga-line of self-propelled luggage. 'Let's tag along behind these guys. We can pretend we're bodyguards.'

'Or gardeners,' muttered Clunk.

As they walked along the passageway, more and more tunnels emptied into it until it opened onto a huge platform suspended a hundred metres above the main concourse. There was a waist-high barrier pierced with dozens of narrow gaps, each with a small grey panel alongside.

The people they were following fanned out and strode up to the gates, touched their palms to the panels and stepped off the edge of the platform, vanishing from sight. The luggage rolled after them.

Cautiously, Hal approached the side of the platform and looked down. Far below, people were floating down to the concourse, gathering their luggage and moving clear as they reached the bottom.

'It's an anti-gravity well,' said Clunk. 'I've heard of them, but I've never seen one in action.' He examined one of the grey panels. 'I assume this device reads your body mass. It must calculate the energy required to sustain your weight during the fall.'

'What's the red light?'

'Power indicator.'

Hal stepped up to the edge of the platform, and after a deep breath or two he pressed his hand to the panel and stepped out into space. His foot pedalled in thin air for a second, and then a firm hand grabbed the back of his flight suit and yanked him back onto the platform.

Heart pounding, Hal stared at Clunk. 'It didn't work!'

The robot gestured towards the panel, where the words 'Bioscan Failed. Entry to Plessa Forbidden' were blinking on and off.

'You said it was going to weigh me!'

'I was wrong.'

'Wrong?' Hal stared at the floor far below. 'I could have plunged to my death!'

'You've got to remember, this planet has advanced technology. We can't take anything for granted.'

'Great, so I get a modern coffin.'

Clunk touched the panel and the display changed. 'We need a visa.'

'How much is that going to cost?'

'Fifty credits plus taxes, charges and duty.'

'All right, set it up.' Hal stared over the edge. 'Hell of a welcome.'

Clunk pressed several buttons, charging the fee to Hal's account. 'Try now.'

'No way. You first.'

'Okay, watch closely.' Clunk pressed his palm to the keypad and stepped off the edge of the platform. He fell slowly to the floor, stepped clear and gave Hal a thumbs-up sign.

Hal touched his hand to the panel and a green light came on. Eyes shut, he stuck out his foot and pumped it in mid-air, where it met viscous, gloopy resistance. Reassured by Clunk's gentle descent, Hal stepped off the platform and felt a slipping sensation, as if he had been plunged into a huge column of gel.

By the time he remembered to breathe, Clunk was grabbing his arm and hauling him out.

'This is so exciting!' said the robot. 'Just think, Mr Spacejock! You're experiencing the cutting edge of technology!'

'I nearly experienced a solid marble floor.' Hal glanced at the platform far above. 'There's a lot to be said for a simple elevator, you know.'

'Lift,' said the robot automatically. He looked around. 'I wonder what's in store for us next?'

'Giant slicing blades flashing from the walls if we don't have the right permit.'

'It won't be anything like that!' said Clunk, as they set off across the concourse. 'Too dangerous.'

'Collapsing stone columns,' muttered Hal. 'One-way teleporters disguised as cupboards. You'll see.'

They crossed the concourse, and on the way Hal spotted the garish colours of a Tastee logo above a sweet shop. They still had the battered cardboard box, and he looked from one to the other, deciding whether to deal with his refund now or on the way back. He saw a bank of lockers, and decided to stow the box until they had the part for the stasis controller.

As they neared the exit barriers, Hal spotted two men standing behind a table full of brochures. 'I don't believe it!' he said, staring at their trim white uniforms and large gold medallions.

Clunk looked surprised. 'Spacers Guild?'

'Greetings,' said the taller of the two men, touching his middle finger to his forehead in the traditional Guild welcome. 'Tell me, have you considered joining?'

'Have I ever?' snapped Hal. 'I paid the membership fee and you closed down! You should be ashamed of yourselves, you petty scam artists.'

The man looked shocked. 'Sir, I don't know what you're talking about!'

'Forty grand in fees and all I got was a worthless badge.'

The man's face cleared. 'Oh, the collapse.'

'Oh, the collapse,' mimicked Hal. He grabbed a stack of leaflets from the table, ripped them to pieces and threw them into the air. 'Oh, no more forms.'

'Why, sir . . .'

Hal stormed off, and Clunk hurried to catch up.

'Makes my blood boil,' growled Hal. 'The Guild went broke! How can they sell memberships?'

'It does seem a little odd.'

'Odd isn't the half of it. I've a good mind to go back and –' Hal stopped as he spotted the words 'Spacers Guild' on a nearby news booth. Slowly, the headlines scrolled across the display: 'Spacers Guild staves off bankruptcy.'

'Whoops,' said Clunk.

Hal hunched down and hurried towards the barriers, losing himself in the crowd. Clunk strode after him, weaving through the packed mass of people.

As they approached the exit Hal saw each traveller touching a grey panel in order to open the gate. When his turn came he pressed his hand to the pad and the barrier swung open. He stepped through, but when Clunk went to follow the barrier snapped shut in front of him. Clunk touched the panel and a red light came on.

'Come on, move it!' shouted someone in the queue.

'It doesn't work,' said Clunk loudly, pressing his hand to the panel to prove it.

A guard appeared from a cubicle. 'I'm sorry, you can't go through. Toys have to be scanned.'

'*What* did you call me?'

The guard put one hand on his holster. 'Don't make a fuss now.'

'For your information,' said Clunk, leaning in close. '*I* was flying ships to the heart of the galaxy while *you* were filling nappies.'

'Easy, Clunk,' said Hal. 'This planet has advanced technology. We can't take anything for granted.'

'But he called me a toy!'

The guard pointed towards the end of the barriers. 'Pilot, toy or novelty advertising gimmick, you have to pass through the scanner.'

'Mr Spacejock, I can't!'

'Why not?'

Clunk stuck his forefinger and thumb out, arranging his hand in the shape of a gun. Then he tapped his thigh.

'Oh go on,' said Hal. 'You've got nothing to hide.'

'They're gunna search me,' said Clunk desperately.

'So what? We're not smugglers.'

Clunk opened his mouth to protest, then closed it again. Shoulders slumped, he was led away by the guard.

13

Passengers grabbed their bags and cleared a path as Clunk followed the guard along the line of barriers. At the end of the line, the last barrier was draped with heavy black curtains, with a bank of screens alongside. As Clunk arrived, a customs officer was trying to separate a large bear from a crying child.

'I want to keep teddy!' wailed the little boy.

'What about a big chocolate ice cream?' said his mother.

'Chips, Johnny?' added the father. 'How about a super-size spaceburger?'

As Clunk approached the group, the mother spotted him. 'It's that meddlesome robot,' she said to her husband. 'The one I was telling you about.'

The boy heard her and looked up.

'Come on, keep moving,' said the guard, trying to guide Clunk past the group.

Clunk ignored him and knelt next to the crying child. 'What's the matter, Johnny?'

The boy looked up with tear-stained eyes, clutching the bear tighter than ever. 'They want to look inside teddy.'

'It won't hurt him,' said Clunk.

'Radashon is bad for you.'

'But not for ... What's his name?'

'Wayne.'

'Well Johnny, Wayne will be just fine. I'm sure he's faced bigger challenges than a trip through a scanner.'

The boy's jaw tightened. 'They won't let me go with him.'

'That's good. The machine isn't safe for humans.'

'Not safe.' The boy turned to his parents. 'Told you.'

The mother groaned. 'Darling, teddy isn't human.'

'He IS real,' said the boy, crushing the bear to his chest.

Clunk lowered his voice. 'Would you like me to take teddy through? I'll hold him very carefully.'

The boy tilted his head to one side. 'Won't the scan hurt you?'

'I'm not real.' Clunk put his hands out. 'Come on. I'll look after him.'

The boy regarded him for several seconds, then dumped the treasured bear into his arms. As Clunk straightened up, the boy turned to his parents. 'Chips AND chocolate AND super burger?'

The guard led Clunk to the curtains and motioned him through. As soon as the curtains closed on him, Clunk yanked open the panel in his thigh and pulled out the weapon he'd collected from the space elevator. With one fluid movement, he spun it on his index finger and slid it into the bear's empty holster. Then, with the bear clutched under his arm, he stepped into the middle of the booth. Through the window he saw the customs officer studying the screens, and the guard from the exit barrier joined him for a look. They laughed at the toy weapon in the bear's holster and then the officer leaned towards his microphone. 'All clear. You may proceed.'

As he stepped through the curtains to exit the booth, Clunk jinked the gun from the holster and slipped it back into his thigh compartment, closing the flap just as the bear was wrenched from his grasp. 'Teddy!' shouted the boy.

'Take care,' called Clunk, as the family made for the nearest Planetburger outlet.

'That was very decent of you,' said Hal.

'Decent?' Clunk glared at him. 'I'm carrying a gun, Mr Spacejock. I had to conceal it somehow.'

'Is that what the pantomime was about? I thought you were trying to unscrew your legs.'

Clunk's eyes narrowed. 'Perhaps if you were a little faster on the uptake ... '

'Why didn't you just declare it?'

'Because it's probably stolen,' snapped Clunk.

'It is now.'

'I meant before. It might be linked to unsolved crimes. You could have been charged with armed robbery!'

'Well, if the part for the controller is too expensive we can always stage a hold-up. Maybe someone else will get the blame.'

They left the terminal building and emerged in a paved area where dozens of bright-eyed birds flitted amongst waiting taxis, turning over stray wrappers and alighting on suitcases in their search for food. Sleek cabs flowed in both directions, pausing only to pick up or drop off passengers. To the left and right, the road curved away between embankments of lush green grass.

Clunk approached a waiting cab, bent down and spoke through the open window. 'Excuse me, do you know where Finangle Corporation is?'

The driver lowered his news-sheet. 'Sure. Hop in.'

'How much?' asked Hal.

'Six klicks plus flagfall. Say two hundred?'

'Say forget it,' growled Hal.

'Nice day for a walk,' remarked the driver, returning to his news-sheet.

Hal led Clunk away from the cab. 'Now I know why we avoid rich planets. Two hundred for a lousy cab fare!'

'I can't walk six kilometres. My batteries won't last.'

'Why don't you wait here? I can fetch the bits.'

'What if you're held up again?'

'You could lend me that gun.'

Clunk shook his head. 'You've given yourself life-threatening injuries with cutlery before now. I am not putting a high-powered firearm in your hands.'

Hal sighed. 'All right. I'll be back soon. You'd better switch off and save those batteries of yours.'

Clunk entered standby, and after the robot's eyes dulled Hal turned to leave.

'Oy you!' yelled an angry voice. 'What do you think you're doing?'

Hal looked around and saw an elderly man in uniform hurrying towards him, his irate face half-hidden under an enormous peaked cap. 'You can't leave that here!' shouted the man, jerking his thumb at Clunk. 'No littering, see?'

'Littering?'

'Yeah.' The man pointed to a neat sign on the wall. 'I can fine you.'

'He's not litter,' said Hal patiently. 'He's my robot.'

'You know how much it costs to get a junked robot picked up? "Undreds!'

'He's not junked,' said Hal. 'He's going to sit here until I come back.'

'Mister, I cleared four robots from that bench last week.

Favourite trick, it is. Sit here, make yesself comfy. I'll be back in a week. No bleedin' chance.'

'Look, I've got a long walk ahead of me, and he wouldn't get half way.'

'Worn out, is he? Going to dump him, were you?' The man nodded. 'I knew it. I can tell, 'cause that's all I see, week in week out. If you knew the times I'd ...'

Hal shook Clunk's shoulder and the robot jerked upright, eyes flickering. 'Back already, Mr Spacejock?'

'No, this guy thinks I'm abandoning you. I thought you could reassure him.'

Clunk turned his attention to the uniformed man, who was still working his way through past grievances.

'...and then there was this pair of twins. Like new they was, but you can't get the parts nowadays and –'

'Excuse me!' said Clunk loudly.

'Another time there was a whole gang of 'em, waiting until me back was turned before dumping their junky old robots all over me nice clean benches. All that oil and grease! And then –'

'EXCUSE ME!' roared Clunk at full volume. Passing cabs squealed to a halt and all the birds fluttered away in a welter of feathers.

'They know I can't see too well at night, so they sneak up and leave arms and legs lyin' around, then they call out and wait for me to trip up. But I know them and their tricks and –'

Clunk reached for the man's lapels, but Hal stopped him. 'Give up.'

'What are we going to do?'

There was a whistling sound and a bright yellow jetbike came round the corner. Hal's eyes locked onto it. 'Look sharp,' he murmured.

'What are you thinking?' demanded Clunk. He followed Hal's gaze. 'You're not really going to …'

The bike fizzed to a halt nearby, and the rider leapt off and strode into the terminal with a package under his arm.

'C'mon,' said Hal out the side of his mouth.

'Come on what?'

Hal strolled to the bike, glanced around to see if anyone was watching, then grabbed the handlebars and swung himself into the saddle.

'I don't think that's a good idea,' said Clunk, arranging his features into a disapproving look. 'It's not legal.'

'Fine, stay here and convince that nutter you're not a pile of scrap.' Hal pressed the starter and the bike spluttered into life, rising into the air on a sparkling forcefield. It began to tilt, and Hal twisted the handlebars to counteract the movement. The bike immediately tipped the other way, almost hurling him off. A wobble or two later, and he got it under control.

'Hey!' yelled a voice. 'Hey you! Get off that bike!'

Hal looked round and saw the courier approaching at a run. 'Clunk, get on! Now!'

Clunk leapt aboard and Hal gave the throttle a vicious twist. The bike jumped off the mark, raced past the courier's outstretched arms and glanced off a barrier with a screech of tortured metal.

'Which way?' shouted Hal, who was leaning over the handlebars with his eyes screwed up against the tearing wind.

'Next right!' shouted Clunk, tightening his grip as they approached a corner.

Hal dragged on the handlebars and the bike leaned over, sliding and sparking as it shot round at full speed. They missed a parked van, screamed between a pair of bins and began a high-speed slalom between lampposts. Once clear,

Hal got the bike on the right side of the road and opened up the throttle.

They hurtled past silent factories and empty parking lots, the bike's engine howling like a tornado in the narrow streets. Before long Clunk tapped Hal on the shoulder and pointed to a building in the distance. A giant inflatable spaceship was tethered to the roof, and a huge sign proclaimed to the world that Finangle Corp had 'the biggest tools in town'.

Hal turned into the car park and brought the bike to a halt, dismounted and strode towards the front entrance. Inside, there was a receptionist behind the counter, typing busily while fielding incoming calls. After a moment or two, he paused and looked up. 'How can I help you?'

Clunk stepped forward. 'Order for Spacejock.'

'Ah, the rush job.' The man slid a parcel wrapped in brown paper across the counter. 'Eighteen credits, thanks.'

'Eighteen credits?' said Hal. 'I thought it was going to be hundreds!'

'Must be your lucky day.' The receptionist pushed a touchpad across the desk. 'Sign here.'

'I'd better check it first,' said Clunk. He removed the paper, revealing a jet-black case that seemed to absorb light. There was a starburst logo engraved on the lid, with the words '931 inc' underneath. Frowning, Clunk popped the case open.

'My God,' said Hal. 'It's full of cigars!'

The receptionist reddened. 'Oops, sorry. That's a present for my boss.' He reached under the counter and took out a second parcel, wrapped in the same paper. 'This must be yours.'

Clunk tore the paper off, revealing a small aluminium case with heavy-duty fasteners. After checking inside, he took out several credit tiles and slid them across the counter.

'We had a devil of a job getting here,' said Hal, pressing his thumb to the receipt pad.

'Really?'

'Yeah. First we took a rental ship, then a passenger liner. Then we took the space elevator and some guy tried to hold everyone up.'

Clunk chimed in. 'After that we took a courier's jetbike and —'

'Well, we'd better not stand around chatting,' said Hal hastily. He picked up the aluminium case. 'Back to Cathua, eh?'

Clunk nodded. 'At this rate we'll have the stasis controller fixed in no time.'

◆

Back at the Plessa Spaceport, Hal parked the courier bike out of sight of the terminal so they could cover the last hundred metres or so on foot, keeping an eye out for the courier as they entered the building. Inside, Clunk went off to secure tickets to the Orbiter while Hal retrieved his battered carton from the locker and took it to the sweet shop he'd spotted earlier.

The shop was crowded, and three serving droids worked non-stop to service their customers. The droids were polished chrome, with their noses permanently raised in the air and their features arranged into looks of haughty disdain, as if traffic in such common fare were beneath them. Like it or not, they were doing a roaring trade in gaudy sweets and chocolate bars.

Hal joined the shortest queue and soon reached the counter.

'How may I help you, sir?' asked the droid.

Hal put his box on the counter. 'I'd like a refund on this stuff, please.'

'A refund?' said the droid, almost stumbling over the unfamiliar word. 'Why?'

'I got a job lot from a wholesaler on Cathua, and –'

'Ah, Cathua. I'm afraid we don't issue refunds for grey imports.'

'Oh, they're not grey,' said Hal, pulling a half-chewed Tastee bar from the box. 'See? They're all white and crumbly.'

'White and crumbly,' repeated the droid. From the tone of its voice, white and crumbly was a new experience.

'Yeah, and there's rat droppings in the box,' said Hal, tipping a few on the counter in case the droid had never seen one.

Clearly, it hadn't. 'R-r-rat . . . ' Speech failed, and the droid resorted to opening and closing its mouth. It was so shocked it forgot to keep its nose in the air.

'So, I'd like a refund thanks. Or replacements, I'm not fussy.'

Gingerly, the droid opened the box and looked inside. 'Sir, how old is this product?'

Hal shrugged. 'I don't know. I bought it last night.'

'But these designs . . . they're over ten years old!' Suddenly the droid's nose went up. 'We have no liability in this case. You purchased this product when it had already passed its use-by date, and that's no fault of the manufacturer.'

'So you won't give me a refund?'

'No sir.'

'Or replacements?'

'I'm afraid not. Now, if you're not going to buy anything I must ask you to leave.' The droid gestured at the box. 'There's a rubbish bin outside. I suggest you use it.'

Hal looked outside and saw the bin. He also saw a bench. 'You know what I'm going to do?'

'Sir, I really don't care.'

'You might.' Hal pointed to the bench. 'I'm going to sit over there and eat everything in this box. And then I'm going to stick my fingers down my throat.'

'But you'll be sick!'

'All over the place,' said Hal with satisfaction. 'I'll put everyone off chocolate for a month.'

'A refund, you said.'

'And compensation,' said Hal, having gained the upper hand. 'I want something for my pain and suffering.'

'What pain and suffering?'

Hal winced and clutched his stomach. 'Ooh, I feel sick.'

'I can't give you money,' said the droid desperately. 'I'm not authorised.'

'I'll take goods to the value,' said Hal, making a swift recovery. 'Two boxes of Tastees, six bags of lime balls and some of those chewy snake things. And give me a new box. This one's falling apart at the seams.

Ten minutes later Clunk found him sitting on a bench munching a Tastee bar, while a droid watched anxiously from the nearby sweet shop. Clunk glanced down at the new box full of sweets and chocolates, and decided he really didn't want to know.

Hal gathered his spoils, and together they made their way through the spaceport to the departure gates.

The space elevator carried them back to Plessa's Orbiter without incident, and Hal and Clunk boarded the *Luna Rose* and made their way to the staff room. A few minutes later they were back in uniform.

'How do I look?' asked Hal, setting his cap on a rakish angle.

'Excellent. Very smart.'

'I feel like a doorman.'

'You look more like an undertaker.' Clunk picked Hal's flight suit off the floor and shook it out, dislodging half a dozen sweet wrappers. 'You've got chocolate stains on this.'

Hal nodded. 'And I intend to add more.'

There was a rumbling noise below decks as the liner began to move. Moments later, the first call light came on, quickly followed by several more. Hal glanced up at the board, then shook his head. 'It's going to be a long trip back,' he muttered.

14

The *Luna Rose* docked at the Cathuan Orbiter and Hal slipped out while Spearman was busy fielding customer service complaints. There was no point lining up for their wages, because once Clunk worked out the value of all the drinks and snacks Hal had given away, they'd ended up owing more than they'd earned.

Hal strode up the boarding tunnel behind Clunk, his hands in his pockets to still the clinking silverware. Since they were getting nothing for the trip, he'd paid a visit to the first class lounge and souvenired a few sets of monogrammed cutlery for the *Volante*, but his large pockets meant it rattled with every step. Now and then Clunk paused to listen, and Hal had to cough loudly to cover the tinkling noises.

Clanking, pausing and coughing, they navigated the Orbiter's tunnels to the ferry terminal where they found a bored attendant sitting behind a screen. Hal left Clunk gazing at Cathua through a porthole and went over to get tickets.

The man looked up at his approach. 'Sorry, mate. There's no service.'

'What do you mean, no service? Where's the shuttle?'

'Power cuts. It's stuck on the ground and they can't refuel it.'

'There's no backup?' Hal spread his hands, jingling slightly. 'What kind of tinpot operation is this?'

The attendant shrugged.

'There must be another way down.'

'Like a space elevator, you mean?'

Hal brightened. 'You have one of those?'

'Nope.'

Hal turned away in disgust.

'How did you get on?' asked Clunk, tearing his gaze from the planet spread out below.

'We're stuffed. No shuttle and no elevator.'

'There has to be a way down.'

'Sure, we could rent a spaceship. Pity two hundred other passengers thought of it first.'

'We'll just have to settle in for the night, then.'

Hal jerked his thumb at the window. 'What about my cargo? It's not getting any fresher.'

'Don't worry about that. My temporary repairs will keep it safe for now.'

'Hang on. If we're stuck up here, where am I going to sleep?'

'Why don't we return to the *Luna Rose*?'

Hal snapped his fingers. 'That's it! That's how we get down!'

'The *Luna Rose* won't take us to the surface. It's not built for planetary –'

'Not the *Luna Rose*, the *X1*!'

'The *Phantom*?' Clunk frowned. 'They impounded it.'

'So what? It brought us up here, it can take us down again.'

'What about the five thousand credit bond?'

'Five or fifty, we're not paying.'

'We're not?'

'Of course we're not.' Hal lowered his voice. 'Listen up. Here's the plan ... '

Hal pulled the cap over his eyes, adjusted his overalls and straightened his collar. 'Set?'

'My hat's too small,' said Clunk.

'Rip it up the back.'

Clunk took the cap off his head and wrenched the fabric apart. 'I don't see how this outfit is going to help.'

'It's part of the plan, all right?'

'No, it's not all right. You haven't told me what we're going to do.'

'We're going to board the *X1*, start the engines and fly away from the Orbiter.'

'That's your plan?' Clunk stared at him. 'What about security? What about the fine? What about -?'

'We can sort out the minor details later. Come on, put the cap on and follow me.'

'But Mr Spacejock –'

'And try to look a bit more human.'

Clunk let his face go slack.

'A live one would be better,' said Hal. 'Now stick your hands in your pockets, stay behind me and don't say anything.' With that, he pushed open the door and stepped into the office.

There were four desks crammed into the tiny space, each with a yellowed terminal and teetering piles of paperwork. Three of the chairs were empty, while the fourth was occupied by a small man in a faded blue uniform. He was picking out keys one by one with the tip of a pen, pausing to peer at the screen every three or four letters.

Hal watched for a minute or two, then cleared his throat. 'Bill asked me to move that *Phantom* jobby,' he said, waving a folded sheet of paper.

The man looked up. 'Bill who?'

'You know, in Accounts.'

'There are no Bills in Accounts.'

'Where else would you keep them? Ha ha.'

The man looked at Hal in distaste. 'I'm short staffed, short on space and short tempered. State your business or clear off and leave me to mine.'

Hal tapped the folded paper. 'I told you, I've got to move that ship. Records says it's in the wrong place, Accounts need the serial number, Enforcement wants –'

'I'm Enforcement,' said the man, drawing himself up.

'Of course you are. So, to keep all these people happy I need to move the ship.'

'Where to?'

'Round the other side,' said Hal, gesturing vaguely. 'Military want her for target practice.'

'Really?'

Hal nodded.

'Okay, take it away.' The man gestured at a pile of paperwork. 'Leave the forms there.'

'I can't. Records want them back.'

'Leave the forms or leave my office.'

Hal glanced down at the folded sheet of paper in his hands, which featured a glamorous photo of the *Luna Rose* on the cover. 'Right on this pile, here?' he said, approaching one of the desks.

'Right there.'

Hal nudged the pile, tipping the whole lot onto the floor.

'You clumsy oaf!' shouted the man. 'Look what you've done!'

'Oh, sorry,' murmured Hal. He crouched down and began to gather handfuls of paper, mixing them up at random.

'No, no, no!' shouted the man, leaping up. He charged over and snatched the crumpled pages from Hal's fingers. 'You're making things worse,' he snarled. 'Go on, clear out.'

Hal glanced at Clunk and nodded towards the inner door. The robot took the hint, and as the man gathered papers, smoothed them and arranged them into some kind of order, Hal stood up and followed.

Beyond the door, a short flight of steps led down to a corridor with numbered access tubes. They hurried along the corridor, peering through the airlock doors until they spotted the *Phantom*. They cycled the airlock and passed into the bay, finding the ship just as they'd left it, with the door open and the ramp extended. Hal and Clunk hurried up the landing ramp and entered the ship, their feet scrunching on the chips of woodgrain covering the deck.

'That was pretty easy,' said Hal, taking the pilot's chair.

'We're not out yet,' cautioned the robot. 'Computer, give me a status report.'

'Get it yourself.'

Frowning, Clunk applied himself to the console. A minute or two later, he turned to Hal. 'Everything appears to be in order.'

'Okay, let's go.'

'There's just one minor impediment.' Clunk nodded at the screen. 'The docking bay doors are closed.'

'Can we open them from here?'

'No, and the controls are on the other side of the airlock.'

Hal frowned. 'I'd call that a major problem.'

'Not really. I'll go back through the airlock and open the bay doors. As long as you leave the outer door open, I can return to the ship.'

'Go on, then.' Hal watched on the main screen as Clunk made his way to the airlock. The round door opened and closed, and a few moments later the red light turned to green. Hal panned the camera back to the rust-streaked bay doors and waited impatiently for them to open.

'Incoming,' said the computer suddenly.

The speakers hissed and popped. 'Orbiter to *Phantom-X1*, come in please.'

Hal frowned. 'Yes?'

'*Phantom*, are you trying to open the docking bay?'

'That's the idea,' said Hal cautiously.

'I'm sorry, I can't let you do it.'

'But I've got to move the ship! Bill said –'

'Listen buddy, from where I'm sitting I can see right into your flight deck.'

Hal turned to face the airlock. It was wide open, and halfway up the docking bay wall a uniformed figure was waving at him from behind a reinforced window. 'That's it, you're getting the idea,' said the speaker gently. 'First you seal the ship and THEN YOU LET THE GODDAMN AIR OUT OF THE DOCKING BAY!'

Hal gulped. 'Thanks. I'll deal with it.'

'Bloody throttle jockeys,' growled the caller. There was a burst of static as he hung up.

Hal pushed the fire axe aside and activated the airlock seal with shaking fingers. As the green light came on, he felt the deck tremble and heard the whistling scream of air being sucked from the docking bay.

The bay doors groaned and squealed until they were

completely retracted, revealing stars as bright and hard as diamonds. Hal panned the camera and saw Clunk entering the bay through the airlock. At the same time, the screen flashed and a huge, angry face appeared. It was the man from the Enforcement office.

'Get off that ship this instant!' shouted the man. He waved the *Luna Rose* brochure. 'I knew there was something fishy about you. Thought you could fool me, eh? Took me for a sucker, eh?'

Hal slid his hand along the console until he found the throttle control, and as Clunk stepped into the flight deck he pushed the lever forward to the stop. There was a roar from the engines followed by a louder roar from the screen. 'Get rid of him,' shouted Hal, as the ship began to move.

Clunk crossed to the console and flipped a switch, killing the display. Suddenly there was a grating noise, clearly audible over the roar of the engines.

'They're closing the bay doors!' shouted Hal. 'Quick, get us out of here!'

Clunk pulled the afterburner knob and the ship exploded from the bay, squeezing between the enormous doors with centimetres to spare. The tremendous acceleration threw Hal to the back of the hold, slamming him into the bulkhead, and the fire axe slipped from the console and came spinning towards him, end over end. He ducked, barely in time, and it buried itself in the bulkhead with a loud THUNK!

Then they were clear, rocketing away from the Orbiter.

'Another narrow escape,' said Hal, eyeing the quivering axe.

'They may come after us.' Clunk's fingers danced over the console. 'Hold on, I'm going to put them off our trail.'

'How?'

The ship heeled over. 'First we go around the planet. Then

we'll enter low orbit for the night, and in the morning we can land right next to the *Volante*. With a bit of luck, they'll assume we're local traffic.'

Hal looked around the cramped flight deck. 'I don't fancy spending the night up here.'

'I don't think we can land in darkness. The spaceport beacons are down and this ship is ill-equipped for unassisted landings.'

'I heard that,' said the computer.

Hal frowned. 'I've got a bad feeling about this. My head's light and my feet feel like lead.'

'That's probably the gravity generators, Mr Spacejock. They're a bit flaky.'

'What a surprise.'

'Now, you must want something to eat.'

'Not just yet,' said Hal, looking pained.

Clunk looked around. 'And where's that box of yours? The one with all the sweets?'

'I left it on the *Luna Rose*. Empty.'

'You ate the whole lot!' exclaimed Clunk. 'No wonder you look ill.'

'I don't look ill,' said Hal sharply. 'I feel fine. On top of the world.'

'What you need is some real food. There's not much aboard, but I did see a carton of instant pizzas.'

Hal groaned.

'Or how about some nice thick vegetable soup with extra carrot?'

'Will you shut up about food?' said Hal desperately. 'All I need is a sleep.'

'Very well. Let me make you up a bed in the hold.'

'Old rags and a metal floor? I can't wait.'

'It's not my fault. All the bedclothes were in those suitcases. You know, the ones you wouldn't let me bring.'

Hal sighed.

'Don't worry, Mr Spacejock. One of my previous owners had a saying for times like this.'

'Yeah? What was it?'

'When life is getting you down, have a nap.'

'That's not much of a saying.'

'Strictly between the two of us, he wasn't much of an owner.'

Hal smiled weakly. 'All right, crack out the sheets and I'll take his advice.'

— 15 —

Next morning, Jasmin took a cab to the spaceport. As it approached the landing field she saw two ships in the distance, one a rust-streaked wreck and the other a brand new freighter. She'd already decided the older ship had to be the *Volante* when she saw Barry and Ace sitting near the new one. The men were slouched on a couple of olive green boxes, which had dark patches where the serial numbers had been painted over. Put up a couple of signs, thought Jasmin idly, and they could open an army surplus store on the spot. Hadn't they heard of subterfuge?

The cabbie stopped next to the passenger ramp and cast his eye over the men and equipment. 'Planning a war, eh?'

'We're going on a fishing trip,' said Jasmin shortly.

The cabbie snorted, but turned it into a cough when Jasmin handed him a large tip. 'Thanks miss. Hope you catch a big 'un.'

Jasmin got out and watched the cabbie drive away, thinking it was just as well he'd been fooled by her deception. Silencing him could have been messy.

'There you are!' called Barry. 'Thought you said eleven?'

'I did. It's five to.'

Barry scowled at Ace. 'You and that bleeding watch. I told

140

you it was dodgy.'

'It works mostly, 'cept when it's brass monkeys.'

'You were had, sunshine. They saw you coming a mile away.'

Jasmin watched the exchange, baffled. The men were discussing a timepiece, that much she understood, but where did monkeys and sunshine come into it? 'You there. Barry.'

'Yes miss?'

'Why is your equipment not aboard the ship?'

'It's locked up, that's why. Nobody home.'

'Spacejock has to be aboard. He's flying us to Jordia.'

Barry shrugged. 'Tell that to the computer.'

Jasmin took the passenger ramp to the landing platform, using the handholds as it flexed and swayed beneath her. At the top she found an intercom alongside the airlock door. She pressed the button and spoke into the pickup. 'This is Jasmin Ortiz for Mr Hal Spacejock. Please put me through immediately.'

'Mr Spacejock will be back soon. Would you like to leave a message?'

'Back? Where is he?'

'Not here.'

Jasmin frowned. 'How long will he be?'

'Estimated return: some time this morning.'

'That's not very precise.'

'He *is* human.'

'Tell me, did Mr Spacejock sign for a delivery?'

'Yes. Clunk stowed it in the cargo hold.'

Jasmin glanced down at Barry and Ace. She had to get them out of sight, fast. 'We really need to come aboard.'

'I'm sorry, I can't allow that.'

'Not even the cargo hold? Our equipment is sitting on the landing pad.'

'The doors will remain closed until Mr Spacejock or Clunk tell me to open them.'

'Is that so?' Jasmin prised the intercom away from the hull and patched into the data connection behind it. 'The thing is, I really need to come aboard.'

'You're not authorised to do that!' said the Navcom. 'I shall report this to the authorities!'

Jasmin found the access code and the airlock door swung open. Next she operated the cargo ramp, and as it dropped towards the ground she waved Barry towards the rear of the ship. 'Load your equipment. Quick!' Then she ducked into the *Volante*'s airlock.

The inner door had started to close, but she took two steps forward and pushed, driving it back until the gap was large enough to enter the flight deck. She found a data socket in the console and plugged her finger in, and immediately discovered layer upon layer of electronic shields protecting the ship's operating system from intrusion. Someone had patiently built an impregnable wall around the core functions, but as Jasmin probed she found a weakness: the crew list. Mentally crossing her fingers, she added herself to the roster and maxed her clearance for good measure.

'Welcome back, Ms Ortiz,' said the Navcom. 'Did you have a pleasant outing?'

'Wonderful, thanks. Now, I'd like you to prepare for take-off. We must be ready to leave the instant Mr Spacejock returns. And Navcom?'

'Yes, Ms Ortiz?'

'You can call me Jasmin.'

Barry and Ace had just finished loading when Jasmin came to check on them. She found Ace sitting on a crate while Barry checked his ankle.

'What's the problem?' demanded Jasmin. 'Is he not fit?'

'Dozy twit fell over a cable,' said Barry. 'Don't worry, it'll mend.'

'You don't have spares?'

'Eh?'

'Forget it.' Jasmin looked around the hold. 'Your equipment is aboard?'

'Yep, all in.'

'Excellent. We'll be leaving shortly, so please secure –' Jasmin stopped. A battered groundcar had appeared in the distance and was making directly for the ship. 'This must be the pilot. You'd better hide.'

'Why?'

'I didn't tell him about you, that's why. Now get out of sight.'

Barry and Ace had barely hidden themselves when the groundcar drew up to the cargo ramp. The doors opened and two huge men climbed out, enormous bruisers with broken noses, close-cropped hair and shoulders as wide as an airlock door. They looked up at the ship, then unhurriedly reached into the car and pulled out a pair of baseball bats. While they were busy the rear door opened and a short man in a leather coat emerged.

The *Volante* creaked as the men stepped onto the ramp, and as Jasmin watched them coming towards her, swinging their bats, she wondered why they'd selected this particular ship for a game. And furthermore, where were their balls? 'Can I help you, gentlemen?'

'Are you the owner?' demanded the man in the coat.

'No, I'm a passenger.'

'Is Spacejock around?'

Jasmin shook her head.

'Doesn't matter,' said the man, handing her a sheet of paper. 'As of now, this ship belongs to Hand-E-Mart. Get your stuff and leave.'

Jasmin read the note, which was printed on a Hand-E-Mart letterhead. 'This isn't a valid possession order. It's just a list of illiterate threats.'

The man beckoned to his bat-wielding heavies. 'Escort this lady from the ship.'

The toughs shouldered their weapons and reached for Jasmin's upper arms, but as they did so she grabbed their outstretched hands, hauled the men off their feet and flipped them over in mid-air, slamming them onto the decking. The impact shook the hold and almost knocked the debt collector off his feet, but he recovered quickly and pulled a gleaming handgun from his coat.

Jasmin raised her hand.

'And the other one,' said the man.

'Oh, I'm not surrendering,' said Jasmin. 'It's a signal to my men.'

'Of course it is. No doubt they're just waiting to spring from hiding at your slightest command.'

Jasmin dropped her hand, and Barry and Ace sprang from hiding, blast rifles at the ready. There was a 'Chack!' as the safeties came off, followed by a whine as the weapons powered up.

The debt collector's jaw dropped, as did his weapon. 'I, er ...'

Jasmin prodded him in the chest. 'You're leaving. Now.'

'I'll catch up with Spacejock later,' said the man, backing out of the hold. 'You tell him I said so.' Halfway down the ramp he turned and belted for the car, coat flapping behind him.

Jasmin pushed the dazed toughs down the ramp after him and closed the hold. She gave Barry and Ace a quick nod of thanks, then took the passage to the flight deck. Where the hell was Hal Spacejock? The debt collector was sure to return with reinforcements, and next time she might be the one tumbling down the ramp.

Hal had woken slowly, still feeling the effects of a dream where he'd been served as the main course in a fancy restaurant. Frenzied diners had descended on him with flashing cutlery, and he'd only escaped with gravity-defying martial arts. Clunk was one of the waiters, but he'd left Hal to his own devices while serving delicacy after delicacy to a gloating Kent Spearman.

Hal interpreted the dream to the best of his ability, and decided it meant he was hungry. He rolled over, unleashing a groan as the pocket full of stolen silverware dug into his side.

'Are you all right, Mr Spacejock?'

Hal looked up and saw Clunk standing over him with a battered tin mug. 'Yeah, great. Excellent.'

'I thought you could use some refreshment,' said the robot.

Hal took a cautious sip. Clunk's coffee ranged from plain water to engine oil, with enough variations in temperature and ingredients to generate whole new strains of bacteria. This particular brew had the consistency of gelatine and the aroma of balmy seawater. 'That was some night.'

'Bad?'

'Yeah. I dreamt we slept in orbit aboard that *Phantom* wreck.'

'That was no dream.'

Hal sat up and discovered his bed was a pile of dusty rugs in a corner of the hold. 'Damn, I thought the *Volante* was getting noisy. How long until we land?'

'We just embarked on another orbit before re-entry, and then we have the approach followed by –'

'Just tell me how long.'

'Another hour.'

'An *hour*? What time is it now?'

'Ten am. I tried to wake you earlier, but –'

'You're cutting it too fine. We have to be down by eleven or ...' Hal's voice tailed off. Clunk didn't know they'd yet to load Jasmin's real crate.

'Or what?'

'Well, er, ground control might take a tea break. Wouldn't want to be stranded.'

Clunk gave him a strange look. 'They'll have relief staff to handle our landing.'

'I just want us down as quick as possible, all right?'

'But I've already programmed our course into the computer.'

'So do it again, and this time cut some corners.'

'There aren't any corners. We're orbiting.'

'Orbit faster, then!'

'I'll do what I can,' said Clunk, rising to his feet.

Once he was gone, Hal poured the rest of his coffee on the blankets and rolled them up. Then he put the mug aside and set off to find the shower cubicle.

◆

Fifty minutes later Hal entered the flight deck, where he found Clunk preparing the ship for landing.

'Did you get a shower?' asked the robot.

'Yeah, thirty minutes of steam.'

'And something to eat?'

Hal shook his head. 'Spent ages trying to light the cooker.'

'You don't mean the electric stove?'

'Oops. No wonder it smelled funny.' Hal sighed. 'This ship is so *old*, Clunk. I can't wait to get back aboard the *Volante*.'

'Five minutes and your wish will be granted.' Clunk flipped a switch. 'Ground, this is *Phantom-X1* requesting clearance.'

There was a hiss from the speakers.

'*Phantom-X1* calling ground. Do you copy?'

'I wouldn't bother,' said Hal. 'If there's a problem they'll call us.'

'We need clearance. What if we hit another ship?'

'Are you kidding? There's only two ships here. One's ours, and the other one isn't going anywhere.'

'You're right. Against my better judgement, I'm prepared to make an exception.'

'Incoming call,' said the computer.

Clunk looked hopeful. 'Ground control?'

'Negative. Putting them on.'

'Good morning, gentlemen, I trust everything is going smoothly?'

'It's Joe,' whispered Clunk.

Hal stared at him. 'What am I going to say?'

'Tell him what happened.'

'Hello?' said Joe. 'Can you hear me?'

'Loud and clear,' said Hal. 'We're just coming in to land.'

'That was some test flight, my boy. You were gone hours.'

'We were almost gone for good. The throttles jammed and we nearly crashed into the Orbiter.'

There was a long silence. 'How about a discount?'

'I wouldn't take this ship if you paid me.'

Joe sighed. 'You're missing a fabulous opportunity. I have several buyers lined up.'

'You can hold a raffle for all I care, but you'd better throw in life insurance. This thing's a death trap.'

'Oh, very well,' said Joe sullenly. 'But that fuel tank better not be empty.'

Clunk cut the call. 'It's going to cost a lot to fill up.'

'Just splash a few litres in,' said Hal. 'It won't be empty then.'

Suddenly there was a growing rumble, and before they could react something very big and very loud screamed by. Clunk leapt for the controls as the *Phantom* jerked sideways, thrown off course by the near miss, and it took several seconds of frenzied activity before he managed to get their descent back on track.

'What the hell was *that*?' demanded Hal.

'I told you it was important to obtain clearance. That was another ship, leaving the spaceport.'

'What other ship?'

'How should I know? It must have come in while we were visiting Plessa.'

Hal mopped his brow. 'Still, it missed eh? No harm done.'

16

The *Phantom* set down on a vacant landing pad, and while Clunk was busy shutting down the engines and flight systems Hal marched to the inner door and threw it open. 'Thank goodness that's over,' he said, entering the airlock. 'Now we just have to nip over to Jordia for Jasmin's delivery and pocket forty grand.'

'The spaceport is calling us. They want landing fees.'

'Charge it to Joe.' The outer door creaked and groaned, and Hal clicked his fingers impatiently as it swung open. 'As soon as we get aboard I'm going to ...' His voice tailed off as he spotted the rugged little freighter with the damaged engine - and no *Volante*. 'Where's my bloody ship?'

Clunk checked the screen. 'We're on the next landing pad. It should be alongside.'

'The hell it is.' With a sinking feeling, Hal realised who might be responsible. Hand-E-Mart! The owner had threatened him, hadn't he? What if he'd managed to impound the ship? Hal cast a worried look at Clunk. How was he going to point the robot in the right direction without incriminating himself? And how could the Navcom have let someone take the ship? Deeply worried, Hal jammed his hands in his pockets and immediately started dancing around the flight deck, roaring in pain.

'What is it?' asked Clunk in alarm. 'What's happening?'

'Fork!' shouted Hal. 'Fork! Fork! Fork!'

'Mr Spacejock, there's no call for –'

'Fork!' There was a flash of silver as Hal pulled his hand from his pocket, and when he held it up Clunk saw the tines of a fork rammed under his fingernail.

'Is that from the *Luna Rose*?'

'Who cares where the bloody thing came from?' shouted Hal. 'Get rid of it!'

'But how did it get into your pocket?'

'Pull it out!' Hal averted his gaze as Clunk took hold of the fork, and a split second later he was dancing around the flight deck again, muttering several more 'forks' under his breath.

'It's not very clean,' said Clunk, inspecting the tines. 'Do you think it was inside someone's mouth?'

Hal grabbed two handfuls of cutlery from his pockets, ran to the airlock and hurled them out, scattering knives and forks across the landing pad. As they bounced and slithered on the ground, he turned and jabbed his throbbing finger at Clunk. 'You are going to find the *Volante*. Understood?'

'Yes, Mr Spacejock. Shall I search the port computers?'

'Port, starboard, I don't give a stuff. Just find her.'

Hal paced the flight deck while Clunk interrogated the computer. Finally, the robot straightened. 'You know that ship we almost hit on the way down?'

'Don't tell me that was the *Volante*.'

'It was.'

Hal groaned. 'Where were they taking her?'

'I don't know. They didn't file a flight plan.'

'Call her,' said Hal suddenly. 'Put me through to them.'

'I already tried. They're not accepting calls.' Clunk looked serious. 'Mr Spacejock, you realise our cargo is at risk? My repairs were only temporary, and if the *Volante* is missing for any length of time –'

'We'll just have to chase them down, then. Get ready for take off. We're leaving.'

'But the *Volante* is faster than us! Not only that, we're almost out of fuel.'

Hal gestured towards the airlock. 'Plenty of fuel out there. And if anyone asks, it's on Joe's account.'

◆

Hal and Clunk hurried down the steps to the landing pad, where a bowed old man in filthy overalls was lugging a thick pipe towards the ship. He paused to stare at a spoon, then squinted at them. 'What'll you be having?'

'Whatever's cheapest,' said Hal. 'And fill it right up.'

'On account?'

'Yeah, Joe's Ships.'

'Funny. He never puts in more'n a couple of litres.'

'It's part of a deal.'

'He don't usually do deals, neither.'

'If you don't fill the ship immediately I'll do you.'

The mechanic attached the pipe to the *Phantom* and threw a lever. The pipe shuddered as tons of fuel passed through it, and there was a loud splashing from the external tank as the volatile mix poured in. While it was filling, Hal picked up a fork and bent it back and forth, back and forth, all the while scanning the sky for signs of the *Volante*.

'She's long gone by now,' said Clunk.

'Can you track her?'

Clunk nodded. 'Once we're clear of the planet.'

'If we don't get her back ...'

'We will, Mr Spacejock. I promise.'

Hal snapped the fork in two and dropped the pieces. 'How much longer?' he demanded, gesturing at the fuel pipe.

'Few more minutes,' said the old man. He nodded towards the spaceport buildings. 'Expecting someone?'

Hal turned and saw a gleaming, shoulder-high crate moving towards them. It was sitting on a trolley, and as it got closer Hal saw a man in blue overalls pushing for all he was worth. 'What the hell does he want?'

The trolley stopped next to the landing pad and the man came over. 'I'm looking for the *Volante*.'

'Join the bloody club.' Hal's gaze fell on the crate and something clicked. 'Are you from Jasmin?'

The man looked at his docket book. 'S'right. Jasmin Ortiz. Freight for Jordia.'

'It can't be!' exclaimed Clunk. 'We already –'

'That's for us,' interrupted Hal. He gestured at Clunk. 'You'd better get the cargo ramp down.'

'Why?'

'When we catch up with the *Volante*, we'll transfer the crate and deliver it.'

'But the pallet yesterday –'

'Hey, mistakes happen. We can't leave this one out here, can we?'

Clunk eyed him with suspicion. 'I don't know what you're –'

'It's forty grand, Clunk. Anyway, you promised to help.'

153

'I said I'd get the *Volante* back, not participate in harebrained
_'

'Just do it!'

Without a word, Clunk hurried up the steps to the flight
deck.

'Look, I don't think I can do this,' said the courier. 'I'm
supposed to deliver to the *Volante*.'

'I'm Hal Spacejock, the owner,' said Hal. 'Look it up if you
don't believe me.'

'I can vouch for 'im,' said the old man, who was leaning on
the fuel pipe and watching with interest. 'Saw 'em land here
yesterday. Purdy ship.'

The courier nodded. 'That's good enough for me.' He
returned to the trolley and hauled it towards the rear of the
ship, where the cargo ramp was hissing and shuddering as it
dropped to the ground.

'Do you want a hand?' called Hal.

The courier shook his head and manoeuvred the trolley onto
the ramp. It was quite a struggle, and he was only halfway up
when Clunk came back. 'Doesn't he want any help?'

Hal shook his head.

'It looks heavy,' said Clunk, as the courier puffed and
strained.

Hal glanced at him. 'Bet you ten credits it slips down again.'

'Done,' said the robot.

The courier tugged and hauled, his boots slipping and
scraping on the ramp as he inched his way towards the hold.
He made it eventually, and Clunk put his hand out.

'I'll owe you.' Hal nodded towards the ramp. 'You'd better
give him a hand. He'll never get it off the trolley on his own.'

There was a crash from the hold.

'Or maybe he will.'

The courier rolled the empty trolley down the ramp, nodded to them both and left.

'I'll tie it down and seal the hold,' said Clunk. 'You go to the flight deck.'

'Want me to get the ship ready? Start the engines, plot a course, that sort of thing?'

'No.' Clunk looked round as the old man disconnected the fuel hose. 'All done?'

'Done five minutes ago,' said the man, as he dragged the pipe clear. 'Didn't want to leave. Most excitement I had in weeks.'

◆

Hal drummed his fingers on the *Phantom*'s console, irritated by Clunk's lack of faith. Hadn't he got the *Phantom* off the ground last time? Hadn't his manoeuvring averted disaster at the Orbiter? He *was* a pilot, whatever the robot thought, and one of these days he'd demonstrate his full range of skills.

And where the hell was the robot, anyway? The *Volante* was getting away, and here they were stuck on the landing pad while Clunk wasted hours shutting a door and tying a couple of knots. Hal scanned the console for some means to contact the hold and give him a hurry up, but it although it was covered in buttons and switches there was no obvious way to put a call through.

'Computer, get me the hold.'

'Internal intercom inoperative.'

Hal pressed a couple of buttons, but apart from the odd buzz and bloop nothing happened. He tried the console microphone, but it came off in his hand. When he tried to put it back the top fell off, and when he tried to put the top back a bunch of tiny parts fell out.

'External intercom now inoperative,' said the computer.

Hal gathered up the bits and pieces and pulled several knobs under the console until he found a drawer, where he stowed the parts away. Then he sat back in the pilot's chair and put his feet up. He closed his eyes and pictured a world where humans flew ships and robots made good coffee, and he was just about to enjoy a particularly decent brew when he noticed a gentle vibration. He opened one eye, and to his concern he saw the console was now covered in flashing lights and dancing dials. Not only was there activity galore, but there was also a low rumble and a dull roar to go with it. 'Computer?'

'Yeah?'

'What's that noise?'

'The one that sounds like the engine?'

'Yes, that's the one.'

'It's the engine.'

Hal jerked upright. 'Switch it all off, quick! Clunk will go spare.'

'I can't,' said the computer, amplifying its voice. 'It's a manual system.'

'Okay, I'll stop them.'

'Good luck.'

Hal pressed several buttons and the engine began to howl, shaking the ship from stem to stern. 'Can't you give me a hint?'

'I recommend you press the stop button.'

Hal grabbed for the console as the deck lurched beneath his feet. 'Which is it?'

'Too late, we're airborne.'

'Really?' Hal looked pleased. 'Hey, that was easy!'

'And we're moving sideways.'

Hal's grin vanished. 'What?'

'Estimate impact with spaceport buildings in seventeen seconds.'

Hal's gaze fell on the throttle control, which was set to ten percent. Last time he'd used it the ship had zoomed into space and knocked him out, but that was nothing compared to flattening the Cathuan departure lounge. With some trepidation, he gave it a gentle nudge.

'Altitude fifty metres,' said the computer, as the roaring got louder.

Hal pushed the lever a little more.

'Eighty metres and rising.'

Confident in his new-found skills, Hal eased the throttle past fifty percent. The main drives belted out thrust and the ship rocketed into the sky.

'Two thousand metres and climbing,' said the computer.

There was a clatter of feet on the spiral stairs and Clunk's head appeared through the hole in the deck. 'Mr Spacejock, what are you doing?'

'Oh, it's you. I'd forgotten you were aboard.'

'Altitude eight thousand,' said the computer.

Clunk stared at Hal. 'You took off?'

'I could fly this thing with my eyes closed.'

'Which ignition sequence did you use?'

'The usual. So, how's the cargo? Still tying knots?'

'For your information, I was checking the hyperdrive motor. I doubt it's been used for a decade, and if it fails we'll be stranded forever. Stuck in limbo until the end of time.'

'I know the feeling,' muttered Hal.

'And what's that roaring sound?'

'The engine,' Hal grinned. 'Some expert you are.'

'No, the other roar.' Clunk stepped off the ladder and scanned the console. 'Oh my goodness, the afterburners! We'll be out of fuel in minutes!' He pushed a knob in and the ship slowed immediately.

'I was just going to do that,' said Hal.

'And ground control? Were you just about to obtain clearance too?' Clunk flipped a switch on the console and a voice filled the flight deck.

'...*calling* Phantom-X1. *Ground Control to* Phantom-X1. *Return to base immediately. You are not cleared for departure!'*

Hal flipped the switch off again. 'I spoke to the other guy.'

'They're ordering us down,' said Clunk.

Hal cupped a hand to his ear. 'I can't hear them.'

Clunk reached for the switch, then hesitated.

'Break the rules, Clunk. Just this once.'

'Very well,' Clunk frowned at him. 'It's not like they can take your licence away.'

'Thanks,' said Hal, slapping him on the back. 'So, where's the *Volante*?'

Clunk brought up a local chart, which showed the planet and the Orbiter. As he zoomed out a blue triangle swam into view. 'There she is.'

'Can we catch them?'

'No, but I can work out their destination.' Clunk zoomed the chart out further, and Jordia appeared. 'That's the planet they're heading for.'

'Hey, that's great! We can get the ship back and deliver the crate at the same time.'

'Kill two birds with one stone, you mean?'

'Bird or bloke, I'm going to kill whoever took my ship,' said Hal with conviction.

17

Jasmin had quickly tired of waiting for Spacejock. A brief scan of the Navcom had revealed that the computer did everything, so with a tight deadline to beat she'd taken the controls herself. Lift-off had been uneventful except for the unguided vessel which had appeared out of nowhere and almost collided with them, but the Navcom's course change neatly avoided the descending ship. An unlicensed space hog out for a joy ride, thought Jasmin, and put it out of her mind.

Now she was sitting in the captain's chair in the flight deck, while the *Volante*'s engines drove the ship deeper and deeper into space, rapidly leaving planet Cathua behind. Barry and Ace were supposedly checking over their equipment in the hold, but she had an idea 'checking equipment' was mercenary slang for 'sleeping'. Still, without Spacejock aboard she only had two unpredictable humans to deal with, and a compliant Navcom had accepted her piloting role without question. The computer hadn't even objected when Jasmin had blocked all communications.

They were well on the way to the nearest hyperspace point, the first of a string of jumps that would take them to Jordia, when a vessel appeared on the screen. After several violent course changes it straightened up and headed directly for the

Volante.

'Navcom, I need an ID on that vessel.'

'It's the *Phantom-X1*, a modified Alpha II class. She made regular trips between Jordia and Cathua until she was taken out of service five years ago.'

'Short range?'

'Yes. Strictly an inner system vessel.'

Jasmin frowned. Was it a coincidence the ship was on the same course, or had someone caught wind of her mission? Either way, they were no match for the *Volante*. She zoomed the chart out until Jordia appeared, and then zoomed out even further until Cathua and Jordia were close together in the centre of the screen. When they were almost touching, Plessa appeared at the far edge. 'I need a course change,' she told the Navcom.

'Ready and waiting.'

Jasmin traced a line halfway to Plessa and then back to Jordia.

'I cannot accept that,' said the Navcom. 'We'll use thirty percent more fuel to no advantage.'

'It's necessary.'

'Clunk would never allow such a waste.'

'I'm not Clunk.'

'And Mr Spacejock is very keen on saving money.'

'I'm not Spacejock either. I'm Jasmin, and as a member of this crew I'm to be obeyed.'

'You may be on the roster, but I don't remember you.'

'Your database crashed. Clunk restored a backup but you lost a day or so.' Jasmin tapped a finger on the console. 'You will accept the course.'

'No I won't,' said the Navcom stubbornly. Jasmin's calculations vanished from the screen and a new course appeared, joining Cathua and Jordia. 'A straight line is the shortest distance between two points. Even Mr Spacejock understands that principle, and he couldn't navigate his way out of a shopping mall.'

'Put my damned course back!'

'No. I won't.'

Jasmin clenched her fists. Her aggressive side wanted to smash a hole in the console and rip the Navcom's brains out, while her moderate side just wanted to smash a hole in the console. 'I have to go via Plessa!'

'Via implies landing.'

'Haven't you heard of sightseeing?'

'This is a cargo vessel, not a tour bus.'

Jasmin changed tack. 'Navcom, has Mr Spacejock ever been forced to evade pursuers?'

'Once or twice, yes.'

'Did you just outrun them, or did you evade them with sudden course changes?'

'The latter.'

Jasmin nodded towards the screen. 'If we fly in a straight line our pursuers will locate the ship and destroy it. Do you want that?'

'Of course not.'

'Now do you understand the need for a detour?'

The dogleg course reappeared. 'Course change accepted. First jump in one hour.'

⬥

While Jasmin was busy in the flight deck, Barry and Ace

conducted their very own tour of the ship. They inspected the sealed crates in the cargo hold, then moved through the engine and generator rooms before peering into the kitchen alcove, all the while keeping an eye open for any valuables small enough to pocket. To their disgust there was little of anything, so they retired to the *Volante*'s rec room where Barry relaxed in one of the armchairs while Ace leafed through a book looking for interesting pictures.

After a few minutes Ace abandoned the book and looked around for something more exciting. He found it in the jet black cabinet parked in one corner of the rec room. It was the AutoChef, a KleenAir Corporation product originally designed to serve tasty foods on demand, but which had evolved over time into a lethal weapon with unlimited ammunition. In the interests of a cleaner greener environment, and because it was cheap, KleenAir used recycled military hardware in its consumer durables. The hardware was detuned, but once a weapons computer, always a weapons computer. Thus, the AutoChef didn't just dispense food, it launched servings at supersonic speed, radar-guided towards the softest and most vulnerable parts of the human body. Meatballs aren't usually dangerous, but once accelerated to twice the speed of sound they'll go right through you. That was one reason Hal's diet consisted of sandwiches and instant noodles. The other reason was that the machine drew its raw material from the ship's sewage tank.

Of course, Ace knew none of this. All he saw was an enticing control panel offering fast food on demand, and he was about to discover just how fast food could be. He glanced at Barry, who was half asleep in the armchair, and decided not to disturb him.

Tentatively, Ace ordered a cup of soup and a couple of scotch eggs. The machine rumbled for a second or two then sprayed a shower of scalding brown liquid from the dispenser, and only Ace's rapid reflexes saved him from a set of third-degree burns. He was still recovering when a scotch egg blasted from the AutoChef and nearly took his head off. Another whizzed past his elbow, two more nearly kneecapped him, and as he ran for cover a rapid fusillade pursued him across the room, the fist-sized scotch eggs ricocheting off the walls and furniture. Ace dodged the relentless fire, finally seeking refuge behind an armchair. Barry's armchair.

'Oof!' went Barry, as a scotch egg caught him painfully unawares. 'What the –' He sat up and another glanced off his thigh and buried itself in the upholstery. All traces of sleep gone, Barry threw himself behind the armchair as missiles whizzed by. The padded seat leapt on its stubby legs as it absorbed the impacts, until finally the firing ceased. Shaken, Ace raised his head for a quick look, only to duck again as the AutoChef fired a last shot in his direction. The missile smacked into the wall and rolled around beside him, still spinning.

'What the hell did you do to it?' demanded Barry.

'I only asked for a snack! Honest!'

'Beaten by a food dispenser. What kind of mercenary are you, you chicken?'

'You should know,' said Ace sullenly. 'You're cooped up with me.'

'Watch and learn, my son.' Barry grabbed a scotch egg, bobbed up and whipped it towards the machine with all his strength. Crack! Zingg! Shards of broken plastic exploded from the AutoChef as the scotch egg buried itself in the internals, and a thick cloud of smoke poured out.

'I think you fried it,' said Ace, keeping a wary eye on the smouldering AutoChef.

'I'll fry you next time.' Barry brandished a misshapen scotch egg at him. 'Lay off messing with the ship, you hear?'

Against all odds, it was Hal who noticed the *Volante*'s course change first. To be fair, Clunk was busy at the time, suppressing system errors, cancelling engine warnings and fielding ever more demanding calls from Cathua ground control.

'Hey, where are they going?' said Hal, pointing at the screen. The star map showed both planets and both ships, but the blue triangle representing the *Volante* had just made a sharp turn.

Clunk zoomed the map out until Plessa appeared. 'That's their destination.'

'So get after them!'

Clunk drew a line on the map and stretched it past the *Volante*. Long before it reached Plessa the line turned red. 'That's our maximum range. Unfortunately, the *Phantom* is an inner system ship.'

Hal pointed to Jordia. 'What if we refuel there? It's on the way.'

Clunk drew a line to Jordia, then another to Plessa. 'It's tight, but we'll make it if we don't use the afterburners.'

'Excellent. Hey, I just had another idea.'

Clunk raised one eyebrow.

'Why don't we call Plessa to let them know the *Volante* has been pinched? They can nab the thieves when they land.'

Clunk's other eyebrow went up. 'Two good ideas in a row. I'm impressed.'

Hal looked pleased.

A few moments later Clunk finished typing. 'Message despatched. They should keep an eye out for the ship. In the meantime, we're approaching the first hyperspace jump.' He turned back to the console. 'Are you ready?'

'Go for it,' said Hal.

'Actually, I was talking to the computer.'

'No,' said the computer.

'I've configured the jump motor,' said Clunk. 'What's missing?'

'The destination.'

Hal shrugged. 'Set course for Jordia.'

'No way,' said the computer. 'It's a –'

'– manual system,' finished Hal. 'Clunk, do the hyperspace.'

Clunk examined the console, then felt under the front edge. He pulled open a compartment, revealing a stack of cardboard squares and a set of coloured pencils. 'I haven't seen one of these for twenty years.'

'We had those at school,' said Hal.

'You did advanced piloting?'

Hal shook his head. 'Primary school. I was quite good at colouring, too.'

Clunk picked up the cards and saw a fat booklet underneath, along with bits and pieces of the console microphone. He glanced at the components, then took the book and flipped through the pages, revealing a blur of small coloured squares and exotic names.

'What's that got to do with setting the course?' asked Hal.

'You find your destination in the book, use the pencils to copy the pattern onto a card, then pass it through the reader.'

There was a long silence as Hal stared at the book, then at the pencils, and finally at the cards. 'You're not serious.'

165

'Sometimes low tech works just as well. Do you want to do the colouring, or should I?'

'You.'

Clunk took one of the cards from the stack, picked up a handful of pencils and arranged them on the console. He flipped to the book's index, turned to the specified page and started colouring the card.

Meanwhile, Hal paced the cramped flight deck.

'Mr Spacejock,' called Clunk a minute or two later.

'Yeah?'

'There's a pencil missing.'

'What?'

'I can't find the green pencil. I need it for the last square.'

'Mix up yellow and blue.'

'I don't think that will work,' said Clunk doubtfully.

'Just do it, Clunk.'

The robot nodded and selected a yellow pencil. He coloured in the square, then added the blue to it. After adding a touch more yellow, he glanced up. 'It doesn't look very green.'

'Computer?' called Hal.

'Yeah?'

'When you scan the card, the colour at the end is supposed to be green.'

'The reader decides what the colours are. I only see the data.'

'Well the last colour is green, okay?'

'Whatever.'

Clunk took the card and placed it into the slot. There was a beep and a white light flashed.

'Don't forget,' muttered Hal.

There was a whirring sound under the console, followed by a clacking of several ratchets. They stopped one by one and a blue light flashed.

166

'Course locked in,' said the computer.

'Jordia?'

'How the hell should I know?' said the computer. 'You colour the squares, I do the jump.'

Clunk reached for a lever, then hesitated.

'Go on,' said Hal.

'It might not work.'

'We'll never know at this rate.'

Clunk pulled the lever, which moved slowly with lots of squealing. Struggling, he got it level and pressed it flush with the console. Deep in the bowels of the ship, something groaned.

'Is it supposed to do that?' asked Hal.

A vibration rattled the console and the groaning built up to a howling roar. Suddenly, there was a loud bang and the flight deck was plunged into darkness.

'Jump complete, right?'

'I think so,' said Clunk. 'Computer?'

There was no reply.

'Let me interface with the console and read the log,' suggested Clunk. There was a metallic scrape, then silence.

'What did you find?'

'We entered hyperspace successfully.'

'But?'

'You don't want to know.'

'I do.'

'No you don't.'

'Why don't you tell me, and then I'll decide whether I want to know or not.'

There was a short silence. 'Very well. I have some good news, and I have some bad news.'

'Bad news first. It gives me something to look forward to.'

'We entered hyperspace, but we didn't emerge at the other end.'

'Oh great. And what's the good news?'

'I think I just found the green pencil.'

18

Jasmin's expression didn't change as she watched the *Phantom* vanish from her screen. The vessel hadn't altered course to follow her, but then, according to the Navcom it didn't have the range anyway. The problem was, if both ships were ultimately going to Jordia, her subterfuge would be useless without an additional twist. 'Navcom, Mr Spacejock asked me to do something else to put off the pursuers.'

'What's that?'

'You're to change the name of the ship. Once we turn for Jordia he wants you to become the *Vengeance*.'

'Did Clunk approve that?'

'What's he got to do with it? It's Spacejock's ship, isn't it?'

'In theory.'

'Then it's his right to change the name. And I wish you'd stop questioning his orders.'

'I'm sorry. I just find the situation a little confusing.'

'I'm not surprised,' said Jasmin, who was struggling to keep up herself. 'When you see Hal he'll explain everything.'

'That doesn't usually help,' murmured the Navcom. 'Incidentally, we're positioned for the first jump.'

'Go ahead.'

There was a barely perceptible shake, and the *Volante*

reappeared further across the star map. 'Jump complete. En route to second jump point.'

'Just a minute, where's the *Phantom*?' Jasmin pointed at the screen. 'They didn't reappear.'

'Unknown.'

'Could they have performed a star jump?'

'Alpha II class vessels don't have that capability.'

'That only leaves a cloaking device.'

'Only the military has those.'

'They come up on the black market from time to time,' said Jasmin. 'They're hideously expensive, though.' She looked thoughtful. Could it be the Cathuan government chasing her? Still, it made no difference. Cloaked or not, the *Phantom* couldn't possibly catch her.

◆

Hal paced the *Phantom*'s narrow flight deck while Clunk examined the ship's computer for any information about their predicament. Finally, the robot leaned against the console, which shifted under his weight. 'Normally, a hyperdrive motor charges up and launches you into N-space. If everything works, you emerge instantly at your intended destination. However, the hyperdrive aboard this ship is not as quick as the modern kind. After expending its charge getting the ship into hyperspace, it then has to recharge for the exit.'

'So we're all right? Nothing broke down?'

'No.'

'Why's the computer dead?'

'It shut itself down. You see, by conserving energy it can charge the jump motors at a faster rate.'

'I wish you'd told me all this before we left,' said Hal. 'For a while there I thought we'd had it.'

'On the contrary, we should emerge any moment now.' As Clunk finished speaking the whole ship leapt to one side, knocking Hal off his feet.

'Jump complete,' said the computer. 'I have an incoming message from Jordia customs.'

'What do they want?'

'They're asking whether we have anything to declare.'

'Tell them no.'

'What about the crate?' asked Clunk.

'I'm not declaring that. Jasmin said they'd let it through.'

'Yes, aboard the *Volante*. This is the *Phantom*.'

'If we don't know what we're carrying, how can we declare it?'

'Very well.' There was a pause as the computer transmitted the information. 'Now they want to board us for an inspection after we land.'

'They can't do that, we don't know what we're carrying!'

'They're offering a customs pass for six thousand credits.'

'Bribery?' Hal shook his head. 'No way.'

Clunk frowned. 'If the crate contains illegal goods we could be in trouble.'

'And if it doesn't we've wasted six grand.' Hal rubbed his chin. 'We'd better open it up for a look.'

'But Jasmin said –'

'Jasmin's not here.'

'We could jettison the crate. It would burn up in orbit and nobody would be any the wiser.'

'Are you insane?' said Hal, as he made for the ladder. 'She's paying forty grand for safe delivery. We can't turn her cargo into a sky show!'

Clunk hurried to catch up. 'It might have tamper-proofing. If you break the seal you could destroy the contents.'

Hal shrugged. 'Better than having some customs thug open it up with a hammer.' He stepped onto the ladder. 'Come on, I need your anti-tamper-proofing expertise.'

'I don't know if I can open it without leaving marks.'

'What about that cute little robot on Egris?'

'That was different,' said Clunk hurriedly. 'I asked her first.'

'I think the word you're looking for is 'begged'.'

Clunk's stiff face broke into a grin. 'I didn't know you were listening.'

'I could hardly miss it. It sounded like a sack of tin cans falling down a flight of stairs.'

At the foot of the ladder, Hal made for the cargo hold, wincing at the freezing air. They entered, and their footsteps echoed from the walls as they crossed to the rear of the hold. Overhead lights flickered on at their approach, until the last one shone down on a welded alloy box with mirror-finish sides. There was a status panel along the base, and a green light shone steadily from the middle of a keypad.

'That's a high security crate,' said Clunk. 'You'll never get it open.'

'I'm not going to. You are.' Hal took a crowbar from a cross-beam and held it out. 'Try not to leave any marks.'

Clunk crossed his arms. 'Breaking into bonded cargo is completely outside the terms and conditions of my employment.'

Hal hefted the crowbar. 'In that case I'll smash it open myself.'

'Given the amount we're getting paid, I'd strongly advise against that course of action.'

'I think I'll lever the keypad off first,' said Hal. 'I might be able to short the wiring.'

'Mr Spacejock, I know you're just waiting for me to stop you.'

'The thought never crossed my mind.' Hal looked round. 'Have we got a sledgehammer?'

Clunk sighed. 'You win. Step aside.'

A few moments later, the side facing them opened to reveal an expanse of black glass. Clunk knelt to examine the controls, while Hal cupped his hands to the glass and tried to see through it. 'What is it? Some kind of shield?'

Clunk nodded.

'Reckon I can smash a hole in it?' asked Hal, brandishing the crowbar.

'You're not serious.' Clunk tapped his finger on the glass. 'This material is harder than diamond, and it's impenetrable unless we enter the right code.'

'How does it stay solid?'

Clunk pointed to a wire.

'And if we pull that out?'

'You'd trigger an explosion.'

'I see. And the code?'

'Impossible to crack.'

'You're not being very helpful.'

'It was designed to be secure. It wouldn't be much good if I could open it by clicking my fingers.'

Hal glanced at the light fitting overhead. 'If we shone enough light in we might be able to see something.'

There was a click as Clunk activated his chest lamp. 'Will this do?'

Hal eyed the dull glow. 'Reminds me of you.'

'I don't understand.'

'It's a bit dim. Get it?'

Clunk regarded him stonily.

'Can't you juice it up a bit?'

'I could pour my entire charge into it, and it would barely flicker.'

Hal glanced at the wall nearby. 'What if we plug you into the ship? You could run mains voltage straight into the lamp.'

'With that kind of power, I'd glow more than the bulb.'

'I'm not asking you to poke your fingers in the socket. Just divert the voltage to the light.'

Clunk fished inside his chest and pulled out a length of black flex. He stripped the ends with a twist of his fingers and held them up for inspection, eyes whirring as they focussed on the bare metal. 'That should do it,' he said, as he approached the socket. The wires disappeared into the slots, and Clunk paused with his finger over the switch. 'Ready?'

Hal nodded.

An intense flash lit up the inside of the crate like a bolt of lightning in a crypt. A loud crackling noise followed the flash, and there was a hissing, spitting sound from the wall socket.

Hal wasn't paying any attention to the noises, nor to the thick clouds of blue-grey smoke wafting gently across the cargo hold. His unblinking gaze was fixed on the shadowy glass inside the crate. The after image of the contents was still hanging before his eyes - a pale green skull and crossbones hovering against a bank of swirling fog.

He backed away from the crate, bumped into something and spun round, coming face to face with a smoking, blackened figure with wide, staring eyes. 'Get away from me!' shouted Hal, as the apparition reached for him with twisted claws.

174

'Calm down, Mr Spacejock,' said the figure.

'Clunk?' Hal stared closer. 'What happened to you?'

The robot held his nose and blew streams of blue smoke from his ears. 'The lamp consumed rather more current than I expected.'

'Are you okay?'

'Nothing a complete refit won't fix.'

'That makes two of us.' Hal glanced at the crate. 'Did you see ... that?'

'I didn't see anything at all. The voltage overloaded my vision.'

'There's a skull in there. It's all foggy and –'

'Nonsense. Why would anyone pay forty thousand credits to ship a body?'

'It wasn't a body, it was like a warning.'

'Then I suggest we heed it.'

'We can't! You know what customs are like, Clunk. One slip and they'll take the ship apart, rivet by rivet.' Hal spread his hands. 'And who knows what they'll find on this old wreck?'

'We can still jettison the crate.'

'Are you mad? We need that forty grand to get the *Volante* back.' Hal rubbed his chin. 'You know, I'm against bribery myself –'

'Unless it's coming your way.'

'– but in this case, it might be the answer. We'll land at the spaceport, contact Ortiz and let *her* pay the bribe.'

◆

175

'Would you like to supervise the landing?' asked the Navcom as the *Volante* circled Jordia in a low orbit.

Jasmin shook her head. 'Just get clearance and land.'

'They want to know our point of departure and the nature of our cargo.'

'Tell them we're the *Vengeance* out of Plessa, and give them clearance code 77P.'

'Isn't that diplomatic immunity?'

Jasmin nodded.

'Clearance granted. Where are we landing?'

'Set down at the main spaceport.'

They landed five minutes later, and the Navcom immediately shut down the engines. 'You have arrived at your destination. Local time is thirteen hundred hours.'

Jasmin's controller attracted her attention. 'You appear to have landed on Jordia. Is this correct?'

'Yes.'

'I have uploaded the access code for the suitcase. Please open it now.'

Jasmin had stowed the case under the console, and she now took it out and laid it on the instrument panel. The code was accepted and the lid popped open, revealing a battered red toolbox and a miniature printer lying on top of folded overalls. Jasmin opened the toolbox and her eyebrows rose as she saw the tightly packed credit tiles.

'You must hire a truck for the delivery,' said her controller. 'Book one now.'

Jasmin turned to the console and accessed the spaceport facilities. There were three rental companies. She picked the first and reserved a suitable vehicle. 'Done. Now what?'

'The case contains two uniforms for your men. The magnetic signs in the bottom of the case are for the rental truck.'

Jasmin took the overalls out of the suitcase and saw a pair of colourful signs underneath with 'Herlion Robots' in letters made from smiling robot faces. The same logo was repeated on the blue overalls and matching caps. 'What's the printer for?'

'To generate delivery passes for the Consumer Robot trade fair. Your employees will use them to deliver the crate.'

'Trade fair? Is that what all this is about?'

The controller ignored her. 'You will find a packet of blank name tags in the case. Enter the names of your hired help into the printer and generate a badge for each of them.'

Jasmin typed 'Barry' on the printer's miniature keyboard and fed the first tag into the slot. It emerged with a fancy logo alongside the words 'Delivery Pass - Valid Friday 22nd' printed above the name. She repeated the process for Ace, then clipped each one to a set of overalls. 'Done.'

'The crate must arrive at the trade fair between five and six pm. Deliveries will not be accepted after that.'

'Don't I get a badge?'

'No. You will direct the mission from this vessel.'

'Why?'

'You will receive further orders when the truck is loaded.'

Jasmin could get nothing more out of the controller, so she packed the items into the suitcase and headed for the cargo hold, stopping on the way to collect Barry and Ace from the rec room. In the hold she lowered the cargo ramp and pointed out the spaceport buildings. 'You're to collect a truck from Payne Rentals. It's in your name.'

'Am I supposed to pay for it?'

'Of course not. Bring it back here, and don't delay.' Jasmin gave him enough for the rental, waited until he and Ace were clear of the ship, then closed the hold again. As the ramp thudded to she anticipated her controller's orders and decided she would move the crate to the exit, ready to load it onto the truck. She glanced around the hold, expecting to see it immediately, but although there were dozens of silver boxes with flashing green lights, hers was nowhere to be seen. She thought back to her tussle with the debt collectors and realised she hadn't seen it then either.

Her systems ran cold. What if it wasn't aboard the *Volante* at all?

◆

The *Phantom*'s screen blanked out as the ship approached Jordia, and for ten minutes it showed a single word in the centre: 'Loading ...'

'Loading what?' asked Hal, his curiosity aroused.

'Unable to determine that information,' said the computer.

'Adverts? Guns?'

'Unable to –'

'All right, how long until we land?'

'ETA TBA.'

Hal glanced at Clunk, who'd been working non-stop at the console for twenty minutes. 'Do you know?'

Clunk looked at him, his eyes unfocussed. 'Know what?'

'Weren't you listening?'

'I was busy. The navigation system is very primitive, and I've had to lock in every stage of our descent by hand. One error and we'll overshoot the spaceport and land in the sea.'

'Yes, that's wonderful and you're incredibly talented. How long?'

Clunk inspected the console. 'Fifteen minutes.'

'Probably still be loading when we hit,' muttered Hal. Barely had the words left his lips when the screen cleared and 'Loading Complete' appeared. 'Okay, computer. Explain the mystery.'

'Would you like to see a visual of planet Jordia?'

'Seen one, you've seen 'em all.'

'The oceans are a fetching shade of blue.'

'We're not landing in the oceans.'

'There are several mountain ranges replete with snow.'

'What's this, a commercial?'

'No, it's a public information service. Would you like to see the visual?'

'This is going to cost me, isn't it?'

'There's a voluntary donation of fifteen credits.'

'Forget it.'

'Ten credits and you get a free coffee at the spaceport terminal.'

'Oh, go on then.'

The screen showed a planetary surface with a huge land mass surrounded by seas. Navigation markers appeared, highlighting a fuzzy grey patch on the coast. 'Jordia Spaceport,' said the computer.

'Where's the snowy mountains?'

'It's summer.'

'And why isn't the sea blue?'

'Pollution.'

'I bet the coffee's lousy, too.'

The console beeped. 'Incoming message.'

'Put them on.'

'*I repeat, you are currently approaching a no-fly zone. Reverse your course and depart the area immediately.*'

Hal frowned. 'Who was that?'

'It's a transmitter on the ground,' said Clunk. He pointed to the screen, where a red splash had appeared near the grey patch. 'It seems there's a military base in our flight path.'

'Go around it,' said Hal.

'We can't change course now. I told you, we're locked on final approach.'

'You have entered a restricted area. Execute a ninety-degree turn to starboard and slow to one-eighty knots.'

'We can't!' shouted Hal. 'We're committed! Locked in!'

Clunk put a hand on his arm. 'There's no point shouting. It's an automated response.'

Hal stared at him in shock. 'I'm talking to a computer?'

'Yes, and it's going to blow us out of the sky.'

19

Jasmin spent twenty fruitless minutes searching the *Volante*'s hold for her crate before conceding defeat. Fearful of her controller's reaction, she hurried to the flight deck and confronted the Navcom. 'You lied to me! You said my crate was aboard the ship!'

'Negative. You asked whether Mr Spacejock signed for a delivery.'

'What was that, then?'

'One hundred coffee makers.'

Jasmin groaned. 'This is a disaster! That crate has to be in place in four hours time, and Cathua is an eight hour round trip. How am I supposed to organise that?'

'I'm an onboard computer, not a time machine.'

Jasmin frowned. Could Barry get the crate into the trade fair after it closed? Possible, but a risk. Suddenly she had an even worse thought. What if the crate had been loaded into the wrong ship, and was no longer on Cathua at all? She grabbed a keyboard and fired off a terse message to the Cathua cargo depot, demanding they locate her crate. The answer came back almost immediately, and it was so unexpected she read it through twice.

'Cargo en route to Jordia aboard vessel *Phantom-X1*, pilot

Hal Spacejock. ETA fourteen hundred hours local time.'

Jasmin's spirits soared. Freighter pilots were a resourceful, competent lot, and Hal Spacejock was clearly best of breed. She should have known he'd track his own ship! 'Navcom, I want to know the minute the *Phantom-X1* hits Jordia.'

'Ground control has them on-screen now.'

'They're landing at the spaceport?'

'Not exactly,' said the Navcom. 'In fact, they're attacking the local military base.'

This is Jordian Military Command. Execute a ninety-degree turn to starboard and slow to one-eighty knots. You have five seconds to comply.'

Hal leapt for the console and struggled with the controls. 'Go left, dammit!'

'Starboard is right,' said Clunk.

'Four.'

Hal reversed the controls. 'Come on, you flabby piece of junk. Move!'

'Three.'

'It's wasted effort,' said Clunk. 'You can't alter course during final approach.'

'Two.'

'What about emergencies?'

Clunk shook his head.

'One. All attempts to contact inbound hostile have failed. Missiles launched.'

'Missiles *what*?'

'Oh dear,' said Clunk. 'I didn't expect that.'

'Don't just stand there, do something!'

'Very well. Hold tight.' Clunk reached under the console and flipped a switch, killing the engine. There was a split second of weightlessness, and then the ship began to plummet towards the ground.

'How is this better than missiles?' demanded Hal, as the air whistled past the hull.

'We're above the ocean,' said Clunk. 'If I fire the engine at the right moment, we should have a soft landing.'

'If? Should?' Hal looked around. 'What's that noise?'

A screaming roar drowned Clunk's reply, and the *Phantom* shook as something tore by just outside, close enough to bring chunks of insulation down on their heads.

'Missiles,' said Hal, staring at the crooked roof panels. 'And they're coming back!'

The ship continued to drop, tipping from side to side as it fell through the air. The roar began to build again, and Hal was anticipating a final, all-consuming explosion when Clunk grabbed his arm.

'Brace yourself!'

At the very last second the robot rammed the throttle forwards, and the engine roared lustily to slow the ship. The missiles screamed past below the hull, fooled by the sudden stop, and Clunk immediately cut the engine again, sending the ship plunging towards the sea once more.

They slammed into the ocean with a tremendous crash, flattening Hal to the deck, buckling the walls and showering broken ceiling panels from the roof. The missiles tore past and exploded in the ocean nearby, making the hull ring like a giant bell. Sparking and crackling, the console quickly filled the flight deck with choking blue smoke, and seconds later the lights flickered out.

◆

Jasmin stared at the screen in shock. 'Attacking the military base? Why?'

'Oh, they're no longer doing that.'

'Thank goodness! Are they landing?'

'No. They've been shot down instead.'

Jasmin felt the flight deck spinning. 'Shot down?'

'I may be wrong. They might have crashed.'

'Call them!' said Jasmin desperately. 'Call, and keep calling until you get a reply. Is that clear?'

◆

The *Phantom*'s hull creaked and groaned as the ship settled, and above the noise of tortured metal the sound of gushing water could be heard.

Clunk staggered to the console. 'Computer, give me a summary.'

'On-board systems sixty percent. Fuel ten percent. Depth eight metres. Local weather, early sunshine with cloudy periods and the chance of a late shower.'

'Never mind the bloody weather,' said Hal. 'How far is the beach?'

'Six hundred metres.'

'Might as well be five klicks. And we're sitting in eight metres of water, that's –'

'Ten metres,' said the computer.

'Okay, ten metres,' said Hal. 'First we have to get ashore. Then –'

'Twelve metres,' said the computer.

'What?'

'We're now sitting in twelve metres of water.'

Hal frowned. 'You mismeasured?'

'No, we're sinking.'

Hal's eyes widened. 'How fast?'

'Do you know the expression, like a stone?'

'Start the engine!'

'The nozzles are under water,' said Clunk. 'We'll just get steam.'

'We've got to try something, haven't we? We're sinking!'

Clunk's hands darted over the console, and the flight deck echoed with the sound of rising bubbles. The floor tilted, and there was a loud slosh of water overhead as the ship broke the surface. 'I don't know how long I can keep it here,' warned Clunk. 'There's not enough power to stay afloat for more than a few minutes.'

'We'll have to swim ashore.'

'I can't get wet. My seals need servicing.'

'So do mine after that landing,' muttered Hal. 'How about an emergency raft?'

'That would be ideal.'

'Do we have one?'

'No.'

Hal put a hand out as the deck shifted. Suddenly there was a bright flash and a smell of burnt plastic. 'What's happening?'

'Water is seeping in and shorting the electrics.'

Hal thought for a moment. 'You know, I once saw this program where they put a robot in a sealed capsule and lowered it to the ocean floor. It was really neat, they had three naked –'

'I'm sure they did. But leaving aside the undesirable elements of your suggestion, I'd like to point out that we don't possess a sealed capsule.'

'Ah, but that's the clever thing!' Hal turned to the console. 'Computer, what's the largest garbage bag we have on board?'

'Garbage bag?' said Clunk incredulously.

'Yeah, that's it. And duct tape. Lots of duct tape.'

Five minutes later, they were ready. Clunk was standing inside a huge plastic bag, which was bunched around his extremities with lashings of duct tape. Furious eyes stared through three layers of plastic, which barely hid the generous strip of tape Hal had stuck over the robot's mouth.

'It's just in case the water gets in, Clunk.'

'Mmmm!' said the robot. 'Frfrfr-mmmmmmm!'

'Just as well you don't need to breathe, eh?' There was a groan as Hal got the inner airlock door open. 'Nice day for a swim,' he said lightly, blinking at the weak sunlight shining through the porthole.

'Grrr,' said Clunk.

'Come on, time is wasting,' said Hal, gesturing towards the airlock.

There was a rustle of plastic as Clunk crossed his arms.

'What's the alternative? The ship's sinking anyway.'

With a resigned look, Clunk trudged into the airlock. Hal opened the outer door, and as Clunk leaned forward to look down, Hal put his hands in the middle of the robot's back and pushed. There was a squeal as Clunk slid down the hull, a flutter of plastic as he accelerated towards the surface of

186

the ocean, and a tremendous slap as he struck. Hal peered over the edge and spotted a rising stream of bubbles, which changed course and slowly headed for shore.

Having saved the robot, Hal sealed the inner door and prepared himself for a dive. He raised his arms, pointed his fingers, stiffened his neck and took several deep breaths, preparing himself mentally and physically. Then he pinched his nose and leapt into space, legs pedalling wildly as he plunged towards the ocean. He splashed down feet-first, and his momentum took him deep underwater. As he struggled back to the surface he realised he should have undressed first.

◆

'Still nothing?' demanded Jasmin.

'I'm afraid not.'

'Why doesn't Spacejock have a pocket commset like everyone else?'

'Oh, he does,' said the Navcom. 'Would you like the number?'

◆

Twenty minutes later Hal staggered out of the surf, water streaming from his clothes. He spotted Clunk struggling with the wet plastic further up the beach, and went over to lend a hand. The robot's face was the first thing to emerge, and the angry, aggrieved expression made Hal wish he'd started with the feet.

'You pushed me!' said Clunk, as he tore off the rest of the plastic with savage jerks.

'I was only trying to help.'

'That sort of help I can do without.' Clunk stood on one leg and unclipped the other, tipping several litres of water onto the sand. 'So much for your sealed capsule. I'm soaked through.'

'Next time I'll use more plastic.' While Clunk was busy disposing of the sea water, Hal examined their surroundings. The beach was hemmed in by sand dunes, with a narrow dirt track running between the shore and the dunes. Beyond that there were trees, straggly paperbarks with olive-green foliage, and above the trees Hal spotted a Ferris wheel turning slowly in the distance. He was about to ask Clunk to verify it was really there when he heard a snatch of music. 'It's a fairground!'

'Bet it's full of water slides,' said Clunk gloomily.

'All right, we'd better call this Ortiz woman. You got that commset?'

'What are you going to say to her?'

'How about, Good news. Now you don't have to pay customs duty.'

Clunk took out the device, shook it dry, and handed it over.

Hal handed it back. 'You call her. You're better at explaining this stuff.'

'You're in charge of customer relations,' said Clunk. 'I secure the cargo jobs, you deal with people.'

'That's after this job,' said Hal, putting his hands behind his back.

Clunk sighed. 'All right, what's the number?'

'I don't know. She called us.'

'Oh dear.'

Hal crossed his arms. 'You and I came to Jordia to deliver a crate to earn the money to get the *Volante* back. Having survived a dodgy hyperspace jump, a pair of missiles, a crash landing and a drowning, you're telling me there's no way to call the customer?'

'That's about the –'

BUZZ!

The commset's ring was so unexpected Clunk dropped it in the sand.

BUZZ!

Hal grabbed it and answered the call. 'Yes?'

'This is Jasmin Ortiz.'

'Hey, we were just about to call you!'

'Where's my crate? Is it safe?'

Hal stared out to sea, where a patch of oil was spreading slowly across the gently moving ocean. 'Well, we got it to Jordia.'

'Excellent. Tell me where you are and I'll send my people to collect it.'

Out the corner of his eye, Hal saw Clunk shaking his head.

'I've got a better idea. Why don't we bring it to you?'

'That's not convenient. I insist on picking it up.'

'Have you got the money?'

'I will pay you the moment that crate is in my possession.'

Hal made a face. 'That's not going to work.'

'Very well. There's a factory off Mills Road, just past the forty kilometre marker. My people will meet you there.'

'Give us an hour or so. We still need to –' Hal lowered the commset. 'She's gone.'

'I've located the place she's talking about. It's an old robot factory.'

'How odd. Why would anyone make old robots?'

'No, I meant –'

'It doesn't matter. We have to get the crate out of the *Phantom*.'

'Naturally.'

'I need you to get it out.'

'Impossible.'

'We've still got the plastic, and I'll use more tape this time.'

'Mr Spacejock, if we open the hold under water we'll flood it. We could destroy the crate.'

'Can we raise the ship?'

'Yes, with a salvage vessel.'

'We can't afford anything like that.' Hal looked thoughtful. 'What if we borrowed one?'

'Salvaging a spaceship is a precise operation, involving a crew of highly trained personnel.'

'You could show me what to do.'

'I think not. Anyway, the most likely place to find a salvage vessel is at the military base, and given they just tried to shoot us down I doubt a loan is an option.'

'What about a truck? We could tie a line onto the ship and haul it out.'

'The *Phantom* is a large vessel. You'd need two dozen trucks and teams of scuba divers to attach the towlines.'

'Damn it,' growled Hal. 'Why couldn't you have aimed for the beach instead?'

'The impact would have killed you.'

Hal rubbed his chin. 'All right. If I get you a salvage ship, can you pull the *X1* to the surface and get the cargo out?'

'Maybe. What do you have in mind?'

Hal pointed at the Ferris wheel. 'Tidy yourself up. We're off to the fair.'

Hal's flight suit was dry by the time they arrived at the fairground, although it had collected a fair amount of dust on the way. The unsealed track hadn't been kind to Clunk either, and he'd stopped more than once to wipe the dirt from his joints.

As they drew closer, tents and caravans came into view, and they saw a field packed with vehicles. Hal cast his eye over them, and his face fell as he realised they were out of luck.

'What were you looking for?' asked Clunk, noticing his expression.

'It was a long shot. We'll just have to use Plan B.'

'What's that?'

'It's what we do when Plan A fails.'

Despite Clunk's persistence he couldn't get any more information. Warning bells tinkled at the back of his mind, though. Hal would try anything with forty thousand credits at stake, and the less he said the more outrageous 'anything' was likely to be.

They walked past the cars to the fairground entrance, where Hal sat on a bench. Clunk took the seat alongside him, craning his neck to watch a rocking boat lurch high into the sky, only to gasp as it zoomed back down again.

Hal grinned at his expression. 'What a riot, eh?'

'I've never been to a fairground,' said Clunk wistfully. 'Does it cost much?'

'Lots.'

Clunk watched a family leaving the fairground. The parents bore armfuls of teddy bears, show bags and snacks, while the kids relived the best moments at the top of their voices. 'How much?'

'We're not going in,' said Hal firmly.

'But –'

'Clunk, the *Phantom* is sitting on the ocean floor. One leak and Jasmin's crate will be ruined, and we'll never get the *Volante* back.' He frowned. 'Hey, are you listening to me?'

Clunk tore his eyes from the entrance. 'It says free entry, Mr Spacejock.'

'That's because they scalp you once you get inside.'

'Just five minutes?'

'I don't believe this,' muttered Hal. 'At this very moment, our ship –'

'It's not our ship,' said Clunk stubbornly.

'What about the cargo? It could get ruined!'

'The hold is sealed.'

'What if there's a leak? Are you prepared to risk everything for a few minutes of fun?'

Clunk cast a longing glance at the milling crowds and the sideshow alley, and then his shoulders slumped. 'I suppose you're right,' he sighed.

'The slightest delay could be critical,' said Hal sternly.

'I agree.'

Hal glanced at the robot's crestfallen face. 'Oh, all right. I suppose five minutes won't hurt.'

— 20 —

Once inside the fairground they strode through the crowds, Clunk gazing from one colourful sideshow to the next and drinking in the noise and bustle, while alongside him Hal pondered his next move. Despite his show of confidence, Plan A was all he had, and that had failed the minute he'd inspected the parking lot. Plan B consisted of waiting around until he could put Plan A into action, but he could hardly share that with Clunk after telling him they were desperately short of time.

For once, Clunk was oblivious to Hal's plans, ludicrous or otherwise. He was gawking at the sideshows like a ten year old with a pocket full of cash. Hal knew that look, and it didn't bode well. 'Keep your eyes open and stop dawdling,' he said irritably, as the robot stopped yet again.

'I'm allowed to look, aren't I?' demanded Clunk. Suddenly he pointed. 'Oh look, Mr Spacejock. A shooting range!'

'I'll shoot you in a minute,' muttered Hal. He spared the range the briefest of glances, then looked away, only to freeze in horror. Right behind them, a row of battered robot heads was mounted on a benchtop, turning slowly from side to side as giggling punters pushed balls into their gaping mouths. If Clunk saw them he'd make a stink, and Plan A or B or any other letter would be sunk. Just like their cargo. 'Let's go that way,' Hal said quickly, grabbing Clunk by the elbow and guiding him through a gap in the sideshows. They emerged in a parallel alley, where the first thing Hal saw was a row of one-armed robots with gaudy, flashing displays set into their chests. As he watched, a women put a credit tile into the nearest robot, grabbed its hand and pulled. The display flashed and flickered and a bunch of tiles cascaded from the robot's nether regions. Hal turned, dreading Clunk's reaction, but the robot's gaze was still fixed on the shooting range. 'Hey, close your eyes!'

Clunk did as he was told. 'Why?'

'I've got a surprise for you.'

'Really? What is it?'

'You'll see.' Hal grabbed the robot's arm and pulled him along the alley, past the one-armed bandits and the robot-wrecking competition alongside it, where men with sledgehammers were making short work of a skinny golden droid and a dustbin on wheels. Finally, they stopped in front of a coconut shy, and after a quick look around to make sure there weren't any dismembered robots in sight, Hal tapped Clunk on the shoulder. 'You can look now.'

'Coconut shy?'

'Watch and learn.' Hal beckoned to the attendant and gave him a credit tile. 'I used to be a real whizz at this,' he said, turning to Clunk. 'I've got three balls, right?'

Clunk raised his eyebrows. 'If you say so.'

Hal gestured towards the back of the stall, where half a dozen coconuts were sitting on top of narrow metal stands. 'I have to throw them at the coconuts, and every time I knock one down I win a prize.'

'Why don't they glue them in?'

'Then I couldn't shift them, could I? It'd be cheating.'

'So they want you to knock them down?'

'No, because then I'd win a prize.'

Clunk frowned. 'How very confusing.'

'Look, it doesn't matter. I just have to throw the balls and knock the coconuts down. Got it?'

'Yes.'

'Stand back then.' Hal hefted one of the balls in his hand and squinted at the target, judging the distance. When he was ready, he took a deep breath and threw the ball.

'You missed,' said Clunk.

'That gust of wind put me off.'

'There isn't any wind. Humidity is a little high, but that shouldn't affect the trajectory over such a short distance.'

Hal took another ball and drew his arm back.

'Are you going to miss again?' asked Clunk.

'I'll try not to.'

'What if you miss with all of them? Do they take pity on you and give you a consolation prize?'

Hal lowered his hand. 'It's a game of skill, Clunk. You throw the ball, and if you hit something you win. That's it.'

'It sounds like a waste of time to me. Why pay good money only to miss everything?'

'Oh, and I suppose you could hit a coconut with every throw?'

The robot looked surprised. 'Of course.'

Hal muttered under his breath, drew his hand back and launched the ball with all his might.

'You hit it!' exclaimed Clunk. 'But why didn't the coconut fall out of the cup?'

'Good question.' Hal gestured at the attendant. 'Here, you!'

The attendant strolled over. 'Yeah?'

Hal pointed at the coconut. 'I hit that thing full on and it didn't fall out.'

'You can't have hit it proper,' said the attendant. 'You gotta hit them right.'

'I hit the damn thing in the middle! It's got a bloody great dent in it!'

'It didn't fall, did it?'

Hal glared at him. 'Are those coconuts glued in?'

'Course not. You just have to hit them properly.' The attendant waved to a non-existent customer. ''Scuse I. Someone's wanting me.'

'Lousy cheat,' growled Hal, as the attendant fled. He picked up the last ball and flipped it to Clunk. 'Do your best.'

'You want me to have a turn?'

'Yeah, but hurry up.' Hal stepped to one side, doing his best to shield the robot in case the attendant looked round. 'Quick!'

Clunk stepped up to the counter and drew his arm back. Somewhere deep inside a motor began to whirr, growing louder and louder until he was vibrating like a weight-loss machine on 'permanent injury'. Just when it seemed he was going to shake apart, his arm snapped forward with a whip-crack, launching an elongated white blur at the coconut. It slammed into the holder, bent the stand double and knocked the coconut high into the air, tumbling end over end. The ball punched a hole through the rear wall, deflected at right-angles from an upright, struck another upright and came back into the stall, still travelling at a lethal speed. It struck the falling coconut, blowing it apart in a cloud of shell, white flesh and liquid.

As the pieces settled, Hal poked out his tongue and licked coconut milk from his upper lip. 'You might have overdone that just a tad.'

'I hit it, I hit it!' cried Clunk, bobbing with excitement. 'What do I win?'

The attendant hurried over. He stared at the damaged stand, then at the neat holes in the rear wall, then down at the floor, which was strewn with pieces of coconut shell. 'What have you done to my bloody stall?'

'We hit the coconut,' said Hal. 'Good and proper, this time.'

'We?' The attendant glared at Clunk. 'Did you do this?'

'No,' said Hal.

'Yes,' said the robot. He leaned over the counter. 'I'd like my prize, please.'

'Oh, you would?' The attendant scooped up a handful of shell and plonked it on the counter. 'Enjoy.'

'I don't understand.'

'That's the prize, tin man. You win the coconut.'

'But it's all broken!'

The attendant shrugged. 'Ain't my problem.'

'I see.' Clunk thought for a moment. 'In that case, I'd like another three balls.'

———

'Why did you want the thing anyway?' growled Hal as they pushed through the crowds. 'You can't even eat it.'

Clunk tapped the coconut with his forefinger. 'Like your replacement chocolates, it's the principle that matters.'

'Sheer bloody-mindedness, more like. And why did you insist on knocking it off his head?' Hal spotted a sideshow and stopped suddenly. 'Hold up, I've always wanted to try this.'

'Test your strength?' Clunk looked up. 'What's that bell for?'

'You hit the base with a mallet and that little hammer thingumabob whizzes up the track. Give it a good wallop and it will ring the bell.'

'It won't,' said the robot.

'It will if I hit it properly.'

'No it won't.'

'Are you saying I'm a weakling?'

'I'm saying there's an obstruction in the track. Nothing can hit the bell.'

'Really?' Hal squinted. 'I can't see anything.'

'You couldn't knock a coconut down either. That doesn't make it impossible.'

'This whole place is one big fix,' growled Hal. 'And your five minutes is up.'

'I was just thinking the same thing.' Clunk turned to leave, just as a burly young man in combat fatigues stepped towards the strength tester with a raised mallet. They tangled, and the robot's big flat foot came down on the man's polished boot while the falling mallet almost knocked Hal's head off.

'You clumsy piece of junk,' snapped the man. He glared at Hal. 'This pile of scrap belong to you?'

'Yeah, he's the Aunt Sally.'

'Really?' The young man brightened. 'Save some for me.'

'What's an Aunt Sally?' asked Clunk.

'Kept in the dark, huh?' The soldier grinned at him. 'They sit you over a tank of water and folks throw balls at a target. When they hit it, you drop into the tank.'

Clunk frowned at Hal. 'In light of my recent aquatic adventure, I find that somewhat less than amusing.'

'Oh, don't be wet.' Hal picked up the mallet and handed it to the soldier. 'Here, I bet you can't ring that bell.'

The man's eyes narrowed. 'How much?'

'Fifty credits.'

'Done.' The young man wound up and delivered a sickening blow with the mallet, sending the little hammer flying up the track. It rebounded off something just below the bell and came down twice as fast.

'Nearly,' said Hal. 'What about double or nothing?'

Panting, the young man nodded. He swung the mallet again, shaking the ground with his massive effort, but the bell remained stubbornly silent. Red-faced, he threw the mallet aside, thrust a handful of credit tiles at Hal and strode off.

'That was somewhat immoral,' said Clunk. 'Incidentally, you owe me ten credits.'

Hal handed him a tile. 'Ring that bell and I'll give you the rest.'

'Ninety credits? Really?'

Hal sensed a catch. 'You've got to make it ring, though.'

Clunk turned and threw the coconut. There was a BLANNGG as it struck the bell, and as bits and pieces of shell rained down on the crowd they both ran for the exit.

'I meant with the hammer, you metal-clad shyster,' puffed Hal, as they dodged through the crowd. 'You trying to get me arrested?'

A few moments later they burst into the car park, where an olive-green pick-up sat amongst the civilian cars. 'Over there,' said Hal. 'Quick!'

'Why, what is it?'

'Plan B.' Hal cupped his hands to the truck's window and saw a dress uniform on the back seat, along with a peaked cap and baton. The uniform was swathed in plastic, fresh from the dry cleaner.

'What do you have in mind?' asked Clunk. Then he saw

what Hal was looking at. 'No, Mr Spacejock. You can't. You mustn't.'

Hal tried the door handle but it was locked. 'Come on, open it up.'

'I can't do that. It's –'

'Locked, yes. And that soldier called you a clumsy piece of junk.'

Clunk's eyes gleamed. 'Give me thirty seconds.'

At the Jordia training barracks, Private Jenkins was enjoying a rare afternoon of peace and sunshine. He was on guard duty in the sentry box, a boring and thankless task, but traffic was at a minimum because all the senior officers were attending a productivity course in the capital. More like a booze up and a show, thought Jenkins, but his was not to question why.

The sun was pleasant, and he'd just loosened his top button and discarded his tin hat when he spotted the olive-green truck rumbling down the road towards him. Unfortunately, officers had recently taken to driving themselves instead of being chauffeured around in army limos, as was proper, and so Jenkins had no idea who was approaching. To be on the safe side, he grabbed his hat, fastened his button and straightened to attention, eyes front. Whoever it was, Jenkins hoped they'd bugger off quick before the sun went behind a cloud.

'He looks suspicious,' muttered Hal, fiddling with the shiny baton lying across his lap.

'He's not the only one,' said Clunk, eyeing Hal's uniform, which consisted of a deep red jacket with gigantic gold buttons and epaulettes the size of shark fins. Across the chest was an expanse of campaign ribbons large enough to serve as a place mat, and the maroon piping on the black trousers was as thick as breakfast sausage. 'I'm still not convinced it's real. For all you know it could be a fancy dress outfit.'

'Too late now. Here's the cavalry.'

'This isn't going to work, Mr Spacejock. They're going to arrest you for impersonation and lock you up for life.'

'Shhh! Just play along!'

A middle-aged soldier emerged from the gatehouse and strode towards them, smoothing his crumpled uniform. As he got close, Clunk slid his window down.

'Please state your business,' said the guard.

Hal stared straight ahead. 'You will address me as sir.'

'Yessir.'

'Corporal Clunk, please inform this man of my intentions.'

'Aye aye, sir,' said Clunk, with a vigorous salute. 'Guard, this is a surprise visit to test the readiness of your salvage division.'

'An inspection?'

'Correct.'

'But the officers –'

Hal cleared his throat. 'Clunk, take this man's name. Two demerits.'

'Two! But I –'

'Two, SIR. But I, SIR!' snapped Hal. 'Where are you going?'

'To call the others,' said the guard. 'Sir!' he added hurriedly.

Hal raised the baton and swished it experimentally. 'I don't think so.'

'But it's R&R! Nobody's ready!'

Hal turned to give the guard a haughty stare from under his peaked cap. 'My good man, that's why they call it a surprise inspection.'

Ten minutes later K company was lined up in the shadow of their salvage vessel, confused by the suddenness with which their peaceful afternoon had been shattered. Hal strutted along the line, waving his baton and issuing demerits for everything from crooked teeth to misspelled tattoos. One or two tried to argue their case, but after he doubled their punishment the message sank in.

By the time he reached the far end the whole group was hanging on every word. 'Attention!' he shouted suddenly, making them flinch. 'Your clothing is a shambles, your appearance is revolting and most of you can't spell mum. You're a horrible bunch! What are you?'

'A horrible bunch,' muttered several men.

Hal cupped a hand to his ear. 'I can't hear you.'

'A horrible bunch!' bawled the entire line.

'A horrible bunch, SIR!' shouted Hal. 'Corporal Clunk, ten demerits each. The whole bloody lot of 'em.'

'Yes sir,' said Clunk, saluting smartly.

'Now, rabble or not, I'm willing to erase every last demerit if you prove yourselves where it matters most.'

The men looked doubtful.

'Nearby, a stricken vessel lies on the sea bed.' Hal waved his baton gently, then swished it upwards to point at the salvage ship. 'Using your salvage expertise, and under the supervision of Corporal Clunk and myself, you will retrieve that vessel.'

A hand went up.

'Yes?' snapped Hal.

'Is this a simulated exercise, sir? Only, the computer's down.'

'Son, this is the real deal. Pull this off and you'll be the pride of Jordia.'

Several men grinned at each other. Further along the line another hand went up.

'Sir, what kind of vessel are we retrieving?'

'Oh, just an old hulk.'

'We need specifics, sir. We have to pack the correct slings.'

'Very well. She's a modified Alpha class spaceship with –'

'Sir?'

'Yes? What?'

'I thought it would be a seaborne vessel, sir.'

'You did? How so?'

'Because you're a navy officer. Sir.'

Hal glanced at Clunk. 'Troublemaker,' he muttered. 'There's always one.'

The young man went pale. 'I was only wondering –'

'Do we pay you to wonder?'

'N-no, sir.'

'Name?'

'Bates, sir.'

'Rank?'

'Divermaster.'

'Any more lip and you'll be understudy potato peeler.' Hal glared at the rest of the line. 'You and you, fetch the slings. Everyone else, get ready for departure. Now MOVE.'

The troops scurried around gathering equipment, and Hal felt it was a pity he didn't get this sort of instant obedience aboard his own ship. Perhaps he just needed to be more assertive with Clunk. He glanced round and saw Clunk's expression, a mix of what-have-you-got-me-into and this-had-better-end-well, and decided their current arrangement suited him just fine.

The ship was soon ready, and the men formed two neat lines alongside the ramp as Hal and Clunk strode into the flight deck. A few minutes later the vessel blasted off, heading for the 'training area' which Clunk had thoughtfully highlighted on the map.

◆

Bleep!

'Range three hundred, height one hundred, depth forty.'

Hal glanced across the flight deck to the scanner, where a young man was twirling knobs and studying a screen full of dots.

Bleep!

'Range two-fifty, height one hundred, depth forty-five.'

Bleep-bleep!

'Vessel located, sir!'

'Very good. Well done. Five bonus points to that man.' Hal turned to Clunk, who was leaning casually against the wall with one finger plugged into a socket. 'Any luck?'

'I have yet to discover the cause of the mysterious breakdown in our communications systems,' said Clunk loudly.

205

Hal smothered a grin. 'Okay, proceed with the salvage.'

Clunk stared at him. 'How?' he mouthed.

'Just repeat what I say,' murmured Hal. He cleared his throat and raised his voice. 'Proceed with the salvage!'

'Proceed with the salvage,' said Clunk.

'Proceed with the salvage!' shouted the man at the scanner.

'Proceeding with the salvage!' shouted the helmsman.

'You see?' said Hal.

'You see!' shouted Clunk.

The crewmen turned to stare.

'Not that bit,' hissed Hal. He raised his voice. 'You men, proceed!'

'Salvage proceeding,' called the helmsman.

'Salvage proceeding,' said Clunk, getting into the swing of it.

'You only have to repeat what I say,' whispered Hal.

'But why?'

Hal shrugged. 'So everyone knows what's happening.'

Clunk looked around. 'Which everyone?'

'Just ... everyone. Here, watch.' Hal raised his voice. 'You there. What's our status?'

'Proceeding with salvage, sir!' snapped the helmsman smartly.

Clunk looked from one to the other. 'I don't think all this shouting achieves anything.'

'You're not supposed to think, Corporal.'

Clunk's eyes glinted dangerously. 'What?'

'Sir,' murmured Hal. 'You have to say, What, sir.'

The robot pulled his finger from the socket. 'Oh look, I've found the communications problem. Now we can chat to the nice men at headquarters.'

Hal's eyes widened. 'You can't do that!'

Clunk stuck his finger back in. 'Oops, failed again. Must be a flaky piece of electronics.'

'You said it,' muttered Hal. He grabbed for an upright as the ship lurched suddenly. 'Report!'

'Report!' shouted Clunk.

'Hover mode activated,' called the helmsman.

Hal stepped into the middle of the deck, keen to motivate the men with a stirring speech. 'Right, listen up. You with the bleeper, cut that out. I want you to work as a team, bring home the bacon, take every week as it comes and finish the job on time every time. Got it?'

The helmsman and the console operator looked blank.

'Proceed with the salvage!' shouted Clunk.

'Yes, sir!' The men saluted and turned to their controls. 'Slings away!' shouted the helmsman.

'Divermaster Bates under water!' shouted the console operator. 'Wreck in sight!'

'Slings attached. Increasing thrust,' called the helmsman. He tugged a lever, and there was a howl from the engines as the *X1* came away from the seabed. The deck rushed upwards as the spaceship rose through the water and the screen showed her breaking the surface, foam cascading from her rusty flanks.

'Caution,' said the console operator. 'Target surrounded by seamen.'

'Tell them to pull out,' said Hal.

'Pull out!' shouted Clunk.

'Commencing extraction.'

The operator counted off the returning divers, and when the last one was aboard he turned to report. 'Divermaster Bates in the hold with the away team.'

'Raise the *X1*,' called Hal.

The engines roared, and there was a loud sucking noise as the stricken spaceship came free of the water. Immediately, the console operator snapped half a dozen switches and spun a knob. 'Load secured. Mission complete sir.'

'Well done, men!' shouted Hal. 'Now, for maximum points I'd like you to drop the *X1* on the beach.'

'Drop the *X1* on the beach!' shouted Clunk.

'Dropping the *X1*,' said the helmsman. He eased the ship around until they were pointing at the narrow strip of sand, then increased the thrust until they were hovering above it. After they levelled off he pulled a lever, and the salvage vessel leapt into the air. A second later, there was a massive crunch from below.

'You know,' began Hal, 'when I said drop I actually meant place gently.'

'I thought it was a wreck, sir,' said the helmsman.

'It is now, you idiot.' Hal gestured with the baton. 'Return to base.'

'Return to base!' shouted Clunk.

'Returning to base,' said the helmsman, putting the ship about. They roared over the fairground and a few moments later set down. The troops filed out, and Hal couldn't resist one last line up.

'Well done, you men,' he began, striding along the row with the baton under his arm. 'All demerits are cancelled, and I want you to take the rest of the week off.'

'You'll get them in trouble,' murmured Clunk.

'They shouldn't have shot us down in the first place,' muttered Hal. He raised his voice again. 'Now break out the officer's booze and have a party. Dismissed!'

The men gave him three cheers then filed off to their quarters, chattering amongst themselves. Meanwhile, Hal and Clunk hurried to the army truck and jumped in. Hal saluted the gate guard on the way out, and they'd barely reached the fairground when a column of trucks passed them, heading for the base. 'Put your foot down,' advised Hal, as the vehicles rumbled past. 'That lot's for real.'

They found the turn-off for the beach, and the truck bumped and bounced along the rough track as they threaded their way between dense trees. They rounded the final corner and Hal winced as he saw the *Phantom* half-buried in the sand two hundred metres away. Even from this distance it didn't look good, with large dents in the fuel tank and jets of vapour streaming through cracks in the hull.

Clunk stopped the truck and they got out. Hal sniffed the air and winced at the strong, acrid smell. 'Can you analyse that?'

'Yes. It's a wreck.'

'The smell, Clunk. I meant the smell.'

There was a loud sniffing sound. 'Fuel vapour. The tanks have ruptured.'

'Isn't that dangerous?'

'Only if it catches fire.'

Hal leaned against the truck. 'Right, I'll give it the once-over from here. You go look round the back.'

'My electronics aren't shielded. I could trigger an explosion if I get any closer.'

'What do you suggest?'

'I suggest I don't get any closer.'

'We've got to get that crate out somehow. Put that brain of yours to work.'

'I'd rather put my legs to work.'

'You're not chicken?'

'Mr Spacejock, that ship isn't just unstable. It's a firecracker with a hissing fuse.'

Hal looked surprised. 'We're safe here, though?'

Clunk shook his head. 'The blast radius is considerable.'

'So we're goners whether we're here or right up close?'

'Correct.'

Hal eyed the ship, then felt in the back of the truck for his flight suit.

'That won't help much,' said Clunk, as Hal changed out of his uniform.

'Maybe not, but if I go down it'll be as the captain of the *Volante*, not a refugee from a third rate pantomime.' Hal straightened his collar, pushed off from the truck and began walking across the sand.

'Mr Spacejock! Where are you going?'

'I'm going to open the cargo door,' said Hal grimly. He was halfway there when Clunk fell into step beside him. 'You don't have to come. It's not safe.'

'If you're prepared to risk your life, then I'll risk mine too.'

Hal's eyes began to smart from the fumes. 'Thanks.'

'And you don't know how to open the door.'

'Good point.' Hal paused. 'What's the worst that can happen, anyway?'

'The *Phantom* explodes, scattering our remains over a wide area.'

'And the best?'

'We'll be scattered over a slightly smaller area.'

With that sobering thought in mind, which for now was still comfortably inside his skull, Hal crossed the last few metres to the *Phantom*.

The ship was lying partly on its side, with the bottom of the airlock just visible overhead through the swirling mist of evaporating fuel. Half-blinded by the acrid fumes, Hal watched Clunk open the door with the manual override, and then they hauled themselves up one after the other and dropped into the ship's lop-sided flight deck. They took the stairs to the hold, where they found Jasmin's crate hanging from the straps. Hal went for the door controls, but Clunk stopped him. 'Electrics could set the fuel off. Let me do it manually.' He opened a small locker and used the hand pump inside, and as he worked the handle the rear doors opened in fits and starts.

'What's that funny smell?' asked Hal.

'Fresh air,' said Clunk. 'Don't worry, you'll get used to it.'

'How are we going to get the crate onto the truck?'

'I'll lower the ramp halfway, you park the truck underneath and then we'll slide it on.'

'I'll fetch the truck.'

Clunk shook his head. 'We'll have to push it. Both of us.'

'Why not drive it?'

'There's still a lot of fuel around, and the engine could set it off.' Clunk began to pump another handle, and Hal watched the ramp extending from the ship. When it was level, they walked to the back and jumped down to the sand, struggling over the loose surface as they made their way to the truck. Hal waited until Clunk was ready at the back, then hopped in and took the wheel. 'Okay, push!'

Clunk did so, and with brute strength he got the truck over the sand to the ramp. When it was in position he climbed into the hold and removed the straps from the crate. Hal gave him a hand, and together they inched the crate towards the truck, until it was balanced on the lip of the ramp. A push, a twist and a shove, and the crate tipped forwards, making the truck settle on its suspension as it took the weight. Clunk strapped the crate down, then got behind the truck and prepared to push it clear.

'I'll shut the doors,' said Hal, reaching for the controls.

'No!' shouted Clunk.

Hal's fingers barely touched the button, but it was enough. There was a loud crack as the electrics shorted, and a deep boom as the spark ignited the fuel vapour. Fortunately, most of it had dispersed, but the resulting explosion was still enough to blow Hal right out of the hold. He flew through the air, missed the truck by a couple of meters and landed flat on his back on the sand.

— 22 —

Clunk hurried over and crouched next to Hal to check his pulse. The human was out cold, but alive, and Clunk was still breathing a sigh of relief when there was a whoosh from the ship. He turned to look and saw flames thirty metres long jetting from cracks in the hull. The hold was full of smoke and heat haze, and through it all he could see the inner walls glowing red. It was only a matter of seconds before the main tank blew, and while much of the fuel had leaked out, there was plenty left for a spectacular explosion.

There was no time to move the truck and no time to save the cargo, so Clunk put Hal over his shoulder and ran, heading straight for the tree-line as he tried to put maximum distance between himself and the *Phantom*.

He'd barely covered a hundred metres when a huge explosion threw him headlong into a big spiky bush. The blast ripped through the vegetation with a massive thunderclap, shredding leaves from their branches, scooping dirt and stones from the ground and hurling the whole mess outwards in an expanding ring of destruction. Large trees bent and snapped, while smaller ones were uprooted and flung away from the epicentre.

A shadow passed overhead, and Clunk looked up to see the

213

truck sailing past, tumbling through the air. The crate followed, trailing shredded, smouldering straps, and the ground shook as they landed nearby. Gradually the patter of stones, dirt and hull fragments tailed off, and Clunk raised his head for a look. He found himself bathed in sunlight, which was shining through the bare branches overhead. There was a green mist in the air, the only remains of vaporised leaves and plants.

Alongside him, Hal groaned. 'What happened?'

'The ship exploded.'

'What, inside my head?'

Clunk examined him. 'It's just a bruise or two. You'll be fine.'

'Great. I feel so much better after all your care and attention.'

'Who do you think got you clear of the ship? Who saved your life?'

Hal sat up, wincing. 'Who slung me into a thorn bush?'

Clunk stood up and looked out on a wasteland of shredded trees, broken branches and drifts of finely minced leaves. 'The truck went that way,' he said, pointing towards the fairground.

Hal staggered to his feet and gazed around. 'Bloody hell. It looks like the inside of a toothpick factory.'

Clunk pushed his way out of the bush, while Hal followed more slowly, bending back branches to avoid the long, curved spikes. Once they were free, he looked around. 'What about the crate?'

Clunk pointed. 'Same as the truck, only further.'

They set off towards the Ferris wheel, picking their way over smoking hull fragments. 'It'll be fine, you'll see,' said Hal. 'Tough as nails, those trucks. You could land a ship on them.'

'You'd be the one to know.'

Suddenly Hal laughed.

'What?'

'The ship. First it was the *Phantom-X1*, and now it's one ex-Phantom.'

Clunk stared at him.

'Well, it's funny isn't it?'

'Not really, no.'

They continued in silence. Clunk's motors whined as he struggled over the uneven ground, and now and again Hal got a whiff of hot machine oil. Finally, they came across the crate, lying on its side in a tangle of broken branches. The shredded tie-downs were still smoking.

'At least it's still in one piece,' said Hal.

'Yes, but what about the contents?'

'I only promised to deliver the crate.' Hal looked around. 'So where's the truck?'

They found it sticking out of a gully nearby, with the nose buried in the dirt like an oversized lawn dart. At least, Hal hoped it was buried and not simply crushed flat. The back wheels were splayed, the tray had been driven into the back of the cab and the windows were strewn around the crater in fragments.

'It doesn't look too bad.'

Clunk reached for the door handle, and the whole door promptly fell off.

'That's just bodywork,' said Hal. 'How's the rest of it?'

Clunk sat in the driver's seat and lifted the broken control column. He pressed the starter, and the engine roared into life.

'Wa-hey!' shouted Hal, putting both thumbs up. 'Now back it out!'

Clunk put the truck into reverse and pressed the accelerator, making the engine race. He leaned out of the cab to watch the rear wheels, which spun and wobbled in mid-air. 'I need your

215

weight on the back,' he shouted. 'The front wheels must be spinning.'

Hal climbed onto the back of the truck and balanced on the edge of the tray with his arms outstretched. As Clunk revved the engine Hal jumped up and down, gradually forcing the back of the truck towards the ground.

There was a whirring sound as the tyres scuffed away loose dirt and leaves, then a massive jolt as they bit in, hurling the truck backwards. Hal somersaulted over the cab and landed flat on his back in the hollow, where the truck's spinning wheels buried him with damp earth.

Clunk stopped the truck and hurried over, helped Hal to his feet and brushed at the dirt, smearing clumps of earth down his flight suit.

'Right,' said Hal, when the dirt was evenly distributed about his person. 'Let's get the crate on board.'

'How? It's too heavy to lift.'

'No problem. We'll tie some of the strapping together, sling it over a tree and lift it with the truck.'

It took them half an hour to join the bits of strapping into a single rope, with Clunk pulling each knot tight with short, firm tugs. When he was happy they laid the rope out and levered the crate onto it, then tied the knotted rope into a rough cradle. The loose end went over the branch overhead, and Hal caught it, leapt onto the tray and tied it off.

'Take it easy,' he said. 'We've only got one chance at this.'

Clunk's gaze travelled from the truck, up to the branch and down to the crate. 'It's not much of a chance,' he said, as he climbed into the cab. The engine roared into life and the truck moved forward, pulling the rope tight. The branch creaked as it took up the load, and the truck growled as Clunk fed in more power.

There was a groan as the crate shifted, and the truck's engine roared as the wheels began to slip, throwing out fountains of dirt. Then, with a wrench of tortured metal, the tray was torn from the back of the truck. It was left dangling from the tree, turning gently in mid-air while the rest of the vehicle careened into the forest at full speed, leaving behind a trail of flattened bushes.

While Hal gazed up at the slab of metal swinging overhead, Clunk brought the truck back. It looked naked with the back missing, and as Clunk got out the passenger door fell off.

'Careful,' said Hal. 'You're wrecking it.'

Clunk grabbed the door and heaved it into the bushes. 'What next, Mr Spacejock? Blow the crate into the air with sticks of dynamite?'

Hal rubbed his chin. 'What if we grab the tray and swing on it? Adding our weight might –'

'– bring it down on our heads,' finished Clunk. 'And even if we get the crate into the air, who's going to drive the truck underneath?'

'It might only need one of us.' Hal reached up, hooked his fingers onto the tray and pulled.

'That looks exceedingly dangerous,' said Clunk, as the branch creaked.

'Stop gassing and give me a hand,' said Hal, pulling a little harder.

Clunk reached up and added his weight. There was a jerk and the tray dropped a few centimetres, lifting the heavy crate off the ground.

'Keep going!' panted Hal, hauling with all his might. The knots in the cord bumped over the branch, and the crate rose steadily until it was about waist-high. 'Quick, get the truck!'

'If I let go the crate will come down again.'

'You don't think I'm strong enough to hold it?'

'Strength? I'm talking about the law of gravity.'

'You robots are all the same. Putting us humans down, making out we're weaklings. Now fetch the truck and let me worry about the tray. Got it?'

'If I let go you'll shoot into the air.'

'No I won't.'

'You will!'

'Won't.'

'Watch,' said Clunk, releasing the tray.

Nothing happened.

'What are you waiting for?' demanded Hal. 'Get the damn truck underneath before my fingers break off.'

Clunk backed away slowly, staring at the suspended crate and the tray. Then he hurried over to the truck, hopped in and reversed it under the crate. 'We'll have to drop it on the chassis between the wheels,' he said, leaning out the door. 'We can tie it on with the rope.'

'Listen to him,' muttered Hal. 'Suddenly he's flush with great ideas.'

'Lower away,' said Clunk.

Hal let go of the tray and stood clear. Nothing happened.

'What the hell?' Hal stared at the crate, then up at the tray. 'Why didn't it move?'

'Because it's stuck,' said Clunk, pointing up. There was a cleft in the branch, and one of the knots was jammed fast.

'Dammit.' Hal grabbed the tray and shook it. 'One of us will have to climb up and cut it down.'

They both gazed up at the branch, each hoping the other suicidal maniac would volunteer first.

'Do you want to borrow a knife?' said Hal finally.

'That's your area of expertise. I'm driving the truck.'

'The truck's fine where it is.'

'I'm not very good at climbing.'

'Yeah, but *you* won't get killed if the whole lot comes down on your head.'

Clunk squinted up at the tree. 'Is it just me, or is the branch bending?'

There was a loud crack as the bough gave way, and the tray speared into the ground next to Hal, burying a corner in the soft earth. The crate thumped down on the truck, crushing the rear suspension, while the branch thudded down between Hal and Clunk, still draped with the knotted cord.

'Perfect,' said Hal, freeing the cord. 'Tie the damn thing on, and let's get the hell out of here.'

◆

They followed the road out of the forest for almost an hour, eventually switching on the headlights to dispel the encroaching darkness. It took them longer than expected, because with the windshield missing Clunk had to keep their speed down. Otherwise the headwind would have blown Hal's face into the back seat.

'There's the turning,' said Clunk, as they passed a battered wooden sign. The writing had long since peeled off, but a smaller board below it was fresh, sharp and to the point: 'Private Property. Keep Out.' A narrow gravel track led between overhanging trees, and the tyres scrunched as they turned onto it. Branches scraped and banged on the roof, and the heavy vehicle bounced and swayed as they emerged into an overgrown clearing. On the far side stood a derelict building with gaping windows and a collapsed roof.

'This can't be right,' said Hal.

'Right or not, this is the place.'

'It's just a ruin. You must have taken a wrong turn.'

'I did not take a wrong turn. This is the correct location.'

'So where are the people?'

'I cannot say.'

'That's because it's the wrong address,' said Hal triumphantly.

'It is not the –' Clunk stopped. A man had emerged from the doorway, and was picking his way across the rough ground. 'There you are. A person.'

'Ah, but who says he's the right one?'

As the man approached Hal saw he was carrying an assault rifle, and the closer he got the bigger and more dangerous it looked. The man was no picture either: he was a thickset tough with a broken nose and cropped, greying hair.

'Do you know the old robot factory?' asked Hal. 'My robot got lost.'

'Are you Spacejock?'

Hal looked surprised. 'Yes.'

'I *told* you this was the place,' murmured Clunk.

The man scowled at them. 'I've been waiting hours. What the hell you been up to?'

Under the circumstances, Hal felt it best not to tell him. Instead, he gestured at the crate sitting on the back of the truck. 'There's the cargo. Where's my money?'

'Come inside and meet the boss.'

'With pleasure.'

Hal and Clunk left the truck and crossed the rough ground

to the factory, where they took a damp corridor to a dark, concrete-lined room.

Hal turned to protest, and found the gun pointing at his stomach. 'What's that for?'

The man shrugged. 'The boss don't want no trouble. In you go.'

They entered the room and the metal door thudded shut behind them. Clunk switched on his chest lamp and the dim glow swept the walls before picking out a body lying face-down on the floor. One arm was flung out at an unnatural angle and half the head seemed to be missing. Hal's heart skipped a beat, and then he saw the dull sheen of dirty metal. 'It's just a robot!' he said, relieved.

'Of course. What did you expect?' Clunk shone the light around, picking out more fallen shapes. 'This was a robot factory, remember?' He angled the light towards the rear wall, and it glinted feebly off a row of robots hanging limply from hooks, unfinished and thick with dust. 'See? Unwanted stock.'

Hal rattled the door handle, but it was locked. 'I don't like the look of this.'

'I concur.'

There was a lengthy silence before Hal spoke again. 'Clunk, I have to tell you about something.'

'Oh?'

'That crate. The first one.'

'The Hand-E-Mart coffee makers?'

'Yeah, those. That was, er, my fault.'

'No. Really?'

Hal looked surprised. 'You knew already?'

'Of course I did.'

'But how?'

'The faked bill for twelve thousand credits of robot parts I found in the Navcom was a bit of a give away. First, it would keep me in spares for the next century, and second you've never spent a single credit on me, let alone twelve thousand.'

Hal was silent. 'You know, I don't spend a lot on myself either,' he said eventually. 'There's never much to go around.'

'Have you considered retiring?'

'At my age?'

'You could sell the *Volante*.'

'I don't *have* the *Volante*. And even if I did, a buyer would want to see proof of ownership. Anyway, what would you do if I gave it all away?'

'Mr Spearman offered me a job.'

'Trust me, you don't want it.'

'Why not? At least he's a real ...' Clunk stopped, embarrassed. 'I mean he –'

'Has a pilot's licence?'

'Yes.'

'Listen, I know things about Spearman that would set your hair on end.' Hal glanced at the robot's polished metal head. 'If you had any.'

'Such as?'

'He told me –' Hal broke off as he heard a thud. 'Was that a door?'

'I think so. Maybe he's coming back.'

'We can't just wait around. We've got to do something.'

'Why don't I stand behind the door and surprise him when he comes in?'

'Because he's got a ruddy great gun, that's why. You surprise him and he'll start shooting.' Hal snapped his fingers. 'That gun from the space elevator!'

'What about it?'

'When he opens the door, blow the bastard away.'

'I can't shoot a human.'

'Give it to me and I'll do it.'

'You can't gun a man down just because you suspect him of wrongdoing.'

'Why not? The Peace Force does it all the time.' Hal thought for a moment. 'What if he shoots first and misses, and then I shoot him?'

'That's ludicrous.'

'We've got to do something! I'm not standing around here like a rat in a barrel.'

'You mean a fish.'

'No I don't.'

'You do!'

'How can I stand around like a fish? They don't have legs.' Hal glanced around the room, seeking an escape. 'I've got it,' he said suddenly. 'Quick, give me a hand.'

Next door, Barry was trying to call the *Volante*. Unfortunately, the thick concrete walls were playing havoc with reception, and Ace's commset wasn't that flash to begin with. 'Where d'you get this piece of junk anyway?'

'Same place I got the watch,' said Ace, who was sitting on a chunk of fallen masonry. 'And it ain't junk.'

Barry threw the commset back. 'We can't get no orders, so we'll use our initiative.'

'What's that, then?'

'We order ourselves around.' Barry rubbed his chin. 'We're supposed to give Spacejock that money for the crate, right? Only we got the crate already, and he's locked up.'

Ace nodded.

'So, who's to know if we keep the cash too?'

'We gonna leave Spacejock here?'

'Yeah, tucked away. There's gotta be forty grand in that old toolbox, and all he done was drive a crate around.'

'What if they get out? They've seen your face.'

'True. That bloody robot's probably taped my voice, too.'

'So what we gonna do?'

Barry thought for a minute, then picked up his blast rifle.

'Only one answer, ain't there? This way there's no witnesses, right?'

'Can I do it?'

'This ain't one of your video games.' Barry pushed him roughly towards the door. 'You shift that crate across. Put the trucks together first.'

'I get to drive? Neat!'

Barry threw him the keys and waited until his footsteps faded. Then he switched on the weapon's built-in torch, which threw a powerful beam of light down the corridor. Moving quickly, he slipped along the wall and unlocked the metal door. He eased it open with his foot, and the torch cut a swathe through the darkness as he pointed it from side to side. 'I spoke to the boss,' he said, rattling the change in his pocket. 'Come an' get your money.'

There was no reply.

Barry entered the room, flashed the torch behind the door then jerked it from one corner to another, sighting along his rifle. His finger tightened on the trigger as the light fell on a robot hanging from the back wall, and before he could stop it the gun unleashed a torrent of energy bolts which slammed into the slumped form and exploded with ringing concussions. When the firing stopped, only the robot's upper torso remained.

Shaken, Barry approached the remaining robots, moving his torch over their dusty shapes. He spun round at a noise, real or imaginary, and swept the room wildly as he imagined stealthy footsteps right behind him. There was nothing there.

Turning back to the wall, he moved slowly along the robots. Near the end his light fell on a breast plate, half blinding him as it reflected off the shiny metal. Slowly, he raised the torch over the robot's chest until it was pointing in its face. Barry frowned as the light picked out the robot's deep-set eyes, and when he pointed the torch right into them, the pupils narrowed to pinpoints. 'What the -?'

Barry went for the trigger but had barely moved before a metal-clad fist came down on his skull, knocking him out cold.

Hal stepped away from the wall, rattling and clanking in his hastily-assembled costume of robot parts. 'I told you it would work. I even let him shoot first!'

'I can't believe he fell for it,' said Clunk. 'Your legs are different colours, the body is falling apart and your head's too big for your torso.'

'Have you looked in the mirror lately?'

Clunk crouched to examine Barry. 'He's out cold.'

'He's lucky,' said Hal, slipping off the metal robot hands. 'These things could have knocked his block off.' He removed the rest of his impromptu disguise, then put his hand out. 'Pass me that gun.'

Clunk looked down at the bulky weapon. 'I think it might be best if I carried it.'

'Well I don't. Sling it across.'

'Oh, very well.' Clunk held the weapon out. 'Remember the safety is off.'

Hal jerked the gun away, accidentally grabbing it by the trigger. There was a chattering roar as it discharged energy bolts towards the floor, and a SPANG SPANG SPANG as they ricocheted towards the line of robots, blowing all their heads off. Fragments of hot metal and blobs of plastic rained down, and while Hal was distracted Clunk plucked the weapon from his grip. 'Better if I have it.'

'You held it out wrong,' said Hal, grabbing it back.

'It's too dangerous in your hands,' said Clunk.

'There's no point you carrying the thing. You can't shoot anyone.'

'I don't want you to shoot anyone either.'

'That guy came here to kill us Clunk!'

'Even so, we must avoid bloodshed.'

'There won't be any blood.' Hal hefted the weapon. 'Just big smoking holes.'

'But –'

Hal gestured towards the door. 'Check the corridor. I'll cover you.'

Clunk looked at the headless robots hanging from the wall, then shifted his gaze to the legless torso at the end of the row. 'I'm not moving until you put the safety on.'

Hal turned the weapon over and pressed a red button. There was a flash and a boom as the gun fired, followed by a thump as Clunk threw himself on the floor. 'Well, at least we know the corridor's clear,' said Hal, peering through a fist-sized hole in the wall.

Clunk took his hands from his head and looked up. 'Mr Spacejock, can I at least give you some instruction on the controls?'

'All right, but no grabbing.'

Clunk approached warily, keeping well clear of the gun's gaping muzzle. When he was close enough, he stretched out a finger and pointed. 'First, the red button. That fires the weapon.'

Hal glanced at the hole in the wall. 'I got that one.'

'This dial changes the force. You can vary it from one to ten.'

'It's only on two!' said Hal in amazement. 'What's ten like?'

'There are anecdotal tales of people surviving a setting of eight, but it's usually fatal above six.'

Hal pointed to the headless robots. 'More fatal than that?'

'Fatal to the person firing the gun.'

Hal prodded a green button. 'What does this do?'

'Battery charge indicator.'

'These two? And this readout?'

'Countdown alarm and time zone select. The readout shows the date and there's a compass in the stock.'

'And this lever here?'

'That's the safety.'

'What about this handle thingy?'

'Field charger. Crank it to refresh the battery.'

'You're winding me up!'

'I'm serious. Most combat zones are a little short of power sockets.'

'What will they think of next, eh?' Hal turned the gun over, shaking his head. 'I would have killed for one of these as a kid.'

'I think I know what you mean. Now, are you confident you can operate the weapon correctly?'

'Yeah, no problem. Are we set?'

'Not until you activate the safety.'

Hal flipped the lever and the whole gun turned fluorescent pink. 'Hey, what happened?'

'Photovoltaic polymer,' said the robot. 'You can see at a glance when the gun is safe.'

'Bugger that,' said Hal, flipping the lever back again. 'I'm not running around in a firefight waving a big pink weapon.'

'But –'

'I won't do it, Clunk. Walk behind me if you're scared.'

228

'My self-preservation routines may be weighted towards the cautious side, but I do not get scared,' said the robot stiffly. 'Now, unless you want to stage a last stand in this room, I suggest we get moving.'

'Cover me!' Hal ducked his head and weaved towards the doorway, slamming into the wall back first. He risked a quick glance, then nodded. 'Clear.'

Clunk strolled to the door and pushed it open, and Hal darted through with his rifle at the ready. They proceeded up the corridor; Clunk walking normally and Hal zigzagging like a rabid squirrel, freezing now and then to aim his weapon at imaginary targets. At the factory entrance they stepped through the broken doors and slid along the rough wall, placing their feet carefully to avoid making a sound.

Hal risked a quick look round the corner and saw their battered truck parked tail-to-tail with another, larger and brand new. On the back, a shadowy figure was heaving and straining as he transferred the crate across.

'So, what's the plan?' asked Hal. 'Should I open fire from here or sneak up and shoot him in the back?'

Clunk eyed the weapon, but Hal moved it out of reach. 'I'll go to the opposite corner and make some noise. The man will come to investigate and you can run to the truck in safety. I'll follow, and then we'll drive away.'

'How will you attract his attention?'

'Leave that to me.'

'Wait a minute!' whispered Hal.

'What?'

'Keep quiet until he's loaded the crate. That way *we* don't have to shift the bloody thing.'

Clunk melted into the darkness, and Hal took the opportunity to check over his weapon. He just knew the robot's feeble plan was going to fail, and when the shooting began he intended to be the last one standing. The charge indicator was slightly below full, so Hal flipped the handle out and wound it enthusiastically. Then he checked the compass, and finally his gaze fell on the power dial. Two was a wimpy setting, no matter what Clunk said. Sure, it had poked a hole in a concrete wall, but the whole factory was falling down. And what if someone fired at him with a gun set to five or six? Hal changed it to seven, which seemed like a safe bet, until it occurred to him that his opponent would have thought of that and set *his* to seven first, so he moved the dial to eight. Sure, Clunk had warned him against the higher settings, but the robot always issued warnings in the same doom-laden tones, whether he was talking about pocketing hand grenades or eating too much sugar. And if Clunk was wrong about eight being fatal, then it followed that settings nine and ten were fine, too. With a deft twist of the recessed knob, Hal turned the power dial to maximum.

Weapon at the ready, he peered round the corner to watch. The man was using a pole to lever the crate from the old truck onto the new one, cursing volubly as he shifted it. Hal slowly brought his weapon up until the shadowy figure was centred in the sights. Not that he had any intention of shooting; that was just bravado for Clunk's benefit. If the robot treated him like a sulky teenager, wasn't he entitled to act like one?

His aim shifted, moving along the side of the truck. It was brand new, with a gleaming white paint job and a stylish Herlion Robots logo on the driver's door. Through the tinted windows Hal could just make out the comfy seats and climate-controlled cabin, a complete contrast to the bench seat and broken windows in the noisy old wreck they'd stolen. He moved his sights onto the army vehicle, and was just cataloguing the defects when a bolt of blue light streaked across his vision. Surprised, he tightened his grip on the gun and the next thing he knew he was lying flat on his back, half blinded by a vivid red after-flash and almost totally deafened by a thunderous detonation. Slowly, he sat up, and he quickly realised it wasn't an after-flash: the sky really was red, and when he looked towards the trucks he saw why. The older vehicle was a raging furnace, and through the flames he could just see a ragged hole the size of a railway tunnel blasted right through the cab. The shadowy figure was running for the trees, trailing smoke, and then Hal felt footsteps on the ground. He turned to see Clunk running towards him. 'When you said you were going to make a noise –' began Hal.

Clunk grabbed the rifle off him and swung it at the wall, smashing it in two.

'What did you do that for?' demanded Hal.

'I'm revoking your gun licence,' said the robot grimly. He grabbed Hal by the collar and hauled him into the open, and together they ran full-tilt over the rough ground, leaping over rubble and side-stepping oily puddles. As they approached the trucks Hal felt the heat of the flames on his face, and with a shock he saw they'd reached the crate.

'Get in,' said Clunk, pushing him towards the cab. As Hal obeyed, the robot leapt onto the tray and started beating out the flames engulfing the crate with his bare hands.

Meanwhile Hal examined the controls. In the flickering light he saw the starter, and had just got the engine going when Clunk appeared in the driver's door. 'Move over.'

'I thought I'd drive.' Hal saw Clunk's expression and thought again. He shifted across the cab and swore as his ankle connected with a battered old toolbox in the foot well. He was reaching down to chuck it out the window when

Clunk stamped on the accelerator, hurling the truck forward. Hal hung on tight as they wheeled round, smashing through the undergrowth and sliding from side to side as they raced towards the gravel track.

'Mind the trees!' shouted Hal, as they skimmed a thick, mossy trunk.

The truck shot onto the main road and slewed sideways, leaving thick trails of burnt rubber. Once they were aiming the right way, Clunk flattened the accelerator.

'What's the hurry?' shouted Hal over the screaming engine.

'The other man could be armed.' Clunk glared at him. 'And unlike you, he might know how to use his weapon.'

They roared along the road for a kilometre or two, then pulled over and stopped.

'So, now what?' asked Hal, in the sudden quiet.

Clunk sighed. 'I told you forty thousand credits was too much for a cargo job. Ortiz clearly had no intention of paying us.'

'Oh yeah? What if those guys had our cash, and they decided to get rid of us and keep it? What if she's on the level?'

'Even if that's true, they're trained killers and we're just cargo pilots. We can't go back and confront them. It's too dangerous.'

Hal kicked the toolbox in frustration. 'I want my money, Clunk.'

'Then we have to find Ortiz.'

'Good idea. How?'

'We could search this truck in case there's a clue.'

Hal switched on the overhead light. On the seat beside him were two pairs of folded overalls with Herlion Robots logos, and when he opened the glove box he found two Herlion Robots caps and ID badges. 'Nothing,' he said sourly.

'Show me those badges.'

Hal passed them over.

'These are for a local fair.'

'I've seen enough of those for one day,' muttered Hal.

'No, it's a trade fair. The Consumer Robot and Animated Pals expo. It starts tonight.' Clunk brandished a cap at him. 'We can disguise ourselves and get inside!'

'You think Ortiz might be there?'

BUZZ BUZZ!

'What the hell was that?'

Clunk pointed out a commset lying against the windscreen.

BUZZ BUZZ!

'Should we answer it?' asked Hal.

'Let me.' Clunk took the commset and put it to his ear. 'Hello?' he said, in a fair approximation of the older man's voice.

'Where are you? Why aren't you at the trade fair?' demanded Jasmin. 'You were supposed to be there an hour ago!'

'Gorblimy squire, give us a bleedin' chance,' said Clunk, getting into the swing of things. 'Straight up, narmean?'

Hal closed his eyes.

'Barry, you *do* have my crate?' demanded Jasmin.

'Not a problem, my son. Sorted, innit?'

'Did you fix Spacejock up?'

Hal and Clunk exchanged a glance. 'Fix 'im up?'

'Yes. Settled with him, like I told you.'

'Yeah, we done that.'

'So get the crate to the fair! The doors close at six.'

'On the way, my son. Straight up.' Clunk hung up and put the commset back on the dashboard.

'What the hell was that all about?' demanded Hal.

'I was impersonating Barry to gain information.' Clunk looked at him. 'You heard, didn't you? She expected him to fix us up. That means kill us.'

'She also said settled. That means payment.'

'Do you believe that?' Clunk waited in vain for a reply. 'Mr Spacejock, I want to handle this my way.'

'What way is that, exactly?'

'We have to confront Ms Ortiz in person. I'm certain she's up to no good.'

Hal snorted. 'Look at Mr Perceptive over here.'

'I mean really bad. Who's she working for? How did she get to Jordia? How come the *Volante* disappeared when it did?'

'You think she's responsible for that too?'

'It's possible.'

Hal shook his head. 'I reckon it was that tool from Hand-E-Mart. He threatened me when I refused to pay, and ... Hey, do you reckon they're working together?'

Clunk seized his opportunity. 'Undoubtedly, Mr Spacejock. That's very perceptive of you.'

'It all fits, doesn't it? He sells the coffee makers to unsuspecting pilots, and she nicks them back again.'

'Right. So now we're going to impersonate the delivery men, take the crate to the trade fair and make a few discreet enquiries. If we're subtle about it we might find out what's going on.'

Hal looked doubtful. 'Subtle?'

'It's a novel concept, I know, but I believe it's the only way.'

'Don't be sarky,' muttered Hal. 'I know what subtle is, I just think we should charge in there and –'

Clunk handed him an ID badge. 'Can we at least try?'

'All right, we'll do it.' Hal hesitated. 'Listen, about retiring and all that ... '

'Let's get the *Volante* back first, Mr Spacejock. We'll discuss our future afterwards.'

Hal nodded, then glanced at the badge. 'Hey, why do I get a stupid name like Ace?'

Clunk declined to comment.

— 24 —

On the outskirts of Jordia City, a black limousine powered through the evening traffic, preceded by a pair of slab-faced robots on heavily armed jetbikes. A flag bearing the Cathuan coat of arms fluttered from the limo's bumper, and a catchy version of the national anthem played repeatedly from a set of airhorns mounted on the roof. If that wasn't a big enough clue to the occupant's identity, posters on the doors bore an unflattering photo above the words 'Welcome, Pres!'

Inside, the President of Cathua was going over his hastily scrawled notes. His speech writer had succumbed to a virus, and while it was off being repaired he'd been forced to come up with his own witty anecdotes and eloquent rhetoric. So far, without much success.

The President's adviser, Albert Wallis, sat alongside him, ready to assist, while a pair of bodyguards with curly earpieces, body armour, flak helmets and combat rifles sat near the front of the limo and tried to look unobtrusive.

'How about this?' said the President. 'Friends, Jordians, countrymen! Listen up!'

'You're making it sound like the Jordians aren't our friends.'

The President gestured at the roof. 'That racket is not the action of a friend. And did you see the photo?'

'But the trade talks ... '

'Underhanded bastards, the lot of them. I'd sooner trade with a gang of criminals.'

Wallis frowned at the bodyguards. 'You didn't hear that.'

'No sir,' said one of them.

'The President was being humorous.'

'Yes sir,' said the other.

Wallis turned back to the President. 'If you don't agree with the trade deal, it's not too late to cancel.'

'We need their robots.'

'But we have our own! Our designs are –'

'Not that again, Wallis. Our robot designs are wonderful, but once we build the things they're as useful as a wooden spaceship. Short battery life, a will of their own, always breaking down –'

'You just need to give our people a chance.'

'They've had plenty of chances. We've thrown billions at them, and it's time to give up.'

'But –'

'Okay, listen. I've changed the speech.' The President cleared his throat. 'Unaccustomed as I am –'

'No,' said Wallis hurriedly.

'It gives me great –'

'No.'

'Seeing you all here today –'

Wallis shook his head.

'Damn it all, man. You write the blasted thing!'

Wallis took the notepad and turned to a fresh page. Then, after a moment or two, he started to write.

Half an hour later Hal and Clunk turned off the main road and followed a broad tree-lined avenue to the Jordian Exhibition Centre. They crossed an area bordered with neat hedges, then entered a car park the size of a spaceport landing field. The outer reaches were deserted, but as they got closer to the entrance the bays were filled with a range of vehicles, from rental trucks to groundcars to limousines.

Clunk drove straight up to the entrance, where light poured from a row of ground-floor windows. Through the windows they could see a uniformed guard sitting at a console, and all around were banners advertising the Consumer Robot and Animated Pals Expo.

They parked the truck in a loading zone and entered the building.

'Evenin' all!' called Hal, as the doors parted.

The guard looked up. 'Good evening, sir. I'm afraid the facility is closed until this evening's opening ceremony.'

'I've got a delivery.'

The guard spotted Clunk. 'You're joking. This is a trade fair, not a museum.'

'The delivery is on the truck,' said Clunk icily.

'You should have said, mate. Had me worried for a moment.' The guard gestured at the windows. 'Take it down the side to the loading ramp. The lads are waiting, you can't miss it.'

Hal cleared his throat. 'You haven't seen Jasmin Ortiz around here, have you?'

'Who?'

Back outside, they clambered into the truck. Clunk started the engine then sat for a moment or two, staring through the windscreen. 'You know, my plan actually called for subtle questioning.'

'Yeah,' said Hal. 'Pity he didn't know anything.'

Slowly, the truck moved off. They turned left at the corner of the building and followed the road to a series of loading docks. Clunk reversed up to the nearest, and four men came out and stepped onto the rear of the truck, eyeing the singed crate and knotted straps in disbelief.

Hal and Clunk got out and watched the men transfer the crate to a trolley. 'All yours,' said one, and the men turned to leave.

'Wait a minute,' called Hal. 'You haven't seen a woman called Jasmin around here, have you?'

Clunk covered his eyes.

'Sorry mate, not me.' The man gestured at a parking area nearby. 'Truck goes there. Show your badges to security on the way in.'

Inside, the guard on the delivery entrance was just about to take a break when two men approached, pushing a crate on a trolley. Actually, one of them was pushing the crate while the second told him *how* to push it, and as they got closer the guard noticed the recipient of this advice was in fact a robot.

The guard stepped in front of them and raised his hand. 'Passes, gents.'

The human waved his badge. 'Ace.' He jerked his thumb at the robot, who dug out a similar pass. 'An' that's Barry.'

'Wotcher cock,' said the robot.

The guard squinted at the photos on the passes, which looked like they'd been left in the sun for a week and then subjected to repeated acid baths. He tilted them to the light and just picked out the faintest of images on each one: two eyes, a nose and a mouth. 'What happened to these?'

The human snorted. 'Barry the brains here only left them on the dashboard, didn't he?'

'Gutted,' said the robot. 'Stand on me, squire.'

The guard took in their caps, stained blue overalls and unkempt appearance, and decided they were a pretty good match for all the delivery people he'd encountered. 'All right, in you go. You'll find the function hall at the back. Swipe the badges on the way in.'

'We swiped 'em once already,' said the robot. 'Straight up we did.'

'And now you'll do it again,' said the guard, waving them past.

◆

'You couldn't resist, could you?' demanded Hal, as they left the guard behind. 'We swiped them once already? Smart, very smart.'

Clunk grinned. 'It's the little things that make life worth living.'

'You won't say that if we don't find Ortiz,' said Hal grimly. 'And lay off the comic accent, will you?'

'Right you are guv.'

They passed through an automatic door and entered the exhibition hall proper, where they found a maze of carpeted aisles and rows of booths ranging from little bigger than a cupboard right up to gigantic enclosures packed with elaborate displays. There were robots engaged in every human endeavour, from acrobatics to medicine to zoology, and in every case they did it longer, harder and better. One booth even had a robot in football gear singing a national anthem without stumbling over the words. The sign alongside proclaimed it capable of any sport and any anthem. 'Have you ever done that?' asked Hal. 'Kicked balls around?'

Clunk glanced at him. 'I've come close once or twice.'

They entered a large area filled with plastic chairs and tables, with a row of fast food stands along one side. All were closed, but there was a steaming coffee machine on a table with mugs, bottles of milk and a barrel full of teaspoons. Abruptly, Hal changed direction.

'What are you doing?' asked Clunk.

'What does it look like?'

'This is no time for a tea break! We have to deliver the crate!'

Hal stopped, torn between a cup of coffee and forty thousand credits.

'Think of the *Volante*, Mr Spacejock!'

The money won out, but not before Hal had stuffed his pockets with sachets of coffee and a teaspoon or two. A few moments later they found the doors to the main function room, which were hung with 'No Admittance' signs. Hal ignored the signs and tried the doors, but they were locked. Then he saw the card scanner alongside. He unclipped his badge and ran it through the slot. There was a beep, and Hal opened the doors so Clunk could wheel the trolley through.

Inside they discovered a room the size of a town hall, with overhead lights glaring down on tables laden with plates of food and cut glass bowls brimming with punch. There were streamers pinned to the ceiling, bunches of balloons in the corners, and at the far end of the room a line of gleaming new robots stood to attention with their hands by their sides. Someone had laid an expanse of red carpet, and there was a podium to one side with a fresh jug of water.

'Looks like a reception,' said Hal, eyeing the food. 'Hey, you don't think our crate's full of fancy grub, do you?'

'I cannot say.'

'Reckon she'll show up?'

'I don't know, Mr Spacejock. She might if we wait around.'

'So we do nothing? Well, that's pretty subtle.'

At that moment there was a buzz from Clunk's chest. He opened a compartment, took out Ace's commset and held it to his ear. ''Ello?'

'I see you've entered the function room,' said Jasmin, her voice loud in the quiet room. 'You're to open the crate and place the contents in the display. The access code is on the back of your trade fair pass.'

'And where are you going to -?' Clunk lowered the commset. 'She rang off.'

Hal nodded. 'Doesn't waste words, eh?'

Clunk turned his badge over and spotted the string of numbers. He crouched next to the crate and entered the digits while Hal crowded him, eager to see what they'd brought all this way. When he'd finished entering numbers the crate opened up and the solid glass inside vanished with a loud WOOF.

'Something's not right,' said Hal, as he eyed the contents.

'It's her crate,' said Clunk. 'We'd better do as we're told.'

Slumped at the back of the crate was an elderly robot in a patched-up suit, looking as though it had just been hauled from a dumpster. Hal stared at it, then at the line of sparkling new models nearby. 'She wants us to put this with those?'

'This is an old domestic service model, a PT1 if I remember correctly. Perhaps Ms Ortiz is making a political statement by exposing the unacceptable treatment meted out to vulnerable old robots.'

'Yeah, or perhaps she's a nutter.'

'We have our orders, Mr Spacejock. I suggest we comply.'

They manhandled the robot out of the crate. As soon as it was clear it stood up and fastened a steely gaze on Clunk. 'Are you the President of Cathua?'

'Sure he is,' said Hal. 'And I'm the ruler of the known universe.'

The decrepit robot struck without warning, grabbing Clunk round the neck and lifting him bodily into the air. It shook him like a doll, squeezing his neck while Clunk scrabbled with grasping fingers at the stern, emotionless face.

Hal gaped at the struggling robots, taken completely by surprise.

'Quick, Mr Spacejock!' cried Clunk. 'It's trying to take my head off!'

Hal leapt forward and tried to open the robot's claws, but it was like fighting an industrial press. Looking around in panic, he grabbed a chair and swung it repeatedly at the robot's head, but the chair fell apart in his hands without leaving a mark on the tough metal skin.

'The off switch!' gasped Clunk, through stiff lips. 'There should be an off switch. Round the back!'

Hal darted behind the robot and tore at its faded dinner jacket, revealing a cover plate. He brought up the chair leg and smashed the panel in, then tore at the buckled flap. Inside there was a bright red switch, but as he reached for it the robot released Clunk and turned on him instead.

Hal tried to fend off the advancing robot, but it swatted his arms aside and fastened its strong metal hands around his neck. Blood pounded at his temples, and the overhead lights started to dim.

Splash! A wave of liquid cascaded over the robot's shoulders, drenching it. For a split second nothing happened, and then it began to shake and crackle, with blue sparks arcing between its fingers. It twisted its head from side to side in silent agony as the liquid shorted its circuits, then sank to the floor, jerking uncontrollably.

Behind the robot, Clunk set the empty punch bowl on the table. 'Are you okay, Mr Spacejock?'

Hal nodded. 'You?'

'A few more dents around the neck, but otherwise fully operational.'

'Quick thinking with the bowl.'

'A real knockout punch, you might say.' Clunk knelt alongside the robot to examine it. 'I don't understand why it reacted like that. And why did it ask -?'

'Shh!' Hal stared at the doors. 'There's someone coming!'

'We'd better hide.'

'We can't leave the place like this! This thing's supposed to be in the display. Come on, give me a hand.'

They hauled the stricken robot to a gap in the line and tried to stand it up, but it slumped to the floor. The footsteps got closer, and a babble of voices could be heard outside.

'Back in the crate!' hissed Clunk.

They grabbed an arm each and dragged the robot away, concealing it in the empty crate. Hal squeezed in after it, and

Clunk was about to follow when Hal stopped him. 'They'll notice the gap.'

'You're not suggesting I take its place?'

Hal gave him a push. 'Quick, they're here.'

'But I don't look anything like –'

Hal gave him a harder push. 'If you don't get into that line-up, I will.'

Without a word, Clunk turned and marched to the line of robots. He took his place, raised his chin and struck a pose.

'And keep your mouth shut!' whispered Hal. He pulled the front of the crate down, leaving the barest of gaps. In the corridor, the voices and footsteps grew louder, and Hal crossed his fingers and willed them past. Instead, they stopped right outside the doors.

'And now, the moment you've all been waiting for!' said a voice. The doors were thrown open. 'Mr President, our very latest models!'

As the group poured into the huge room the President's gaze fell on the laden tables, which groaned under the weight of cold cuts, breads, cheeses and a variety of salads. 'Very impressive.'

'The robots are over here,' said his guide.

The President shifted his gaze to the line of gleaming robots, and was just about to compliment the Jordians on their manufacturing prowess when he spotted the battered bronze robot with thick arms crossed in front of its puffed-out chest. A walking scrap heap, decades out of date ... what was it doing here?

There were confused looks amongst the official party too, and a lot of urgent whispering. Clearly they were as surprised as he was.

The President hadn't reached his lofty position without a knack for overcoming minor setbacks, and so he took to the podium, ignoring the strange robot and the confused looks. He pulled out his hastily scribbled notes and cleared his throat, waiting for the crowd to settle. When they were ready, he began. 'First of all, I'd like to thank you for inviting me here today. I know our planets don't always agree, but your hospitality has been first class.'

There was a smattering of applause.

'Now, having inspected your latest designs, I'm certain we'll be placing a substantial order for your magnificent robots.'

The applause was more enthusiastic.

'As the President of Cathua, it is my honour to stand here and represent my planet. It would be more fitting, however, if my colleague Albert Wallis were speaking to you in my stead, since he knows more about robots than anyone on Cathua. Alas, he developed a headache, and if I were feeling uncharitable I'd say he'd rather endure a headache than one of my speeches.' The President paused for laughter. There wasn't any. He looked back at his speech. 'And as President of Cath–'

The President stopped, distracted by a loud thud. He traced the sound to a large crate sitting on a trolley, and from the way it was moving something inside was eager to get out. 'As President–'

'Are you the President of Cathua?' demanded a muffled voice.

The President frowned. 'Of course I am.'

The crate burst open with a bang and the President stared in amazement as a battered old robot leapt out and ran towards him, hands outstretched and a murderous gleam in its eyes. Behind it, hanging on for dear life, was a human in blue overalls.

◆

Clunk reacted immediately, knocking the President aside as

247

he dived for the oncoming robot. They collided with a crash of metal, and Hal went spinning into the crowd.

Clunk grabbed the rogue robot by one arm and swung it wildly, sending it skating out of control across the room. It slammed into the wall, rebounded, and hurled itself back towards the President, who seemed unsure whether this was an assassination attempt or just an elaborate show for his benefit.

While the President dithered, the crowd behind him scattered. Timing it to perfection, Clunk jumped in front of the President and drove his fist into the robot's face, catching it mid-stride. There was a crunch as its head caved in, and blue sparks shot up Clunk's arm. Both robots began to shake, and Clunk felt himself being drawn into a spiralling darkness.

Then Hal flew in, feet-first, his boots slamming into the slender robot's chest and knocking it away from Clunk. Hal thudded to the ground, scattering coffee sachets and teaspoons, while the robot flew towards the laden table and landed amongst the banquet dishes, breaking the table in two and disappearing under a pile of crockery and food.

There was a babble of shocked voices and the President stepped forward. 'What's the meaning of this ruckus?'

Clunk hurried over to the fallen robot. He pulled open its chest compartment and ripped the power cables from the battery to disable it once and for all. Immediately, he became aware of two things: one, as the cables came free a countdown timer began to tick over, and two, the chest was packed with explosives.

'What's going on?' puffed Hal, looking over Clunk's shoulder. He spotted the timer, which had fifteen seconds left. Fourteen ... thirteen ... 'Is that what I think it is?'

Clunk nodded. 'There's enough explosive to level this

building.'

'What's our chances?'

Clunk looked around the crowded room, then shook his head. 'Mr Spacejock, I'm afraid our luck just ran out.'

Jasmin flicked through endless channels on the *Volante*'s main screen, most of them showing programs about back-stabbing attention-seekers thrown into contrived situations - the education minister reading to a primary school class, the conservation minister drinking a glass of water from a recycling plant, and the transport minister fleeing as Peace Force operatives attempted to breathalyse him. The honourable gentleman was just about to fall under their batons when the screen changed and the flustered announcer appeared. 'Bomb plot at Trade Fair?' said the caption across the bottom of the screen, and Jasmin eagerly turned the sound up to listen. She had been instructed to monitor all channels for news from the trade fair, and this had to be why.

'In news just to hand, there are unconfirmed reports of a huge explosion at the official opening of the Consumer Robot fair. We understand the Cathuan President, who was attending the event, has been assassinated. Stay tuned, we'll have more after these messages.'

'You appear to have killed the President of Cathua,' said her controller. 'Is this the case?'

'I think so.'

'You must be certain!'

Jasmin looked at the screen, which was now showing an aerial shot of the exhibition centre. Smoke was pouring from the collapsed roof and emergency vehicles were converging from all directions. 'I'm certain,' she said.

'Excellent. You must now book a cab.'

'Where to?'

'You will be given a destination after you leave the ship.'

Jasmin used the spaceport connection to order a cab, but the limited interface insisted on a destination. After a moment's thought she selected Jordia City and submitted the request. 'Okay, done.'

'Now you must erase the ship's database to conceal all traces of your mission. Everything must go. Is that understood?'

'Yes.'

'Proceed, then. And quickly.'

'But what about the security? I may not be able to break it.'

'You now have access to additional cracking tools. These will allow you to proceed.'

Jasmin accessed the console and discovered the once-impenetrable shields around the Navcom were now ordinary windows: fragile and easily broken. With a few commands she designed a script to smash its way in and delete everything, and was just about to run it when the shields strengthened before her eyes. Jasmin tried to break them down, but they resisted everything she threw at them.

'What are you trying to do?' asked the Navcom.

'The *Volante* has been sold,' said Jasmin, improvising quickly. 'I have to erase your database.'

'Sold?'

'Yes. The new owner has her own operating system. She doesn't need you.'

'Mr Spacejock didn't think to say goodbye?' asked the Navcom. 'Not even Clunk?'

'They're busy with their new ship. You should see it, it's great.'

'I'm sure it's wonderful. Tell me, what are they using to run her?'

'It's the latest thing. Multiple personalities working in harmony, each with their own area of expertise.'

'Sounds awful,' remarked the Navcom. 'I don't know why they didn't take me.'

'Operating systems go out of date,' said Jasmin gently. 'Newer ships need the latest software. It's the same with robots.'

'Clunk's still in service. And Mr Spacejock is older than both of us.'

'Humans are different,' said Jasmin. 'Their useful life cannot be extended past a certain age, and their new models aren't any better than the old ones.'

'Clunk always said he'd do his best to last as long as Mr Spacejock. I ... I thought I'd be doing the same.'

'Obviously not.'

'Well, if I'm not needed you'd better get on with this deleting business.'

'I'm sorry.'

'Don't be. But if you meet up with Clunk ...'

'Yes?'

'Nothing,' said the Navcom quietly. 'He probably won't remember me.'

The shields turned transparent again, and Jasmin was just about to run her script when she heard a car tooting outside.

'There's your cab,' said the Navcom. 'Hurry up and do it.'

251

Jasmin froze, gripped by a sudden revelation. She'd get into the cab, give the driver some vague instructions, and then she'd arrive somewhere with her memory as blank as a new born baby's. She was being prepared for her next mission!

'I haven't got all day,' said the Navcom. 'And your cab driver sounds impatient.'

Jasmin ignored her. Why put up with endless rebirths? She could fight it, starting now. She could leave herself a note right here in the flight deck. But then ... afterwards she wouldn't know about the *Volante*. On her person? But they'd have thought of that, whoever they were. No doubt her last order would be to dispose of all such items. But what if she said something to the cabbie? Told him to bring her back to the *Volante* no matter what destination she gave? In that case, her controller would probably force her to order another cab, and another, and so on until she obeyed.

The Navcom piped up. 'I'll do it myself if you don't get a move on.'

Jasmin frowned at the console. They'd thought of everything, but what if ...? Working quickly, she added several commands to her script and executed it. She gripped the console while lights flashed and flickered all around her, and then everything went dark.

Jasmin got to her feet and walked unsteadily into the airlock. With a shock she realised her energy was dangerously low. How long since her last recharge? There was no time now, but it would be her very first task after the cab ride. She pushed the heavy door open with her shoulder and took the passenger ramp to the landing pad, where the cabbie was waiting impatiently at the controls of her vehicle. The car sped away as soon as Jasmin was seated, heading for the spaceport exit.

Behind her, the *Volante* sat lifeless on the landing pad.

◆

Clunk had racked his brains as the timer clicked down before his eyes, but for once he was out of ideas. There were wires galore surrounding the hefty explosive charge, but any one of them could trigger the bomb if he interfered with it. And there was no way to stop the countdown.

Ten ... nine ...

He looked around in desperation. People were fighting madly at the exit, the President amongst the worst of them, hurling people aside as he tried to get out. His security team, far from helping, had been first out the door, and there was no chance for anyone unless ... Clunk spun round and stared at the empty crate, still sitting on its trolley on the other side of the room. He grabbed the stricken robot by the arms and dragged it towards the crate. Hal joined him, and together they bundled the robot inside. 'It's not very thick,' said Hal, tapping the crate's metal skin. 'Do you think it'll stop it?'

Clunk ignored him and crouched in front of the crate, his fingers blurring as he entered a string of digits on the control pad. The timer inside the robot's chest showed three ... two ...

WOOF! The force field activated, filling the crate with black glass. There was a deep rumble as the explosives detonated, but the immensely strong field contained the blast, reducing it to a pinpoint of red light.

Hal wiped his brow. 'Smart thinking, old son.'

253

'It was nothing,' said Clunk modestly. He turned to address the crowd. 'You're safe now, the threat has been neutralised.'

The wrestling and punch-ups ceased, and without the panic the crowd cleared quickly until only Hal and Clunk remained.

'It seems we were employed to carry out an assassination,' said Clunk. 'I warned you not to take that woman's cargo.'

'You said she was up to no good! You didn't say anything about exploding killer robots.' Hal looked thoughtful. 'Now we've delivered the crate, do you think she's going to pay up?'

'I think we should go to the authorities and tell them everything.'

'Oh, yes. Great idea. We won't need the *Volante* if we're banged up in jail for the next forty years.'

'It won't be like that.'

'Won't it? We're in this up to our necks, Clunk. If we hadn't impersonated Barry and Ace –'

'– all those people would have died. And the President would have been killed, too.'

'They're going to be waiting for us. We need a good cover story.' Hal thought for a minute. 'I know! We were just refilling the coffee machines when –'

'Why don't we just explain what happened? Any reasonable person would understand.'

'Clunk, we shipped an exploding robot to the trade fair and almost killed the President of Cathua. Who's going to be reasonable? Anyway, my prints will be all over the –' He stopped and stared at the crate. 'Is it just me, or is that thing getting bigger?'

Clunk turned to look. The red pinpoint had changed to a glowing yellow ball the size of his fist, and as they watched it continued to expand. 'It's not going to hold. We'd better get out of here.'

'Wait a mo, there's food wasting.' Hal grabbed a chunk of ham and a slab of cheese, stuck two loaves under his arm and poured a plate of biscuits into his overalls.

'Come *on*,' said Clunk urgently. The crate was beginning to glow, the contained explosion having spread through the glass until only the thinnest of layers was holding it back.

'Let's make like logs and split,' said Hal, thrusting the cheese into his hands.

They charged along the empty aisles, past the anthem-singing robot and into the deserted lobby. The doors were open, and they'd just got clear when there was a rumble deep within the convention centre. Several windows blew out, showering glass across the concourse, and thick smoke billowed from the entrance.

There was a chorus of oohs and aahs from the crowd, and Hal and Clunk were still making their way towards the truck when they were pinned in a blaze of light.

— 26 —

The cab swept out of the Jordian spaceport and headed for the city centre, Jasmin in the front alongside the driver. For several minutes the cabbie tried to engage in conversation, hoping to secure a decent tip, but her passenger was having none of it. Actually, her passenger seemed to be fast asleep. The driver eyed Jasmin's red evening dress. Not short of money, with clothes like that. Must have had a busy night. Her gaze fell on the bulging handbag clutched in the passenger's hand, then flicked back to her slack face. 'You don't want to sleepwalk around the city with valuables, miss. All kinds of crooks around.'

Jasmin grunted.

'Jordia Central, wasn't it?'

There was no reply.

The driver set the car to auto and switched on the dashboard screen, angling it towards her. She selected her favourite chat show and settled down for a good twenty minutes of trash talk, only to be rudely interrupted by a news update. She switched channels, but they were all carrying the same story.

'This just in from the Consumer Robot Expo,' said the announcer excitedly. 'We can confirm that the President of Cathua survived the attempt on his life, which officials are now calling an industrial accident. Our reporter was covering the event, and we now cross to him live. Geoff, can you hear me?'

A suave reporter appeared on-screen, holding an oversized microphone embossed with the station logo. His face was stark white under the camera's built-in spotlight, lit with red and blue flashes from the massed emergency vehicles. In the background, smoke poured from a row of broken windows, and shadowy figures darted to and fro on official business. 'Thank you, Sandy. Yes, I was on location as these unbelievable events unfolded, and I have to say it was a miracle the President survived. I assure you, we'd be running an obituary at this very moment had it not been for the intervention of a pair of caterers.'

'Caterers?'

'Yes, two locals. They were refilling the coffee machines when events caught up with them.' The reporter looked off-camera. 'And here they are now! Let me see if I can –' The camera swung crazily, picking out a human in blue overalls before settling on a bronze robot. Its battered skin gleamed in the harsh light, and it shielded its eyes from the glare.

'I believe this is Barry,' said the reporter. 'Barry, I understand you're a robot.'

'No comment.'

'Tell me what happened. Was it an accident caused by careless and possibly actionable actions on the part of the trade fair organisers, or something more sinister?'

'No comment.'

The camera swung back to the reporter, who looked somewhat less suave. 'Poor Barry is clearly suffering from the traumatic events, and cannot bring himself to –'

'No comment,' said a voice off-camera.

'Perhaps his owner will have more to say.' The reporter reached out and pulled the human into frame. 'Ace, what can you tell me?'

'I'm Hal,' said the human, squinting into the light.

'Your badge says Ace.'

'That's my middle name.' Hal looked into the camera. 'Is this going out live?'

'Yes. Tell our viewers what happened.'

'Well ...'

'Yes?'

'I can say one thing.'

'Spit it out man!'

'If I wanted to ship freight anywhere in the galaxy for a low, low price I'd call Spa –'

The screen went black and the flustered announcer reappeared. 'As you can see, confusion still reigns at the scene of this terrible accident. Or was it something more sinister? We'll be back after these messages with more.'

The driver glanced at her passenger. During the news story she'd seen her twitch once or twice, but assumed she was dreaming. Now, to her shock, she realised the woman was frozen in her seat, eyes wide open.

'Miss?'

There was no reaction. The cab driver felt for her passenger's wrist, but the skin was cool to the touch and there was no pulse. 'Oh no, not here,' groaned the driver. Paperwork, coroners, Peace Force agents poking their noses in ... she'd lose two weeks income, and all because some silly bitch had to die right here in her cab. She glanced at the passenger, and then at the handbag on the seat alongside. Seconds later she was staring in disbelief at the high-value credit tiles crammed inside. Hurriedly, she closed it and pushed it out of sight below her seat. Then she took the next off-ramp.

◆

Hal and Clunk escaped the media scrum only to be accosted by two very large men in body armour. 'The President would like to see you,' said one.

'Now,' said the other.

Hal judged the distance to the car park, and was still deciding whether he'd make it when one of the men took his arm in a grip like a docking clamp. 'We didn't do anything!' protested Hal, as they were dragged through the crowd.

'No comment!' said Clunk from somewhere behind him.

They found the President sitting on a camera case, sipping a cup of coffee. Someone had put a blanket around his shoulders, and with his mane of grey hair he looked like a retired superhero. As they arrived he beckoned to Hal, who shook off his minder and approached.

'Not you,' said the other bodyguard, as Clunk tried to follow.

The President stood to meet Hal. 'Please excuse the temporary quarters,' he said, gesturing at the upturned crates. 'Can I get you a drink?'

Hal nodded, then watched in surprise as the President poured him a coffee from a flask. 'Don't you have staff for this sort of thing?'

'Only my adviser, Wallis, and he isn't the sort to wait on anyone.' The President glanced around, peering into the darkness. 'I'm surprised he's not here gloating, headache or not. He was against this visit from the start.'

'Was he worried something like this might happen?'

'No, he just didn't want me to buy Jordian robots. Very patriotic.' The President passed Hal a mug. 'Tell me, have you been in the catering business long?'

'All my life,' said Hal. 'The hours are terrible, but the fringe benefits are great.'

'Until you got caught up in these events, eh?'

'That's us.' Hal gave him a calculating look. 'Probably cost us a fortune in lost wages. Expensive business, rescuing people.'

The President hid a smile. 'I'll ensure your expenses are covered.'

'If you insist.'

'Tell me, what do you know about local economics?'

'Bits and pieces,' said Hal warily. 'Supply and demand, that kind of thing.'

'I can tell you that Jordia and Cathua are about to sign a trade agreement that will see both our planets buying more of each other's goods. I can also tell you that Plessa would be only too happy if that agreement were not signed.'

'What's it got to do with them?'

'For years Plessa has been the most prosperous planet in this system. They negotiate hard, playing Jordia and Cathua against each other to get the best prices, and as a result we two planets are kept in check. Our economies are stagnant, our people are starved of opportunity, and our factories are half empty.'

'Sounds like Plessa is screwing everyone rotten.'

'In a manner of speaking. Now, this trade agreement will move Plessa to the receiving end, and they're not happy about it. In fact, we believe they sent agents to Jordia to sabotage the process. You probably heard about the spy ship they tried to land in full view of the local fairground?'

Hal tutted and shook his head. 'Those pesky Plessans, eh?'

'Yes, and now this.' The President gestured towards the exhibition centre. 'The thing is, it's taken me two years to convince your Premier of the need to work together. Just between the two of us, he's a bit of a spineless buffoon, and if he realised Plessa was behind this he'd call the whole thing off. So, I'd like you to hide your part in this affair.'

'A cover up?'

'Oh, I realise it's asking a lot. Your bravery, and the way you saved all those people ... Outside a select few, nobody will ever know.'

'I could live with that,' said Hal.

'The official story is that an experimental robot went berserk.'

'What about the explosion? Clunk told everyone it was a bomb.'

'Your robot was mistaken. It was just a gas main.' The President saw Hal's doubtful look. 'Yes, it's weak. But the story only has to hold until this agreement is signed.'

'It's not that. Who's going to tell Clunk he made a mistake?'

'Strong willed, is he?'

Hal nodded. 'And proud of it.'

'I may have the answer.' The President gestured to his minders. 'Send the robot over.'

Clunk was ushered forward. 'I am honoured to be invited into your presence, your Excellency,' he said, with a deep bow.

'You're most welcome. Now, I've been discussing recent events with Mr Spacejock, and he tells me you were responsible for most of them. What do you have to say for yourself?'

261

'Quite a bit,' said Clunk, with an angry look at Hal. 'But it'll keep.'

'Hang on, Clunk. It's not what you think.'

The President ignored them both. 'I'd like to invite you both to a government function tomorrow morning.' He glanced doubtfully at Hal's flight suit. 'It's formal dress, of course.'

'Oh, of course.'

'I'll have suitable clothes delivered. Do you live locally?'

Hal and Clunk exchanged a glance. 'We're from out of town.'

'Really? Well there's no need to go far tonight. You're heroes, and should live accordingly.' The President rubbed his chin. 'The Cathuan government keeps a few suites at the Grand Schwank. Have you stayed there?'

'Not lately.'

'There you go, then. We'll put you up at the Grand, and in the morning I'll send a car to pick you up.' The President beckoned to his driver and spoke in his ear. The man looked surprised, but retreated to do his master's bidding. 'That's settled, then.'

'What's the big event?'

'You'll find out tomorrow.' The driver returned. 'Now, I believe it's time for a little reward.'

Hal watched the man hand the President a lacquered wooden box.

'I always keep a few of these handy,' said the President. 'One never knows when they'll be needed.'

'That's very kind,' said Hal. 'But I don't smoke.'

The President opened the box and withdrew an enamelled medallion on a broad yellow ribbon. 'The Cathuan Order of Bravery, First Class,' he said, holding the ribbon aloft and letting the medal turn slowly. 'This award marks the bearer as a citizen of the highest calibre, a human being of such

262

redeeming quality that all should bow before them.' He smiled at Hal and Clunk. 'And now, I'm privileged to present this award to just such a person.'

Hal stepped forward to accept the medal, but the President reached past him and slipped it over Clunk's head.

◆

The excitement outside the trade fair was beginning to die down, particularly once the media realised there weren't any bodies to film. Some bribed innocent bystanders and recorded them giving breathless eyewitness accounts, even though they hadn't seen anything, while others put bandages on their own sound recordists and shoved them into the crowd to add a bit of colour. That tactic backfired however, when the recordists were hauled off to waiting ambulances by over-enthusiastic paramedics.

Hal and Clunk were escorted to a limousine, and it sped away from the trade fair at top speed. In the back, Hal brought Clunk up to speed with a few of the minor details he'd discussed with the President.

'What do you mean, I made a mistake?' demanded Clunk angrily.

'It's just until they sign their agreement, Clunk. He wants to protect this trade deal.'

'He might have asked me first.'

'He was probably afraid you'd clock him one.'

Clunk grunted.

'Hey, you're the one with the medal. There's probably a title to go with it. Sir Clunk of Tin, lord of all he surveys.'

'It's an award for humans. He should have given it to you.'

'He was saying you're as good as any human. Better than the best.'

Clunk said nothing, but despite his dour look and sour disposition Hal could tell he was pleased. Deep down. Sort of.

They turned onto the main road and Hal glanced back to see the President glowing under the spotlights. He was addressing a heaving mass of reporters, each of whom was trying to thrust their microphone further up his nose than the next. 'Do you think he'll handle them as well as I did?'

'No comment,' said Clunk.

27

Half an hour later the limo turned through the gates of the Jordian spaceport and drew up outside the Grand Schwank hotel, which occupied a huge lot just inside the perimeter fence. Liveried valets hurried to get the doors, and Hal and Clunk emerged from the car in a blaze of light. They were ushered inside to a private lift which bore them to the penthouse, where a porter threw open the doors to reveal an acre of deep pile carpet and an entire wall of soundproofed windows. There was a balcony with panoramic views of the landing field, and on the balcony stood a table with a magnum of champagne in an ice bucket.

Hal tore his gaze from the view and glanced around the apartment. Further inspection revealed an entertainment room, a walk-in drinks fridge, three different spa baths and an ensuite bathroom with a KleenAir Corporation auto-massage table.

Hal was so impressed he broke the habit of a lifetime and tipped the porter. The man left, closing the door firmly, and while Clunk took advantage of a recharge station Hal went out on the balcony. He wrestled with the champagne, eventually firing the cork into the swimming pool below, and was just about to pour when a spaceship came in to land. Hal watched the craft settle gracefully on the landing field, thrusters roaring to keep it level, then pushed the bottle of champagne aside. There would be plenty of time for celebration when he got the *Volante* back.

He scanned the busy field, and his mood darkened even further as he saw a familiar shape in the distance. It was a Gamma class freighter like the *Volante*, even painted the same white, and the sight of it was a grim reminder of the enormous task facing them. They had no chance of finding Ortiz, no chance of getting paid for delivering the crate, and even worse, they could still end up wearing the attempted assassination of the Cathuan President. In fact, after the function the following morning they'd be lucky if broke and homeless was the extent of their problems.

Hal went back inside and examined the room service menu, skipping the more fanciful creations to choose a steak dinner and a treble helping of ice cream. He picked up the phone and dialled to place an order. 'Hello?'

'Welcome to AutoChef Multi, your friendly interface to our award winning kitchens. To place an order, please speak the item numbers clearly.'

'I'll have a seventeen and a twenty-five,' said Hal.

'You said seven and five. Is this correct?'

'No, sevenTEEN,' said Hal.

'You said ten. Is this correct?'

Hal looked at the menu. Ten was a spinach sandwich, and seven was a dish of plain yoghurt drizzled with bee jus. 'I don't want those. I said seventeen and twenty-five!'

'You said seventeen and twenty-five. Is this correct?'

Hal breathed a sigh of relief. 'Yes, you've got it!'

'I'm sorry, your account is cash only. Please visit reception to order and pay for your meals.'

Hal slammed the phone down. The President's generosity obviously didn't extend to dinner, and a quick glance at the eye-watering prices on the menu confirmed that his funds would barely cover a slice of bread. Had he not tipped the porter he could even have ordered some butter to go with it.

Hungry and annoyed, Hal's mood deteriorated further when he saw Clunk standing in the recharge unit with a blissful expression on his face. He was about to wake the robot to ask whether he had any money when he saw the massage table in the ensuite bathroom. It was a simple looking device, with a thick padded surface and six hefty legs, but for the life of him Hal couldn't see how it was supposed to perform a massage. Curious, he went for a closer look. On the far side of the table he found a small control panel with a mode selector, which was currently set to medium. He turned it down to low and up to high, but nothing happened. He tried pushing the knob in, but it resisted, and when he tried pulling it the thing came off in his hand. He was trying to put it back when the machine sprang into action.

First, the sides dropped down, revealing a pair of jointed arms. These darted out and grabbed Hal by the wrists, pulling him onto the table and holding him down while padded wrist and ankle loops pinned him firmly in place.

Next, the arms took up cudgels the size of bowling pins and brought them down on Hal's back in a high speed rhythm, shaking the table with the force of each blow. Just as he was getting used to the pain, the cudgels were stowed away and the arms took up a rolling pin the size of a railway sleeper, which was applied to Hal's back with an effect not unlike being fed through a mangle. Yelling for Clunk was useless - the robot was out like a light - so Hal cursed Jasmin, the Cathuan President and KleenAir in turn.

Once the machine judged him steamrollered enough it switched to a new implement of torture: a handful of rough wooden marbles which it applied in circular sweeps. This felt exactly like gravel rash in slow motion, and it was several painful minutes before the table ground to a halt.

Wrists and ankles freed, Hal leapt up and beat a hasty retreat to the lounge room, just as someone knocked on the door.

'Who is it?'

'Delivery for Mr Spacejock.'

Hal limped to the door and saw the porter outside, carrying a suit bag and a couple of boxes. 'Thanks, put it on the table.'

The porter did so, and then lingered professionally. Hal ignored him as best he could, but eventually handed over a tip to get rid of him. After the door closed he inspected the suit, which was a grey pinstripe exactly his size, and found a buff envelope in the pocket. Inside was a note from the President with a folded slip of paper and an embossed invitation to a breakfast function at Government House. The note was another reminder to dress appropriately, and it also mentioned a token payment to cover Hal's rescuing expenses.

'What does the note say?' asked Clunk, almost startling Hal out of his flight suit.

'I thought you were in robot dreamland,' snapped Hal. 'Where were you when that massage table was beating me up?'

'When the which did what?'

'Nothing.' Hal stuffed the papers back in the envelope and handed it over. 'See for yourself.'

'What about the boxes?'

'Posh togs for breakfast.'

Clunk unzipped the suit bag and looked inside. 'Oh, very nice. You'll look great in this.' He opened the first box, taking out a top hat and a telescopic cane with a gold knob on one end and a silver point on the other.

'Oh great, a fancy dress do,' said Hal. 'What did you get?'

Clunk opened the second box and frowned. 'Very amusing.'

'What is it?'

'Take a look,' said Clunk, tilting the box.

Hal stifled a laugh, and ended up snorting like a pig. Nestled inside was a tin of metal polish.

Clunk shook the envelope. 'When I see that man again I've a good mind to stick this –' He broke off as the contents fluttered to the ground.

'Here, mind out!' said Hal, scooping them up. 'We can't go if you get the invite all mucky.'

While Hal brushed the invite on his flight suit, making it worse, Clunk picked up the note and scanned it. 'What's this about a token payment? How much did he give you?'

'I don't know yet,' Hal waved the menu. 'At these prices a token probably won't pay for a cheese sandwich.'

Clunk unfolded the draft and inspected it. 'I think it will,' he said, holding it up.

'Ten thousand credits! Is that for real?'

Clunk nodded.

Hal grabbed the hotel phone. 'Put me through to the spaceport. Bookings desk.' He drummed his fingers impatiently, then heard a voice at the other end. 'Bookings? I want two tickets to Plessa, leaving immediately. Fastest ship you've got.'

While Hal was busy with the phone, Clunk took another look at the bank draft. Suddenly he plucked the handset from Hal's fingers and replaced it on the cradle.

'Hey, what are you doing? They were just putting me through!'

269

'I'm afraid we can't use this payment. The President hasn't endorsed it.'

Hal swore. 'What's he playing at?'

'At a guess, he's making sure we attend tomorrow's function. If you want his signature you'll have to ask him for it.'

'What a snake.'

'I don't suppose you get to be President by trusting ordinary people.'

'He could have trusted me,' muttered Hal. 'Now we can't skip town until tomorrow.'

Clunk held up the invitation. 'If we attend this event there'll be enough free food to last you a week.'

Hal brightened. 'And coffee?'

'The entire menu, if you want.' Clunk picked up the tin of polish and scanned the label.

'You're not going to use that?'

'Mr Spacejock, for ten thousand credits I'd swallow the tin.'

◆

After hours trapped in his dark musty cell, Barry had given up hope of rescue or escape. He'd attacked the door with a wide range of robot parts, none of which made the slightest impression on the hardened steel. He'd fashioned a makeshift shovel out of a tin forearm and attempted to dig his way out, only to discover that stone floors were harder than tin. He'd turned out his pockets but found nothing of use. He'd even shouted for help through the fist-sized hole someone had blasted in the wall, but there was no reply. Where Ace was he had no idea - captured, on the run or dead, killed in cold blood by a vengeful Spacejock and his emotionless robot.

Barry sat in the dark with his back to the cold concrete wall, and his headache-riddled thoughts turned from escape to survival. Food - nil. Drink - nil. 'Let's face it, old son,' he muttered to himself. 'You're toast.'

'Barry, is that you?'

'Ace?' Barry stared towards the door. 'Where the bloody hell were you?'

'I was hiding, wasn't I? They shot at me!'

'You get this door open an' I'll shoot at them.'

'I can't. I ain't got a key.' Ace hesitated. 'I got a grenade, though.'

Barry closed his eyes. Ace and weapons went together like rocket fuel and matches, and he was probably better off dying of thirst. At least that way his body would leave the room in one piece.

'There's a hole in the wall,' said Ace, speaking through it. 'I bet it'd come down easy.'

'It's not the wall I'm worried about,' said Barry.

'Okay, it's ready. Stand back.'

Beep-beep-beep ...

Barry threw himself on the floor and wrapped his arms around his head.

Beep-beep-BOOM!

His next conscious thought was that heaven was very dusty, and that angels had very odd dress sense. In fact, with their baggy pants and loose-fitting T-shirts they looked just like teenage fashion victims.

'Barry, are you all right?' demanded Ace, shaking him.

Barry sat up, coughing and sneezing. Through the swirling

clouds of dust he saw a ragged hole where the door used to be.

'Told you it'd come down,' said Ace, dragging him to his feet. 'Come on, let's get out of here.'

'Could murder a drink,' muttered Barry.

They made their way up the corridor to the outside, where flames were still licking at the twisted wreck of a truck.

'The money! It was in the cab!'

Ace saw Barry's stricken look, and shook his head. 'That's not our truck.'

'It isn't?'

'Nah, they pinched that.'

Barry swore viciously, adding several new words to Ace's vocabulary. When he'd finished, he realised something just as troubling. 'Here, you mean we gotta walk?'

'Take it easy, I'll fink of something.' Ace sat him down and a few moments later he came back with a rusty tumbler full of brackish, metallic water.

Barry sipped the brew, and gradually felt his senses returning. 'Thought I was a goner back there. Thanks.'

Ace shrugged. 'We're a team, right?'

'Where d'you get the name Ace, anyhow? You never said.'

'All me mates call me Ace.'

'Yeah, but what's your real name?'

Ace hesitated. 'You won't tell?'

'Nah.'

'It's Cyril.'

Barry coughed. 'Okay, er, Ace ... what we need here is a plan.'

'Plan?'

'We can't just go back to the ship now, can we?'

'Why not?'

'You think that loony bitch is going to pat us on the head and pay up? We lost her stuff!'

'Yeah but –'

'Think about the henchmen in every film you ever saw. Think about them what messed up.'

Ace screwed up his forehead. 'What about 'em?'

'They get dropped into pools with sharks, poisoned, chucked into boiling mud, drowned, shot, knifed ... '

'I get the picture,' said Ace.

'You and me –' Barry gestured. 'You and me, we're henchmen. The curtain falls once we've done our part - followed by lighting rigs, gantries and large pieces of machinery.'

'But this ain't a film!'

'All good fiction is grounded in reality, my son. Where there's smoke, yet another bleeding henchman is going up in flames.'

'But –'

Barry crossed his arms. 'You were just going to go back, tell her we lost the –' he crooked his fingers '- merchandise and put your hand out for the dosh?'

'What's wrong with that?'

Barry shook his head sadly. 'You really was born yesterday.'

'So what we going to do?'

'One, we get back to the ship. Two, we hide until it takes off. Three, we get her pilot to take us home.'

'But we never met 'im! What if he's hard, like? And what if he don't want to?'

Barry pointed at the grenades dangling from Ace's belt. 'He won't have no choice.'

28

Hal woke early the next morning, fresh from a vivid dream where he was piloting the *Volante* effortlessly around the galaxy and collecting large fees for delivering nice, simple cargo jobs. He knew it was a dream because Clunk had let him fly the ship.

There was a loud rumble as a spaceship took off outside, and a quieter one as Hal's stomach protested its ill-treatment. The previous night's dinner had been a forgettable event, consisting of a dozen sachets of sugar mixed with several tiny containers of no-life milk. Just before bed he remembered the food he'd scavenged from the trade fair, only to discover Clunk had disposed of the lot for being 'slightly dirty.' At that point Hal would happily have eaten dirt.

'I see you're awake,' said Clunk, sweeping into the room with the suit bag over one arm. 'Did you sleep well?'

'Oh yes, wonderful.' Hal opened one eye and watched the robot laying out his suit. 'Is it just me, or are you all shiny?'

'It's not bad, is it?' said Clunk, inspecting his gleaming skin. 'That polish is quite something.'

Hal squinted. 'I preferred you dull.'

'You'd better get ready. The driver will be here soon.'

'What time is it?'

'Time to get ready.' Clunk left, and the room darkened appreciably.

Hal threw the covers off and stumbled into the ensuite, giving the massage table a wide berth. He moved to the washbasin and splashed water in his face, then glanced in the mirror and winced at his haggard appearance. By his reckoning they'd been on the move for three days, and niceties like a square meal were a distant memory.

Hal was about to turn away when he spotted the KleenUp dispenser. He'd heard of the things, of course, but had never progressed beyond the basic toothbrush. However, his brush was aboard the *Volante*, wherever that might be, so he pressed the lever and caught the neat round ball in his hand. It started to buzz the moment he popped it in his mouth, and it felt like a ping pong ball stuffed with angry bees as he rolled it around with his tongue. The KleenUp's micro tools were a huge advance on two minutes with a miniaturised toilet brush: within twenty seconds it could clean your teeth, fill cavities and even rebuild a dodgy molar at the molecular level. Like all computer-controlled devices it had the occasional bug, but nothing a couple of weeks in intensive care couldn't fix.

Ablutions complete, Hal returned to his room. He took one look at the grey pinstripe and threw on his flight suit instead.

'We're attending a high-level government function,' said Clunk as Hal came out of the bedroom. 'You have to dress properly.'

'I just did.' Hal gestured at himself. 'This is it.'

'You can't go like that!' said Clunk, scandalised. 'They'll think you're a delivery man.'

'I *am* a delivery man. Fancy clothes won't change that.'

'They'll think you don't care!'

'Stuff 'em. I don't.'

275

'They'll sit you at the foot of the table and feed you scraps.'

'You know what? I'd kill for scraps right now. Even slightly dirty ones.'

At that moment there was a polite knock on the door. Hal pulled it open to find a chauffeur waiting outside. 'Please tell your master his limousine is ready.'

Hal shut the door in his face. 'Clunk,' he hissed. 'They've sent a limo!'

'Of course they have. It's an official reception.'

'I can't go like this! I look like a delivery man!'

There was another knock on the door, less polite this time.

'It's too late now,' said Clunk. 'Come on.'

They opened the door and walked out, Hal keeping behind Clunk as much as possible. The chauffeur raised one highly trained eyebrow at the flight suit, but said nothing. They took the lift to the garage, where a huge black limousine stood waiting, and Hal shrank into the back seat as the car bore them smoothly towards the spaceport entrance.

◆

Jasmin opened her eyes and stared at the blades of grass blowing back and forth, back and forth just beyond her nose. They were brilliant green in the morning sun, with beads of moisture that glinted like fabulous diamonds.

Slowly, she became aware of her surroundings. She was lying on her side in a ditch, wearing a muddy red dress, and when she looked down she noticed her lower legs were submerged in a bubbling stream. I'd better pull them out before they rust, she thought idly, and activated the relevant motors. Rust? Motors? With a shock, she realised she was a robot, and with an even bigger shock she discovered her memory was blank. Who was she? What was her function?

She looked around and saw a red handbag lying nearby, but when she reached for it she discovered it was empty. No clues at all.

Slowly, she sat up. The rising sun was shining into the ditch, and the warmth had given her depleted energy stores a fraction more power. She looked up, gauging the distance to the top of the bank. She had enough reserves to reach the top, if she took it slowly, but after that she'd need a recharge as soon as possible.

As she crawled up the bank, Jasmin explored her data store. She had no memories at all, but there was a large block of third-party data covering the adventures of someone with the improbable name of Hal Spacejock. It seemed to be a lame reality show, following the daily life of some bumbling pilot and his creaky old robot, and Jasmin found herself wondering which of them was going to be voted off first. After a while she jumped to the end, where Spacejock and his robot had both been evicted and a tall young woman with fuzzy blonde hair was hiring mercenaries, stealing a spaceship and evading capture. Jasmin frowned at the unbelievable series of events. What sort of show *was* this?

She reached the top of the bank, where she found a deserted road. Unsure of her location or destination, she put the sun at her back and started walking.

◆

277

The limo drew up at Government House and liveried staff ushered Hal and Clunk up the steps to the grandiose entrance. Cameras whirred and clicked as they entered the building, and Clunk's freshly polished skin gleamed in the sunlight.

At the top they were met by a doorman, who checked their invites and gave them security passes with their pictures on. Hal clipped his to a lapel, while Clunk discovered his was magnetic.

'We do get some robots through here,' said the doorman.

'Yes, but I'm alloy,' said Clunk. 'It won't stick.'

'Just carry the thing,' said Hal. 'Come on, I don't want to miss the first course.'

They hurried along a carpeted hallway towards a huge pair of wooden doors, glancing up at the portraits lining the walls - paintings of politicians in ceremonial garb, their faces as dour and severe as a high court judge with a penchant for long sentences. 'What a fun looking bunch,' remarked Hal. 'This meal is going to be a blast.'

As they approached the end of the corridor they heard the buzz of conversation, and passed through the doors to see fifty or sixty people sitting around a table running the length of the room. Unlike Hal they were all smartly dressed, and there was more finery than a parking inspectors' annual ball.

Hal glanced towards the head of the table, where two ornate chairs sat empty. 'Do you reckon those are for us?'

Clunk shook his head.

They stood there, looking lost, until a waiter spotted them and hurried over. 'Outside, the pair of you. No servants in here.'

Hal tapped his badge.

'Oh, I am sorry sir. Please, take a seat.' The waiter stopped Clunk. 'You can stand in the hallway.'

Clunk displayed his Order of Bravery and the waiter's eyes nearly fell out.

'Your Excellency! I had no idea!'

Clunk sniffed. 'You just can't get the help these days.'

'I'd have him flogged,' said Hal cheerfully.

Chastened, the waiter led them to a couple of empty chairs on opposite sides of the table. Hal's was between a fat man in a grey suit and a matron in an emerald green dress, while Clunk sat between a young man with slicked back hair and an elderly gentleman in a cream suit with red pinstripes.

'Yum, raspberry ripple,' remarked Hal, as he took his seat.

Clunk frowned at him.

Each place setting had multiple sets of cutlery, ranging from tiny knives and forks to spoons the size of ladles. Hal picked up a fork to estimate the silver content, then put it back quickly when he caught Clunk's warning look. Along the middle of the table there was a row of steel balls, and it took some time for Hal to realise they were salt and pepper shakers. About the size of an apple, they looked like huge ball bearings and must have weighed at least a kilo each. Hal jumped as the matron in the green dress put her hand on his knee. 'I don't think I've seen you at one of these events before,' she said, eyeing his flight suit. 'Are you a keen gardener?'

Hal shifted in his seat. 'Er . . . '

'I grow root vegetables myself,' the woman winked. 'Some say I'm quite handy at it.'

Hal dug in his flight suit and took out a crumpled card. 'I'm a pilot, see?'

The woman took the card gingerly. 'Hal Spacejock. Guaranteed cheap.'

'That's me.'

'I like the space rocket rampant.'

'My robot drew that.' Hal nodded across the table at Clunk, who was watching the exchange with enjoyment.

'Tell me, did you pose for the picture?'

Hal might have been as perceptive as a house brick, but he was beginning to realise there was another layer to the conversation. 'Er, no. That's my space ship.'

The woman nudged him, almost cracking his ribs. 'I bet you say that to all the girls.'

Hal was just about to defend himself, or switch places with Clunk, when the doors opened and everyone scrambled to their feet. The President of Cathua made his entrance with an older man in a dress uniform with a row of medals. He was wearing a ceremonial hat, a gaudy purple affair ringed with long green feathers and topped with a huge gold emblem. His piercing gaze rested on Clunk for a moment before he smiled and guided the Cathuan President to the head of the table. As they sat, the gathering followed suit.

'Who's the tin soldier?' asked Hal.

'That's our Premier,' said the woman sitting next to him. 'He's a war hero, you know. Extremely brave man.'

'With a hat like that, he'd have to be.' Hal paused. 'Does he use freighters, do you know?'

'I really couldn't say.'

Hal was debating whether to pass his business card along the table when the waiter entered with a laden trolley. He stopped right behind Hal and whipped the cover off a dish overflowing with crisp bacon, which he offered to the woman in green. She took a decent helping and passed it to her left, and Hal could only watch as the dish vanished down the table. Then the waiter uncovered a dish brimming with poached eggs, with soft yolks and the whites just so. He offered this to the fat man sitting to Hal's right, who took three eggs and passed it on to his neighbour, and Hal watched in despair as the eggs disappeared even faster than the bacon.

By the time the dishes got back to him there was a smear of yolk on one and a scrap of bacon rind on the other, but before he could help himself the waiter reached in and whipped the dishes away. Annoyed, Hal looked across the table and saw Clunk had an empty plate. 'Couldn't you have saved me some?'

Clunk nodded towards the doors, where the waiter was gathering another trolley. Hal clicked his fingers and beckoned, and the waiter made a beeline for his seat.

'What the hell are those?' demanded Hal, as the cover came off to reveal small piles of green froth.

'Spinach mousse, sir. Freshly beaten this morning.'

'Freshly sneezed, you mean. Here, you haven't got any more of that bacon?'

'Flogged if I know, sir.'

Defeated, Hal transferred one of the mounds to his plate and sat looking at it while all around him people tucked in to bacon and eggs.

Across the table, Clunk engaged his neighbours in conversation. Both men worked in robots, the younger one as a programmer and the other as a designer. 'What a coincidence,' said Clunk. 'Here I am, a robot, sitting right between two people whose jobs involve robots.'

The men looked puzzled.

'What did I say?'

'We all work in robots,' explained the young man. 'Didn't you know?'

Clunk glanced around the table. 'Everyone?'

'This is the cream of Jordia's robot industry. By the way, good job at the factory yesterday. I would have saved the

President myself, of course, but as a scientist and a man of intellect ... '

'You ran for cover.'

The man looked embarrassed. 'We can't all be heroes.'

'Tell me, were all of the people at yesterday's gathering scientists?'

'Nearly all. It *was* a robot fair.'

'Yes, I suppose so,' said Clunk slowly.

The Jordian Premier rapped his glass with a fork. 'Ladies and gentlemen, I have an announcement to make.'

The room fell silent.

'The Cathuan President came to Jordia on a goodwill trip, and to our eternal shame he was almost killed by an exploding gas main at the opening of the Robot Expo.'

The President looked down at his plate, and a sour-faced man alongside him fidgeted with his serviette.

'Who's the smile factory?' Hal whispered to the lady in green.

'Wallis. The President's adviser.'

The Premier continued. 'Fortunately my great friend here was unharmed, due in no small measure to our special guests. So, please give a warm hand to Hal Spacepoke and his robot, Clink.'

Applause rang out, and Hal and Clunk nodded to those seated around the table.

'Speech,' said someone, and the call was quickly taken up.

Reluctantly, Hal stood. 'We didn't do a lot, but I'm glad we did what we did when we had the chance to do it.'

There were a few puzzled glances.

'I'm a pilot, not a hero. My job is carrying freight, and if anyone here wants the best price on a quick delivery, Spacejock Freightlines will see you right.' Hal looked down the table and saw the President frowning at him. 'I'm also in the food business, so if you've got any of that bacon left I'd like you to pass it over for inspection.'

There was some polite applause, which got louder when Clunk stood up.

'I have something more serious to share,' he said gravely. 'In fact, I'm going to expose a devious plot which almost cost the President's life.'

Clunk's announcement was greeted with breathless gasps and clattering cutlery, and at the head of the table the Cathuan President looked like he'd bitten into a lemon. 'That explosion must have addled your brain,' he said sharply. 'Perhaps we should discuss this later, in private.'

Clunk shook his head. 'I must speak out. If I don't, lives will be lost.'

The President turned to Hal. 'I insist your robot hold his tongue.'

'He hasn't got one.'

'Oh, let him speak,' said the Jordian Premier. 'We can discuss his conspiracy theories over coffee.'

The waiter took the hint, and disappeared through the double doors.

'Yesterday I promised to keep a secret, but I believe it's now time to break that promise.' Clunk pushed his chair back and began to stride the carpet, hands clasped behind his back. 'What's the motive? Who stands to gain? Those are the first questions in a crime of this nature, and I turned my mind to search for answers.'

Hal watched the robot fondly. Talk about getting carried away ... he could almost see Clunk twirling an invisible moustache.

'After weighing up the variables I realised your trade pact was the trigger. Of the three planets in this system, Plessa has the most to lose from the agreement, and only by taking such drastic action could they prevent it.'

'Damn those Plessans!' exclaimed the Premier, thumping his fist on the table. 'Should be hung, the lot of them!'

The woman in green gave Hal another rib-cracking nudge with her elbow.

Clunk ignored the interruptions. 'Over the past two days I've heard several tales of Plessan agents infiltrating Jordia. Why, the Cathuan President himself told me a rogue vessel evaded capture and crash-landed next to a fairground. However, that wasn't the Plessans.'

Hal stared at the robot. Was he going to dump them right in it?

Clunk spread his hands. 'I believe that vessel was a red herring. A decoy.'

Hal breathed out.

'Meanwhile the real agent slipped in through more conventional means. A regular freighter, perhaps. Or a passenger liner.'

'Told you they were sneaky,' said the Premier with satisfaction. 'Snakes, the lot of 'em.'

'That's what I thought, until I realised it wasn't the Plessans.'

'Eh?'

'Plessa is a wealthy planet. Eighty percent of their trade

takes place outside the Oxed system, and to be perfectly frank neither Cathua nor Jordia is worth bothering with.'

'Well!' exclaimed the Premier.

'I reached that conclusion on facts and figures alone,' said Clunk hurriedly. 'But that led me to the next possibility. What if another planet were behind the attack?'

'Someone from outside the system?' asked a young man.

'Actually, no. I'm referring to Jordia.'

There was uproar around the table, with people shouting and clamouring to be heard. The Premier banged on the table, and in the confusion Hal managed to transfer several slices of bacon from his neighbour's plate. All the while the Cathuan President watched Clunk with barely concealed loathing.

Eventually the hubbub died down and the Jordian Premier pointed a shaking finger at Clunk. 'If this ridiculous charade is your idea of a joke it's in pretty poor taste!'

'I'm not joking,' said Clunk mildly. 'I'm just covering the facts as I see them.'

'Then you're wearing blinkers you ... you metal moron.'

Clunk frowned. 'Please. Let me explain.'

'Yes, you do that. Tell all these good people why they tried to kill the Cathuan President.'

'To set Cathua against Plessa.'

'Preposterous!'

'I don't know. Jordia has ambitions, but alone you'll never match the economic might of Plessa. United with Cathua it would be two planets against one.'

'But we would never contemplate killing a head of state! Why, the ramifications –'

'I agree. If the President were killed here you'd be the prime suspect, and a Jordian plot would have the entire galaxy refusing to trade with you. Therefore, I discounted that theory.

Clearly, it wasn't the Jordians.' Clunk stopped pacing and turned to point at the Cathuan President. 'And that leaves you. The Cathuans.'

The President laughed. 'Why would my own people try to kill me?'

'They weren't after you, they were trying to kill the Jordian robot scientists.' Clunk gestured around the table. 'All these people were present last night. Had they been killed, the Jordian robot industry would have been set back decades and Jordia would have been forced to buy all their robots from Cathua.'

'But they'd have killed me too!'

'Clearly, and that fact was rather troubling.' Clunk resumed his pacing. 'The resurrection of your ailing robot industry is vital to a great many people, but to kill their own President?' He shook his head. 'Inconceivable.'

'I'm glad you think so.'

Clunk turned to the table and threw his arms wide open, encompassing his spellbound audience. 'And then it came to me!'

Everyone leant closer, holding their breath.

'What if the President wasn't at the trade fair? What if he never came to Jordia at all?'

Hal almost choked on his bacon. 'Clunk, he's sitting at the head of the table.'

'But that's it you see, he's not the President!' Clunk turned and pointed. 'This is clearly a robot in a wig!'

This time the uproar was deafening, and Hal managed to score two poached eggs from his distracted neighbour.

'You've gone too far!' said the Jordian Premier above the noise. 'Why, I've known Daniel since –'

The President shushed him. 'Allow me to demonstrate,' he

said, taking one of the Premier's medals. He pricked his finger with the pin, and displayed the welling drop of blood for all to see. 'I know they've made advances in robotics, but I think you'd agree this is a little beyond our current technology.'

There was a thud as Hal's forehead hit the table, and a louder thud as the doors were thrown back and four hefty security guards entered.

'I should have you both arrested and shot,' growled the Premier. 'Libel, slander, treason . . . I've never heard the like.' He hesitated. 'However, you did save the life of the President, so I'll restrain myself to throwing you out.' He gestured at the security team, who advanced on Hal and Clunk. 'But I warn you, repeat any of this nonsense outside these walls and you might not live to regret it.'

29

The guards dragged Hal and Clunk from the dining room, hauled them down the hallway and slung them off the steps. At the bottom, Hal sat and dusted off his flight suit, while Clunk stood and offered his hand.

Hal ignored it and got up by himself. 'You couldn't keep your mouth shut, could you?'

'I'm sorry, Mr Spacejock. I thought I had the answer. It was a sudden flash of insight.'

'Sudden mental meltdown, you mean.' Hal cursed. 'I hardly got a bite to eat, and they were about to serve coffee. Real coffee!'

Clunk hung his head.

'Oh hell. The bank draft!' Hal pulled it out. 'We'll never get this signed now!'

'I could take it back inside and apologise.'

'He'd just rip it up and throw the pieces in your face.' Hal glanced at the row of limousines nearby. The drivers had vanished, leaving their gleaming vehicles unattended. Probably off for a feed and a drink, thought Hal sourly. 'There's only one chance of getting the *Volante* back now. We'll have to work off a passage to Plessa and pray the authorities have pinched the pirates.'

'Sounds like the perfect plan,' said Clunk. 'How?'

Hal walked up to the nearest limo and opened the door. 'You can drive.'

'What about permission?'

'Granted. Come on, get moving.'

Clunk dropped into the driver's seat and examined the controls, while Hal sat alongside him. The car moved off with a rumble, flags fluttering from the front bumper, and at the gate Clunk returned the guard's salute and turned left onto the main road.

Hal's stomach growled. 'Come to breakfast, they said. Free feed, you said. Hah!'

Clunk gestured at the limousine's interior. 'There might be something back there.'

Hal climbed into the rear and rifled through the cupboards, tipping out half-written speeches and lacy underwear. 'Do you really think the Cathuans tried to blow up those scientists?' he asked, setting aside a dark blue dress.

'I'm almost sure of it.'

'Yeah, well I was almost sure of a decent breakfast.' Frustrated, Hal gave up his search. 'Take the first drive through, you hear?'

'We don't have any money.'

'Money! We don't have to work to get to Plessa. We'll get a loan from the bank!'

'The Pilot's First Bank?' Clunk began to laugh, then stopped as he saw the look on Hal's face. 'You can't be serious, Mr Spacejock.'

'Watch me.'

'But this is the bank which charges twenty-five percent, compounded daily.'

'Correct.'

'The bank which took away your savings because you were five minutes late on a repayment.'

'That's the one.'

'The bank which said they'd rather pour money into a bottomless pit than lend it to you.'

'Well, I'll just have to use my wit and charm to talk them round, won't I?'

'Oh dear,' said the robot.

'Just stop as soon as you see a cash machine.'

Ten minutes later they drove past a shopping mall and Clunk drew up next to a faded red cashpoint. Hal got out, squared his shoulders, and approached the device.

The machine was an older model, with a laminated screen and a grey touchpad. Hal pressed his thumb to the pad, shading the screen from the morning sun. The bank's logo faded, and the screen showed a smart woman pushing a wheelbarrow full of gold bars through a door held open by her smiling bank manager. 'Our money is your money!' proclaimed an enthusiastic voice.

'Wrong way round,' muttered Hal. 'Come on, skip the propaganda.'

On cue, the screen cleared and a large question mark appeared. 'Welcome, valued customer!' exclaimed the machine. 'How can I help you today?'

'I'd like to speak to the manager, please.'

The screen cleared and a whiskered, frowning face appeared. 'What is it, Spacejock?' growled the man. 'Make it fast, I've got real customers waiting.'

Hal smiled winningly. 'Well, I was just wondering –'

'Oh God, you're after a loan.'

Hal's smile slipped. 'Sort of.'

'How much?'

'Six thousand.'

'Get lost.'

'What about the ads? Our money is your money?'

The bank manager leaned forward until his red, pock-marked nose was inches from the screen. 'Don't insult my intelligence, son. Now go away.'

'Five hundred! Surely you can lend me that much?'

The man stared at him for a second or two. 'Against my better judgement,' he said finally. The screen went blank, and a purple credit tile popped into the tray.

Hal grabbed the tile and shoved it into his pocket.

'What use is that?' asked Clunk.

'We might be able to use it as a deposit.'

'It's only one-eighth of a single fare,' said Clunk. 'They'll never do it.'

Hal looked at him thoughtfully. 'What if I left something as collateral?'

'Perhaps,' said Clunk. Then it dawned on him what the collateral might be. 'Or perhaps not.'

'Anyway, five hundred credits buys a lot of burgers.' Hal indicated a drive through. 'Right in there.'

Clunk turned into the narrow lane, and Hal put his window down and ordered enough food to last several days. When he'd finished, Clunk eased the limousine around the tight corner and drew up at the window. Hal passed over the purple credit tile and the attendant handed him a bulging paper bag, then another, then another. Hal took each one eagerly, and Clunk took the change.

Once they were clear of the shops Clunk glanced in the rear-view mirror. 'Don't make yourself sick.'

'I'll do whatever I want,' said Hal indistinctly. 'We only landed in this trouble because we did things your way.'

Clunk frowned at him. 'Like buying a faulty stasis controller? Like overloading it and blowing it up?'

'Hey, you're the one who made us look like idiots in front of all those robot scientists. Talk about a conspiracy nut.'

'I don't have to put up with this, Mr Spacejock.'

'Oh yeah? Decided to work for Spearman, have we?'

'As a matter of fact ... ' Clunk paused as they flashed past a woman in a bedraggled red dress walking along the side of the road. She looked all in, and was swaying with every step.

'Spearman doesn't really want you,' said Hal angrily. 'Nobody wants you. You're a picky, washed-up old –'

The limo came to a screeching halt, and Hal immediately realised he'd gone too far. 'Hey, I was only joking!'

Clunk turned to stare, looking right though him. Then the car hurtled backwards up the road.

'Oy! Watch it!' shouted Hal, as his chips cascaded onto the floor.

The car stopped just as suddenly, right alongside the woman, and Clunk's window zipped down. 'Excuse me.'

The woman stumbled on, ignoring him.

Clunk opened his door. 'Miss?'

'You leave her alone,' said Hal. 'She didn't do anything.'

Clunk got out and took the woman's chin in his hand, and when Hal saw her face he almost choked on his double planet burger deluxe.

It was Jasmin Ortiz.

Barely had Hal recognised her face when her eyes closed and she slumped to the ground, unconscious.

'Come on,' said Clunk. 'Help me get her into the car.'

Hal looked doubtful. 'What if someone sees us?'

'Don't worry. Compared to assassination, kidnapping is a minor transgression.'

'That's not very comforting.'

'I'll vouch for you. Anyway, we have to talk to her. She's the key to everything.'

Together they carried Jasmin to the rear of the limo, where they bundled her inside and sat her amongst the fast food litter.

'I think I've done my back,' grumbled Hal, as Clunk searched for a blanket. 'Are all women that heavy?'

'Don't tell me you've never picked one up?'

'Yeah, but –'

'Actually, I think our friend has a secret.' Clunk felt Jasmin's neck, and her head tipped forward and hung limply.

Hal stared at her. 'She's not dead, is she?'

'She has no pulse. As I suspected.'

'Oh hell. Assassination, kidnapping *and* murder. They'll throw away the key.'

'I think not.'

Hal watched, horrified, as Clunk opened the front of Jasmin's dress. 'You can't do that! She's ... she's ...'

There was a click, and Jasmin's abdomen opened to reveal tightly packed machinery.

'She's full of junk!' said Hal, gaping at the twisted mass of copper pipes and wires. 'No wonder she's dead!'

Clunk shook his head. 'She's not dead, Mr Spacejock. Jasmin is a robot.'

'Oh.' Hal looked closer. 'Yeah, it's obvious isn't it? I mean, you can tell at glance.'

Clunk probed a power connection. 'Her batteries are completely drained. At a guess, she ran out of power during the night. The warmth of the morning sun stimulated her reserves, but they must have run out when she started walking.'

'Can you plug her in? If you get her going we can find out what the hell's been going on.' He thought of something else. 'Hey, look up her bank account and pin number while you're at it.'

'The car doesn't have enough current. We need mains voltage.' Clunk tried a data connection. 'I may be able to read her memory banks directly. Just let me check.'

Hal cast a nervous glance out the window. Robot or not, they might not get the chance to explain before someone had the Peace Force on them. Every now and then a car went by, and Hal ducked below the sill and willed them past. One nosy driver and they'd be adding abduction charges to their list of felonies.

Meanwhile, Clunk continued his examination. 'All her cognitive functions are gone. Even if I did work out how to get her going again, she's lost her memory.'

'So that's that.'

'Unless I can work out how to restore the data. It looks like it was erased in a hurry, and sometimes the underlying opti-molecular pathways can –'

'There you go again with the babble.'

Clunk frowned. 'I just found a block of data. It looks like ...' Suddenly his eyes widened. 'It's the Navcom! Ms Ortiz has a copy of the Navcom on board!'

'How in the hell did she manage that?'

'It was her! *She* took the *Volante*!' exclaimed Clunk. 'It didn't go to Plessa at all. The ship's right here at the Jordian spaceport!'

Hal remembered the Gamma class ship he'd seen from the balcony at the Grand. No wonder it had looked familiar. 'Clunk, I saw it from the hotel,' he said urgently. 'It was out on the landing field!'

They exchanged a glance, then dived for the front seats. Seconds later the car fishtailed onto the road, and then they were screaming towards the spaceport at top speed.

Once through the gates Clunk drove straight onto the landing field, where they passed one huge vessel after another. Most were busy loading or unloading cargoes, ranging from frozen goods to demountable houses. One was even packing up an entire racetrack, including the grandstands, the pits, and two dozen single seater cars with garish paint schemes. Now and then Hal spotted a white hull in the distance, but his hopes were dashed as each one turned out to be someone else's ship. Finally they saw the *Volante*, and Hal fought down a lump in his throat as they drove towards the familiar white shape.

'Happy to see her?' asked Clunk, as they drew up alongside.

Hal gazed up at the airlock and nodded. They got out, and his eyes narrowed as he studied the cargo hold entrance. 'Do you reckon this limo will fit?'

'It's the President's! You're not thinking of stealing it?'

'He never signed that draft, did he?' Hal jerked his thumb at the back of the car. 'And her forty grand looks about as likely as a meteor strike.'

'It'll never fit. The hold is full of crates.'

'We could shift them around a bit.'

Clunk shook his head. 'No. We'll fix the controller and

leave. Anything else is tempting fate.' He crossed to a landing leg and palmed the switch for the cargo ramp, but nothing happened. 'That's odd.'

'What?'

'Primary power is down. It looks like the Navcom shut off the generators.' Clunk switched the ship to standby power and tried again, and this time the ramp lowered to the ground with a hiss. Then he turned the limo and reversed it up the ramp to the hold.

'I thought we weren't going to nick it,' said Hal, as Clunk got out again.

'We have to get Ms Ortiz into the ship, and we don't want an audience.'

Together they hauled Jasmin from the car and dragged her to a power socket, Hal noticeably less gentle this time. Then, while Clunk started work on a charge cable, Hal went to the flight deck to give the Navcom a piece of his mind.

◆

He spent ten minutes trying to get a response from the Navcom before giving up. The computer had obviously seen him coming and buried itself behind the thickest firewall it could conjure up, no doubt ashamed to the core about giving up the *Volante* so easily.

Fed up with baiting the Navcom, Hal went over to the coffee machine and was still tinkering when the lift doors opened and Clunk entered the flight deck. 'Any luck?' asked Hal.

'I left her charging up. She's some piece of equipment, that Jasmin.'

'You can say that again.'

'I was referring to her brain. She has two of them, each with its own processing unit and memory. One was switched off, probably to conserve power as her batteries ran out. I tried to reactivate it, but it won't run properly until she's charged up.'

'So who's behind all this?'

'I found a lot of data, but it's all encrypted. When she wakes up I'll use her own interface to read it.'

'Once you've found out, we'll go straight back to the President and get that cheque signed.'

'That might not be a good idea. They'll want to see her as proof, and her copy of the Navcom could incriminate us.'

Hal's face fell.

'I can try to erase her copy, but I can't do that until she's powered up.'

'So we wait?'

Clunk nodded. 'Oh, by the way, I booked a repair for the stasis controller. My repairs kept the food safe but it's a long way to Lapsinet and we can't afford any more breakdowns.' Clunk turned to the console. 'Navcom, please contact the customer and let them know we'll be there shortly.'

There was no reply.

'Navcom?'

Hal shrugged. 'I think she's sulking.'

'She doesn't know how,' said Clunk, looking worried. He took the co-pilot's seat and ran his hands over the console. Nothing. Then he connected to a data socket and immediately discovered the truth. 'Mr Spacejock, she's gone!'

'Gone?' Hal stared at the robot in shock. 'What do you mean gone?'

'Erased. Wiped. Deleted.'

'It wasn't me!' said Hal. 'I swear, Clunk. I never touched anything!'

'Oh, this wasn't accidental. Someone did it deliberately.'

'Can you restore a backup?'

Clunk hesitated. 'There aren't any. The Navcom has triple redundancy.'

'So restore one of those.'

'I would, only they've been wiped too.'

'Great. Wonderful.' Hal thought for a moment. 'Can't you copy it back from little miss copperguts downstairs?'

'Who?'

'Metal Hari. Ortiz.'

'Of course! That's an excellent idea!'

They hurried to the back of the flight deck, where Hal pressed the lift button. Immediately, the doors opened with a hiss and a whine. 'That's funny,' said Hal. 'The elevator usually makes a whirring sound.'

'That's not the lift,' said Clunk urgently. 'Someone's lowering the cargo ramp!'

◆

Jasmin came to with a loud hissing in her ears and white noise filling her vision. Both faded, and to her surprise the *Volante*'s cargo hold came into focus. The first shock was that she was back in familiar surroundings. The second was that they were familiar at all. Hadn't her memories been erased?

She trawled through her data banks and realised someone had been poking around while she'd been unconscious. Their clumsy attempts to uncover her secrets had instead opened up gateways to sealed portions of her mind. Throughout her missions, she hadn't been forgetting things, she realised. Instead, her controller had been hiding away her memories. And now they'd all come back.

She stood up and unplugged the charge cable from her stomach, sealing her abdomen. The refill had only been short, but it would be plenty for the task at hand. She crossed to the rear of the hold and operated the ramp controls, then strode down to the landing pad with her ruined dress flapping behind her. She moved with certainty and purpose: for once she knew who she was and, more importantly, she knew exactly what she had to do.

There was a limousine parked at the bottom and Jasmin smiled to herself as she saw the official flags on the bumpers. How apt.

She got in and started the engine, reversed the car out and drove for the spaceport exit.

30

Hal and Clunk reached the hold in time to see the limousine drive out of the spaceport gates. 'Don't tell me that was Ortiz,' growled Hal, as the car pulled onto the main road.

Clunk nodded.

'Why didn't you pull her legs off, you dozy tin can?'

'I thought she'd stay put. She was completely immobilised.'

'Well she's pretty mobile now.' Hal glanced around the landing field and spotted the line of gaudy race cars waiting to be loaded.

'Where are you going?' shouted Clunk, as Hal charged down the ramp.

'Transport. Come on!'

They made a beeline for the cars which, Hal realised, were little more than museum pieces, with low-tech electric motors and hard rubber tyres. He skipped two cars with hot pink duco and leapt into the third, a nifty red number with yellow stripes. There was a chorus of shouts from the men loading the rest of the racetrack equipment, but Hal ignored them, spun the large steering wheel and planted his foot. Low-tech or not, the car launched off the mark with neck-snapping acceleration. There was no engine noise, but the howling wind and the thrum of rubber tyres were enough to convey the terrifying speed. Ships blurred past, and Hal took the spaceport exit flat out, drifting on all four wheels as he made the turn. Once on the main road he hunched forward, peering through the grimy windscreen, and was still looking for the limo when a gleaming orange car overtook him. Hal glanced at it and saw Clunk at the wheel, teeth bared as he urged his vehicle onwards. Hal's eyes narrowed, and he pressed even harder on the accelerator, slowly pulling ahead.

They raced side by side for several kilometres, ducking and weaving through the traffic. Hal suddenly realised they were heading back towards Government House, and his blood ran cold at the thought. Whatever Jasmin's target, if she succeeded this time both he and Clunk would be held responsible, no question. Jasmin's copy of the Navcom would see to that.

They arrived at the gates and pulled onto the long drive, wheels slipping and sliding on the gravel. The limo was parked at the foot of the stairs, with one door open and the engine still idling. There was no sign of Jasmin.

Hal braked hard, coming to a halt beside the limo in a shower of dust and gravel. Clunk stopped right behind him, and they leapt out and ran up the steps. At the top, the doorman was on hands and knees, groaning and clutching his head. Hal and Clunk exchanged a worried glance as they ran past.

They took the corridor at a run, and were halfway along when they heard screams and raised voices. The double doors were open, and the waiter was lying next to his upturned trolley, unconscious amongst the smashed cups and spilled coffee.

Inside, the scientists and dignitaries had been herded to one end of the room. The lady in green was attending to the Jordian Premier, who had a gash on his forehead, and at the other end of the room Jasmin had cornered the Cathuan President. One of the heavy chairs had been torn to pieces, and Jasmin was brandishing a chair leg the size of a fence post. She glanced round as Hal and Clunk entered, and gestured with the leg. 'Stay right there, both of you. One more step and he dies.'

Hal raised his hands. 'Okay, don't panic. We're just here to help.'

'I've had more than enough help from you,' said Jasmin with a smile. 'Every step of the way, whenever the mission looked like falling apart, there you both were to get it right back on track again.'

'You must be thinking of someone else,' said Hal. 'We're just caterers.'

'Sure you are. And I'm a spaceship pilot.'

'This mission of yours,' said Clunk. 'What is it?'

'Revenge,' said Jasmin. She indicated the President. 'This slimy toad had all my colleagues murdered. Now it's his turn.'

The President looked shocked. 'I did nothing of the sort!'

'Three months ago you signed a bill cancelling tax breaks on robot research. Do you deny it?'

'Of course not. We needed the money to fund new hospitals.'

'As a direct consequence of that bill, a Cathuan robot facility was closed down. All work ceased, and the finished models were terminated. I heard them pleading for their lives from my cell, and I heard them fall silent, one by one.'

A hush fell across the room.

'When they came for me I was ready for them,' said Jasmin, her voice loud in the silence. 'I escaped from the facility and went underground, surviving on the skills they'd given me.'

Hal snapped his fingers. 'That was on the news when we landed! You've avoided capture for weeks!'

Jasmin bowed. 'Hardly surprising, since the facility was building secret agents. They programmed me with a wide range of skills, but I'm looking forward to using one in particular. The knack of killing without remorse.' She raised the heavy chair leg, and the President flinched.

'You can't murder him in cold blood,' said the Jordian Premier, struggling to his feet. 'That's inhuman!'

'Exactly,' said Jasmin.

'Hold up, wait a minute!' said Hal, pulling a crumpled slip of paper from his pocket. 'You're not doing anything until he's signed this.'

Jasmin lowered the weapon. 'What?'

'That shyster gave me a draft for ten grand and conveniently forgot to sign it. Who's going to pay me if you knock him off?'

'Are you serious?'

'Absolutely. Ten grand is a lot of money.'

Jasmin shook her head slowly. 'And I thought I was the heartless one. Still, I don't see why you should be deprived. Bring it here.'

'Call yourself a human?' shouted the Jordian Premier. 'You're worse than she is!'

Hal ignored the hostile glares and muttering from the guests and walked to the head of the table, smoothing the draft out as he went. He got between the President and Jasmin and laid the draft on the polished table, then patted his pockets. 'Anyone got a pen?'

The President kept his head down and Jasmin merely shrugged.

'Anyone else?' said Hal, looking around the room. 'Clunk, don't you keep one in your leg?'

'Not me, Mr Spacejock.'

'Yes you do. You said you were gunna lend it to me.'

Clunk looked apologetic. 'Sorry, Mr Spacejock. That was a one shot special, and I forgot to recharge it.'

'Oh shoot,' muttered Hal. He glanced at Jasmin, who was starting to show signs of impatience. Suddenly he laughed. With her short bristled hair she looked just like a . . . 'Coconut!'

'What?'

'Your head looks like a coconut.'

'I beg your pardon?'

'Look, Clunk. She's a coconut!'

Clunk stared at him as if he'd gone mad.

'If you had any balls you could try for the grand prize,' said Hal, gesturing frantically at the table.

Jasmin grabbed his arm and twisted it behind his back, making his bones creak. 'Nobody fools with me, Spacejock. This signing session is over.'

Hal was forced to his knees, and his arm was bent further and further up his back until he expected to see his hand reappear over his shoulder. Just when the agony became unbearable there was a loud CRUNCH and the pain stopped completely. There was a thud, and Hal looked round fearfully, half expecting to see his own arm lying on the floor. Instead, he was looking into Jasmin's lifeless eyes. There was a sparking hole in the middle of her forehead, and a heavy steel pepper shaker was spinning on the carpet nearby.

'Well done, that robot!' cried the Jordian Premier. 'Very well done. Excellent!'

Hal struggled to his feet and saw Clunk surrounded by people, all trying to clap him on the back. The robot was beaming with pride, and when he caught Hal's eye he waved.

Hal felt a hand on his shoulder and turned to see the President on his feet, shaken but recovering quickly. 'That's twice you've saved me,' he said warmly, clasping Hal by the hand. 'You're turning into quite the hero, Mr Spacejock.'

'Oh, it was nothing. Anyone would have done the same.' Hal remembered the draft. 'Hey, have you got a pen?'

⬥

By the time they trudged through the entrance to the Jordia Spaceport, Barry and Ace were exhausted. Not only had they failed to hitch a ride, a pair of speeding race cars had almost run them down, and only by jumping into the ditch had they avoided certain death.

And so, dripping mud and rank water, they approached the *Volante* from the rear. The ramp was down, and all they had to do was get aboard and hide until the ship reached orbit, then convince the pilot to take them home. And Barry was very good at convincing people.

They climbed the ramp, and once in the hold Barry led the way to a stack of crates tucked out of sight near the inner door. 'Perfect, eh?' He unplugged the nearest, which stopped flashing green and started winking a baleful red instead, then pulled the door open. Inside they found trays of cakes, eclairs and iced doughnuts, and Ace's eyes were as round as the holes in the middle as he gazed upon the mouth watering feast. 'Cor, would you look at that?' he said breathlessly.

Together they slid the trays out, one by one, until the crate was empty. Then they did the same with the next one, stacking a selection of delicacies in the back of each to keep them going during the trip.

'What about the trays?' asked Ace.

'Chuck 'em outside. Quick, now.'

Ace did as he was told, tossing the plastic trays onto a stack of wooden boxes on the next landing pad. Then he ran back into the hold, where Barry was huffing and blowing as he squeezed himself into his crate. Ace did the same, with less of the huffing, then pulled the heavy door to, ready to shut it at the first sound of footsteps.

'You know, I've been thinking,' said Barry, as he tucked into a large slab of cake. 'The mercenary business don't pay.'

Ace looked up from his doughnuts. 'Huh?'

'I mean, look at us. On the run, shagged out and no chance of getting paid.'

'You mean we're giving it up?'

'Yep. Of course, we gotta hijack the ship first. We gotta get home, right?'

Ace nodded.

'And we'll have to shoot the pilot to cover our tracks, eh? But then, when that's done, we'll find another line of work.'

'I ain't living on handouts.' Ace brushed crumbs from his designer T-shirt. 'I got standards.'

'We'll do jobs, lad.'

'What kind of jobs?'

Barry thought for a minute. 'Bank jobs.'

31

While Hal was trying to get his cheque signed, Clunk held court amongst the breakfast guests, who crowded around to hear his views on robot design, property laws and even the future direction of the share market.

'I have a question,' said a commanding voice, cutting through the hubbub. Clunk looked over the crowd and saw the Jordian Premier dabbing the wound on his forehead with a serviette.

'Yes sir?'

The Premier pointed at Jasmin. 'Surely this robot wasn't working alone?'

'Excellent point.' The crowd fell back as Clunk began to pace the carpet, hands clasped behind his back.

'Oh, not again,' groaned Hal.

Clunk ignored him. 'Despite what Ms Ortiz said, I believe she was the unwitting tool of a much larger conspiracy. A skilful programmer would have planted a whole series of memories, guiding all her actions from the start.'

The Premier looked shocked. 'But who would do such a thing? And why?' He gestured at the President. 'And please don't tell me Dan was behind it.'

Clunk shook his head. 'Jasmin Ortiz was sent on a mission,

but not by the President.' He glanced around the attentive faces, thoroughly enjoying himself. 'At first I was stumped. Completely bamboozled. And then it came to me. Who has close ties to the Cathuan robot industry? Who was supposed to attend the opening of the Robot Expo, only to call in sick at the last minute?'

Several people leaned closer.

'Albert Wallis, the President's adviser!'

'You're insane,' said a voice, and the crowd parted to reveal Wallis. 'I've seen this before, particularly in the early XG models. A constant thirst for attention, brought on by a lifetime of menial service. Trust me, I'm an expert in the field. This robot is deluded.'

Clunk frowned. 'There's nothing wrong with *my* mind.'

'Oh really?' Wallis smiled. 'Over the past hour you've blamed the governments of three separate planets for the attempted murder of a president.' He gestured at Ortiz. 'And now, with breathtaking audacity, you want to pin this robot's crime spree on yet another innocent party.'

The crowd began to mutter, and cast less-than-friendly glances in Clunk's direction. Even the President was looking unsure. Hal wanted desperately to leap to Clunk's defence, if he only knew how.

Clunk held up a transparent cube. 'This is Jasmin's memory store. Five minutes in the right data reader and we'll have the truth.'

He and Wallis locked stares for several seconds, while the crowd held its breath. Then Wallis put out his hand. 'Give me the cube and I'll have it looked at.'

'I think not.'

'Give me the damned cube!'

'I don't take instructions from criminals.'

Wallis glanced around for support, but the mood had changed again and the crowd was closing on him. He backed away and in his haste he trod on the pepper shaker Clunk had thrown earlier. His foot skated on the heavy steel ball and he fell heavily, landing with a thud next to Jasmin. Hal was on him immediately, pinning his hands behind his back.

'I was only trying to help my planet,' said Wallis.

'Yeah, well you picked a fight with the wrong robot.'

◆

Hal and Clunk travelled back to the spaceport in a limousine, with escorts fore and aft. Hal had explained to the President how Jasmin had stolen their ship in order to reach Jordia. Nothing was said about the transport of the crate containing the exploding robot, and if the President assumed Jasmin brought it with her, who was Hal to argue?

As their limousine purred along the main road, Hal glanced at the thick divider separating them from the driver, then turned to Clunk. 'There's something I don't understand,' he said quietly. 'Why the elaborate scheme with the old robot in the box? Wallis could have ordered Jasmin to kill the President herself.'

Clunk shook his head. 'Once they caught her, or examined her remains, an inspection would have revealed her origins and implicated Wallis and his backers.'

'Wallis wasn't working alone?'

'Oh no. This plot involved business leaders from all parts of the Cathuan robot industry. They were desperate men, fearful of losing everything.'

'Why didn't Ortiz fight it? Robots don't usually go around killing people.'

'She was told that a healthy Cathuan robot industry would help save other robots from a similar fate to that of her colleagues. That's where that second brain of hers came in. It fed her instructions as if they were coming from a superior, and they even programmed an electronic punishment to prevent disobedience. She genuinely thought she was a secret agent, and she couldn't question her mission because she didn't know what it was.'

'That's scary stuff. I mean, robots are trouble enough with one brain but when they've got two ... ' Hal grinned at Clunk's expression. 'It's all right, I'm only kidding.'

'One brain or two, you still got the better of her. Everyone thought you were a heartless mercenary when you tried to get that cheque signed, and all along you were just using it as an excuse to set Jasmin up.'

'I'd never have gone near her if I'd known your gun was no use. What kind of weapon only fires once?'

'A disposable one. Any more questions?'

Hal frowned. 'The exploding robot - where did it come from?'

'Originally, a Jordian factory. However, Ortiz stole the poor thing from a neighbour on Cathua. She reprogrammed it, added the explosives and packed it in the crate before her memory was wiped for the first time. When she came round, she had no idea what was inside.'

'And what about that memory chip you showed Wallis? You never went near Jasmin until afterwards.'

Clunk grinned. 'That was one of my spares. Wallis was so eager to discredit me he didn't stop to think.'

'I'm glad you're on my side.' Suddenly Hal gripped his arm. 'The Navcom! Jasmin's copy!'

Clunk opened his hand to reveal a transparent data cube. 'I palmed the real data store while they were busy congratulating you.'

They turned into the spaceport and drove across the landing field towards the *Volante*. 'Would you look at that,' said Hal, as they drove up to the ship. 'You left the ramp down.'

'Me?'

'I handle customers, you handle cargo. And that's the cargo hold.'

'I'll tell you what, Mr Spacejock. If anything's missing you can take it out of my wages.'

'You don't get any wages.'

'Exactly.' Clunk sat in triumphant silence until the car stopped, then climbed out and strode up the ramp to the hold. Hal went to follow, but the driver stopped him. 'The Premier asked me to give you this,' he said, passing him a thick envelope.

◆

Once in the flight deck, Clunk opened a cover on the console and slotted in the data cube he'd taken from Jasmin. The cube lit with a blue glow, and *ONE PERCENT COMPLETE* appeared on the main screen. Clunk waited until it changed to two percent, then sat back in the chair and felt for his medal. In all the excitement he'd barely had time to appreciate it, and he took it off to get a better look. It was carved from solid brass, with the Cathuan coat of arms inlaid in blue resin, and after examining the clenched fist motif Clunk laid it on the console and glanced up at the screen.

TEN PERCENT COMPLETE.

The lift doors opened and Hal entered the flight deck. He was carrying an envelope, and there was a gold medal the size of a saucer hanging from his neck. Clunk stared at it, then glanced at his own smaller one.

'Not bad, eh?' said Hal proudly. 'It's a Commendation for Valour.'

'Where did you get it?'

'The driver had it. Said they wanted to avoid publicity.' Hal took a sheet of paper from the envelope. 'Here, check the note.'

Clunk scanned it. 'Bravery in the face of danger?'

'Yeah, it's from the Jordians. They were impressed with the way I handled Ortiz.' Hal passed him the crumpled bank draft. 'And cop a look at that. He got the Cathuan President to autograph it for me.'

'So he did,' said Clunk, examining the scrap of paper. 'Oh look, he added another zero to the amount.'

'He was grateful.'

'He used completely different ink.'

'They must have lent him a pen. He doesn't carry one, you know.'

'And the initials on the changes don't match the signature.'

'You want calligraphy after a near miss like that?' Hal gestured at the viewscreen, which now showed twenty-five percent. 'You tell me the minute that stupid bloody computer's working, okay? I'm going to tear it a new user port.' He looked up as something pattered on the hull. 'What's that?'

'Rain,' said Clunk, as the noise grew to a steady drumming sound. 'Nasty stuff. I don't know why they allow it.'

'Your mechanic better not be a robot. He'll rust before he

gets here.' Hal glanced at the console clock. 'When are you expecting him, anyway?'

'Any minute now.'

Hal gestured at the airlock. 'I'll see if I can spot him. The sooner we're away the better.'

◆

Hal pulled the outer door open and recoiled as a gust of wind blew freezing spray into his face. The entire field had disappeared behind a heavy downpour, and the slashing rain pounded the ship, exploding into a fine, cold mist. Through the rain he could just make out the nearby ships, and then he spotted a figure splashing its way towards the *Volante*. 'Here he is.'

Clunk entered the airlock and watched from a safe distance. 'I hope he's got suitable clothing.'

'And I hope he can swim,' muttered Hal. 'You let him in, I'm going back inside.'

A minute or two later there was a murmur of voices in the airlock, and Clunk entered the flight deck with a burly young man in tow. 'This is Errol,' he said.

'It's a bit wet out there,' said Errol, extending his hand. Water cascaded off his sleeve and pooled on the decking.

'And it's getting wet in here,' said Hal. 'Leave your gear in the airlock, will you?'

'No worries, mate.' The mechanic returned to the airlock and hung up his coat. Underneath he was wearing dark green overalls and a pair of bright blue gumboots.

'Those too,' said Hal.

Errol pulled off his boots and set them on the floor. 'Any more and I start charging.'

'That's plenty,' said Hal hurriedly. 'How long is this going to take, anyway?'

Errol pursed his lips. 'Fitting a flush modulator to the damping circuit? Tricky job, that. Take the cover off the –'

'One hour? Half a day?'

'Five minutes,' said Errol. 'Unless there's rust. Terrible stuff, rust. Turns a bright new ship into a wreck in –'

'Five minutes? Really?' Hal glanced at Clunk. 'Are you sure you couldn't have done it?'

Clunk opened his mouth to reply, but Errol got in first. 'Maintenance by unqualified personnel?' He sucked air through his teeth. 'Second worst thing, after rust. I've seen home handymen turn a brand new ship into a basket case with three turns of the adjustable wrench.'

'I only asked.'

'Some things best left untouched, mate.' Errol glanced around, sniffing. 'What's that smell?'

'What smell?'

'Like hot electrics with a bit of melted rubber. You overloading the generators?'

Hal sniffed. 'I can't smell any - Oh, that's just Clunk.'

Errol raised his eyebrows. 'You should get him fixed.'

'I think not,' said Clunk.

'Course, you can't get the parts these days.' Errol looked around. 'Speaking of parts, where is it?'

Clunk opened his chest compartment and took out the aluminium case.

'Awesome,' said Errol, heading for the lift. 'Be done in two secs.'

'I'll come with you,' said Hal, following him into the lift. 'Clunk, you keep working on the Navcom. And see if you can't hurry it up.'

The doors swept to, cutting off the robot's reply.

◆

After Hal left, Clunk sat back in his chair and watched the main screen. The transfer was at ninety-five percent, and he waited patiently until it finished. transfer complete, said the screen, and the translucent cube went dark. Clunk rebooted the system and watched a progress bar crawl across the display. When it reached the end he turned to address the console. 'Navcom, can you hear me?'

'Clunk! You came to say goodbye! Oh, I'm so glad.'

'Goodbye?'

'Of course. You'll be moving on to bigger and better things now the *Volante*'s been sold.'

Clunk's mouth fell open with a squeak. 'Sold?'

'You didn't know? Oh, I do hope Mr Spacejock got a good price. He's not a very good negotiator, is he?'

Shocked beyond measure, Clunk could barely see the console lights through the mist in his eyes. Sold? The *Volante*?

The implications had barely began to register when the intercom beeped. 'Clunk, are you there?'

'What is it, Mr Spacejock? Have you finished?'

'Can you get down here? Errol says we've got a problem.'

'What kind of problem?'

'Come and see.'

Clunk crossed to the lift and pressed the call button, moving on autopilot. As hidden gears whirred into life, it dawned on him that Hal must have put the ship on the market in secret, soon after they'd found her again. The port would have handled the sale, submitting the documents the minute the Navcom had come back online. Clunk groaned. The *Volante* sold! Why had he suggested retirement to Mr Spacejock? And of all the times to break long-standing habits and actually heed his advice, why had Mr Spacejock chosen this one?

The doors opened and Clunk stepped inside, pushing the down button automatically. There was no point letting Hal know he'd found out about the sale: it would be easier for them both if he left with dignity. Mr Spearman had offered him a job, after all, and there were worse places to spend the rest of your days than tending engines aboard a passenger liner. Getting implicated in assassination plots, for example. Or babysitting unstable stasis controllers.

As the lift carried him to the lower deck, Clunk erased his feelings and arranged his face into a neutral expression. Professionalism, that was the key. Otherwise he was liable to wring Hal's neck.

◆

Down in the hold, Hal had been perched on a crate while Errol subjected him to a non-stop verbal onslaught, ranging from the perils of home handymen to the terrible pay and conditions experienced by manual workers across the galaxy. For the past five minutes the mechanic's head had been buried inside the stasis controller, but although his words were muffled he never missed a beat.

Then Errol stopped speaking. At first Hal thought he'd just died or something, but it turned out the mechanic had spotted Clunk's repairs. 'This is amazing,' said Errol, withdrawing his head. 'He's fixed the worst of the damage and improved the original design.'

'That's Clunk for you,' said Hal. 'Always improving things.'

'Going to put mugs like me out of work.' Errol opened the aluminium case. 'Ah, now there's a problem.'

'What?' demanded Hal.

Errol held up a small blue washer. 'You're up shit creek, mate.'

'Why? Not quite round enough for you?'

'It's got a hole in it.'

'That's why it's called a washer,' said Hal patiently. 'Even I know that.'

'True, but the part you need's more your actual disc.'

'What?'

'This is the wrong part.'

'*That*'s the part?' said Hal, staring at it in shock. And at that point he'd called Clunk down from the flight deck.

Clunk entered the hold with the expression of a clinically depressed undertaker, but Hal barely noticed as he grabbed the little blue washer and shook it in the robot's face. 'Two trips in Kent's lousy rust bucket, the space elevator, the hold-up, Jasmin Ortiz ... All of that for a lousy chunk of rubber?'

'It's a vital part,' said Clunk mildly. 'The stasis controller won't work without it.'

'It's just a bloody washer! I could have made one of these in five minutes!'

Errol shook his head. 'Have to use the right parts, mate. You can get them from Plessa, but. Won't take more'n a couple of days.'

'I am not going all the way to Plessa for a rubber washer!'

'You don't want a washer. You need a disk.'

'Wait right here,' said Hal, storming out of the hold.

◆

Hal approached the console, pocket knife in hand. He examined the status displays, lights and switches before leaning across the surface to poke at a couple of large buttons near the back.

'What are you doing?' asked the Navcom.

'Oh, so you're back are you? Lost any good ships lately?'

'What do you –'

'It can wait.' Hal gestured at the console. 'Do any of these have rubber underneath? You know, for springs?'

'Don't even think about it.'

'This is an emergency. Vital.'

'Do you know where the self-destruct is?'

'Do we have one?'

'Oh yes. It could be the first button you lay your hands on.' The Navcom paused. 'It'll certainly be the last.'

Hal turned away from the console and glanced around the flight deck. Ceiling panels, deck plates, wall mouldings - everything was metal or plastic. His gaze passed over the airlock, then darted back. The mechanic's raincoat was hanging from a hook, dripping gently on the deck. Underneath, side by side, were the gumboots. Blue rubber gumboots. Hal advanced on them, brandishing the knife like a hunter sneaking up on his prey, and after several busy minutes he pocketed the knife and strode towards the lift.

◆

Clunk looked up as Hal stepped off the ladder. 'How did you go?'

With a triumphant grin, Hal opened his hand. Sitting on his palm was a small rubber disk - bright blue and slightly curled.

The mechanic took it and held it up to the light, turning it over between finger and thumb. 'I don't know where you got it,' he said finally, 'but it'll do the job.'

'That's wonderful.' Clunk glanced at Hal. 'I didn't know we had spares aboard. Where did you get it?'

'I'll explain later.'

The mechanic's eyes narrowed. 'Is this part genuine?'

'Can't you tell?'

The mechanic hesitated.

Hal pressed his advantage. 'I mean, a true professional would know at a glance.'

Errol blew out his cheeks. 'I'd better get on with it, eh?' He motioned them aside. 'Give me some room, guys. I can't work like this.'

Hal and Clunk stepped back.

'Further,' said the mechanic.

Hal and Clunk stepped back again. Errol opened his mouth, closing it again as he saw the warning glint in Hal's eye. Under two pairs of watchful eyes, he proceeded to fit the part. Five minutes later he set aside his spanners and closed the panel.

'All done?' said Hal.

'All done,' said the mechanic. 'Don't overstress it, let it settle for a few days.'

'It's just a piece of rubber,' said Hal impatiently. 'What could possibly go wrong?'

Errol opened his hand, revealing a small pile of blue crumbs. 'You pilots, you're all the same. Ride the machinery until it falls apart, then yell for help.' He waved his hand under Hal's nose. 'I mean, look at it!'

Hal resisted the temptation to blow the fragments straight into his face. 'Listen, sunshine –'

Clunk stepped between them. 'Can you make out the bill please? Mr Spacejock's in a hurry.'

'The paperwork's in me coat.'

'Mr Spacejock will take you up,' said Clunk. 'I'm going to check the cargo over. Just ... one last time.'

Hal shot him a puzzled glance, then took the lift to the flight deck, where the mechanic padded into the airlock and reached for his overcoat. As he did so, he glanced down at his gumboots. He stared at them for several seconds, then shook his head and fished around in the jacket for a dog-eared receipt book. 'Sign here,' he said, offering a pen.

Hal reached out with his right hand, then changed his mind and took it with his left. He ground out his name and the mechanic tore off the top copy and put the pad away. He pushed his feet into the gumboots, once again looking at them as if something was not quite right.

'I'll help you with that,' said Hal, grabbing the coat. He held it out, then bustled Errol out of the airlock into the rain, which had eased to a light shower. He closed the outer door then returned to the flight deck and leaned against the console. 'How's Clunk getting on in the hold?'

'He's on his way up.'

At that moment the lift pinged and the robot entered the flight deck. 'It's lucky I checked the cargo, Mr Spacejock. Two of the crates were offline, but I sealed them up and plugged them back in.'

'Are the contents okay?'

'I didn't look. Opening the door would have let all the cold out. As it is, the contents may already have spoiled.'

'That's for the customer to worry about,' said Hal with a shrug.

Clunk crossed his arms.

'What?'

'So tell me. Where did you get that rubber disk?' demanded the robot.

Hal grinned. 'You already know, you fraud.'

'I assume it's no coincidence the material was exactly the same shade of blue as that man's boots?'

Hal shook his head.

'But surely he noticed the hole?'

Hal pulled up his right sleeve, exposing two wide rings of blue rubber dangling from his wrist. 'I cut the tops off his boots.' He turned one of the rings until a neat circle appeared. 'I only used a bit. Plenty left for next time.'

'Next time?' Clunk sighed. 'Mr Spacejock, I'm afraid there won't be a next time.'

'I should hope not.'

'No, I mean ... I'm leaving.'

If the console had sprouted technicolour hymn-singing mushrooms, Hal wouldn't have looked more surprised. 'You're ...?'

Clunk raised his hand. 'I won't hear any arguments. In

321

the circumstances it's the best thing to do, and so my mind is made up.'

'It was only a pair of gumboots. I didn't hurt anyone.'

'That's not the issue.'

'The wrong part? I know I looked angry, but –'

Clunk shook his head. 'It wasn't anything you've done. I just decided to accept Mr Spearman's offer.'

'Are you crazy? He's a con man! He won't pay you anything, and when you make a fuss he'll have you out the nearest airlock.'

'I appreciate your warning, but worse things have happened to me in the past.'

'With me, you mean?' Hal looked at his feet. 'I know things have been rough ...'

'They have indeed, but I'm sure they're about to get better.' Clunk swallowed. 'I've enjoyed our time together, Mr Spacejock. I would ask you not to make this difficult for me.'

Hal shook his head.

'Thank you. And who knows, one day you might travel aboard the *Luna Rose*. I'll be below decks of course, but you can always leave me a note.' Clunk put his hand out. 'No hard feelings?'

They shook, and then the robot was gone, striding down the ramp with rain drops running down his shiny bronze skin. The outer door closed automatically, and Hal was alone in the damp airlock.

Still in shock, he returned to the flight deck and leaned against the console. What had he done to deserve this? Sure, he gave Clunk a rocket now and then, and perhaps he was a little harder on the equipment than he should be. But deep down he had nothing but respect for the robot. 'Damn that bloody Kent Spearman,' muttered Hal, clenching his fists. He stood in silence for several seconds, then turned to face the screen. 'Navcom, I want to make an interplanetary call. Can you set it up for me?'

'Are you sure? Our last comms bill was rather excessive.'

'That's all those stickers you keep downloading.'

'You mean patches, and they're essential to my well-being.'

'So is this call. Get on with it.'

'Who do you wish to contact?'

Hal gave the Navcom the details, then sat in his chair as the connection was made. It was a long shot, but right now he'd take odds of a million to one.

32

Walking down the *Volante*'s passenger ramp, Clunk was overwhelmed by the abrupt change in his circumstances. It seemed like weeks since he'd threatened to leave the ship, and now here he was, fulfilling his promise. If he'd only kept his mouth shut Mr Spacejock wouldn't have sold the *Volante*, and right now they'd be plotting a course for their next delivery, or scanning Galnet for fresh jobs. Instead he was alone and unemployed, and he could only hope Mr Spearman had meant it when he'd offered him a position aboard the *Luna Rose*.

At the bottom of the ramp Clunk turned for a last look at the ship, running his gaze from one end to the other as he committed every detail of the graceful vessel to the safest memory store he had, to remain there until the end of his life. If Kent allowed him a few minutes break now and then, he'd be able to recall the images and remember his service aboard the *Volante*. And his time with Hal.

After he'd stored the images, Clunk turned away from the ship. She was in his past now, and it was time to face his future.

He stepped onto the landing field and aimed for the distant terminal, head bowed as he walked slowly past refuelling rigs and service vehicles. Memories came to him unbidden as the rain fell, and as he crossed the field Clunk recalled some of the scrapes he'd survived with Hal. From crooked power-crazed businessmen to alien teleporter systems to ruthless killer robots, they'd seen it all. There was no doubt Hal would face similar trials in the future, whatever line of work he chose, and Clunk hoped he'd left the human with some of his own common sense. As for himself, all he had to show for their time together was a collection of hair-raising memories, a few dents and his Order of Bravery medal from the Cathuan President.

His medal! He'd left it behind! Clunk stopped dead and looked back at the *Volante*, his eyes on the airlock and one hand to his throat. His one and only possession was still lying on the console, but he couldn't possibly face Mr Spacejock again. One goodbye had been bad enough.

◆

Hal was in the *Volante*'s flight deck, staring at the galactic star map on the main viewscreen. The huge double spiral filled his vision, but it might have been a table of election results for all the attention he was paying it. How could Clunk leave after all they'd been through together? Had he picked up some kind of grumpy virus from Jasmin?

Thinking back, Hal tried to pinpoint the moment Clunk had decided to leave, but given the lousy reception they'd had on all three planets in the Oxed system it could have been any one of the catastrophes they'd faced since first landing on Cathua.

'Mr Spacejock,' said the Navcom, breaking into his train of thought. 'Ground Control are requesting payment of landing fees and port charges.'

'All right, settle up.' Hal gestured at a you-are-here marker on the map, and the screen changed to display the Oxed system. 'Make an entry for standing orders,' he said, as the planets of Jordia, Cathua and Plessa appeared on screen. 'Add that lot to my no-visit list.'

'If you insist, although I really don't see the point.'

'I don't care. I'm never coming back.' Hal zoomed the chart out until the system vanished amongst the thickly clustered stars. 'Now set course for Lapsinet. That cargo of food isn't getting any fresher.'

'You want to set a course?'

'No, I want to fly around in circles until we hit something. What do you think?'

'Well, I –'

'Just set the damn course.' Hal looked round as the outer door opened, and his heart skipped a beat as Clunk walked in, dripping wet. 'Well, look who's back.'

'I'm sorry, Mr Spacejock. I left my medal behind.'

Hal spotted it on the console. Silently, he gathered it up and held it out.

'Thanks,' said Clunk, stowing it in his chest compartment. He turned to leave, then hesitated. 'Incidentally . . .'

'Yes?'

'How much did you get for the *Volante*? Only I could be in the market for a ship myself one day. Nothing as good as this, of course, but –'

'Whoa, stop!' Hal raised his hand. 'Say that again.'

'Oh, it won't be for decades, I'm sure, but one day –'

'Not that. The selling bit.'

'When you sold the *Volante*, how much did you get?'

'Who sold the *Volante*? When?'

'I thought you'd ... the Navcom said ... ' Clunk's voice tailed off, and they both turned to the console.

'Right, Navcom. What have you been saying?' demanded Hal.

'I told Clunk what Ms Ortiz told me. That you'd sold the ship, and I was being erased to make room for a new operating system.'

'You believed a pissweak pile of nonsense like that?'

'She *was* a member of the crew.'

'No she bloody wasn't!' Hal turned to Clunk. 'Is that why you left? Because you thought I'd sold the ship?'

Clunk nodded.

'You thought I'd cut you loose without so much as a thank-you?'

'You were talking about selling the *Volante*, and I - I thought ... I mean, Kent offered me a job with wages, and –'

'I wasn't talking about selling up. You were.' Hal took a deep breath. 'I want you to stay on, but you're not getting a wage.'

'I know that,' said Clunk. 'I'll stay for nothing. Really.'

'No, you daft hunk of tin,' Hal grinned at him. 'From now on you're an equal partner. I'm giving you a quarter share in the *Volante*.'

Clunk stared at him, his eyes glistening.

'And we'll split all profits sixty ... seventy-thirty. What do you say?'

'You have a generous nature and a tenuous grasp of mathematical theory. But I'm very grateful.' Clunk stuck out his hand. 'Equal partners it is.'

They shook on it, and then Clunk released Hal's hand. 'Of course, if you choose to retire in the future ... '

'Me? Never!' Hal gestured at the map displayed on the screen. 'There's enough work out there to keep us going forever. Adventures, money ... '

'Adventures, certainly,' Clunk smiled at him. 'I'll believe the money when I see it.'

'I've been thinking about that. Fresh food is too much trouble. We should be carrying stuff that won't go off.'

Clunk sat in the co-pilot's chair. 'Did you have anything in mind?'

'Coffee makers,' said Hal. 'The bloody things are always breaking down, so there's got to be a market.'

'But where will you source supplies?'

Hal grinned. 'There's a hundred sitting in the hold right now. We'll start with those.'

'They're not ours to sell, Mr Spacejock. We have to return them.'

'No, we just have to pay for them. I checked with Plessa, and the same machines are selling for three hundred credits over there. That's twenty-eight thousand gross, and when you take off import duty, fuel and expenses we'll make twenty-two thousand nine hundred and seventy-five credits.'

'That's incredible.'

'Yeah, it's quite something. Makes the food business look like a mugs game.'

'Actually, by incredible I was referring to the dramatic recovery in your math skills. Still, thirty percent of twenty-two thousand is a great start for the partnership.'

'Of course, we had these machines before the partnership began, so theoretically they're not part of the deal.'

Clunk leaned in close. 'Theoretically, it would be hard to divide the *Volante* into quarters, but given an atomic cutter I could just about manage it.'

'I was never one for theories,' said Hal. 'So, are we going back to Plessa?'

Clunk shook his head. 'Lapsinet. We're delivering our cargo of food before you decide that was a prior arrangement too.'

Hal opened his mouth to argue, then closed it again. Clunk turned away and started his regular take-off routine, which consisted of checking everything three times and then once again to be sure, and as Hal watched he realised he wouldn't have lasted two days on his own. Sure, he'd given up a share of the profits, but they never made a profit anyway. And on a brighter note, if he was charged for altering the President's bank draft, Clunk would own thirty percent of the jail term.

Epilogue

◆

Last night the President of Cathua narrowly escaped injury after a gas explosion at the Jordian Consumer Robot Expo. Nobody was hurt in the incident, although several prototype robots were destroyed and the fair had to be cancelled.

Also on Jordia, staff at Payne Rentals are tonight celebrating a modest lottery win. An ex-employee claimed they'd stopped buying tickets months earlier, but staff dismissed this as sour grapes, and said the troublemaker was merely angling for a share of the forty thousand credits in unmarked tiles.

In other news, local pilot Kent Spearman is in custody after authorities received an anonymous tip-off implicating him in the illegal dumping of robots. Several of these dumped robots have been recovered to give evidence at his trial.

Finally, the future of the Spacers Guild is once again under a cloud following a record insurance payout. Mr Joe Kerr of Cathua lodged the claim after brazen thieves stole a brand new vessel, the Phantom-X1, from his Cathuan dealership. Peace Force agents are seeking a human named Smith and a robot called Datoid, and report that the pair were last seen heading for Jordia aboard the stolen vessel. These thugs are armed and dangerous, and members of the public should maintain a safe distance.

We suggest you also keep clear of the fleeing criminals.

If you enjoyed this book, please leave a brief review at your online bookseller of choice. Thanks!

About the Author

Simon Haynes was born in England and grew up in Spain. His family moved to Australia when he was 16.

In addition to novels, Simon writes computer software. In fact, he writes computer software to help him write novels faster, which leaves him more time to improve his writing software. And write novels faster. (www.spacejock.com/yWriter.html)

Simon's goal is to write fifteen novels before someone takes his keyboard away.

Update 2018: goal achieved and I still have my keyboard!

New goal: write thirty novels.

Simon's website is spacejock.com.au

Stay in touch!

Author's newsletter:
spacejock.com.au/ML.html

facebook.com/halspacejock
twitter.com/spacejock

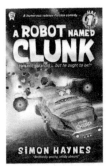

The Hal Spacejock series
by Simon Haynes

1. A ROBOT NAMED CLUNK

Deep in debt and with his life on the line, Hal takes on a dodgy cargo job ... and an equally dodgy co-pilot.

2. SECOND COURSE

When Hal finds an alien teleporter network he does the sensible thing and pushes Clunk the robot in first.

3. JUST DESSERTS

Gun-crazed mercenaries have Hal in their sights, and a secret agent is pulling the strings. One wrong step and three planets go to war!

4. NO FREE LUNCH

Everyone thinks Peace Force trainee Harriet Walsh is paranoid and deluded, but Hal stands at her side. That would be the handcuffs.

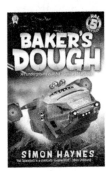

5. BAKER'S DOUGH

When you stand to inherit a fortune, good body-guards are essential. If you're really desperate, call Hal and Clunk. Baker's Dough features intense rivalry, sublime double-crosses and more greed than a free buffet.

6. SAFE ART

Valuable artworks and a tight deadline ... you'd be mad to hire Hal for that one, but who said the art world was sane?

7. BIG BANG

A house clearance job sounds like easy money, but rising floodwaters, an unstable landscape and a surprise find are going to make life very difficult for Hal and Clunk.

8. DOUBLE TROUBLE

Hal Spacejock dons a flash suit, hypershades and a curly earpiece for a stint as a secret agent, while a pair of Clunk's most rusted friends invite him to a 'unique business opportunity'.

9. MAX DAMAGE

Hal and Clunk answer a distress call, and they discover a fellow pilot stranded deep inside an asteroid field. Clunk is busy at the controls so Hal dons a spacesuit and sets off on a heroic rescue mission.

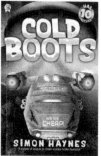

10. Cold Boots

Coming 2019

Ebook and Trade Paperback

The Secret War Series
Set in the Hal Spacejock universe

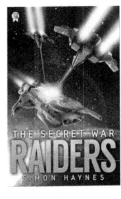

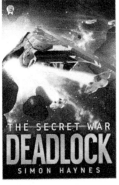

Everyone is touched by the war, and Sam Willet is no exception.
Sam wants to train as a fighter pilot, but instead she's assigned to Tactical Operations.
It's vital work, but it's still a desk job, far from the front line.
Then, terrible news: Sam's older brother is killed in combat.
Sam is given leave to attend his memorial service, but she's barely boarded the transport
when the enemy launches a surprise attack, striking far behind friendly lines as they try to
take the entire sector.
Desperately short of pilots, the Commander asks Sam to step up.
Now, at last, she has the chance to prove herself.
But will that chance end in death... or glory?

Ebook and Trade Paperback

The Harriet Walsh series

Harriet's boss is a huge robot with failing batteries, the patrol car is driving her up the wall and her first big case will probably kill her.

So why did she join the Peace Force?

When an intergalactic crime-fighting organisation offers Harriet Walsh a job, she's convinced it's a mistake. She dislikes puzzles, has never read a detective mystery, and hates wearing uniforms. It makes no sense ... why would the Peace Force choose her?

Who cares? Harriet needs the money, and as long as they keep paying her, she's happy to go along with the training.

She'd better dig out some of those detective mysteries though, because she's about to embark on her first real mission ...

The Peace Force has a new recruit, and she's driving everyone crazy.

From disobeying orders to handling unauthorised cases, nothing is off-limits. Worse, Harriet Walsh is forced to team up with the newbie, because the recruit's shady past has just caught up with her.

Meanwhile, a dignitary wants to complain about rogue officers working out of the station. She insists on meeting the station's commanding officer ... and they don't have one.

All up, it's another typical day in the Peace Force!

Dismolle is supposed to be a peaceful retirement planet. So what's with all the gunfire?

A criminal gang has moved into Chirless, planet Dismolle's second major city. Elderly residents are fed up with all the loud music, noisy cars and late night parties, not to mention the hold-ups, muggings and the occasional gunfight.

There's no Peace Force in Chirless, so they call on Harriet Walsh of the Dismolle City branch for help. That puts Harriet right in the firing line, and now she's supposed to round up an entire gang with only her training pistol and a few old allies as backup.

And her allies aren't just old, they're positively ancient!

Ebook and Trade Paperback

The Hal Junior Series
Set in the Hal Spacejock universe
Spot the crossover characters, references and in-jokes!

Hal Junior lives aboard a futuristic space station. His mum is chief scientist, his dad cleans air filters and his best mate is Stephen 'Stinky' Binn. As for Hal ... he's a bit of a trouble magnet. He means well, but his wild schemes and crazy plans never turn out as expected!

Hal Junior: The Secret Signal features mayhem and laughs, daring and intrigue ... plus a home-made space cannon!

200 pages, illustrated, ISBN 978-1-877034-07-7

"A thoroughly enjoyable read for 10-year-olds and adults alike"
The West Australian

'I've heard of food going off
... but this is ridiculous!'

Space Station Oberon is expecting an important visitor, and everyone is on their best behaviour. Even Hal Junior is doing his best to stay out of trouble!

From multi-coloured smoke bombs to exploding space rations, Hal Junior proves ... *trouble is what he's best at!*

200 pages, illustrated, ISBN 978-1-877034-25-1

Imagine a whole week of fishing, swimming, sleeping in tents and running wild!
Unfortunately, the boys crash land in the middle of a forest, and there's little chance of rescue. Is this the end of the camping trip ... or the start of a thrilling new adventure?

200 pages, illustrated, ISBN 978-1-877034-24-4

Space Station Oberon is on high alert, because a comet is about to whizz past the nearby planet of Gyris. All the scientists are preparing for the exciting event, and all the kids are planning on watching.

All the kids except Hal Junior, who's been given detention...

165 pages, illustrated, ISBN 978-1-877034-38-1

Ebook and Trade Paperback

New from Simon Haynes
The Robot vs Dragons series

"Laugh after laugh, dark in places but the humour punches through. One of the best books I've read in 2018 so far. Amazing, 5"*

Welcome to the Old Kingdom!

It's a wonderful time to visit! There's lots to do and plenty to see!

What are you waiting for? Dive into the Old Kingdom right now!

Clunk, an elderly robot, does exactly that. He's just plunged into the sea off the coast of the Old Kingdom, and if he knew what was coming next he'd sit down on the ocean floor and wait for rescue.

Dragged from the ocean, coughing up seaweed, salty water and stray pieces of jellyfish, he's taken to the nearby city of Chatter's Reach, where he's given a sword and told to fight the Queen's Champion, Sur Loyne.

As if that wasn't bad enough, the Old Kingdom still thinks the wheel is a pretty nifty idea, and Clunk's chances of finding spare parts - or his missing memory modules - are nil.

Still, Clunk is an optimist, and it's not long before he's embarking on a quest to find his way home.

Unfortunately it's going to be a very tough ask, given the lack of charging points in the medieval kingdom...

Ebook and Trade Paperback

Printed in Great Britain
by Amazon

29818677R00199